# A COLD
# TREACHERY

***Also by Charles Todd
in Large Print:***

A Test of Wills

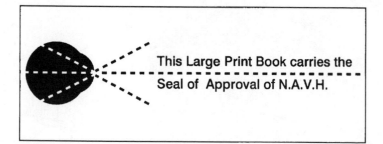

This Large Print Book carries the
Seal of Approval of N.A.V.H.

# A COLD TREACHERY

*Charles Todd*

**Thorndike Press • Waterville, Maine**

Map illustrated by Laura Hartman Maestro

An Inspector Ian Rutledge Mystery.

Published in 2005 by arrangement with The Bantam Dell Publishing Group, a division of Random House, Inc.

Thorndike Press® Large Print Core.

The tree indicium is a trademark of Thorndike Press.

The text of this Large Print edition is unabridged.
Other aspects of the book may vary from the original edition.

Set in 16 pt. Plantin by Ramona Watson.

Printed in the United States on permanent paper.

**Library of Congress Cataloging-in-Publication Data**

Todd, Charles.
    A cold treachery / by Charles Todd.
       p. cm. — (Thorndike Press large print core)
    ISBN 0-7862-7655-X (lg. print : hc : alk. paper)
    1. Rutledge, Ian (Fictitious character) — Fiction.
2. Mass murder investigation — Fiction.  3. England, Northern — Fiction.  4. Police — England — Fiction.
5. Missing children — Fiction.  6. Child witnesses — Fiction.  7. Large type books.  I. Title.  II. Thorndike Press large print core series.
PS3570.O37C65 2005b
  813′.54—dc22                     2005005300

For Cassandra,
who appears here as Sybil . . .
1990–2003

And for Biedermann,
who always believed he was one of *us* . . .
1989–2004

Good night, dear friends.

As the Founder/CEO of NAVH, the only national health agency solely devoted to those who, although not totally blind, have an eye disease which could lead to serious visual impairment, I am pleased to recognize Thorndike Press★ as one of the leading publishers in the large print field.

Founded in 1954 in San Francisco to prepare large print textbooks for partially seeing children, NAVH became the pioneer and standard setting agency in the preparation of large type.

Today, those publishers who meet our standards carry the prestigious "Seal of Approval" indicating high quality large print. We are delighted that Thorndike Press is one of the publishers whose titles meet these standards. We are also pleased to recognize the significant contribution Thorndike Press is making in this important and growing field.

Lorraine H. Marchi, L.H.D.
Founder/CEO
NAVH

★ Thorndike Press encompasses the following imprints: Thorndike, Wheeler, Walker and Large Print Press.

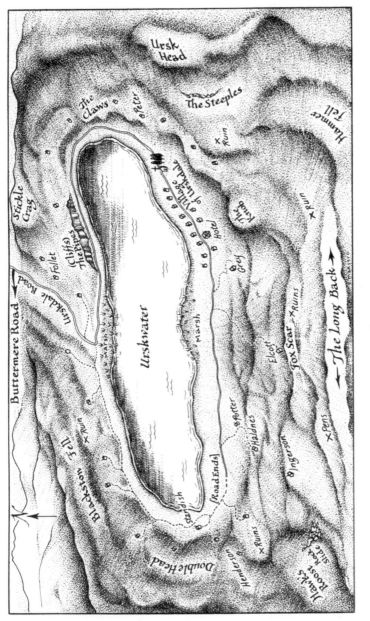

Greeley's Map

# Chapter One

The North of England
December 1919

He ran through the snow, face into the swirling wind, feet pounding deep trenches into the accumulating drifts. Rocks, their shapes no longer familiar under the soft white blanket, sent him sprawling, and he dragged himself up again, white now where the snow clung, and almost invisible in the darkness. He had no idea what direction he had taken, enveloped by unreasoning panic and hardly able to breathe for the pain inside him. All he could hear was the voice in his head, shouting at him —

*"You will hang for this, see if you don't. It's my revenge, and you'll think about that when the rope goes round your neck and the black hood comes down and there's no one to save you —"*

The sound of the shot was so loud it had shocked him, and he couldn't remember whether he had slammed the door behind him or left it standing wide.

He could still smell the blood — so much of it! — choking in the back of his throat like feathers thrown on a fire. He could feel the terror, a snake that coiled and writhed in his stomach, making him ill, and the drumming wild in his head.

They would catch him. And then they'd hang him. There was nothing he could do to prevent it. Unless he died in the snow, and was buried by it until the spring. He'd seen the frozen body of a dead lamb once, stiff and hard, half rotted and sad. The ravens had been at it. He hated ravens.

Half the countryside knew he'd been a troublemaker since the autumn. Restless — unhappy — growing out of himself and his clothes. They'd look at what lay in that bloody room, and they'd hate him.

He was crying now, tears scalding on cold skin, and the voice was so loud it seemed to be following him, and he ran harder, his breath gusting in front of his face, arms pumping, pushing his way through the snow until his muscles burned.

*"You'll hang for this — see if you don't —— !"*

He would rather die in the snow of cold and exhaustion than with a rope around his neck. He'd rather run until his heart burst than drop through the hangman's door and feel his throat close off. Even with the ravens eating him, the snow was cleaner. . . .

*"You'll hang for this — see if you don't —— !*

*That's my revenge . . . my revenge . . . my revenge. . . ."*

# Chapter Two

Paul Elcott stood in the kitchen beside Sergeant Miller, his face pale, his hand shaking as he unconsciously brushed the back of it across his mouth for the third time.

"They're dead, aren't they? I haven't touched them — I couldn't — Look, can we step outside, man, I'm going to be sick, else!"

Miller, who had come from a butcher's family, said stolidly, "Yes, all right. The doctor's on his way, but there's nothing he can do for them." Except pronounce them dead, he added to himself. Poor souls. What the devil had happened here? "We might as well wait in the barn, then, until he's finished."

Elcott stumbled out the door. He made his way to the barn, where he was violently sick in one of the empty horse stalls. Afterward he felt no better. He could still see the kitchen floor — still smell the sickening odor of blood —

And the eyes — half closed — staring at nothing the living could see.

*Had Gerald looked at Hell? He'd said the trenches were worse —*

He sat down on a bale of hay, and dropped his head in his hands, trying to regulate his breathing and hold on to his senses. He should have sent the sergeant back alone. He'd been mad to think he could face that slaughter again.

After a while, Sergeant Miller came across to the barn, and the doctor was with him, carrying a lantern. Elcott lifted his head to nod at Dr. Jarvis. He cleared his throat and said, "They didn't suffer, did they? I mean — no one lingered —"

"No. I don't believe they did," the doctor answered quietly, coming to stand by him and lifting the lantern a little to shine across Elcott's face. He prayed it was true. He couldn't be sure until the autopsies. Without moving the bodies, he'd been able to find only a single gunshot wound in each, to the chest, with resulting internal trauma. Sufficient to kill. A surge of sympathy swept Jarvis and he reached out to press Elcott's shoulder. The bloody dead were this man's family. His brother, his brother's wife, their children. An unspeakable shock . . .

The doctor himself had been badly shaken by the scene and found it difficult to imagine how he would answer his wife when she asked him why the police had come to fetch him in the middle of his dinner. Nothing in his practice had prepared him for such a harrowing experience. It was, he thought, something one might see in war, not in a small, peaceful farmhouse. At length he said gently to Elcott, "Let me take you home, Paul, and give you something to help you sleep."

"I don't want to sleep. I'll have *nightmares*." Without warning Elcott began to cry, his face crumpled and his chest heaving. His nerve gone.

The doctor gripped the weeping man's shoulder, and looked to Sergeant Miller over his head. "I wish I knew what's keeping Inspector Greeley — his wife told me he'd gone to see if the Potters needed help getting out. I hope to God he hasn't stumbled on anything like this!"

"We'll know soon enough," the sergeant replied.

They listened to the sobbing man beside them, feeling helpless in the face of his grief.

"I ought to take him home," Jarvis said. "He's no use to you in this state. You can wait for Greeley. When you're ready for me, I'll be with Elcott."

Miller nodded. "That's best, then." He glanced at Elcott, then jerked his head, moving to the door. Jarvis followed him. The two men stood there in the late afternoon light, gray clouds so heavy that it was difficult to tell if dusk was coming, or more snow. It had been a freak two-day storm, fast moving with a heavy fall, and the skies still hadn't cleared. The roads were nearly impassable, the farm lanes worse. It had taken Miller a good hour to reach the house, even following in the ruts left by Elcott's carriage.

"There's one still missing." Miller pitched his voice so that Elcott couldn't hear him. "I daresay Elcott's not noticed. I've walked through the rest of the house. He's not there."

"Josh? By God, I hadn't — Is he in the outbuildings, do you think?" Jarvis shivered and glanced over his shoulder at the unlit interior of the small barn, with its stalls, plows, barrows, tack, and other gear stacked neatly, the hay in the loft, filling half the space. Two horses and a black cow watched him, ears twitching above empty

15

mangers. "Gerald Elcott was always a tidy man. It shouldn't take long to search."

Miller counted on his gloved fingers. "Elcott penned his sheep, against the storm. I could see them up there to the east of Fox Scar. Stabled his horses, and brought in the cow. At a guess, then, he was alive this time Sunday, when the snow was coming down hard and he knew we were in for it. But the cow's not been milked since, nor the stalls mucked out, nor feed put down."

"That confirms what I saw inside. I'd say they've been dead since Sunday night." Jarvis frowned and stamped his feet against the cold, torn. "I should stay until you've found Josh. In the event there's anything I can do. . . ."

"No, take Elcott back. If the rest are dead, the boy is as well. I'll manage."

The doctor nodded. He was moving towards Elcott again when Miller cautioned, "Best to say nothing about what we've seen" — he gestured to the house — "in the village. Until we know a little more. We don't want a panic on our hands."

"No. God, no." Jarvis handed the lantern to Miller and settled his hat firmly on his head against the wind. Raising his voice, he said, "Now then, Paul, let's take you home,

16

and I'll find something to help you get past this."

"Someone has to look after the animals," Elcott protested. "And I want to help search. For whoever it was killed them. *I want to be there when you find this bastard.*"

"That's to your credit," Miller answered him. "But for now, I'd go with the doctor if I was you. I'll see to the beasts, and there'll be someone to care for them tomorrow. Leave everything to us. As soon as we know anything, I'll see you're told."

Elcott walked to the barn door and stepped outside, unable to turn away from the silent house just across the yard. "I wish I knew *why*," he said, his voice ragged with grief. "I just wish I knew why. What had they ever done to deserve — ?"

"That'll come out," Miller told him calmly, soothingly. "In good time."

Elcott followed Jarvis to the horse-drawn carriage that had brought the doctor out to the isolated farm. The only tracks in the snow were theirs, a hodgepodge of footprints around the kitchen door of the house, and the wheel markings of the two vehicles, cart and carriage. Beyond these, the ground was smoothly white, with only the brushing of the wind and the prints of winter birds scratching for whatever they could find.

As if only just realizing that the cart was his, Elcott stopped and said, "Dr. Jarvis — I can't —"

"Leave it for Sergeant Miller, if you will. He'll bring it back to town later. I expect he'll need it tonight."

"Oh — yes." Dazed, Elcott climbed into the carriage and settled himself meekly on the seat, stuffing his cold hands under his arms.

By the time Inspector Greeley had completed his examination of the Elcott farmhouse, he was absolutely certain of one thing. He needed help.

Five dead and one missing, believed dead.

It was beyond comprehension — beyond the experience of any man to understand.

In Urskdale, with its outlying farms and vast stretches of barren mountainous landscape, his resources were stretched thin as it was. The first priority was making certain that all the other dale families were accounted for, that this carnage hadn't been repeated — *God forfend!* — in another isolated house. And there was the missing child to find. All the farm buildings, sheep pens, shepherds' huts, and tumbled ruins had to be searched. The slopes of the fells, the crevices, the small dips and swales, the banks of the little becks. It would take more men than he could muster. But he'd have to make do with what he had, summon the dale's scattered inhabitants and work them to the point of exhaustion. And time was short, painfully short, if that child had the most tenuous hope of surviving.

Overwhelmed by the sheer enormity of what lay ahead, Greeley did what his people had done for generations here in the North: He buttoned his emotions tightly inside and grimly set about what had to be done.

It was well after midnight when he got back to the small police station that stood six houses from the church on the main street of Urskdale. The inspector laboriously wrote out a message and found an experienced man to carry it to the Chief Constable. "Make the fastest time you can," the man was told. "It's urgent."

On his drive back to the police station, Greeley had already compiled a mental list of the outlying farms, roughly grouping them by proximity. And then, to keep his mind busy and away from that dreadful, bloody kitchen, he had considered what the searchers would need — lanterns, packets of food, Thermoses of tea, rope.

But that was easier; each man would know from experience what to bring. Locating lost walkers in the summer had taught them all how to plan.

*Jarvis had said two days — that the Elcotts had been dead two days.*

This madman had already had more than sufficient time to track the boy over the snow, and then vanish. Or spread his net to other victims . . .

*What in hell's name would the search parties discover, as they knocked on doors?*

Greeley capped his pen and set it in the dish. A general warning now would come far too late to help anyone else. But the search had to go on. A search for the boy, for the killer — for other victims.

As he rose to leave, turning down the lamp on his desk, an appalling thought struck him.

What if the murderer was an Urskdale man? Where had he spent these last forty-eight hours? Safely at home by his hearth? If he hadn't found the boy after all, would he make certain that he was included among the searchers?

*What if he, Greeley, was about to set the fox amongst the hounds, unwittingly sending the killer out with an innocent man, to search for himself?*

He felt as if he'd not slept for a week — the tension in his body and the nightmare in his mind seemed to envelop him.

In the darkness the inspector rubbed his gritty eyes with his fists. When he walked out the door to face the somber men collecting outside the station, would one of them look away, unable to meet his glance? Would he read suspicion into the turn of a head or the restless stamp of feet?

He knew each individual in his patch too well to believe one of them was a vicious killer. Or — until now he'd thought he did. More to the point, he needed every man he could lay hands to; he couldn't afford to speculate. Still, he would send them out in threes, not twos. Just in case.

As he finally strode down the passage, he could hear the first arrivals talking among themselves, coming in, some of them, as soon as the news reached them. A few at a time, on foot, on horseback, their numbers slowly swelling.

The blast of icy air hit him in the face as he went through the door, a shock to warmed skin. Nothing, he thought, to match his shock at the Elcott farm.

In all his years as a policeman, he had never seen anything like the scene in that farmhouse kitchen. Try as he would, he couldn't imagine the kind of malevolence that could do such a thing. Try as he would, he couldn't shut it out of his mind. He and his men had lifted the five stiff bodies onto blankets and carried each out to the waiting cart. He could still feel the small bodies of the children, resting so lightly in his arms. Blind anger swept him so that he felt sick with it, helpless and for the first time in his life, vengeful.

As the searchers turned towards him, prepared to receive their orders, he winced, his eyes evading theirs, staring over their heads as he began to speak. *How could any man kill like that, and not wear the guilt of it, like an ugly brand?*

Greeley realized he wasn't prepared to read guilt in any face. Not yet. Not until his mind found a way around the horror. Then he would look. . . .

He was moving on nothing but fear now, his legs pounding through the snow that was sometimes as deep as his knees. His heart seemed too large for his chest, but his brain was wild and tormented, refusing to let his body rest. He paused from time to time, listening, his face turned to the wind like an animal, certain he could hear steps behind him, a voice calling to him. But there was no one alive to come after him.

It never occurred to him that it would be easier simply to stop, to lie down in one of the drifts and let himself fall asleep forever. What followed him was so terrible that his dread of its catching up with him ate him alive. Like the ravens, it would pick and dig at him, even in death. Fleeing was his only salvation. Far beyond reach. As far and as fast as he could manage.

He had no idea where he was — in which direction he'd run or how well he'd kept to that line, once out of sight of the lighted windows of the kitchen. He had no idea how long he had been running. Everything was measured by his feet, how far they were taking him, how fast they could go. Away from the menace behind him.

But the voice was always in his ears, in spite of the wind. Always pushing him on when his lungs begged him to stop for breath, always at his heels like a living thing intent on savaging him.

*"You will hang for this, see if you don't. That's my revenge, and you'll think about that when the rope goes round your neck and the black hood comes down —"*

As a goad, the voice was crueler than any whip.

He was terrified of it.

★ ★ ★

Some time later he fell, the air whipped out of his body and his chin buried in the snow. For an instant he lay there, listening. Was it his heart beating so hard that it choked him — or was it the crunch of footsteps coming down the swale after him? Frantic, he clawed his way to his feet again. He turned to stare into the darkness behind him. But the sky and the land seemed inseparable, a blank gray-white swirl that offered neither hope nor sanctuary.

There was no one behind him. There *couldn't* be. And yet he could almost feel the warmth of a body coming towards him. He could see shapes dissolving and solidifying in the wild eddy of flakes caught by the bitter wind. Like a ghost.

*A ghost* . . .

He began to cry again as he ran on, wishing it was over, wishing that he was dead, like the others.

But he couldn't be dead like the others. He would be hanged when they found him, and the last thing he would ever feel was the jerk of the thick rope around his neck. . . .

# Chapter Three

From the village itself, Sergeant Miller had gathered some two dozen able-bodied men with a motley number of horses. The plan was to send these men posthaste to the nearest farms, where they would recruit others to go on to their outlying neighbors. A human chain, adding links at every stage, reaching across Urskdale.

As Inspector Greeley called out each area of search, Miller pulled forward those who knew the ground best, and sent them on their way. As if unperturbed by the dead, the sergeant worked steadily and tirelessly, offering encouragement and answering questions in his deep, gruff voice.

But a slow fury burned inside him, and he kept the faces of the children in the forefront of his mind. For more than twenty years he had been a policeman in Urskdale, and he had taken a personal pride in maintaining the peace through a combination of fatherly persuasion and stern authority. The murder of the Elcotts had forever shattered his complacency.

"And mind you speak to every single person," Miller commanded. "It's not just the boy we're looking to find! The old granny and the newest babe, make certain you see with your own eyes that they're alive and not under duress. Don't be put off with excuses — search every corner of every building, leaving nothing to chance. If there's any trouble, anybody hurt — or dead — send word at once. Don't forget the high pens or any fold or crevice that might hold a frightened lad. And don't forget to look down wells. Up chimneys. In the wardrobes and the coal bins. Comb the lot, anywhere a killer might hide himself as you come into the yard. Don't waste time dwelling on events. That's no help to anyone and will frighten some. Do your best, then come back here to report. Or send for the inspector here if need be. Don't be bloody heroes — keep in mind the killer is sure to be armed! We haven't found the murder weapon yet. Off with you, then."

When Chief Superintendent Bowles was summoned from his bed by a messenger from the Yard, he tied the belt of his robe around his thickening waist and ran a hand over his hair before going down the stairs to find out what was so urgent he had to be awakened from a sound sleep.

He took the folded sheet the waiting constable handed him, and scanned it swiftly, then read through it more carefully.

"Hell and damnation!" he swore under his breath. And looked up at the constable with the fierce glare of a man who needs spectacles and is too vain to wear them.

"Sanders, is it? Any more than this, do you know?"

"That's all Sergeant Gibson gave me, sir. He said we've got a man close by, sir, who could be there in a matter of hours, if you like. Inspector Rutledge has just finished his testimony in Preston and is set to travel back to London in the morning."

"Rutledge?" Bowles scowled. He disliked Rutledge with a fervor that time and various absences had not succeeded in reducing. Mickelson, on the other hand, was a man after his own heart. Careful, never stirring up the wrong people, deferential to his superiors, Mickelson was. Not always clever, but steady. It would take him twice as long to arrive on the scene, but he could be trusted.

27

On the other hand, the Chief Constable who had sent to the Yard for immediate assistance was a man of parts, with connections — a brother in Parliament, and a wife whose father had a title. It would not do to let him discover that Chief Superintendent Bowles had not been as expeditious as he might have been, under the circumstances. *Five dead — bloody hell!*

They were going to attract notice, these murders. . . .

He couldn't afford to dally.

"Rutledge it will have to be, then," Bowles agreed sourly. "Tell Gibson to get word to his hotel and stop him before he leaves Preston. I'll be in my office directly." He read through the message a third time — and had second thoughts.

"Yes, send Rutledge by all means," he repeated. If anything went wrong in the North, it might be just as well to have a scapegoat available. "I'll speak to him myself as soon as I've been put in the picture."

The telephone call that reached Rutledge shortly before dawn was from Sergeant Gibson, a gruff man with a good head on his shoulders.

"A message from the Chief Superintendent, sir," the sergeant said without pre-amble. "You're to stay where you are until he telephones you. There's been a good bit of trouble in the North. Place called Urskdale. And it appears you're the closest man we've got."

"I know the area." Rutledge's voice down the line was wary. He was beginning to take the measure of his senior officer: There was often a whitewash of facts when Bowles sent Rutledge to handle an inquiry. And scant praise when Rutledge succeeded on his own in spite of unforeseen obstacles expected to defeat him. Bowles's cardinal interest was in fiercely protecting his own advancement and making certain his men reflected well on him. More than one am-bitious inspector had learned to his cost that credit often found its way to the Chief Superintendent, deserved or not. And Rutledge had discovered in Kent to what lengths Bowles would go to destroy a threat. "What kind of trouble?"

"Five dead. Shot, all of them. One missing. All in a single family, sir."

"Gentle God! Any other details?"

"No, sir, not that I've been told. They'd just been discovered. The bodies. Late yes-terday, as I understand it. The snow is hampering the local people, but Inspector

Greeley has got parties out searching for miles in every direction. The Chief Constable agrees with him that the Yard should be brought in as quickly as feasible."

"Very well, I'll wait for the Chief Superintendent's instructions." As Rutledge was about to put up the telephone, Gibson's voice came down the line in a last word.

"Sir?"

"Yes, Sergeant?"

"It's likely the Chief Superintendent will have other things on his mind, sir, and forget to tell you. But we've had a call, just last night, from Chief Inspector Blakemore in Preston. He was pleased with your discretion. That's how he put it, sir. Your discretion."

It was rare praise from Gibson, a man not given to unnecessary speech. But then Sergeant Gibson would do whatever lay in his power to irk Old Bowels, as the Chief Superintendent was known among the rank and file. And he always chose his methods with an unerring eye for what would succeed without bringing a reprimand down on his own head. If Bowles disliked Rutledge enough to withhold praise, Gibson took spiteful pleasure in passing it on.

"Thank you, Sergeant," Rutledge replied, a wry smile in his voice, and this time hung up the telephone without interruption.

Blakemore had been kind. But then the Chief Inspector hadn't understood, fully, the impact of the conviction that Rutledge had helped him win. . . .

By ten o'clock that morning Rutledge was well on the road north, a frigid wind blowing through the motorcar and clouds sweeping in again from the west. He was pushing his speed, taking advantage of every empty stretch to make better time, taking risks where he had to, to gain a few extra miles. The towns and villages strung along the road like a haphazardly designed strand of somber beads often slowed him to the point of exasperation, and at one point he was out of the motorcar directing traffic like the rawest constable, sorting out a tangle of wagons in a narrow market square.

A child out in this weather couldn't survive for long. . . .

The thought drove him like a spur.

Hamish reminded him from the rear seat that the search parties were the boy's best hope. *If he's alive, the men in the district will find him, no' us.*

It was true, but the urge to hurry was ever present. If a man had murdered five people, Rutledge knew, he would have nothing to lose by killing more. And what had become of *him* was as important as what had become of the lost child.

He picked up the snow two hours later, at first a dusting that was already muddy and torn, and then growing deeper by the mile. Rutledge swore. A fresh storm on the heels of one that had already left the North buried would make the journey a trial, turning the roads into slippery, unpredictable ruts. It would hinder the search in Urskdale, as well. If they hadn't given it up . . . or already found the child's body. The sooner he got there, the sooner he would know the latest news.

He was tired, and adding to his fatigue, the case in Preston still weighed heavily on his mind. The murderer had been a young man, Arthur Marlton, aged eighteen and mentally disturbed. Driven by voices to attempt to kill himself — and in the end driven to kill someone he had come to believe was stalking him. In his confusion and emotional distress, Marlton had lashed out to deadly effect. The man his wealthy family had quietly set to watch over their distraught son had been his unfortunate victim, allegedly striking his head on a curbstone as he fell and dying without regaining consciousness. The victim's version of the attack died with him. But the circumstances pointed to murder — and witnesses supported it. A tragedy compounded by tragedy . . .

Rutledge wasn't convinced that an asylum was a kinder sentence than facing the hangman. He himself found the thought of being shut away out of the light and air for the rest of one's life an appalling prospect.

But the young man's family had been in tears, grateful, watching their only son with inexpressible relief, striving to be patient in their need to touch and hold him. And the son, barely aware that his life had hung in the balance for a week, wore his chains in bewilderment as he listened to words they couldn't hear.

Beyond the sweep of Rutledge's headlamps, darkness closed down, coming early this time of year. Gray stone villages lining the road had thinned to more open country; and the rising ground that would eventually lead up the fells still lay before him. The air already seemed colder as he pointed the motorcar's bonnet north.

What troubled Rutledge as he had testified against the young man in the dock was that he himself heard voices. *A* voice. Not that of madness, where the mind tricked itself into believing the twisted commands of its own fabrication. Or — at least he prayed it wasn't! What he heard was more fearful — a dead man. Corporal Hamish MacLeod pursued him like the Furies, following him through the last years of the war and into its aftermath as if the man were still alive. So real that the soft Scots accent created a presence of its own, as if Hamish stood just out of sight, where Rutledge would surely find him if he turned unexpectedly. A presence that was the embodiment of too much horror piled on horror. The product of shell shock. The legacy of war.

For two days Rutledge had listened to the testimony of expert witnesses, aware of the difference between himself and the prisoner in the Preston dock. And yet at the same time Rutledge had known with a cold certainty that he was the only person in that courtroom who could fully understand what the doctors and the barristers were trying to describe: a haunting so real it was at times terrifying.

He could even understand why the prisoner had wanted to kill himself. He,

Rutledge, had in the depths of his torment walked into heavy fire as he crossed No Man's Land with his men and waited for the peace of death, and it had eluded him. When, against all odds, he'd survived the war, he had made a promise to himself: When he could *see* Hamish, when the day came that he could feel the dead man's breath on the back of his neck, or the touch of a ghostly hand on his shoulder, it would be finished. By whatever means.

The revolver that had belonged to his father lay in a flannel cloth behind the books in his sitting room in London, where he could reach it at need.

The legacy of war . . . It had left Rutledge so scarred emotionally that the blurred, ghostly faces of men he had led into the teeth of battle seemed to mock him, their useless deaths on his very soul. War, he thought, was madness of a different kind. And the final ordeal had been the death of Corporal MacLeod. Not by enemy fire, like so many others, but by Rutledge's own hand. The epitome of waste, a man who had broken under fire even as Rutledge himself was breaking — a man who preferred dying in shame to leading others into another futile massacre: the long, deadly slaughter called the Battle of the

Somme. Hamish MacLeod's decision had left an indelible mark on his surviving officer. A good man — a lost man — who had perished on the unhallowed altar of Military Necessity. In bald truth, murdered.

And yet Rutledge — and Hamish — had survived the trenches, after a fashion. Haunter and haunted, they had lived through the bloodiest conflict in the history of warfare. It was Peace that had made the presence of the young Scots soldier, invisible and at the same time more real than in life, an even more unspeakable burden for Rutledge to carry.

"You were one of the lucky ones," Dr. Fleming had told him not a fortnight ago. "But you can't see it as luck. In your view it's intolerable, your survival. You're punishing *yourself* because a whimsical God let you live. You think you've failed the dead, failed to protect them and keep them alive and bring them back home again. But no one could have done that, Ian. Don't you see? No one could have brought all of them through!"

*But Hamish had tried,* Rutledge answered Fleming silently. *And so I had had to try as well.*

Rutledge had come to the doctor's

London rooms that fair and windy December afternoon before driving to Preston to ask when — if — his expiation would end. After concluding a particularly unsettling investigation where Hamish seemed to be on the brink of revealing himself at every turn, Rutledge was looking for absolution — hope — from a man he had once hated and slowly learned to respect.

Only eight months before, sleep-deprived, goaded beyond endurance, he had lived in silence and despair, hardly aware of himself as a man. At Rutledge's sister's insistence, Dr. Fleming had taken him out of the military hospital, settled him in a private clinic — and forced him to speak. Reliving the trenches had nearly destroyed him, but out of the ruin of the barriers he had erected in his mind, he had found a way to return to Scotland Yard, slowly and painfully reclaiming himself. A long road, with no end in sight. It had been a hard eight months. And very lonely.

Fleming had added cryptically, as Rutledge stood at the window, staring out at traffic in the street, "It really depends on you, Ian. I don't have an answer. I expect no one does. Time? Learning to forgive? To forgive yourself most of all? I can't cure you.

But you may be able to cure yourself . . ."

Rutledge had had to be satisfied with that.

And now as he drove through the darkness, Hamish kept him company in the lonely silence.

This part of the Lake District was bounded on the east by the Pennines and on the west by the sea where the high country fell away to coastal plains. It was a land of farming and sheep, where damsons ripened in August but apples were gnarled and sour, where a man's nearest neighbor might live out of sight in a fold of the great fells, and such roads as there were often became impassable in winter.

Urskdale was not one of the famous valleys of the lake country. It possessed no poetic views or famous prospects. It was, simply, a rough, lonely, and wildly beautiful place where ordinary men and their families eked an existence in hard soil and harsh conditions, and felt at home. Safe. Until now . . .

What had turned a killer loose in their midst?

He'd had the forethought to add a Thermos of tea to the sandwiches the hotel had put up for him, and stopped only to refuel the motorcar or walk for five minutes in the snow while the wind brought him back from the edge of sleep. In the cold night air, there was only the warmth of the engine to keep his feet from numbness. There was no such help for his gloved hands or the back of his neck.

How long would a child survive in this weather, lost in the open?

*No' verra long* . . . Hamish, at his shoulder in the rear seat, had for miles been making comparisons with the Highlands, the poor ground and narrow valleys, streams that ran crookedly over stones and sang sometimes in the silence. *It's no' the same, but it makes a man homesick,* he added. *In the trenches I sometimes dreamed about the glen. It was verra real. Wi' all my heart, I wanted to come home again.*

"I came to the Lake District as a boy, with my father. For walking holidays." The words were whipped away by the wind, and Rutledge, concentrating on the road running before his headlamps, was unaware that he had answered aloud.

They had driven through Kendal two hours before, one of the handful of small towns that serviced this part of the country. He had seen the bridge by the church, where he had stood with his father and leaned over the sun-warmed stone wall to watch for salmon in the Kent. Years ago. A lifetime ago.

The road just outside Keswick was barricaded by police. Rutledge was stopped and questioned, his papers examined in the light of a torch. Then it swept the rear of the motorcar. Rutledge flinched as it passed over where Hamish sat. But the constable nodded and stepped back.

The sergeant in charge, hands jammed into the pockets of his heavy coat, leaned into the open window and said, "Sorry, sir. Orders of the Chief Constable."

"Any news?"

"None, sir, that we've heard. There's little enough traffic just now, seeing the state of the roads. At least no one's come out since we've been posted here."

"Or he got through long before that," Rutledge answered. "Still, we can't take that chance. Carry on, then."

# Chapter Four

He turned off the Buttermere road soon after, following what was little more than a well-traveled track that looped the flanks of some of the tallest peaks in the district.

They loomed overhead, hidden by the swirls of snow, hulking shadows unseen but always — *there*. It was odd — he could feel them, their presence confining.

Rutledge shivered, fighting a rising panic. Unexpected panic — almost as if it had been conjured up by the prison sentence handed down to the young man in Preston —

But it wasn't that. The heights above him, the encircling fells, once familiar and beautiful, were now watchful and malevolent, pressing in on him, smothering him.

It was the first time he'd come here since the war. And in his concern for the missing child, his concentration on road conditions, it hadn't occurred to him that the very things that made the Lake District what it was — the high peaks and inaccessible valleys — would now threaten him as effectively as the heavy gates of a prison clanging shut at his back.

He had been buried alive in that nightmarish dawn when Hamish was shot. He had felt the earth shift and tilt under his feet as the shell exploded, then he'd dropped far down in the pitch dark of the erupting hole as mud and bodies and debris thundered down on him. All that had saved him was the bloody tunic of one of his men, his face pressed against the still-warm cloth where a tiny pocket of air survived between the living and dead. Deaf and blind, his extremities pinned by the weight of earth, the taste of blood in his mouth, and slow suffocation setting in, he had seen the dying face of Hamish MacLeod. Eyes begging him for the coup de grâce to stop the pain, a thread of a whisper that seemed to be burned in memory. Fiona MacDonald's name . . .

By the time the frantic rescue party had dug down to him, the damage had been done.

He could no longer endure a place from which there was no escape. A shut door, a small room, a crowded train carriage, a throng of people pushing against him. But he hadn't anticipated — he hadn't been prepared for the sense of *walls* around him here. Blinding snow and darkness and that nearly invisible presence above his head cutting him off from retreat.

"Aye, there's only one way in," Hamish reminded him mercilessly. "Ye saw the map for yourself."

The urge to turn around, to go away while he could, swept over him.

Rutledge swore. He didn't need Hamish to remind him that he was a serving policeman. That there was duty to be done. God knew he'd done it in France. At what cost to himself and to others . . .

"I can't change it," he said aloud. "I can't build new roads." Swallowing hard against the panic, he told himself, *Tomorrow when the sun is out, it will be different. Please God, I can carry on until then* —

And then the rough roadbed demanded all his attention, wiping out every other thought.

He drove on, tense, watchful.

The fingerpost offering directions at the next turning had been shifted by the wind, leaning at an odd angle and pointing skyward. But instinct told him he'd found the right place. The track rose and fell with the land, forged by centuries of traffic: hooves of countless flocks, cart wheels, shod feet. He prayed the sheep had been penned up before the storm. Or were hunkered down among the rocks where they could find shelter, out of the cruel wind. They were allowed to roam freely, sometimes clogging the roads, and tonight they would be nearly invisible until he had driven straight into their midst. Even a single animal on these icy tracks could spell disaster for a motorcar.

Herdwicks were a sturdy breed, well suited to the fells, and could survive without fodder all winter, scratching for their own sustenance. Since the time of Edward I, a thriving weaving business had made the North famous. The coarse, wiry fleece yielded a variety of cloth.

There was nothing in his headlamps but the snow-rutted road, the occasional low-lying hump of a stone farmhouse hugging a curve, or the silhouette of an upright box of a house sitting on the slope above. And always trees that somehow seemed determined to thrive in spite of the harshness of Nature.

Ordinarily Rutledge liked the darkness, the isolation, the silence. But now he was fighting fatigue. And keeping himself alert with the image of a lost child huddled in the lee of a wall or crouched in a shallow crevice, terrified and alone.

Urskdale couldn't be much farther. . . .

The road narrowed again just as a heavier snow squall was passing over, obscuring everything.

Rutledge bit back his exasperation, concentrating on maintaining what speed he could, only to find himself defeated by the weather. Already the verge was hardly visible, and in the darkness to his right, there was a black void indicating a long drop and a nasty slide into grief.

He took his foot from the pedal, letting the motor slow his speed as he reached a curve, his eyes fixed on the bright swath of his headlamps. Then his wheels began to lose traction and he fought to accommodate the skid, finally bringing the heavy motorcar back to the crown of the road.

Hamish, behind him, scolded sharply, "It willna' help the lad, if you wreck the motorcar and kill yoursel'. It's no' the time to be sae foolish! There's no' a house in sight."

There hadn't been for some time.

His shoulders ached now, and his face burned from the force of the wind sweeping through the motorcar. His wits were slower, his reactions not as fast. The engine's output of heat, hardly more than a breath of warmth, was losing the battle — his accelerator foot was already growing numb. And beneath it all, the panic of claustrophobia was still there, like a weight.

As the cold penetrated even the heavy clothing he was wearing, he braked, stopping in the middle of the road to drink more of his dwindling store of tea.

" 'Ware!" A sharp hiss of warning from Hamish just as he was reaching for the Thermos.

A little beyond the reach of his headlamps, Rutledge could just make out the telltale marks where a carriage wheel had spun across the road in front of him and veered straight for the drop that lay to his right. Snow had nearly filled in the tracks — he couldn't judge how long they'd been there or where they were heading. Or whether the person holding the reins had recovered in time and driven on, as he himself had just done.

It would have been impossible to see the marks, if he hadn't stopped —

"We havena' met anyone since we left Keswick," Hamish reminded him.

"He may be ahead of us . . . if he got himself righted again."

Rutledge let in the clutch, slowly moving forward a dozen feet, and now could see what appeared to be a jumble of rocks some distance down the slope. Or, no, not rocks! A horse lying quietly in its traces, a good twenty yards below the road's edge. It had thrashed a wide area into a muddy mix of black and white, half obscuring itself as well.

*Where there were traces, there must also be a carriage —*

Again he pulled carefully to a stop, leaving the engine running and setting the brake.

Feet and legs stiff with cold, he got out slowly, holding on to the motorcar's frame as he tested his footing. The icy crust was slick, but the weight of his body broke through to firmer ground. No longer blinded by the brightness of the head-lamps, he could pick out a shadowy tangle of reins and harness and broken shafts. Taking his torch from the pocket of his greatcoat, he shone the light down the sharp incline, sweeping the snow.

A small carriage, its shape already distorted by a shroud of white, was just visible. It lay like an irregular boulder, only its sharper lines betraying the fact that it had been man-made.

Using great care, Rutledge scrambled down to the horse, and laid a gloved hand on its hide. Dead. Still warm . . . but already cooling.

He slipped and nearly lost his footing as he reached the overturned carriage and shone the torch beyond its upturned side.

It was then he saw the woman's form, curled into a knot on the ground, her back pressed against the seat.

She responded so lethargically to the glare of his torch that he thought at first she must be dying, then as she stirred, he realized she was alive but very likely badly injured.

When she tried to turn her head to look up at him, he could hear a soft mew, of pain and pleading.

He moved around the footboard of the carriage, careful not to disturb her body, and came to kneel beside her.

"Can you tell me where you hurt?"

She lifted a white face to him, her eyes so dark they seemed sunken in the sockets. "I —" She was shivering violently and could hardly speak, her teeth clicking together involuntarily. "Ribs," she said, after a moment, "I th-think — ribs. But my f-feet are numb —"

She'd used the blanket to wrap herself, and the seat of the carriage offered some protection from the wind, but she was very, very cold, rigid with it.

Rutledge reached down to touch the hand pressed to her side, and it felt icy through his glove. The woman shook her head, as if afraid he was going to lift her.

"I must get you out of here. Do you understand me? If you stay where you are, you won't live through the night!"

"Please — *no* — *!*"

With the snow deep enough and treacherous enough to make carrying her nearly impossible, he said, "There's nothing for miles — no house, no barn. There's no help." He could feel the wind sucking at his breath, as it had sucked at her will.

"No — I must — *I must* —" She shook her head again, as if her mind refused to work clearly and tell her what it was she must do.

Making certain, he said, "Were you alone? In the carriage? No one has tried to go for help?"

"Yes — alone."

"I'm going to lift you to your feet. I'll be as careful as I can. And then you must walk, with my support. I can't carry you. But I have a motorcar on the road —"

After a moment she nodded. With enormous effort she tried to get her feet under her, and finally, with her hands on his shoulders as he knelt to brace her limbs, she was able to stand. He was afraid to bring any force to bear on her arms or shoulders because of her ribs, and instead took her hands. But it wasn't enough to help her climb. Her feet stumbled in the snow as he pulled her upward, and she cried out again from the pain even that induced.

The road might as well be on the moon, he thought, casting a despairing glance in the direction of his headlamps. With nothing and no one to help them.

Hamish, carrying on a running argument in his mind, urged him to hurry.

In the end, he had to wrap his arms around the woman and almost walk her like a child leaning on its father's legs and body, her shoes on the toes of his boots. It was like dealing with a puppet, no will of its own, yet its very awkwardness seeming to defy the puppet master at every step. The effort exhausted both of them.

She bit her lip until the blood flowed, a dark line running down her chin, and fought not to cry out. But her legs were stiff with cold, and it was almost an act of will on both their parts to climb to the road again.

Once he got her there, in the light from the headlamps, he released her for a moment to see if she could stand on her own. She nearly crumpled, and then managed to hold herself erect, swaying. He went to the motorcar, found the Thermos of tea, and brought her a steaming cup. And had to hold it to her lips because her hands trembled too badly to keep it there.

She took the first sip as if it had burned her, jerking her head away, even though the tea was far from scalding. Then she managed to swallow a little. And the sweet liquid ran through her with life-giving warmth. Not enough to stop her from shaking, but enough to bring her back to her senses. And her pain.

He took the empty cup from her, replaced it on the Thermos, and set it back in the floor of the car under his feet. Fumbling in the rear, without looking in the direction where Hamish always seemed to be sitting, he could feel the fringe of his rug, and he set that in his seat as well.

Going back for the woman, he asked, "Can you walk as far as the car?"

But she was looking back down into the darkness. "My horse — we must do something — I see him there —"

"I'm afraid the horse is dead."

"Oh — a pity —" She went with him docilely then, and with his help was able to lift herself into the high seat. Her own rug was damp with snow, but he left it around her, and added his to cover her.

Hamish said, "She's lost more warmth than she can make."

It was true. Rutledge gave her a little more of the tea, and finally, with great difficulty, got her into his arms, and himself into the passenger's seat.

She lay against his chest quivering, and he could see the tears of pain running down her face.

"I must get you somewhere with a fire. I don't know how far that will be. But first, we've got to make some headway in warming you up."

It took another ten minutes to stop the most violent shivers, and then she seemed to fall asleep against him. He woke her, urging her to fight the cold.

More tea, and then he set her back where she belonged, and took off the brake.

"We can't wait any longer. Talk to me," he commanded. "I don't care what you say, nonsense if you like. Verse. Songs. But talk. Concentrate on that, not the pain."

"I never knew it could hurt so to breathe," she said finally. "I can only —"

"Yes, I understand. And that's all right. Go on," he said again.

"I can't feel my feet —"

"They'll be fine, as soon as we find help. Do you know this part of the country? Is there a farmhouse near here?"

"I — I can't remember —"

He took one hand from the wheel and gripped hers where they were clenched under the blanket. They were still cold, her leather gloves wet through.

"Take off your gloves, and if you can bear it, tuck your hands under your arms . . ."

She did as she was told, cradling her body. "That helps —" she told him. "Except for my p-poor feet." She had twisted herself in the seat to shut the wind out of her face and ease her ribs. He couldn't see her features except as a blur against the dark rug.

"Have you come far? It's foul weather to be on the road!"

"I — I drove down from Car-Carlisle —"

He eventually came upon a lane with wind-drifted snow blocking it, and got out to plow his way up the hill to the porch of a house, his shoes thickly encrusted. Although he knocked with his fist, no one came to the door, and there were no lamps lit. He stepped back, and could see no smoke in the chimney.

"Empty as a drunkard's purse," Hamish grumbled as Rutledge started back down the drive.

"No one at home," he told his passenger as he climbed once more behind the wheel. "We'll find another soon enough." And hoped that he was right.

# Chapter Five

The road rose over a hill and then dipped again. Off to his left Rutledge could see a turning with a fingerpost, and a hundred yards beyond that, the rough shape of a house. The wind carried the heavy scent of woodsmoke to him, and he said cheerfully, pointing, "Over there. You'll be by a fire soon!"

The lane came up so quickly he nearly missed it — no more than a long rutted bit of track that twisted up to the house and around to the yard.

He took it carefully, testing the snow depth with his wheels. But the tires were able to find purchase, and he went up the slight rise with less difficulty than he'd anticipated, the powerful motor coming to his aid.

A dog began to bark with savage ferocity as Rutledge approached the yard behind the house. It was not on a chain and ran bounding beside the motorcar, lips drawn back in a snarl. Even after he'd come to a full stop, it put its forelegs on the motorcar and dared him to step down.

"Set your foot within range, and he'll clamp his teeth on it," Hamish warned.

Rutledge blew the horn. Once and then again.

A lamp flared in an upstairs window. The sash went up and a gray head looked out.

"Who are you? What the hell do you want, waking the family like that?"

"Call off your dog and come down. I'm a policeman, and I have a woman here. There's been an accident. She needs help and she needs it quickly."

"You're no policeman I'm familiar with!"

"Inspector Rutledge, from London. I've come north at the request of the Chief Constable to assist Inspector Greeley in Urskdale."

"And I could call myself the King of Siam, if I was of a mind to. I'm not opening my door this night to any man without proper authority."

The dog was growling deep in its throat, reflecting his master's truculence.

Rutledge shifted the motorcar into reverse. "Please yourself. Inspector Greeley will be expecting you at Urskdale gaol tomorrow at noon." It was the voice of command. "The charge will be obstructing a police officer in the course of his duties." The vehicle began to move.

"Stay where you are!" Cursing, the man withdrew his head and after several minutes, he appeared again at the yard door. He was in no hurry, weighing the situation with the hardheaded prudence of the North. Rutledge waited impatiently but said nothing, nearly certain that there was a shotgun somewhere within easy reach.

"Here, Bieder," the farmer at last called to the dog, and with a final challenging glance at Rutledge, the animal turned obediently to his voice.

Pulling on a pair of Wellingtons, the man came out into the yard, a lantern in his hand. Holding it high, he stared from Rutledge to the pale face of his passenger.

"An accident, you say?" he demanded suspiciously. "Miss?"

"My — my — carriage — went off — the road," the woman managed, her teeth chattering as she raised her head out of the nest of blankets. In the lantern light the blood on her lip was a dark and ominous smudge. "Please — I don't think I can bear the cold much longer. L-Let me sit by your fire for ten minutes, and we'll b-be on our way."

"Ah." He lowered the lantern and said to Rutledge, "Can she walk, then?"

"Her ribs are bruised — possibly cracked. Her feet are numb."

Rutledge got out, walked around the bonnet, and came to the passenger door. Opening it, he said gently, "It will hurt, to help you out. Can you manage?"

A ghost of a smile appeared on the strained face. "If there's a fire —"

The farmer, a burly man, said, "Come along, lass. I'd lift you myself but for the ribs, now. Between us, we'll have you in the kitchen in the blink of an eye. My wife already has the kettle on!" His accent was heavy, the words gruff, but his intentions were kind.

They got her down, and between them on their crossed wrists, to the house, the dog sniffing at their heels. A heavyset woman with a red face, cheeks permanently windburned, was waiting for them in the kitchen, her hands tight together.

As they came through the door, her expression softened. She said, "My sweet Lord! Oh, the poor *lass!* Bring her here, by the stove!" Over the injured woman's head she said to Rutledge, "What's happened to her?" He could see the shadow of alarm in her eyes, as if the older woman expected him to say his companion had been attacked by a murderer.

He explained again as his passenger was urged into a chair, her blankets hastily settled around her like cushions. She tried to lean back and gasped.

The farmer's wife, tightening the sash of her robe about her thick waist, said, "Jim, take the inspector into the sitting room, if you please. I'll just have a look at this young lady."

Rutledge followed Jim into a small sitting room. It was already losing the evening's heat but was still comfortable, compared to the raw night outside. The man lit a lamp on a table, settled the chimney in place again, and motioned Rutledge towards the best chair. The fire on the hearth had been banked for morning, but the farmer stirred it into life, still holding the poker as he turned back to his unexpected guest.

"If you're a policeman, you'll have something to show me."

Rutledge reached into his coat and withdrew his card. The farmer examined it.

"Scotland Yard, is it, then? You've made rare good time!"

"I was in Preston when the summons came."

The farmer set the poker back in its place, shaking his head. "Bad business, this! There was a search party come through early this morning. I asked if they needed me as well, but they said they had enough men for this part of the valley. They hadn't found the boy — more's the pity." He sat heavily in the next chair. "Tonight I put the dog in the barn, with the door ajar. A precaution, belated though it was! I don't put much faith in anyone except myself, out here. There's a shotgun in the entry, behind the pantry door. If I'd needed it." He held out a rough hand. "James Follet."

Rutledge acknowledged the introduction, but couldn't stop himself from casting a glance towards the kitchen.

"Don't worry about the lass," Jim Follet told him. "The nearest medical man is a good twenty mile from here as the crow flies. Jarvis, his name is. My Mary's been doctoring the family and the animals for thirty year or more."

Rutledge believed him. In such isolated farms, the wife was usually the first and sometimes the only help to be had in an emergency.

Follet stretched his legs out to the hearth. "Where did she go off the road?"

Rutledge told him what he could. Follet said, "Aye, I know the place. She's not the first to come to grief there! Even heavy rains make that stretch hazardous. Well. I'll have a team up there at first light. A pity about the horse."

"I don't know if there's any luggage in the back. But if she drove from Carlisle . . ."

"There'll be a valise of some sort. Yes, I'll look."

Follet reached across the table to a pipe rack and began to fill one, tamping it carefully before lighting a spill at the hearth and holding it to the tobacco. His hair was iron gray, his skin toughened by wind and cold. The blue eyes squinting through the pipe smoke were sharp. Rutledge noticed that he'd hastily pulled on his trousers and a sweater over his night clothes, his braces hanging down to his hips.

"Nasty business," Follet said again, referring to the murders. "Not the sort of thing we're used to. An entire *family*, by God. It makes no sense to me!"

"Did the search party bring any other news?"

"As far as I can tell, Inspector Greeley has no idea who's behind these killings. To be honest, that question's plagued me as well. Ever since the men left here. And for the life of me, I can't come up with a satisfactory answer. It isn't as if the Elcotts were troublesome, the sort who'd rub people wrong and make enemies! And Cummins — who keeps the hotel — did tell me it appears nothing was taken. That rules out thievery. The best I can think of is a chance encounter — someone quietly passing through, and Elcott spotted him. Once the man was seen, he might've feared word would get out. But even that's far-fetched! It smacks of something vile, to my mind — killing those children."

"How well did you know the family?"

"Well enough. The Elcott farm lies across Urskwater from us, and I doubt I've been there more than a dozen times over the years. Henry — the father — I knew best, of course. We'd served on church committees together. I'd meet Gerald now and again in Urskdale. He's the older brother, and High Fell went to him when Henry died. Good sheep man. His wife came here in the third year of the war — at the end of 1916, I think, or first part of '17. A war widow, she was, with two children. Late last summer she and Elcott had the twins. Nice enough woman, from all reports. Kept her house well, and Mary claims she was a good cook. A neighbor bought a packet of her sweet cakes at the last church fair, and told Mary they was particularly fine. If the boy's dead, it's a kindness, in a manner of speaking. What's he to do, on his own at that tender age? Besides, I don't see how he could have survived for long out in that storm!"

*But what if the boy could identify the killer? What if the killer and not the storm had already reached him and left him dead? A sixth victim?*

There was nothing to be done tonight, Hamish reminded him. Except to make all haste to Urskdale.

But Rutledge was considering the homey accolades. They were the measuring stick of small towns and villages all across England. The state of a man's stock and the state of a woman's kitchen told neighbors whether they were dependable or slovenly, careful or spendthrift, reliable or slack. Perhaps more so here, where isolation made a knowledge of one's neighbors rudimentary. To stop next door for a cup of sugar often meant a walk of several miles. Still, a man learned soon enough who was to be trusted and who wasn't. . . . Had Elcott had any suspicion at all that he and his family were in danger? Or had Death simply walked in one evening? A knock at a random door . . .

Hamish, who had grown up in another isolated and independent world, the Highlands of Scotland, said, *It's a verra simple life, this. But it can still breed jealousy and murder. Greed, even.*

Rutledge, fighting the tiredness that was nearly overwhelming him as the fire's warmth began to seep into his cold sinews, caught himself in time or he would have answered the voice aloud, from habit.

Instead, he said to the farmer, "I think we ought to see what Mrs. Follet has found. I must be on my way again as soon as possible. There's still some distance to travel."

"The lass can remain with us. It's for the best, if she's bad hurt. And in your shoes, I'd wait until morning myself. But you know your own business —"

He was interrupted by his wife, poking her head around the door and saying, "The ribs don't appear to be broken, but they're badly bruised. I've wrapped them as well as I can. And she's warmed up a bit. If you'd want to speak to her, sir —"

As the two men got to their feet, Mrs. Follet added shyly, "And there's a cup of tea for you as well, if you'd like one."

He followed her down the passage to the kitchen, and found the woman he'd rescued still huddled by the fire. Her face was very tired, her eyes looking into an abyss, as if she had finally realized how close to death she'd come.

Her wet clothes had been replaced by a flannel nightgown, two sizes too large, and the heavy quilt around her served as a robe. Her carriage blanket and his rug had been draped over chairs by the stove to dry, the odor of damp wool strong in the comfortable room. A glass of warmed milk stood at her elbow, half empty. She looked like a child, with the thick dark hair that fell down her back in a braid. A towel around her shoulders had been used to dry it.

Turning her head as the two men came in, she stirred and began to pluck at the edges of the quilt, as if in modesty.

Mrs. Follet handed Rutledge a cup of tea, and he realized with the first swallow that she'd added a little something to it. Grateful, he smiled at her. Then he nodded to his passenger and asked gently, "Feeling better?"

She said, "Yes." But her voice was a polite thread in the quiet room.

"What's your name?"

As if surprised that he didn't know it, she answered with more strength, "Janet Ashton."

"Can you tell us what happened, Miss Ashton?"

That seemed to alarm her, and Mrs. Follet put her hand on the quilted shoulder, comforting her.

"The horse lost the road," Mrs. Follet answered for her. "And dragged the carriage a bit before it went over and pulled him down. He injured himself thrashing about in the shafts and finally was still. She couldn't reach him or coax him to his feet."

Miss Ashton blinked, as if awakening from a dream. "Yes . . . I — it was frightening, I thought he'd crush the *carriage* — but I couldn't get out, not at first —" She shuddered, and took a deep breath, trying to shut the experience out of her mind. Then she looked up at Rutledge. "You said — you did tell me the horse *is* dead?"

"He is." Rutledge pulled a chair away from the table and sat down close to hers. "Is there someone I can contact? Your family must be worried about you."

"No — there's no one. No —"

"What brought you out in this weather?" Follet asked on the heels of her faltering answer. "It was foolishness, a lass like you!"

But she buried her face in the quilt, refusing to answer.

Mrs. Follet scolded, "Don't fret her, now! She's that tired. I'll take her up to bed. Jim, there's a warm bottle for her feet. If you'll bring it up in five minutes." With a soothing croon that would have comforted a child, she coaxed Miss Ashton across the kitchen and down the passage, her arm around the thick wrapping of quilt.

Follet and Rutledge watched them go. "There's my son's bedroom, at the head of the stairs, if you're agreeable to staying what's left of the night. He's over to Keswick, where he's been courting a lass."

"Thank you, but I must be on my way," Rutledge replied with sincere regret. "They're expecting me in Urskdale." He set his cup on the table and went out to the motorcar to bring in the empty Thermos.

As Follet refilled it, Rutledge reconfirmed his directions before stepping out into the cold, windy night. As the farmhouse door swung to, Bieder, the dog, followed the interloper all the way to the motorcar, head lowered and a deep growl in his throat to emphasize a personal dislike for strangers. "I'd not like to come across you unexpectedly," Rutledge commented as he put up the crank and went around to the driver's side. "Murderer or no."

Hamish said, *It's a pity the slaughtered family didna' have a dog like yon.*

"I doubt that it would have mattered, if he was armed. Or the killer might have been known to the animal." Rutledge turned the motorcar with some difficulty and went back down the farm lane in his own tracks. Miss Ashton was safe. He hadn't far to go to his destination. He'd had a chance to warm himself and the whisky had given him second wind. He should have felt revived, eager to go on. But as the darkness encompassed him, isolating him in the bright beams of his headlamps, he could feel the mountains again, out there like Russian wolves beyond the campfire's light. It was a trick of the mind, nothing more, but he was thrown back into the war, when in the darkness an experienced man could sense movement in the German trenches, even when there was no sound, nothing to betray the congregation of enemy forces before a surprise attack.

As it happened Rutledge reached his destination ahead of the dawn. But not before he'd taken half an hour to backtrack to where he'd found the wrecked carriage. The policeman in him, the training that even war hadn't blunted — in fact had honed — made him thorough. Earlier, the need to safeguard Miss Ashton had been his only priority. Now he could examine the scene.

The wind had died and with it the squalls of snow. With his torch in his hand, he surveyed the overturned vehicle, thinking that by this time — if he hadn't come along the same road — Janet Ashton would be dead.

"She was verra lucky," Hamish agreed. "And who will rescue us?"

Ignoring the jibe, Rutledge got out to walk warily to the road's edge. His policeman's brain was registering details even as a part of his mind was picturing himself pinned under the overturned motorcar. It would have been, he thought, an easier way to die than most, to fall asleep in the cold night air. Was this the fate of the missing child? It would be ironic indeed if the weather had claimed the murderer as well! A fitting justice, in a way.

What appeared to be a valise was just a white hump beyond the place where he had trampled the snow to get Janet Ashton out of the carriage. It had been tossed some feet away by the impact of the carriage's tumbling fall. And the off wheel, he noted, was cracked. But the horse, tangled in its traces, was pointing in one direction, the vehicle in another. It was nearly impossible to judge where Miss Ashton had been heading when she had skidded wildly off the road. And he hadn't thought to ask her. She had seemed so vulnerable — detached from the tragedy that had taken place in Urskdale but a victim of the same storm. The miracle wasn't that someone had found her in time, but that she had survived at all. It had been a nasty spill. Satisfied, he flicked off the torch.

Hamish said as Rutledge returned to the idling motorcar, "If she had broken her back, you couldna' ha' dragged her up that slope."

"No." Moving her could have killed her or crippled her terribly.

Releasing the brake, Rutledge turned the motorcar with great care and continued on his way.

But Hamish, responding to the weariness that still dogged Rutledge, was in a mood to bring up unpleasant subjects.

He ranged from the case just ended in Preston to the letter that had come from Scotland the day before Rutledge had traveled north. This had invited him to spend the Christmas holidays with his godfather, David Trevor. And he had answered that the weather was too uncertain to plan on driving north in December.

"It couldna' be any worse than this night."

Rutledge argued for a time and then fell silent, unwilling to be drawn again.

Hamish was not satisfied, and kept probing at what he knew very well was a sore subject. It was not David Trevor that Rutledge was avoiding but his houseguest, the woman Hamish should have lived to marry. . . .

# Chapter Six

The stars were just visible as Rutledge drove into the small community hugging the roadside. Shops and houses mingled against the backdrop of the lake on the right and in the shadow of high peaks to his left. The main thoroughfare was churned into muddy ruts, freezing over in the predawn cold and cracking under his wheels. Another quarter of an hour or so, and it would be morning. But now the windows were dark, the streets empty. The door to the police station was shut, and no one answered his call as he stepped inside. He went back to the idling motorcar and began to search for his lodgings.

A long ridge loomed above the village, its irregular outline smooth in the darkness, the rocky slopes shapeless under their white blanket. As if concealing their true nature. Below, Urskdale was oddly quiet, almost withdrawn. Rutledge soon found the rambling stone house that served as the local hotel — hardly more than a private home with rooms to let in the summer for walkers.

Someone had shoveled out the drive after the earlier storm, and the new fall was not as deep. Rutledge made the turning with ease and continued past the side of the house into the yard behind it. Here there was a motley collection of vehicles between the stable and the sheds — carts, wagons, and one carriage — left helter-skelter as if the arriving searchers had been in great haste. Muddy tracks led from the yard towards the sloping land beyond, soon lost in the darkness.

As Rutledge got out of his motorcar, a light came on in a ground floor window and someone peered out through the curtains. He walked around to the front of the house. After some time the door opened, and a woman asked, "You're the man from London?" Wind swirled up in their faces as she looked up at him.

She was seated in a wheeled invalid's chair, her lower limbs covered by a soft blue blanket, and he found himself thinking that she had been brave to open the door to a stranger when there was a killer at large.

"Inspector Rutledge. Sorry to arrive so late — or so early. The roads —"

She nodded. "Do come in." With accustomed ease she turned her chair and made room for him. "I'm Elizabeth Fraser. All the able-bodied men are out searching for the child. Mrs. Cummins, whose house this is, asked me to keep a fire in the kitchen and the kettle on. She's not well, and I've been staying with her. Inspector Greeley arranged for her to put you up while you're here."

He stepped past her into the hall and watched as she latched the door behind him before expertly guiding the chair ahead of him through another door that led to the rear of the house. He could feel the warmth as he followed her down a passage, as if a stove was beckoning him.

Or was his mind dazed with exhaustion?

Holding another door for her, he found himself in the kitchen.

It was bright with color, the walls a soft cream and the curtains at the windows a faded dark green that complemented the floral-patterned cushions on the chairs around the table. A door led to an entry from the yard.

"Would you care for a cup of tea?" She gestured to the kettle on the stove.

"Yes. Please," he answered, already awash with it but suddenly unwilling to be alone. The kitchen was ordinary, quiet, cozy — it had nothing to do with a murdered family or the faces of a jury or the voice of Hamish MacLeod in the rear seat. Nothing to do with the overwhelming mountains outside or the duty he had come to carry out. He wanted only to sit down in one of the chairs and think about the crackle of the fire and the warmth that was spreading through him and the drowsiness that would follow. Without dreams, because the light kept them at bay and the woman in the chair somehow reminded him of Olivia Marlowe. . . .

But Olivia Marlowe — the war poet O. A. Manning — was dead, buried in Cornwall. Beyond his reach.

Shaking himself awake, he began to take off his gloves, scarf, and coat, setting them with his hat on one of the chairs. Miss Fraser was busy with the tea, and without getting in her way he stood to one side of the great iron stove, absorbing the heat. In the cupboard she found a plate of cakes left from tea and said, "I can make sandwiches, if you are hungry."

"Thank you, no." He roused himself to ask, regretfully shattering the illusion of

75

peace, "Any news? Have they found the boy?"

"Not that I've heard. One of the men fell and twisted his knee. When he was brought down, he said his party had failed to find any signs. And there haven't been signals from the other search parties. Each carried a flare . . ." Elizabeth Fraser glanced at the window, though the curtain was drawn. "I can't see how Josh — the boy — could possibly survive in this weather. It's been brutal — and he's so young, barely ten . . ." Her voice trailed off.

"Early storms are often the nastiest," Rutledge agreed. "I wonder if the killer counted on that to cover his tracks — or if it was a matter of luck." His limbs were on fire as circulation returned to them. The room felt stifling now, and he sat down on the far side of the table from the stove. Forcing his tired mind to concentrate, he said, "London wasn't able to give me the usual briefing. I was in Preston when they reached me. Did you know this family — the Elcotts?" He ought to be in his bed — but he wasn't sure he could stand up again.

"Not all that well." She smiled, her face lighting with it. "Up here, there isn't what you'd describe in London as an active social calendar. We see each other at market or at baptisms and weddings, often enough at funerals. But I've met them. A very nice family. Gerald has" — she stopped and bit her lip — "*had* a sizeable sheep farm he'd inherited from his father."

She set the pot of tea beside Rutledge and then brought him a fresh cup. He had noticed that everything was to hand, rather than on high shelves. It appeared the kitchen had been designed for her. "Go on," he urged.

"Gerald ran the sheep himself — except during the war years, when his brother, Paul, managed the farm for him. Then Gerald received a medical discharge and came home to take it up again. But while he was in hospital near London, he met Grace Robinson, a widow with two small children — the missing boy and a little girl. They fell in love and were married. Only, as it turned out, she wasn't a widow. Her husband had survived in a German camp, and came home to find his family gone."

"And no way to trace them," Rutledge observed, "since she had remarried."

"Exactly so. It was the Army's fault, not his or Grace's. His name had been confused with another man's. Robinson is common enough. I expect it wasn't really easy, at the Front, to keep up with who was captured or wounded, and who had died."

Rutledge remembered the thousands of dead, Hamish among them. Stacked like logs, rank with the stench of blood and rotting flesh. And others blown to bits, listed simply as "missing." "I expect it wasn't," he answered simply.

She sighed. "At any rate, they were married, Gerald and Grace, with twins on the way by the war's end. And then Robinson reappeared out of the blue. It was a shock for Grace. She hadn't seen her husband since Christmas of 1914, and even the boy, Josh, hardly remembered him. And yet — there he was."

"A dilemma of major proportions," Rutledge agreed. "How was it resolved?" He took one of the cakes and bit into it. Rich with egg and sugar and butter, it reminded him of boyhood treats, not the austere cooking of wartime and postwar, when many commodities were hard to come by.

"Amicably, surprisingly enough. I expect a divorce was quietly arranged, because Gerald and Grace were as quietly remarried before the birth of the twins. Robinson gave his blessing, or so I was told. The war had changed him, he said, and he didn't know how to begin again. It was rather sad."

This wasn't the first marriage that had come apart with the long separation of the war. Some couples made do with what they had, especially when there were children, and others lived in silent wretchedness, enduring what they couldn't afford to change, socially or financially.

Hamish said, "It's as well ye didna' marry your Jean. But I'd ha' given much to ha' wed Fiona."

It was a frequent source of contention between the two men — how shallow Jean's love had been, while Fiona had remained faithful to Hamish, even after his death. Rutledge still envied Hamish that depth of love.

Hurrying past that hurdle, too tired to argue with the voice in his head, Rutledge said, "Where does this Robinson live now?"

"Near London. Poor man, someone will have to break the news to him. I'm glad it isn't my lot."

"And Urskdale? Did the village take these events in stride?"

Miss Fraser replied thoughtfully. "It was a nine days' wonder, of course. The whole affair. Gossip flew like smoke. And afterward everyone settled down again into the old way of thinking. Grace is — *was* — a lovely person, and we liked her well enough as herself."

Her words ran together and then faded. Rutledge set his cup down with great care, aware that he was losing his battle with sleep.

"I think," he said slowly, "that if I don't see my bed very soon, you'll have to step over me to prepare breakfast."

He had meant it lightly, but was all at once reminded that Miss Fraser sat in a wheeled chair and was not likely to step over anyone.

Silently swearing at himself, he said abruptly, "I'm sorry —"

She smiled again. "Don't be. I'd rather everyone forgot that I don't walk. Pity is far worse than simple acceptance."

He believed her. He wanted no pity for his shell shock. Nor reminders that he had failed himself and his men. Dr. Fleming had been right — it was better to fight through it on his own, whatever the toll.

Standing, he reached clumsily for his coat and gloves, and watched his hat roll across the floor like an oddly shaped football. Retrieving it, he said, "If you'll tell me where I shall be sleeping — I wouldn't want to walk in on Mrs. Cummins."

"Go down the passage again, and through the second door on your right. It leads to rooms that are kept ready for guests. Yours is at the end. A hot water bottle is over there by the hearth, wrapped in a towel," she added, pointing. "I'd recommend it. The house can be quite cold in the early morning. I'll see that you have warm water for shaving —"

"I can fetch it myself, if you leave the kettle on the stove. You must be as tired as I am, watching for my arrival."

"Fair enough. Well, then, good night, Inspector. I hope tomorrow brings news that Josh is safe. If anyone comes, I'll wake you at once."

"Good night. And thank you."

His luggage was in the car and he retrieved that before making his way to his room. It was, thankfully, commodious, and his windows looked out on the distant lake. But Miss Fraser was right, it felt like ice, and the sheets were cold enough for Greenlanders, he thought when he finally got into bed. The hot water bottle, a welcome bit of warmth, made it possible to slip into quiet sleep, lulled by the wind off the fells brushing the corners of the house.

Dreams came after first light, the candle guttered and the room still dark with the long winter nights. Rutledge awoke with a start, the image of a frozen child lying deep in the snow still with him when he opened his eyes.

# Chapter Seven

There was still no news in the morning.

Inspector Greeley sent a man to the hotel; he arrived just as Rutledge had come down to the kitchen. Shaking snow off his shoes and his coat, he strode through the yard door. His nose was cherry red, and he nodded as he walked to the stove and held out his hands to the warmth.

"God, it's miserable out there," he said without preamble. "And I've lived here all my life. I won't shake hands, sir — the fingers will surely fall off. Constable Ward. Mr. Greeley sends his apologies for not coming in person and asked me to report that there's been no change. And with all respect, sir, he'd as soon not have you searching on your own and getting lost."

"I can appreciate that," Rutledge answered. "But I've walked here from time to time —"

"It isn't the same in winter, sir, when you can't see the landmarks." The constable was a thickset man with graying hair and a square face. "Instead, Mr. Greeley has arranged for all the search parties to report to you here. He doesn't want them trampling the yard at the Elcott farm, and this hotel is as near middle ground as you can find. And a good deal more comfortable than the station."

"Any sign of the boy? Any idea of the direction he may have taken?"

"Sadly, no, sir." Ward glanced around the room, as if worried about being overheard. "He can't have survived. Someone will find what's left of him, come the spring."

"And the killer? Any news there?"

Ward shifted, as if the admission made him uncomfortable. "We're no closer to him than we were yesterday."

"Have you a map? I need a better sense of where I am."

"Yes, sir, a fairly good one as it happens. All the farms are shown, and the elevation, with the names of landmarks. Else, the map sometimes lies — tracks are not always where they're marked. You mustn't count on them."

He reached in his coat pocket and pulled

out a folded square of paper, spreading it out on the kitchen table and weighting it with the salt and pepper, the sugar bowl, and the empty cream pitcher.

"We're here," he said, one thick finger pointing to the line of houses along the road. "And this is the Elcott farm." He moved his hand to indicate an isolated square some miles away. "As the crow flies, it isn't all that far. But see, the terrain has to be taken into account. There's no straight line anywhere. Even when the road curves around the lake, it's still the shorter route."

Rutledge, standing, leaned over the map shoulder to shoulder with Ward. He traced the unmade road he'd followed coming in, noting how it skirted the head of the lake and then came straight into the village, passing through to end somewhere near the bottom of Urskwater, blocked by the rising shoulder to the south that was notched at the top. *Doublehead* was neatly printed above it.

A vast expanse in which to search for one small boy. Or a murderer. But in such a storm, how far could either have got?

As in Wasdale, the road didn't circle the lake here. Urskwater was long and narrow, running east and west but on a tilt that put the head of the lake to the northeast, pointing towards Skiddaw, the highest peak in England. There appeared to be marshes along the shore opposite Urskdale, and craggy cliffs rose at the head, soaring like an eagle's lair. They were marked *The Claws*.

"How do you get to the other side of Urskwater at the southern end?"

"There're tracks, if you know where to look for them —"

Ward broke off as the door opened and Miss Fraser rolled herself into the room. "Good morning, Constable. Inspector."

She looked as if she hadn't slept well, but her spirits were high.

Ward, turning beet red, almost bowed to her. "Good morning, Miss. I hope I didn't wake you, come clumping in at this hour."

"No, I was already awake. If you see her husband, will you tell him that Mrs. Cummins is showing a little improvement? It will set his mind at peace. And you'll stay for breakfast, before you go?"

"Yes, Miss, I'll be happy to do both." His eyes followed her as she rolled the chair around the table and began to prepare breakfast. There was a doglike devotion on his face.

Looking from Ward to Miss Fraser,

Rutledge noted that she was an attractive woman, her hair so pale it was almost silvery, and her eyes very blue, the color of a deep sea under sunlight. There was Scandinavian blood, he thought, here in the North. But hers wasn't a Westmorland accent —

A thick porridge had been steaming on the back of the stove, and as she lifted down bowls and handed them to the constable, she said to Rutledge, pointing to a painted china pitcher on the table, "If you would — the milk is just through there. A neighbor has already seen to our cow and her own."

He nodded and walked through the door she'd indicated. In the narrow stone room that kept milk and butter cool in the summer and warmer than the outside in winter, a large white pitcher stood on the middle shelf.

Miss Fraser was dipping the porridge into the bowls, and Ward was setting spoons and cups on the table for her. Rutledge said, "I made tea when I came down. It should be ready." He filled the smaller vessel that was still holding down a corner of Ward's map, and then returned the foamy milk to the pantry.

"Yes, that's fine, thank you," she said,

handing him a bowl to set on the table as he came back.

"If you're making up a tray for Mrs. Cummins," Ward said diffidently, "I'd be glad to take it in for you, Miss."

"Would you, Constable? I'll prepare it when we've finished here."

Rutledge added sugar and butter to his porridge, and then the milk, while Miss Fraser made toast for them. There was damson preserves for it. Ward set to with an appetite.

It was excellent porridge, creamy and hot.

They talked about the unexpected storms, the scope of the search, the various directions it had taken, but skirted any mention of the farm where the bodies had been found or the fate of the child lost in the cold and dark.

When Ward took the tray to Mrs. Cummins, Rutledge helped Miss Fraser clear away the dishes.

"If Mrs. Cummins isn't well —" he began, thinking it would be better to find other accommodations.

"She — drinks," Elizabeth Fraser told him. "Not to put too fine a point on it. She began to drink while Harry was in France, and couldn't stop when he came safely home. The murders have upset her quite badly — well, all of us, come to that. But any excuse, I suppose, would have done." She grimaced. "I don't mean to sound coldhearted. But Harry needs her help to run the hotel. And instead she frightens people away. If they don't make any money in the summer, what are the Cumminses to do the rest of the year?" She began to dip the dishes into hot soapy water. "It would be a kindness if you stayed, Inspector."

"Then I shall."

Ward returned. "She's got a little appetite this morning, she says."

"That's good news!" Elizabeth answered bracingly. "As soon as I finish here, I'll look in on her and let you confer in peace."

"You mustn't leave on our account, Miss! And you know a good bit about this valley," Ward told her. "It would be just as well if Mr. Rutledge here had someone who could keep him abreast of which parties send messages."

He bent over the map again, continuing to point out landmarks, sometimes sketching in the rough lanes that led to various farms, correcting the lines on the map. Rutledge made an effort to commit the constable's points of reference to memory.

The truth was, he would much have preferred going out on his own, starting at the Elcott farm. Surely there would be something there to tell him which way Josh Robinson had fled! But Greeley was right: It was treacherous on unfamiliar mountainous terrain where weather could be unpredictable, landmarks were half hidden in snow, and daylight was short. There was no guarantee he would be any more successful than the local people, and he could well become another problem for the already exhausted search parties.

Hamish retorted, "As yon lassie last night discovered, to her misfortune."

"Will you show me the Follet farm?" Rutledge asked Ward, remembering Janet Ashton.

Ward glanced at him. "Know them, do you, sir?"

As Ward located the square on the map that represented the farm, Rutledge briefly explained. "There was a carriage accident near there last night."

Ward's pencil stopped moving and he asked quickly, "Not our murderer, by any chance?"

"A woman. I left her with the Follets. Bruised ribs."

"Ah. Mary'll see to her then." His pencil

began to move again. "A good sheep man, Jim Follet," Ward went on, echoing Follet's comment about Gerald Elcott. "And in fact, that's how the doctor can pinpoint the time of death, sir. Gerald Elcott brought his animals in before the storm. But he hadn't fed the cow or horses after that. He was either dead, or in no case to see to them."

Rutledge calculated. "Four days dead now, at the outside. The Elcotts. I understand they were shot."

"Revolver, large caliber. Whoever it was just stood there and cut them down. One at a time. Paul Elcott, who discovered the carnage, didn't look for the boy, but Inspector Greeley did, and Sergeant Miller. No sign of him in the house or the outbuildings. We can't be sure how long the lad has been out in the weather — whether he managed to hide until he saw it was safe to move, or took off straightaway." He paused, and glanced up at Rutledge. "My guess is, the boy wasn't at home. He came back, and ran straight into the murderer. He didn't stand a chance, sir. And the body hidden, likely enough, to keep us searching while that devil made good his escape."

"I'd like to see the farm straightaway,"

Rutledge commented, but Ward shook his head.

"Mr. Greeley wishes to take you there himself, sir." And Rutledge was bound by courtesy not to argue.

"What about enemies? Anyone who might have wanted the Elcotts dead?"

"I've tried not to consider that, sir." Ward's voice had turned cold. "It's not pleasant, searching through one's acquaintance to see who might be guilty of a monstrous cruelty!"

"All the same, we've got to address the possibility that he's local. There can't have been many outsiders in Urskdale, not this time of year."

"True enough. Still, who's to say one wasn't keen on being noticed? But he hadn't counted on the storm, had he?" Ward answered stubbornly. "Has London looked to see if a lunatic escaped from an asylum or a prison? What were the Elcotts to him, if he was desperate and needed sanctuary for a bit, somewhere to stay until the weather had passed?"

Hamish reminded Rutledge that the farmer Follet had made a similar comment.

"Or perhaps he used the storm to his own advantage."

Ward met his eyes squarely. "Shall I leave the map, sir? I shan't need it myself. It might be more useful to you. Inspector Greeley said I should ask."

"Leave it, if you can spare it."

And Ward was gone, brusquely thanking Miss Fraser for his breakfast and pulling on the heavy boots he'd left by the yard door.

# Chapter Eight

After a moment, Rutledge opened the outside door again and walked out into the snow. The small back garden was pretty in a pale light that filtered through the clouds. The humps and arcs of last year's vegetables were etched in white now, a magical landscape in miniature.

This was not agricultural country. The season was brief, the ground stony. Root crops did poorly, but a few hardy varieties such as cabbages and whatever else could be coaxed into growing in the shelter provided by the house survived long enough to be harvested.

The well and then a stable led the eye to the barn that stood at the end of the yard. A stone feeding trough ran along one side of a large pen, a shed next to it. An outbuilding provided cover for a farm cart and a carriage. Beyond a patch of raspberries and gooseberries, bare-branched now, a track made its way out into an open field. Looking up, Rutledge could see the faint outline of the fell behind the inn, a long slope that climbed to a ridge and ran, humpbacked, in both directions. Shadows carved rocky defiles and boulders, tricked the eye with deceptive smoothness where loose scree or crevices lay waiting for the unsuspecting foot, and then changed shape again as the clouds thinned, presenting a different face entirely. Except for the wind, there was only silence.

Now that he could see the open sky, Rutledge found the mountains less oppressive than they had been last night. But there was still that uncomfortable sense of being shut off. A sense of claustrophobia.

"They're treacherous, the fells," Miss Fraser said at his back, startling him. "That's probably their attraction. And Wordsworth, of course, with his belief that pristine Nature holds secrets civilized people have lost. I don't think he tried to make a living here — he never saw how hard life can be for those who do. It's harsh country, demanding, and it seldom offers a second chance. I wonder, sometimes, if their roots didn't run so deep here, holding them back, whether people in these valleys wouldn't rather live in Kent or Somerset or Essex. If there was any choice at all." Her voice was sad.

He turned to see her in her chair, shawl over her hair against the cold air, looking out at the long run of fell faintly outlined against the gray sky.

When he said nothing, she went on, "That child must have been terrified. I can't help but agree with Constable Ward, that the killer had better luck finding him and disposing of him that awful night. That's why the search parties have come up empty-handed. How can a ten-year-old boy outrun a grown man? I want to hope — and dare not! It would be too cruel to have hope dashed."

"Is there any other way out of the valley? From the Elcott farm?"

"There's a track farther to the south that runs over the mountains and is said to meet a road coming up from the coast. Sheep were driven to market that way, a long time ago, or so some of the older men claim. I doubt if many people outside Urskdale know how to find it . . ." She looked up at him, her blue eyes troubled. "Do you suppose he — whoever he is — escaped that way?"

"It's possible. I'm sure Inspector Greeley

sent a party in that direction to look for traces of him." But what would bring a man over such rough terrain to kill and then vanish again? There would be easier opportunities along the coast. A lunatic . . .

"You'll never find him, if he got out of Urskdale. And that brings up the question of whether or not he'll — come back. Whether he's finished — satisfied — or still has other business here . . ."

"We'll find him," he told her. "It may take time, but we will. You needn't worry." But Hamish was not as certain. Rutledge could feel the resistance in his mind. *A comforting lie . . .*

They could hear a raven high on the ridge, the deep call echoing.

Elizabeth Fraser tilted her head to listen. As if following up on an earlier thought, she said, "This is such an isolated valley. Sometimes I find it very lonely. Just now I find it very frightening."

"Why do you stay?" he asked, and then wished he could bite back the words. For all he knew she was dependent on the Cumminses for her keep. A companion-housekeeper of sorts to a drunken woman.

But she smiled. "I like the stillnesses. And the wind. I like the wildness. Everything is pared down to the bone in a place like this. It's a wonderful antidote for self-pity. I'm as bad as the summer walkers, aren't I? They come only for 'splendid vistas and noble panoramas.' I should be telling you that I admire the hardiness of the people or the bracing climate. Something unselfish and fine."

She watched him pace restlessly, his mind on the search parties.

"You aren't used to waiting, are you?" she asked.

"No. I'm afraid it shows." Hamish, still agitating in the back of his mind, was keeping him on edge, and the wait for Greeley was beginning to get on his nerves. There must be people he could speak to, evidence he could begin to pull together. But most of the men of Urskdale were out there on the fells, beyond his reach. And the killer could very well be among them. Had Greeley taken that into account?

A gust of wind came round the corner of the house and brought with it a shower of snow from the roof over their heads. Reluctantly Miss Fraser turned her chair and went back inside. After a moment, Rutledge followed her, closing the door and latching it.

"You know these people, do you?" he asked. "Here in Urskdale?"

"You mean, do I know any of them well enough to point my finger at one and call him a murderer?" She drew her chair to the window, where a rare patch of pale, early sun was reaching through the clouds. She turned her face up to it. "Yes. I suppose I do."

He crossed the room and found a chair near the table, taking up one of the napkins there and folding it into triangles and then squares. It soothed his restlessness, a contrast to her peacefulness. How had she learned to accept her disability so tranquilly? Or was it a hard-won lesson, a victory he knew nothing about? "It may be that there was no outsider . . ."

"I hope I don't know anyone who could kill like that," she began pensively. "A grudge simmers, doesn't it? It grates and warps a man until he can't bear it any longer. Short words — angry looks behind someone's back — glares in the butcher shop or at the smithy. Something he's feeling seeps out, surely? But I can't remember ever seeing anyone show that kind of animosity towards Gerald Elcott. I don't recall anyone telling me that they'd overheard a quarrel or seen indications of bitterness or envy. I don't want to think that someone could conceal such anger so well. It smacks of madness, doesn't it?"

"Even madmen have reasons for what they do." Rutledge remembered Arthur Marlton, the prisoner in the dock in Preston. "Look at it another way. Why the Elcotts? They seemed to have lived a rather ordinary life. Not very different from a dozen other families, surely? Then suddenly someone sweeps down on them in a fury and destroys them. Where did this fury come from? Was it directed at *them?* Or were they merely the closest target?"

"The Elcott family has deep roots here. And it's true old resentments are nursed, kept alive for years." Her back was still to him. "I've told you, this is a hard land, and the people on it are hard as well. They don't have much to give, except perhaps trust, and when that's betrayed, they do know how to hate —"

She was interrupted as the kitchen door opened and a man came in, his boots in his hand.

"Morning, Miss," he said to the woman in the chair, before turning to the man at the table. "You're Inspector Rutledge, then?" His eyes scanned Rutledge from head to foot, as if expecting to find a Londoner wanting in the sheer physical ability to cope with the demands of the North. What he saw seemed to satisfy him, and he held out his free hand.

He was tall and gangling, heavily dressed for weather, his face burned a deep red from the wind. But his gray eyes were clear enough. "My name's Henderson. I've come from the group that's been searching" — he caught sight of the map on the table and walked over to stab a finger at a location — "just here. We've seen nothing. Spoke to this house — this one — this — this, and this. They've not seen nor heard anything suspicious. No strangers about. And they're all able to account for their time two days ago. Three, now. Four."

"And do you believe them?"

"It's hard not to. The whole family tells the same story, all the while looking straight at us. I'm a shopkeeper, not a policeman, and uncomfortable risking my livelihood pushing those who frequent my shop too hard. Still — I'd say they were telling the truth." He glanced at Miss Fraser and back again. "Surely what was done leaves scars? You'd have to read *something* in a man's eyes, if he was guilty of such a crime! And what woman would want to lie for him, knowing he'd slaughtered the children as well?"

Which was, Rutledge thought, a perceptive comment and very much what a policeman would be looking for, asking questions of potential suspects. The eyes were sometimes unable to mask emotions that the muscles of the face could conceal with greater ease.

*You'd have to read something in a man's eyes, if he was guilty of such a crime!*

But not all killers had a conscience. . . . He had learned that, too, in Cornwall.

Henderson stayed only for a cup of tea and then was off again, to be followed within the next hour by three more messengers from the search parties. Each, hovering over the map, filled in another area of countryside, giving the details of what they had seen and where they had searched and how they'd found the isolated inhabitants in their path. Rutledge noted each man's information in pencil.

One of them said wearily, "It's not that we aren't doing our best. It's just that there's too much ground to cover, and no certainty whether the boy was there before us. Or will come there after we've passed the place by. We keep an eye to the skyline as we go, and to the slopes. We find ourselves wondering if the murderer is watching *us* from behind a boulder or in a fold of the land. Even at night, when we know he must be out there somewhere, maybe wanting young Josh as much as we do, and hoping we'll lead him to the lad, we feel uneasy. Nobody falls behind in the search party. Even the stragglers keep up."

"Anyone missing?" Rutledge always asked. "Unaccounted for?"

But the answer was always the same: "Not that we can discover. So far."

Another man reporting in said, "People are locking their doors for the first time in years, barring them as well. Out of fear. You can be sure we make noise, coming into a yard — knowing we're being watched. No one wants a shotgun going off in his face!"

Hamish said, "They ken the terrain. They ken the name of every male in the district. If he's no' a stranger, then the killer has to be one of the searchers, if no one is missing!"

Rutledge followed the various parties along the tracks, jotting names beside each square that marked a farm, sketching in the sheep folds and ruins mentioned in the reports, noting the contours and shape of the valley. Information, Hamish reminded him, that was useless to a man in a kitchen by the warmth of a stove.

It was a challenge, and Rutledge resisted it.

Elizabeth Fraser put it best, when the men had gone again. "You aren't in London. You can't bring London experience to bear up here."

"I know." But Hamish, stirred by Rutledge's own tension, was goading him.

*There's a child somewhere in the cold. . . .*

Some time later he came to a barrier, and his numbed mind tried to identify what his hands and his feet could feel: hard, icy stones blocking his path. Beyond them he could see the snow moving, like an ocean of heavy flakes.

But it wasn't the sea, it couldn't be. A walled pen, then, for the sheep who wintered on the fells. He could smell them now, the heavy odor of wet wool. The bellwether often took the flock to shelter when weather came down. Or the owner and his dog would drive them here, where, huddled together, their own warmth would see them through. It was easier to find and care for them when they weren't scattered about the hillsides, nearly invisible humps in the snow.

With a last spurt of effort he clambered up and over the rough stone wall and slipped in among them. Snow-covered himself, he could crouch here and be safe for a little while, until he got his wind back and the snow slacked off. If anyone came, the sheep would know it before he did.

The shapes closest to him sneezed in alarm as they caught his scent. But they were accustomed to men, and when he made no move to drive them out into the wind, they accepted his presence. Sidling back towards him seeking the shelter of the wall on their own account, they surrounded him and eventually included him as one of their own. Unthreatening and in need, in this storm.

Their warmth as they pressed around him in the lee of the wall saved his life.

The house creaked with the cold wind. The rooms were chill and damp. Rutledge wandered into the little parlor reserved for guests, and considered lighting the fire laid ready on the hearth.

But the kitchen was warmer, Elizabeth Fraser seemed comfortable enough in his company, and the men sent to report came by habit to the kitchen door, their heavy boots and rough clothes unsuitable for the parlor.

He stepped into the cold street, leaving the front door ajar, and looked out at the lake. It lay perhaps a quarter of a mile away. Ice and snow rimmed the edges, and the water seemed dark and secretive in the uncertain light. From the Elcott farm it would be impossible for the boy to reach Urskwater . . . but it was a place where a small body could be *carried,* weighted with whatever the killer had to hand. How long would it take for a child to float back to the surface?

Where was Josh Robinson?

Was he a red herring, already long dead, his body hidden while the killer slipped back into the ordinary life of Urskdale? Or had his murderer disappeared over the fells and into safe havens where no one would think to look?

What could the boy tell the police, if he were found alive? An eyewitness . . .

Or had he come on the scene long after his family had been shot, and simply lost his way in the snow trying to find help?

It was easy to make assumptions . . . but there would be no answers until Josh Robinson was found.

Terrible questions remained. Would

there be other killings? What had set a man on the road to such destruction? What had been done to him, real or imagined, that lighted the dormant fuse of such anger? And would he turn on another neighbor next, when some small slight or uncertainty began to haunt him again? Or was he simply a man with a secret to be protected at any cost? Had Gerald Elcott stumbled onto something too vile to be overlooked? The storm might have given even a reluctant killer the perfect excuse to be absent — the perfect timing for murder.

*"I'll just go and have a look at the sheep, before it's any worse out there. . . ."*

But that would mean someone reasonably close by, within reach of the Elcott farm. It might even be someone who had no need to explain his absences. Or — someone who lived alone and was accountable to no one?

Rutledge remembered what Elizabeth Fraser had told him about the people of Urskdale only a few hours before.

*"They don't have much to give, except perhaps trust, and when that's betrayed, they do know how to hate —"*

Whose trust had Gerald Elcott betrayed? What had he done that would drive a man to kill Grace Elcott and her children as well?

Until he saw that farmhouse kitchen for himself, his experience and intuition had nothing to work with, except the reactions of others. And secondhand knowledge was never to be trusted.

*What was keeping Greeley? Why was he avoiding the Yard man he had so urgently sent for in the beginning?*

# Chapter Nine

Elizabeth Fraser had gone to make the beds. In the silence of the kitchen, Rutledge stood over the map, hands spread on either side, studying what he'd been told by the men reporting to him.

There appeared to be no farms close enough to the Elcotts to offer the child safe haven, even if Josh Robinson could have found his way to one of them in heavy snow and darkness. And the boy hadn't been born here, bred to the tracks and landmarks that his stepfather would have known by heart. But that might also mean that the killer wouldn't have stumbled across them, either, if he had found the Elcotts only by chance.

The first priority of Greeley's search parties would have been to reach these farms, and make certain all was well.

All right then. Where *could* Josh Robinson have gone, if he was still alive?

Rutledge ran a finger across the face of the map. In fact, Urskdale itself was closer, if one came over the shoulder of the ridge. So, why hadn't the boy tried to reach the village? His uncle, Paul Elcott, was here. No, that wasn't quite true. Elcott wasn't an uncle by blood.

If Josh Robinson didn't know Elcott well enough, then why not the rector? Or his schoolmaster?

Even Inspector Greeley or Constable Ward? Or the sergeant — what was his name? Miller.

Or had the child been cut off from the village, and forced to strike out into the darkness without knowing where he was heading?

There was another possibility. Rutledge turned to stare out the window. Josh might have been terrified of coming to the village. Afraid he would run into the murderer here. It would mean that someone —

Hamish objected, "It doesna' signify. He didna' have the time."

Yes. In spite of all their hopes, the boy must be dead. Rutledge bent over the map again. Perhaps the question now was where a body could be concealed?

But why hide it? Why not leave it in

plain sight, to show that the killer had wiped the slate clean —

Lost in thought, he didn't hear the door from the passage open. The woman's voice startled him.

"Good morning . . ." Her hair was crimped and straggling, and her clothes seemed to have been made for another woman, thinner and younger. She cast a glance around the room with an air of vague confusion, as if uncertain if this was where she ought to be.

He straightened, looking up into drained eyes, a pale blue that seemed to be painted in place under paler lashes.

"Good morning. Er — Mrs. Cummins? I'm Inspector Rutledge. Thank you for putting me up while I'm here in Urskdale. It was kind of you."

"It was my husband decided that," she replied. "But I'm glad you're here. It isn't safe for two women to be in a house alone. I told my husband as much before he left. I told him if he didn't worry about me, he should worry about Elizabeth. She's helpless —" After a moment she added in a whisper, "He killed the *babies*, too, you know. This murderer."

"I'm afraid it's true —" he began, but let his voice trail away, for she appeared to have forgotten him.

Unable to settle, she walked to the side-board, her hands busy folding a pile of freshly ironed serviettes lying there. When she'd finished, she stood staring at them, as if unable to think where they ought to go now.

Hamish remarked, "It isna' any wonder she needs a minder. The lass in the invalid chair canna' have an easy time of it!"

Rutledge had seen other women like her. Driven to despair by fear and long months of uncertainty, they had taken comfort in the bottle. And more than one man had come to him to beg for compassionate leave, when a wife or fiancée had been taken up as a common drunk.

Unaware that she was the subject of this silent exchange, Mrs. Cummins smiled distractedly at him. "Is there anything you need, Inspector? Would you like some tea?" Her attention was drawn back to the serviettes. She picked them up, put them in a drawer, and then took them out again. Finally she simply smoothed them once or twice and forgot them.

"I've been well taken care of, Mrs. Cummins. Thank you."

"You might bring in more coal," she said, walking unsteadily across to the window. "That's difficult for Elizabeth."

"I'll be happy to see to it," he promised. He cursed himself for not thinking of offering.

"My room is never warm. There must be something wrong with the chimney's flue. It can't be drawing well," she fretted, clutching her shawl across her body as if needing something to hold to. "This used to be a fine hotel, before the war. I don't know what's to become of it now. Or us."

"I'm sure," Rutledge said gently, "that the climbers and walkers will return next summer."

"I grew up in London. But my grandfather could find his way blindfolded over most of Cumberland and half of Westmorland. He told me more than once he could tell by the smell of the ground where he was. Like the sheep. He said if he ever lost his sight, he could find his way about without it. We had an old dog who was just the same. You could set her down anywhere, and she'd know her way home."

"A gift," Rutledge agreed.

"They say sheep are stupid, but they aren't."

The silence between them lengthened. "Any word of the child?" she asked finally, her voice trembling on the last word. "Have they found the little Robinson boy yet?"

113

"No, I'm afraid not. But several of the search parties have yet to report."

She continued to stand by the window, as if the wintry scene drew her. "I pray for him every night . . ."

"That's kind —" Rutledge began.

Her eyes flicked back to him. "Does anyone hear prayers, do you think? Really — *hear* them?"

"I'm sure someone does," he answered.

"Oh — I can see the Long Back — our ridge," she exclaimed suddenly. "The clouds have lifted." And then with agitation she begged, "Look — there! Do you think that dark spot up there — over to the left, by The Knob — do you think that might be *him?*"

Rutledge came to stand behind her, picking up the faint smell of whisky, lavishly overlaid with rose water.

There was nothing where she was pointing except for a shallow depression that the sun had not found yet.

"Shadows play tricks," Rutledge told her, moving on to the pump for a glass of water. "The boy can't have traveled this far."

"No . . . probably not." She turned, losing her animation, and walked to the passage doorway. "You won't forget about the coal, will you?"

"No —"

But she was gone, a ghost in her own house, flitting between awareness and stupor.

"A pity," Hamish was saying.

And then the soft voice floated down the passage as the door swung closed. "What if *he's* hunting for the child too? What if he finds him first? *I can't sleep for thinking about it!*"

It was barely ten minutes later that Inspector Greeley came striding into the kitchen from the front of the house, his voice carrying, answering Elizabeth Fraser somewhere behind him.

There were dark shadows under his eyes, and his chin was patchy with missed beard, as if he'd shaved quickly, without a mirror. Lines of strain bracketed his mouth, aging him.

"I'm sorry," he said, extending his hand as he introduced himself, "that I wasn't here earlier. I snatched a few hours' rest this morning."

"You look as if you could use more," Rutledge answered sympathetically. "A number of your men reported in when they could. I've noted the names and the areas they've searched. No luck, I'm afraid."

With a nod Greeley walked to the map and glanced down at it. "Yes, that's what I'd expected, more or less. But we had to try, you see. Hard as hell to find your way out there, much less hunt for a veritable needle in a haystack. I don't know how to handle this any differently," he added. "I've never had to deal with anything like it."

He pulled out a chair, and sat down heavily. "I see you've more or less set up your headquarters here. Just as well. The chimney at the station hasn't been drawing worth a damn. Smoked me out again just last week! But I should think the parlor would be more comfortable."

"Men coming and going here are less likely to disturb Mrs. Cummins in her room, and to be honest, it's the only truly warm part of the house." Rutledge took the chair across from Greeley. "You've done what I'd have done," he went on. "The most important task was to locate the boy. And to make certain there were no other victims. After that, to hunt down the killer."

"A boy of ten couldn't survive this long, surely!" Greeley rubbed his face with his fingers, massaging stiff muscles. "It's hopeless."

"It would depend on his resourcefulness and his knowledge of the land. He could have taken shelter somewhere —"

"We don't even know how he was dressed," Greeley said. "Or which direction he took. By the time we got to the farm, any tracks had been well covered by several inches of snow. His and the murderer's." His eyes veered away from Rutledge's. "I suppose you want to see the Elcott house." The reluctance in his voice was only half concealed.

"I shall have to, yes."

"I'd as soon never set foot in it again. I can't close my eyes without seeing them lying there. Shocking, that's the only word to describe it." He heaved himself to his feet. "All right. Let's get it over with. Is that your motorcar in the yard? We'll take that. It's faster. The roads are wretched, but we can manage."

"Let me tell Miss Fraser that I'll be leaving."

Rutledge went down the passage and quietly called her name. She was sitting in the small, chilly parlor, a book in her lap, and the door open.

"I heard Inspector Greeley arrive," she told him, closing the book. "I thought perhaps you'd like a little privacy."

"He's — er — we're going to be away for a time," Rutledge said, trying to spare her feelings. "I don't know if I'll be here for dinner. But don't worry about that. I'll manage well enough."

"Thank you for telling me, Inspector." She smiled, and he noticed again how it lighted her face from within.

From somewhere the thought came, *Olivia Marlowe might have looked like this woman.* . . .

Elizabeth Fraser was saying, "Is there any message you'd like for me to give to anyone who needs you?"

"Just that I'll be back as soon as possible. And you might note on the map whatever information they've brought. If it's urgent, Inspector Greeley can be found at the Elcott farm."

Her expression stilled. "Yes. I'll do that, Inspector."

It was a silent drive. Rutledge was nearly certain that Greeley had nodded off, his head down on his chest, his hat shadowing his eyes. But he could have been lost in thought. Or preparing himself for what was to come . . .

Following the map in his head, Rutledge was able to find the rough road on which the farm stood, but after that asked Greeley for directions.

They drove up a muddy lane and into the back of a tall whitewashed stone farmhouse with nothing to set it apart from dozens of its neighbors except for the traffic that had passed in and out of the yard over the past several days, churning the snow into black muck.

Hamish said, "A stalker couldna' find the lad's tracks in that . . ." He was referring to the Highland gillies who could follow the red deer over bare rock. Or so it was said. They had hunted snipers in France with equal skill and cunning.

Greeley got out stiffly, and stretched his back. More, Rutledge thought, to postpone the inevitable than to ease his tired spine. Then he turned to scan the horizon, almost a reflex action, looking for any sign of movement or activity. But there were no flares, no line of men on the heights. "This way," he said finally, and Rutledge preceded him into the tiny stone entry that led into the kitchen.

It wasn't, he found himself thinking, so very different from the one where he had spent most of the morning. Large, square, with windows looking out on two sides and a great black cooker in one corner, it had been pretty once. Rose-patterned curtains hung at the windows, chintz cushions in a matching style covered the chairs, and the cloth on the table had roses embroidered in the center, great cabbage roses in cream and pink.

In stark contrast, blood marred everything — the floor, the walls, the furnishings — as if flung there by a mad painter. No longer a bright red, but an ugly black. The bodies had been removed, but the tracks of men who had carried them out had of necessity marked the splatters of blood with heel-prints in different sizes.

Hamish said, with feeling, "It brings back the war . . ."

Rutledge thought: "The refugees we found in that cellar —"

There were plates of food on the table, and covered pots on the stove. One glass overturned. A stained fork lying on the floor. A chair on its side. The unexpectedness of the attack witnessed by such insignificant things . . .

Greeley was explaining, as if by rote, "Gerald Elcott was there, by the cooker. From what Jarvis told me, it took him nearly a minute to die. The little girl — Hazel — was lying by the door — She died quickly, thank God. And the twins were close by the table, beside their mother. She was half draped over them, as if to shield them. Jarvis thinks she saw them shot before she herself died. It was ruthless — venomous —"

Rutledge could picture the scramble as the family realized what was about to happen. The father too far from the outer door to stop the killing — the little girl racing to reach safety in another room. The mother flinging herself towards the infants. Shouts and screams — the deafening sound of the revolver — and then silence. And Josh? Where was Josh?

"How many shots were fired?"

"As far as we can tell at this stage, there were six. One in each of the dead, and one there in the wall. It must have missed the boy as he ran out the door. We haven't found the revolver. We've searched the house top to bottom, and the outbuildings. Our man is still armed, wherever he is."

"And the killer stood where?"

"Here, where we are. It would give him command of the room, an open field of fire. No one had disturbed the scene. The murderer made no effort to find out if all of them were dead. He didn't care. Paul Elcott never approached the victims, either. I don't think he could bear it —"

Greeley broke off and then blurted, "You know the worst of it? I helped Sergeant Miller carry them out. And I think if I'd had their murderer within reach, I'd have killed him *myself!*" He cleared his throat in embarrassment before going on in a steadier voice. "It seems to me that he came in from the yard and caught them all off guard. There was no way to tell if there was any exchange before he began shooting. But it must have happened very quickly. Gerald Elcott — the father — was shot first, before he could put up a fight to save his family. That would make sense. And it would have been less than two minutes before the killer turned to go after the boy. Not much of a head start, really." Taking a deep breath, he added, "I have to ask myself if the parents knew why this was happening. Or if it was as senseless to them —"

"Whoever it was, if he came into the kitchen as we did, he must have known the family."

"That's possible. But here in the North, the kitchen is always the warmest room in winter, and we generally go round to the yard door rather than the front of the house. I don't think it signifies. And a stranger would have come to where the lamp was lit."

"Still, Gerald Elcott was standing by the stove. That means the son opened the outside door, and must have known the killer at least well enough to allow him to step inside. Otherwise, Elcott would have been here, where we are, in the murderer's way. Think about it."

Greeley sighed. "Yes, I agree. Not a stranger, then . . ."

"But not necessarily someone *you* may know," Rutledge pointed out. He recognized the propensity of local police to prefer outsiders, not their own.

Brightening, Greeley said, "Yes, that's possible."

"How many members of the family live close enough to call in without notice?"

"Only Gerald's brother, Paul, lives here in Urskdale. Grace has a sister, who sometimes visits in the summer. I've never known her to come in winter. We haven't been able to reach her, but the wires were down for a day and a half. And there's the father of the two older children. Robinson. He lives in London."

"Any close friends, then?"

Greeley shrugged. "Anyone from Urskdale might stop in. And be welcomed." He turned away and stumbled out into the air. "I can't stand the smell in here."

123

Hamish said, "It's no' the smell —"

Rutledge barely heard him. He stood there in the doorway for a moment longer. Even without the presence of the victims, the force of helplessness and terror lingered, like a miasma, as heavy as the acrid taint of blood. He could sense it, and with it, something else.

Surely it hadn't been done without an attempt at justification, the killing. There would have been no satisfaction in that, surely . . . only a massacre.

With a last look at the kitchen, he followed Greeley out into the cold afternoon.

They walked around to the front of the house, where the snow was beaten down by foot traffic.

"It was smooth as glass when we got here," Greeley was saying. "And this door was tight shut." He opened it and they stepped into a small hall, where wet, muddy tracks marred the smooth floor.

Rutledge thought, "Grace Elcott wouldn't care to have strangers see her floor in this condition. . . ."

The style of the furnishings in the parlor was Victorian, but the polished wood was a measurement of pride, and the small touches, a plant on a stand by the window, the coal scuttle filled, matches upright in a narrow blue vase beside it, a collection of picture frames with yellowing photographs of at least two generations, and the spotlessly clean chimneys of the lamps, indicated that Grace Elcott was a good wife. But what else was she?

They climbed the stairs to find that the twins shared a room, while the boy and girl had their own. Each was neat as a pin, with a wooden chest for the collection of toys and games in the boy's room and a small shelf for dolls in the girl's. Clothes were tidily folded in drawers or hung in the wardrobes.

There was a photograph by Hazel's bed, and judging by the Victorian style of dress, it had been taken around 1900. A young girl stood squarely facing the camera almost as one would face an enemy, straight on. Dressed in a plain white gown, her hair pulled back with a ribbon, she seemed to resent the photographer's intrusion, as if she had other things she'd rather be doing. At her feet lay a tennis racket, as if thrown there in anger. The little dog half hidden in her skirts looked up at her in adoration, unmindful of her mood, but Rutledge, holding the frame, could read the stormy face very well. Grace Elcott as a girl?

The master bedroom boasted a great carved bedstead, early Victorian, with a matching washstand and chest. On that was a set of silver-plated brushes with GLR on the backs. Mrs. Elcott's, from her first marriage?

If so, it might indicate that her present husband was a tolerant man, or that they were too expensive to be replaced easily.

Hamish said, "He accepted the children of the first marriage . . ."

Perhaps the initials didn't matter, or the brushes were kept for the daughter.

On the dressing table was another photograph. Rutledge found himself looking down into the faces of the dead. A man of middle height, fair-haired and exceptionally handsome. Beside him a woman who smiled with noticeable joy, her face tilted, her eyes alight. There was something about her that suited her name — Grace. Slim and leaning a little towards her husband, she appeared to be deeply in love. In her arms she held the twins, swathed in blankets, hardly more than tiny features blinking at the sun. Barely a month old when the photograph was taken, Rutledge judged. Grace Elcott had grown from a sulky child into a confident wife and mother.

A shy girl stood between Gerald and Grace Elcott, and Gerald's hand was on her shoulder, as if in reassurance. Hazel. Her eyes were looking up into his face. Next to the woman stood a boy, all legs and arms, scowling at the camera, his chin tucked into his chest, as if in protest. Josh Robinson. In the background was a church door.

Greeley said to Rutledge, "Taken by the rector, after the christening. Mrs. Elcott was that happy, that day. My wife remarked on it, how happy she was." He shrugged his shoulders deeper into his heavy coat, as if to shut out the cold.

And only months later Grace Elcott's happiness had ended abruptly in a whirlwind of destruction. The kitchen was still all too fresh in Rutledge's mind. Here in the bedroom, Grace's bedroom, the house no longer warmed by fire or laughter or the ordinary sounds of a family's life, he could feel the emptiness, and the pervasive silence that would never be filled again. It was, in a sense, far more horrible because in his hand he held the faces of the living family. *Did you know why you became a victim?* Or had his imagination run away with him?

Hamish said, "There had to be hatred behind such murders . . ."

Rutledge set the photograph down, and without comment turned to finish his search.

The contents of the wardrobe were what he'd expected to find — mostly daily wear, with dark coats for market day and for church. One of the hats on the shelf had been worn by Mrs. Elcott the day of the christening, with frivolous silk roses still pinned on the brim. His sister Frances had told him once that a woman's choice of hat revealed her mood.

Hamish reminded him of Elizabeth Fraser's words: *"We see each other at market or at christenings and weddings, more often at funerals."* And the same clothes served for each occasion, but the hats could define the moment.

As if mirroring his thoughts, Greeley said, "The Elcotts were no richer than the rest of us. There's never money for frills here in the North. Still, we're grateful for what we have. And through the war, we managed. We were used to making do. Nobody went hungry."

It was a comment Rutledge had heard often enough. *We managed.* . . . The hardships of war and the ensuing peace had left many families struggling to survive. Few of them complained, making an effort to cope and rebuild their shattered hopes. But there were those who had prospered, and for whom there was no looking back.

Hamish said, "It's no' money, then, that's at the back of this killing."

Rutledge, before he could stop himself, answered aloud, "There's the land —"

Greeley nodded, as if the comment had been directed at him. "We found Gerald Elcott's will. Here's how it stood. The farm has been in the family for generations. There's no one left to inherit now save his brother. Gerald was generally the one who worked with his father, and so Henry passed the land to him. Paul was set up in business as part owner of the licensed house in Urskdale. Of course when Gerald was away in France, Paul came back here to run the sheep. The Ram's Head had all but gone under, anyway, with no one coming of a summer to keep it afloat."

"What does Paul Elcott do now?"

Greeley went back to the head of the stairs, saying over his shoulder, "He's trying to reopen The Ram's Head. On his own. Frankly, it's an uphill struggle."

The inspector was eager to get away from the house, and it showed.

Rutledge followed Greeley back to the motorcar. A watery sun was strengthening, and the snow was beginning to melt. It was slushy underfoot, the first sign of thaw.

As they came around the corner of the house, Hamish said, "Why did yon brother come out to the farm on Tuesday?"

Rutledge asked Greeley as he cranked the motorcar.

"I expect to see if they needed anything. I looked in on two other families myself. One an elderly couple, and the other with very young children. The storm came through in a hurry, and there wasn't much warning. No time to come into the village for lamp oil or staples. There was barely time to bring in the stock." Greeley stepped into the passenger's seat.

"Has it occurred to you that Paul Elcott could have killed his brother and his brother's family?"

Shocked, Greeley simply looked at Rutledge as he drove out of the yard.

"Paul Elcott would inherit the farm," Rutledge pointed out. "There's your motive. And he must have visited the house often enough. Any signs of his presence at the murder scene could easily be explained by that fact."

"That's foolishness! You didn't see him after he'd found them. He was sick as a dog in the barn —" He broke off, his eyes on the road.

A horse and carriage was coming swiftly towards them, moving far faster than conditions on the road warranted.

Greeley said, his voice rising with excitement, "There must be news! By God, they must have found the boy!"

# Chapter Ten

Rutledge pulled on the brake, drawing the motorcar to the side of the rutted verge, out of the path of the horse galloping straight at them.

"No, that's the doctor's carriage," Greeley declared, squinting at the oncoming vehicle. "Gentle God, you don't suppose there's been another *slaughter* — !" He leaned out of the window to shout "What's happened?"

The carriage was near enough now to see the man holding the reins. He wore a heavy gray coat, and his face was half hidden by a hat pulled down tightly against the wind. Greeley swore. "That's not Jarvis or one of my men. It's Hugh Robinson! Grace Elcott's first husband —"

The horse thundered to a stop ten feet short of the motorcar, eyes rolling, as a slender man with a strained, haunted face drew rein. "My God —" he began, and his voice choked. He shook his head wordlessly. "It must be true!"

As the lathered horse sidled in such close proximity to the vehicle, Rutledge switched off the motor. He and Greeley opened their doors and stepped out into the lane.

"Mr. Robinson —" Greeley began.

"I came as soon as I heard —" Robinson was saying as the horse steadied. *"Why in God's name didn't anyone contact me in London!"*

"The blame is mine," Greeley said, with a tiredness in his voice that spoke of something else besides exhaustion. "We've been out looking for your son. All our energies have gone into searching for him. I'd hoped to have —"

"I should have been here — *I should have been out with the searchers* —" Robinson's thin face contorted in grief.

"Mr. Robinson —" Greeley began, and then found nothing to say.

Rutledge said, "If you'll come with us back to the hotel —"

"No! I want to go to the house. I need to see —"

"I don't think it's a very good idea," Rutledge began, but Robinson stared at him with angry eyes.

"It's my family, not yours." He took up the whip and lashed at the horse, sending it flying down the lane.

Greeley flinched as if he'd been struck instead, and ran after him, leaving Rutledge to turn the crank and then catch them up.

Robinson was already in the kitchen when Greeley reached him, leaning against the open door as if poleaxed.

Rutledge was in time to hear Robinson mumbling over and over again, "Dear God — dear God — dear God . . ."

And then he was outside and bending down by the cellar stairs, vomiting as if all the contents of his stomach were being forced out by the horrors he'd just seen.

Greeley looked across at Rutledge, pleading for understanding. Hamish was saying, "I wouldna' be in his shoes — !"

Rutledge said with some authority, "Mr. Robinson. I'm from Scotland Yard."

Robinson fumbled for a handkerchief to wipe his mouth. He stopped to stare up at the man from London, his eyes dazed.

"When did they summon *you?*" Robinson asked.

"I was already in the North," Rutledge replied. "I'm sorry to hear that Inspector Greeley failed to contact you straightaway.

But we were already two days late hunting for Josh, and time was against us."

Robinson leaned back against the side of the house, looking up at the sun. "I was bringing gifts for the holidays — I was coming to bring *gifts*."

Greeley said to Rutledge, "He did come about this time last year. I had forgotten —"

Rutledge said, "How did you get here?"

"By rail, as I always do. And then I borrowed a mount from the smith to ride the rest of the way. Dr. Jarvis overtook me outside Urskdale. He wanted me to come to his house — but I couldn't wait — and he gave me the loan of his carriage. My horse was not as fresh as his." He straightened. "Where's Josh? Why haven't you found my son?"

"We've done all we can — all that's humanly possible. I'm afraid prospects aren't . . . the best." Greeley dug the toe of his heavy boot into the trampled snow by the back door. "The searchers haven't given up."

Robinson began to pace in his agitation. "I want to know who did this. I want to know *now*. Do you understand me?"

"We're no less eager than you are to apprehend the bastard," Greeley told him, stung.

"Inspector," Rutledge intervened, "if you'll take the doctor's carriage back to him, I'll drive Mr. Robinson to the hotel —"

"I want to see them," Robinson said steadfastly. "I want to see Grace and my daughter."

And in the end, there was nothing to be done but to let him have his way.

While Inspector Greeley took Robinson to the makeshift mortuary to inspect the bodies of his dead, Rutledge drove back to Urskdale with only Hamish for company.

Hamish was saying, "It's no' very wise to view the corpses."

"No. But then I don't know him well enough to judge what's best. For some men —"

For some men it could harden their resolve to mete out their own justice. . . .

When he reached the inn, Rutledge reported to Miss Fraser that there would be another guest.

"I don't know how he can bear such a loss," she said with compassion. "I wish we had better news for him, but the search parties, I'm to tell you, have found no one. They're to try again tomorrow at first light, but they need to rest. Mr. Cummins is so weary, he's staying with his men over at the Ederby farm."

That was far down the valley, just before the lake turned.

"And you," Hamish reminded Rutledge as Miss Fraser wheeled herself down the passage, "havena' wet your shoes out on the fells."

Rutledge went into the kitchen to stand by the window, watching the early darkness rise up the face of the ridge like a curtain.

It would be a miracle to find a lone child in such an expanse of empty landscape. The valley, small as it was, was still a vast area to comb. And time had surely run out for Josh Robinson. Even if every farmer scoured his own acres, it would take days to cover them properly. There wasn't even a certainty that the boy would turn up in the spring. His small bones would be carried off by ravens and foxes, leaving nothing to mark how or where he died.

Yet it was not something any man found easy to do: to walk away from a child in need. Greeley would have to make the decision to halt the search, and Rutledge didn't envy him.

Hamish said, "It doesna' sit well."

In the aftermath of a shelling or in the carnage of an attack, men went missing:

dead, lying wounded in No Man's Land, or captured. Rutledge had always done his best to bring back his wounded, young Scots not so many years older than the missing boy, and yet already men. It had felt like a betrayal to post them as lost. As if he could have done more . . . should have . . .

He shook off the darkness that came creeping out of the past to waylay him. This was not his battle, it was Hugh Robinson's.

Elizabeth Fraser had wheeled into the room behind him, and as he looked up, he realized from the odors wafting to him from the cooker that dinner was already well under way. Turning to her, he smiled ruefully.

"I'm sorry. I promised to bring in coal."

"You still may, if you will. One of the searchers helped me earlier."

And he followed her directions as to where to find the scuttles needing filling, and then took them out into the yard where the cellar door led down into the bowels of the house. Shoveling coal from the bin into each, he found the physical effort released some of the tension that had built up at the Elcott farm.

On his last trip the stars were pushing

their way through thinning clouds, and he looked up at them, his breath coming in white puffs.

Hamish said, jarring him, "Ye're reduced to carrying coal, like a dustman."

Ignoring him, Rutledge walked past the barn and into the field beyond, then began to climb the slope of the fell that rose in the darkness like a hunched figure out of some wild mythology. The snow, giving light back to the stars, seemed more sinister in the darkness, as if holding secrets within its white mantle. And there was nothing to show him a path to follow, although in summer when he had come to the Lake Country with his father, there had always been tracks, clear on the ground where thousands of feet — man and beast — had preceded him. Worn ground, giving up its secrets easily in some places, holding to them tightly in others. But the snow obliterated even the clearest signs, offering silence and mystery instead. And it was no use trying to read what the snow shrouded. It would be too easy to find oneself in a place where retreat was as dangerous as going on.

But he had always believed in knowing his enemy. And these fells were his, in more ways than one. Professionally they foiled him, hiding what he needed to know. Personally they threatened him, as if intent on sending him out of the valley before his work was done.

He climbed another fifty feet, and then fifty more. Looking back at the winding street of houses and the lights in the inn, the plain stone church at the far end of the village, and at the head of Urskwater, the great bulge of The Claws black against the sky, Rutledge could see the paper map come to life. Where a light faintly twinkled, he could name the farm, traveling in his mind's eye the track that led there. He scanned the heights for a telltale bobbing line of lanterns traversing a slope, but there was nothing: Either too great a distance lay between them or the searchers were asleep in a house or barn, dead to everything but the needs of their weary bodies.

Like it or not, it *was* time to call a halt to the search. If Josh Robinson had survived this long without shelter, it would be a miracle. Exposure would quickly finish what exhaustion had begun.

If the murderer had also failed to find him, then the boy missing would be in as great a danger as the boy found and in the custody of the police. . . .

And what would he do then, this killer of children?

It would be ironic if the weather that had doomed the boy had also doomed his murderer. Two bodies to find in the spring.

But all the reports claimed that no one else was missing . . . Where had the killer gone to ground? Or had he come here by chance?

Below him, a carriage was turning into the inn's yard. He could see the side lamps gleaming in the darkness, and then the light from the kitchen door as someone opened it.

Rutledge began to walk quickly back the way he had come, his feet slipping once or twice as his boots pressed into the icy crust. Pausing only to pick up the last coal scuttle, he turned towards the kitchen door. And instead of opening it, he looked through the window at the lighted scene inside.

A middle-aged man was there, speaking to Elizabeth Fraser, and at his side was a white-faced Hugh Robinson, his hands gripping a chair's back as if desperate for its support. Then the men followed Elizabeth through the door to the passage and disappeared.

Rutledge stepped into the empty

kitchen, setting the scuttle by the stove, and stood there, warming his cold hands, listening to the sounds of the house. Faint voices, doors opening and closing. Steps coming this way.

The middle-aged man returned, and looked up at Rutledge with some surprise. "Shall I fetch Miss Fraser or Mrs. Cummins . . . ?"

Rutledge introduced himself, and the other man said in his turn, "Jarvis. Local doctor." He shook his head. "I tried to persuade Robinson not to view — but he's a stubborn man. In the end, I think he regretted it. I had to give him some of my hoarded whiskey before he fell on his face." The doctor was clearly irritated, his hands moving restlessly around the brim of his black hat.

"I shouldn't think it was easy for either of you," Rutledge commented.

"No." Jarvis pulled the chair out and sat. "I gather the searchers have come up empty-handed?" He indicated the map, and turned it towards him.

"So far. Reports haven't been promising."

"I can't think where the boy could have got to." Jarvis sighed as he leaned over the map and with one finger traced several routes from the death scene out into the hilly ground that surrounded it. "There's nothing in any direction for miles."

"A sheep pen here," Rutledge said, leaning across the table, "and what appears to be a ruin here."

"Yes, that's the old Braithewaite farmhouse. Long since fallen into ruin. My wife's grandfather knew the family, but they had all died by her father's time. You should have seen the stonework on that house! A marvel of construction, a lost art. My father-in-law took me there to point it out. Couldn't have been comfortable to live in, up at that elevation, but they were hardy Norse stock and never seemed to mind either the isolation or the cold. The old grandmother could weave blankets thick as your finger! Double-sided, they were. My wife's mother had one of them, as I remember. A wedding gift."

"You know the people around here better than I do," Rutledge said. "Any thoughts on who might have killed the Elcotts? Or why?"

"I heal people, when I can. I don't judge them," Jarvis said bluntly. "Why should it be someone local?"

"It's a place to begin," Rutledge responded mildly. "I was under the impression that Gerald Elcott was shot where he stood, by the stove. He wasn't afraid of the intruder in his wife's kitchen, or he would have been at the door, between his family and the unexpected danger."

Jarvis's face changed. "I hadn't considered that. I knew Gerald. He could handle himself. Even before he went into the Army. You're absolutely right, he'd have fought —"

"I understood he was invalided out of the Army."

"Yes, a kidney shot up. Doctors removed it. But he got on well enough, afterward. And he'd have protected his family at any cost to himself."

"Tell me about Paul Elcott."

"There's not much to tell. He'd broken his left leg when he was young — a severe compound fracture that left the bone weak — and the Army wouldn't take him. He spent the war years working with local farms, trying to increase crop yield. And he ran the Elcott place as well. By the time Gerald was invalided home, Paul had lost thirty pounds. The man was a walking skeleton."

"And Robinson? Did he bear a grudge against Elcott for taking away his wife?"

"For one thing, Gerald hardly took away

Hugh Robinson's wife! The Army declared the man missing, then dead, a year before Gerald met Grace. And when he came home, Robinson himself believed that it was for the best to bow out. He hadn't seen his wife in years, and she was carrying Gerald's twins by that time. I hardly think that twelve months later he would slaughter all of them in some sudden craving for revenge. Certainly the man I saw an hour ago, looking at his little daughter's body, was distraught —"

The door opened and Elizabeth entered. "I think he might be able to sleep a little. Mr. Robinson. If not, I told him he could find us here."

Jarvis, rising, nodded. "God knows the powder I gave him ought to do the trick. But after the whiskey, I was afraid to try anything stronger."

"He tells me Inspector Greeley never sent him word —" she began.

"I think Greeley had hoped to offer him a little good news, that his son was safe." Jarvis sighed. "It was an unfortunate oversight."

"I wonder if the inspector has remembered Grace's sister?" she went on.

Jarvis stared at her. "I expect he hasn't. I'll find him and remind him. The roads are better, someone should be able to reach Keswick."

Rutledge said, taking out his watch and glancing at the time, "If she's in Keswick, I'll bring her here myself. It will be faster."

"I think he's speaking of reaching the telephone there," Elizabeth Fraser replied. "As I remember, Miss Ashton lives in Carlisle now."

# Chapter Eleven

Rutledge stood rooted to the floor, his mind flying.

"*Janet* Ashton?" he asked, already knowing the answer.

"Yes, that's right," Elizabeth replied, and picking up a nuance in his voice, added quickly, "What is it?"

"She's not in Carlisle now. Or she wasn't last night. She's *here*, at the Follet farm."

"I wasn't aware that she knew them, the Follets," Elizabeth said. "She hasn't been to Urskdale all that often —"

"She didn't know them. At least, not before last night!" Rutledge turned to Jarvis. "I think you ought to come with me, Doctor. Miss Ashton met with an accident on the road. I need your opinion as to whether or not she's fit to travel."

"My bag is in the carriage. But I should think tomorrow morning —"

Rutledge was already pulling on his coat. "I made it through last night. I can find my way back," he answered. "It's a police decision and I've already made it. You can sleep in the motorcar, if you wish."

They were gone in the next five minutes, heading out of Urskdale and taking in reverse the route Rutledge had followed coming in. The verges were even harder to see now than in the snow, churned and rutted as the unmade road was.

Hamish was already reliving the accident, but Rutledge was too busy keeping his eyes on the swath of his headlamps to satisfy Jarvis's curiosity about Janet Ashton except to say, "She was on the road when the storm caught her. The carriage went off at a steep incline and turned over, killing the horse and leaving her stranded."

"What in God's name was she doing out in such a storm? I doubt we've seen its match since before the century turned!"

"I'd like very much to know the answer myself," Rutledge told him grimly.

*"What about your family? Is there someone I can contact? They must be worried about you."*

*She'd shaken her head. "No — there's no one. No —"*

"We assumed, Follet and I," he went on,

as he passed under The Claws, no more than a looming shape far above him, "that she was what she appeared to be — a traveler injured and in need of help. The fingerposts had been blown about by the wind. It was hard to follow the road. She might have been heading for Buttermere, and missed her turn."

"She wouldna' be lost, if she's been to Urskdale before . . ." Hamish pointed out. "Fingerpost or no'."

Jarvis said, "If she was found close by the Follet house, she had a long way to go before reaching her sister's farm. It might have saved her life, don't you see? That her trip was held up by the storm. If she'd been there Sunday, she'd have been killed along with the others!"

Hamish said, "If Elcott was expecting his sister-in-law, he'd no' ha' thought twice when a carriage turned into his yard."

It would explain why Josh had opened the door. After a moment, Rutledge asked the doctor, "If the boy had survived the shooting that Sunday night, he was out in the worst of the storm. Could you be wrong about the timing of the murders? Could they have happened on Monday night? When he might have had a better chance?"

"I'm not wrong about the timing. I'd take my oath on that. As for his chances, people don't often walk off cliffs when the weather comes down here unexpectedly. But that's not to say there aren't places — nasty ones — where a fall results in serious injury, even broken bones. He could have hurt himself badly enough that he died of exposure where he lay. My wife thinks he made it to the village and is hiding out in someone's barn or cellar, but we've searched too thoroughly for that to be true. A patient told me today that we ought to drag Urskwater — that the killer drowned Josh to conceal the body. On the other hand, there are old shielings about that could offer some shelter from the cold. The question then becomes, how did Josh know where to find them? Why didn't the search parties see signs that he'd been there? And if he did manage to survive, why hasn't he shown himself to one of the search parties?"

"What sort of boy is he?"

"Troublesome. Not surprising. He knew damn all about sheep, and I expect his lack of enthusiasm for them tested Gerald's patience more than once. Grace had her hands full with the house and the twins, and her only help was little Hazel. Grace

150

might not have been sympathetic with him if he failed to do his share about the place." Jarvis grimaced as the tires hit a rut and the motorcar bounced heavily. "Children learn their duty early on. Few of my patients see a great age. Life is inherently hard here, and they begin as soon as they can walk doing what they're told, from feeding the chickens to minding the baby or the bedridden old granny. But Josh came from London and a different life. Look, I've been up for nearly forty hours straight and I've answered your questions. Now I'm making the most of this opportunity to sleep without feeling guilty." Jarvis buried his chin deeper into the collar of his coat and was soon snoring lightly.

Rutledge drove steadily, covering ground that tonight was not as slick nor as dangerous as it had been only twenty-four hours ago, the snow softer, the visibility better. But it was not any easier, and as the temperatures fell with darkness, the slush on the road would refreeze. The sooner there, the sooner safely back at Urskdale.

Jarvis, rousing unexpectedly, asked, "Did the Follets know about the murders?"

"Yes, a search party had come through that morning. They'd put their dog in the barn, a first line of defense. I damned near lost my foot to it."

Jarvis chuckled. "Follet is a careful man. The sheepdogs, I can tell you, are good workers. Faithful and dependable and possessed of amazing endurance." His face sobered. "One or two will turn rogue and kill sheep. It's like a madness setting in on them, without warning. I daresay very like our murderer."

Maggie Ingerson struggled through the snow in the wake of her dog. It turned its head several times to be certain she was still following. Once she called out, "Damn it, Sybil, I've only got two legs to your four, and one of them's half dead already."

But Sybil went bounding on ahead, intent on her destination. Maggie, her breath coming in ragged gasps, shouted at the dog again. "I can't make it, I tell you! Dead sheep or no dead sheep!"

All the same, she did make it, reaching the pen some thirty minutes later, her face flushed with exertion, her graying fair hair straggling out of the man's hat she wore. Sybil was already standing there with tongue lolling and tail beating a tattoo in the air, as if in welcome.

The sheep pen was no more than a rough stone wall built up on three sides, the fourth open to allow the animals to go and come at will.

As her mistress leaned heavily against the nearest bit of snow-encrusted wall, chest heaving as she fought to catch her breath, Sybil dived into the banked flock of sheep, sending them flying in every direction.

Maggie swore with masculine proficiency, but the sheep were circling now, and where they had been clustered was something that was distinctly unsheeplike.

Sybil stood over it. The dog's face all but exclaimed her excitement at finding her treasure still in place. She sniffed at it, looking for enough bare skin to lick.

Maggie stared. Finally, driven by curiosity, she turned and moved into the pen, talking softly to the sheep as she made her way through them. Their sneezes marked her progress.

By the far wall, where the sheep had huddled against the wind, lay the curled figure of a human being.

A child . . .

It was wearing a heavy coat that was quickly turning white as snow blew in on it. And it looked to be dead. Maggie knelt beside it, her face intent, unsure whether or not to touch it.

And then, her gloved hands clumsily moving inside the coat, she felt the steady rise and ebb of the thin chest. The child appeared to have fallen into the deep sleep of sheer exhaustion. Satisfied, she got to her feet with some difficulty.

As if the cold air where the warmth of the sheep had been roused the boy, he moaned a little in his sleep.

Maggie stared down at him. It was no use, trying to wake him.

"I'll have to go back for the bloody sled!" she said aloud to Sybil. "Why in God's name didn't you tell me I needed the *bloody sled!*"

Sybil, grinning from ear to ear, faced her mistress and waited. The main task had been accomplished as far as she was concerned. Any further details were of no interest.

Maggie, making her way back through the sheep, shooed them towards the wall again, and then at the entrance to the pen, stopped stock still and looked around her.

There was only fell and cloudy sky and snow. Nothing that would explain the way the hair had suddenly risen on the back of her neck. The dog seemed oblivious to danger, and the sheep were already settling themselves again. But Maggie felt an inexplicable urgency. She turned swiftly, in haste to reach the small farmyard and the shed where her sled was stored.

More than an hour later Maggie made it back, pushing the sheep aside and staring down again at the unwanted bundle of clothes that had been deposited in her sheep pen. As far as she could tell, it hadn't stirred. With a string of curses to mark the effort it took, she rolled the child onto the sled and began to strap it down. Then she pulled the rope taut and started for the gate of the pen.

Sybil, nosing the sleeping bundle, gave up and trotted beside her mistress, her head looking up for the usual "Well done!" that came with carrying out a task. But Maggie, her back into the rope, paid no heed. The silent lump on the wooden deck was heavier than it had any right to be, and the damned sled, with a mind of its own, wanted to go faster than she herself could manage. She thought, "If I were still young enough, I'd get on it and ride it down." But that was foolishness and she knew it. The fell were not a sledding hill, and the hidden rocks that scarred its face would damage runners in short order, tumbling both rescued and rescuer into the snow. No doubt breaking her bad leg all over again.

With increasing exhaustion dogging her steps, Maggie worked at bringing the sled down, and as the familiar outline of the farm rose up out of the darkness, taking the shape of roof and lighted windows and barn almost under her feet, she was nearly at the end of her strength. Once she sat in the snow and wept from tiredness, and the dog licked her face, chilling her hot cheeks as the air cooled the wetness. Her knee throbbed from so much effort.

But in the end, she got herself and the boy to the yard door of the house.

It wasn't until she was beginning to untie the knotted ropes that had held the boy in place on the journey down to the farm that he woke up and began to scream, the high-pitched cries of a trapped and terrified animal.

# Chapter Twelve

Rutledge found the Follets' dog in no kinder mood than it had been on his previous visit, and blew the motorcar's horn to raise the inhabitants of the house. The doctor, stretching himself, said, "Are they deaf, then?"

"No, just careful." Clouds were banking over the fells, closing him in as surely as shutting a gate. He shook off the feeling and spoke to the dog.

Jarvis nodded. "Follet always was a careful man."

Follet eventually came to the door, lantern in hand, called off the dog, and greeted Rutledge guardedly. Then, with considerable warmth, he added, "Dr. Jarvis! Now you're a welcomed sight. Mary was just saying she wished you was here to have a look at Miss Ashton's ribs."

"How is the patient?" The doctor got

stiffly out of his seat and shielded his eyes from the glare of the lantern.

Follet lowered it. "Well enough. According to Mary."

He led his visitors inside and called to his wife from the kitchen. She came down the passage after a moment, smiling at Dr. Jarvis with a dip of her head — pupil to master — and shyly asked how one of his other patients was.

They exchanged news while Follet said in a subdued voice to Rutledge, "I was unprepared for the damage to Miss Ashton's carriage. My guess is it rolled several times after leaving the road. The incline just there is steep enough to do serious harm."

"Yes, I was of the same opinion." Rutledge paused, made certain that the two practitioners were still busy, and added, "I couldn't even be sure which direction it was traveling in."

Follet answered, "I'd not like to place my hand on a Bible myself —" and then he broke off, as if aware that the reference to sworn testimony was not, perhaps, the proper comparison to make in jest to a policeman. "Any news of the boy? Or the killer?"

"None, I regret to say. The search parties are still out there."

Mary turned to greet Rutledge, and then she led them down the passage to the small sitting room where Janet Ashton sat by the fire, swathed in blankets, cushions, and pillows. She winced as she tried to turn her head to see who her visitors were.

"Miss Ashton. I'm glad to see you're feeling a little better," Rutledge said, though privately he thought she looked tired and still in considerable pain.

"I've had a very fine nurse," she told him, smiling up at her hostess.

"Yes, indeed, you've had that! How are you managing today, my dear?" Jarvis asked, setting down his bag and coming to take her hand. "I'm sorry to find you in such straits."

"Very bruised," she told him wryly. "And quite tender." Her glance slid on to Rutledge, as if half expecting him to argue with her. "It was kind of the inspector to bring you to me."

"Yes, he explained there'd been a nasty accident. Whatever took you out in such a storm? Foolishness, I'd call it! Now let's have a look at you and see what Mary has done for those ribs."

Follet and Rutledge left the patient with her nurse and the doctor, and returned to the kitchen. Follet offered Rutledge a chair and sat down himself, asking about the condition of roads beyond the farm.

Rutledge gave him a brief account, and then asked, "You found the valise? I thought I had seen one, when I drove back to the scene. But I didn't relish going after it on my own and in the dark."

"Wiser not to! As it was, I had to use tackle to keep myself from going arse over teakettle. And her purse was there as well." Follet reached across the table and set the salt and pepper in a line, then looked up at Rutledge with uneasiness in his face. "There was a revolver under the seat," he went on after a moment. "I didn't know what to make of it."

"Where is it now? Have you returned it to Miss Ashton?"

"Lord, no! I've set it in the barn, in the tackle box! Nor has she asked for it. I saw no harm in bringing in the valise and purse. And she was grateful to have them."

"A woman traveling alone," Rutledge suggested, "would be glad of some protection."

"At a guess it's a service revolver," Follet continued. "Not one of them German weapons. They're a nasty piece of work."

"German pistols were much sought after as souvenirs."

"Yes, I'd heard that said, but I've never seen one. Wicked, like their makers, in my book. I never held with the Germans." The farmer leaned back in his chair. "Truth is, I've been unsettled since the search party brought the news of what happened at the Elcott farm. It might have been any one of us — senseless killings such as that — and they say lunatics look no different from the rest of us. How is a man to tell what's outside his door!"

"Did you know, when I brought her to your house, that this woman was Grace Elcott's sister?"

"Lord God, of course we didn't! I doubt I'd ever heard her called anything but 'Mrs. Elcott's sister.' She came to visit from time to time, mainly in the summer, but I never met her face-to-face. Mary passed her once coming out of the tea shop on market day and was told later who she was."

"And Mrs. Follet didn't remember her face?"

Follet grinned. "Only the hat she was wearing. It was new, and London made. And the fact that she was dark."

"What does gossip have to say about her?"

"I was asking Mary that same question

last night after we'd gone up to bed. She said she'd heard that the sister stood up with Grace Elcott when first she married Gerald — that was in Hampshire — but not the second time. There was some talk about that, of course, but the ceremony was private, and the sister was still living in London. She came later for the lying-in."

"Does Miss Ashton know what happened to her family?" Rutledge phrased the question carefully.

"She was saying to Mary as we were helping her up the stairs to her room that she wished there was some way she could send word to her sister Grace — she didn't want her to be worrying. *Grace who?* I asked, thinking she was speaking of the Satterthwaites over to Bell Farm — their eldest is marrying a girl from Carlisle, and for all I knew that's who Miss Ashton was speaking of, being from Carlisle now herself. When she said her sister was Grace *Elcott,* the hair stood straight up on the back of my neck! It was as if we'd been dragged into the midst of something fearful. And how was I to go about breaking such news?"

And yet to Rutledge she had denied having any family at all. "Go on!"

"Meanwhile, my Mary was telling her

162

not to fret, saying that with the storm they'd have expected her to take shelter where she could." He glanced over his shoulder as if afraid of being overheard. "I asked Mary later why she'd held her tongue. She said she was afraid that if Miss Ashton was told, she'd want to go straight to the Elcott farm, and how was we to do that, I ask you? In that weather with a murderer stalking about? And if nothing could be done, it seemed kinder to leave Miss Ashton in the dark, so to speak, until she could be got to Urskdale." He seemed embarrassed by his decision but prepared to stand by it. "What was we to do?" he asked.

"Actually, I'd rather you went on saying nothing. Until Dr. Jarvis tells me she's fit to travel."

Follet looked relieved. "Not that I've seen nor heard anything against the sister, you understand. But we don't know why the Elcotts died, do we? And I'd not be drawn into whatever it is if I can help it."

"I can't blame you," Rutledge agreed, and then after a moment, at Hamish's prodding, questioned, "There's something else, I think. That you haven't told me."

Follet tugged at his earlobe. "We're all at sixes and sevens. You start reading omens

163

in the milk pail, after a time! Still, when I got up at my usual hour that next morning, I tried to be quiet as I went past Miss Ashton's door so as not to wake her. I had my shoes in my hand, and was bent on where I put my feet, when I heard weeping on the other side of her door. And then her voice saying over and over again, 'Why? Oh God, *why?*' It was as if she knew something was wrong." His eyes were worried.

"There was the accident. The wrecked carriage and the dead horse —"

"You don't weep like that over a dead horse," Follet said scornfully. "Or a broken carriage wheel. Even if both belonged to someone else. Something was keeping her awake that hurt her far more than those cracked ribs. The only time I ever heard Mary cry like that was when our youngest died. Inconsolable, beyond any help or comfort."

Dr. Jarvis came into the kitchen at that moment and told Rutledge, "I'd prefer to leave Miss Ashton here a day or two longer. She's badly bruised. But nothing appears to be broken, I'm happy to say."

"Is she fit for travel?" Rutledge asked. "Will it do her any harm?"

"I doubt it will *harm* her," Jarvis answered. "But continued rest will do those ribs a world of good, and in my opinion she needs a little time to grieve as well." He saw the expression on Rutledge's face and added, "I was surprised that no one had told her about her sister. When she commented that she wouldn't be much use to Grace and the twins for the rest of the week, I felt I was obligated to say something. You can't have intended to keep it from her!"

"I would have preferred to choose my own time and place," Rutledge returned curtly. "What did she say?"

"She wept —"

Rutledge stood up, already on his way to the sitting room. Jarvis called after him, something about Mary Follet being the best person to comfort her, but Rutledge ignored him.

The sitting room door was open, and he found Mrs. Follet kneeling on the carpet, her arms around the sobbing woman in the chair. The farmer's wife looked up as he came in, and got stiffly to her feet.

"The doctor told her," Mrs. Follet said.

"Yes. Miss Ashton?"

After a moment Janet Ashton lifted a red and tear-streaked face to him. He walked into the room, pulled a chair closer to hers and said, gently, "This isn't the time to ask you questions, I understand that. But time is what neither of us have to spare. We must find your nephew. Josh may have seen the murderer —"

Something flared in her eyes, a flame of emotion that galvanized her. "Josh is dead. Paul would see to that; he wouldn't leave the work half finished! Paul's your killer, I swear to you he is! Jealous, self-centered, cruel — *he did it!*"

Rutledge stared at the tear-ravaged face. Janet Ashton was a very attractive woman, but the twisted anger in her voice and the savagery with which she denounced Paul Elcott made him flinch. Mary, just at his shoulder, gasped in horror.

"I don't understand —" Rutledge began.

"No, no one ever did! I tried to warn Gerald — I told him over and *over* again —" Her hands over her eyes, she broke down completely, unable to speak.

Rutledge glanced at Mary Follet. "Had she said anything about this before I came into the room?"

"No, oh, no! I can't believe —" Her voice faded and she reached out a hand in comfort. "There, there, my dear —" Looking back at Rutledge, she explained,

"It's the shock. She can't mean what she's saying."

It was several minutes before Rutledge could stem the flow of tears and make Miss Ashton face him again. He said gently, "You've just made very serious accusations —"

"I was bringing a weapon to my sister!" she cried. "She was the only one who believed me. And it's too late! *I'm* too late —"

"You must explain what you're talking about," Rutledge said. "Why did you think Paul Elcott might want to harm his family? Why were you bringing a weapon?"

"The farm," she said fiercely. "It was all about that horrid *farm!* Paul was the heir, don't you see? If anything happened to Gerald, Grace wouldn't be able to run sheep on her own, she wasn't bred to it. Josh couldn't inherit even if he'd wanted to. He isn't an Elcott. Gerald never adopted him — Grace wanted him to keep his father's name. It was always *understood* that Paul — Then the twins were born, and circumstances changed." Janet Ashton shook her head. "They were *his,* don't you see? Gerald's own flesh and blood! And Paul was beside himself."

Hamish was reminding him, "He was the first to find the bodies. After no one came

167

to the house for two days."

And therefore any clues that might point his way would be explained — it was an old ploy, one that sometimes succeeded.

Rutledge leaned back in his chair. Janet Ashton, as far as he could tell, believed what she was saying. And there was the revolver, to back up her account.

Or to explain it away, Hamish countered.

"How did you come by the weapon?" he asked Janet Ashton. Mary Follet glanced at him in surprise. He thought, "Her husband hasn't told her —"

"A friend of mine, in the war. He'd been gassed and gave it to me just before he died."

"Can you prove that?"

"Why should I have to do any such thing! I've just told you —"

"The police are thorough," he said, quietly. "We have to be. I'll need the name of the friend, and the date of his death."

She turned away from him. "I'd like to be alone, please. I've still not — I can't really *believe* —" Taking a fresh handkerchief from Mary Follet, she buried her face in it, as if hiding from his questions.

Rutledge rose, nodding to Mrs. Follet. He found himself thinking that Janet

Ashton had come a long way to hear tragic news . . . and sometimes at that first emotional blow, people said things they later wished they hadn't. Would this woman feel the same way tomorrow?

*Or truth can come tumbling out* — Hamish reminded him.

As Rutledge walked back to the kitchen, he agreed. Murder brought to the surface odd antagonisms and old scores wanting settling.

Jarvis said, hearing his footstep in the passage, "How is she?"

"Quite upset. As you might imagine." He went to the window and looked out. The dog was lying in the barn door, watchful as ever. "How well do you know her, Dr. Jarvis?"

"She was there for Grace's lying-in. I found her to be efficient and levelheaded, which is what I needed at the time. The twins were small and required good care. And there were the other children to think about. I could see that Grace was fond of her, and indeed Gerald depended on her."

"The children got on well with her, then."

"The little girl, Hazel, was Miss Ashton's goddaughter and kept a photograph by her bed. I've seen it while treating her for frequent sore throats. Miss Ashton was younger when the photograph was taken, hardly more than Hazel's age. It wasn't a flattering likeness. I wondered a time or two why it hadn't been replaced. Hazel told me it was a favorite because of the dog, Bones. Seems Miss Ashton made up stories about him at bedtime."

Rutledge himself had seen that photograph — and hadn't made the connection with Janet Ashton. Jarvis was right. The sulky child was nothing at all like the grown woman.

"And Josh?"

"He was at an age where women's apron strings had begun to pall —"

Before he could go on, Follet interjected, "How is Elcott taking the news? Can't be easy for him."

"Paul?" the doctor asked. "I had to sedate him. He wasn't in any shape to join the searchers. More of a hindrance than a help, in my book."

Rutledge turned from the window. "Is Miss Ashton well enough to accompany us back to Urskdale?"

"In my opinion, the cold and the rough ride will not do her any good!"

"On the other hand, it shouldn't do her any harm, if her ribs are sound?"

"That's true, but —"

Rutledge nodded to Follet. "I think we'll relieve you of your unexpected guest. If you'll escort me to the barn, I have some business there. Dr. Jarvis, if you'd be kind enough to ask Mrs. Follet to prepare Miss Ashton for the journey —"

"I'd rather not take the responsibility —"

"Nor would I, Doctor. But we need to be expeditious if we're to find our murderer." He picked up hat and gloves from the table, and prepared to leave.

Shut off from the wind, the cavernous barn was not as cold as Rutledge had expected. Bieder sniffed his heels suspiciously as he followed Follet into the dim interior. Sizeable and sturdily built, the structure was at least as old as Follet himself, and probably well into a generation before that. Looking up, Rutledge said, "You had a fine builder."

"That was my father and his. We have to build solidly, up here. The barn before this was probably well over a hundred years old." He led the way to the tack room where harness and tackle were kept, and opened a wooden box that stood under a shelf. Digging inside, he brought up a revolver and held it out gingerly to Rutledge.

He found that the weapon was fully

loaded and he emptied it, dropping the cartridges in one pocket and sniffing the pistol before adding it to the other pocket. "I'd not mention this to your wife after we've gone," he told Follet. "It would upset her, I think, to know that it had been here."

"I'm not likely to do that," Follet agreed. "I'm just glad to be rid of it!" He didn't add that he could be just as happy to see the back of its owner.

In the yard, Dr. Jarvis was already setting Miss Ashton's valise in the boot, and Mrs. Follet had nearly filled the back of the motorcar with pillows and blankets. Rutledge shivered, thinking of Hamish on the long drive back to Urskdale. It would be crowded, and neither Hamish nor Rutledge himself took pleasure from that.

They managed to get Miss Ashton into the vehicle without causing undue pain, Mrs. Follet fussing around them. Rutledge retrieved his own rug and added it to the array of blankets. A warmed stone was wrapped in towels and set at Miss Ashton's feet, and within half an hour of the time he'd made the decision to carry her with him, Rutledge set out on the road.

She hadn't been willing at first to come with him.

"You can't ask me to walk into that house!" she had said in rising panic. "No, I won't go with you! You can't force me — I'll stay here, or go back to Carlisle if someone will drive me —" She turned to Mrs. Follet. "I'm sorry if I'm such a burden —"

"My dear, of course you're not a burden." Mary Follet cast a pleading glance at her husband. "Jim, tell her —"

"I'll be happy to ask my wife —" Dr. Jarvis was saying, but even Rutledge could hear the doubt in his voice.

"I intend for Miss Ashton to stay at the hotel," Rutledge had said, cutting across their voices. "Dr. Jarvis can treat her there, and she can help me with my inquiries."

Miss Ashton stared at him. "The hotel —" she said. "Yes, that's all right, then."

But something in her expression made him wonder what had really changed her mind. A fleeting moment of speculation — a conscious awareness of opportunity? It was there and then gone so quickly he couldn't decipher it.

Now she sat in the back of the motorcar in what appeared to be grieving silence. It made conversation between the two men stiff and uneasy.

After a time Jarvis drifted into sleep

again, and from the rear of the motorcar an almost disembodied voice, husky and muffled by blankets, asked, "Will you arrest Elcott tonight?"

"No. So far I have only your word that he was a threat to his brother's family. I'll have to look into that and see if I can find evidence that bears it out. And when — if — we find the boy, he'll be my chief witness."

"If he was there," she said, the words drifting away on the wind.

The boy slept for hours. Sybil, curled beside the bed, kept watch, and Maggie herself fell asleep by the kitchen fire, dozing heavily in the chair that had been her father's. She woke once with a start, thinking she'd heard something outside in the snow, then was satisfied when the dog didn't bark. Her eyes closed again.

She had set the red-handled ax by her chair, where she could put her hand to it quickly. It could take a chicken's head off in one blow and chop through wood thick as her wrist. Perfectly weighted, it was all she needed in the way of protection.

Her father had taught her to use it, and had once said lightly, "Your Norse ancestors could cleave a man's skull with an ax.

Right through the helmet. It's a fearsome weapon. Respect it."

And she always had.

As Rutledge neared the inn, he began to wonder if he had overstepped his own welcome by bringing another guest for Miss Fraser to cope with. Certainly Mrs. Cummins was not up to caring for and catering to a house full of people. Now, besides himself, there were Robinson and Janet Ashton. Where he could make do with whatever meals were set before him, he doubted that they would.

Hamish reminded him, "It isna' a weekend in the country."

But Miss Fraser took her new guest in stride and said, "I've a room that's quiet, and I think Miss Ashton will prefer it. Just give me a few minutes to see that all is as it should be."

Dr. Jarvis, after asking if there had been any summons during his absence, helped bring Miss Ashton in from the motorcar and settle her in her room. As soon as he could politely excuse himself, he disappeared in the direction of his own house.

Miss Fraser said to his departing back, "His wife will be glad to see him. She never bargained for murder disrupting their quiet life."

"Where is Robinson?" Rutledge asked.

"In his room. He slept a little, I think, and missed his tea. I've a ham in the pot, and if you could bring in some cabbages from the cold cellar, and the small bag of potatoes, I'll have dinner in an hour."

Rutledge not only brought in cabbages and potatoes but helped scrub and prepare them. It was a surprisingly companionable domestic scene, Miss Fraser busy about her tasks while he, shirtsleeves rolled to the elbows, followed her instructions. As he worked, he asked, "What do you know about Paul Elcott?"

"A quiet man. He was engaged to be married before the war, but the girl ran away with a soldier she met in Keswick. I don't think he mourned her. It was an understood thing, without great passion on either side." She smiled over her shoulder. "We don't see great passion in this part of the world. Most everyone has known each other since they were children. Life isn't easy, and no one expects it to be. A man provides and a wife keeps house and brings up the children. And so they drift into old age, considering they've had a happy marriage. Use the other pan, if you will, for those potatoes. I'll need that one for steaming the apples — Oh! I forgot to ask you to bring them up as well!"

Rutledge went out again to find them, and came back with them, small and shriveled by comparison with those in the south, and with a stronger flavor. He cored and cut them up and passed the bowl to her.

The passage door opened and Robinson came in, his hair awry from sleeping hard, his eyes bleary. He said, "I don't know what the doctor gave me, but I've had better hangovers!" He sat down heavily at the table, as if his body had run out of energy, and buried his head in his hands. "Christ!"

Rutledge said, feeling his way, "It's been a rough day."

Robinson nodded. "I thought many times during the war that I was going to die. I never expected my family would die instead. Have you heard any word about Josh?"

"The search parties are sleeping," Elizabeth Fraser answered him. "They'll start out again at first light, from wherever they are now."

"Greeley wouldn't let me join one of them." He turned to Rutledge as if he were to blame. "I don't understand why I can't search for my own *son!*"

"You're needed here," Rutledge answered, finishing the last of the apples. "When Josh is found, the news will be brought directly to the hotel."

"I can't just sit here and *wait*. There must be something I can do! Even peeling apples, for God's sake!"

Elizabeth Fraser glanced at Rutledge and then said, "You could bring in more coal, if you don't mind. With two extra bedrooms to heat, it would be nice not to have to worry about running out."

He turned, and said, staring at her chair, "What happened?" It was asked simply, as if acknowledging that something had.

Rutledge began to object, but she set aside the knife she was using to slice the potatoes and answered calmly. "It was an injury. Just before the war. I tripped on my skirts, actually, and nearly went headlong under a train. There's nothing wrong with my spine; I just can't manage to walk." With a smile she added, "I've quite grown used to it."

But Hamish said, "She's verra young to accept yon patiently. And she doesna' say where she fell. She doesna' have a northern accent."

It was true, she didn't. Even though she spoke of the fell country as if she had known it all her life and was happy to live here.

Rutledge said, shifting the subject, "We brought Mrs. Elcott's sister to the hotel an hour ago. She'd made it as far as she could in the storm and stopped with a family some miles from here."

"Janet?" Robinson asked, as if she hadn't crossed his mind. "Good God — does she know? I mean, I suppose you've told her —"

"Dr. Jarvis did. She's sleeping now."

"She'll be sick with grief. She and Grace were close —"

"She's living in Carlisle now, she says. Did you know that?"

"Lord, no. I thought — but I haven't kept up with her. I suppose I should have —" He made a face. "There are many things I should have done. I should have seen more of my son and my daughter."

"Your relationship with Elcott was comfortable?"

Robinson looked away. "I don't know that it was comfortable. He was married to my wife. But that wasn't his fault, it was the bloody Army's." With an apologetic glance at Miss Fraser he added, "Sorry. But I can't blame Grace or Gerald. We got on well enough for me to visit the children from time to time, and try to close the gap of being away so long. They'd believed I was dead and it was something of a shock to find I wasn't. Hazel had no idea who I was when I came in the door. Grace handled it well. But Hazel and Josh are — were — too young yet to travel to London on their own, to visit me." He shook his head, remembering. "They won't come at all. Not now. I hadn't gotten around to thinking that far ahead. . . ."

"When you came back to England, how did you know where to find them?" Rutledge asked, curious. "How did you learn they were living here in Urskdale?"

"I made straight for the house where we'd lived. There was another family there, I thought I'd made some mistake. But the woman had corresponded with Grace, over some problem with the drains. And so she had her direction. I didn't know what to think, then. What to write to her. I finally got up the nerve to come north. It was as much of a shock to Grace as it had been to me. I — we managed to settle it amicably. There were twins on the way, that had to be faced. And it was clear she didn't feel the same way about what had been — our marriage and all that. I couldn't hold her to the past. I wasn't sure I wanted that myself. Not anymore." He broke off and then without realizing it, repeated himself. "We managed to settle it amicably."

Abruptly getting up from the table, he walked quickly out of the room, leaving silence behind.

Miss Fraser said, "Poor man! If only they can find his son — that will be such a comfort to him."

But the fells and the precipices and the long cold nights were unforgiving.

# Chapter Thirteen

In the event, only Miss Fraser and Rutledge dined together that night. Robinson asked for a tray in his room, Mrs. Cummins got one out of habit, and Janet Ashton sent word that she didn't feel like eating at all.

The meal was well cooked. Miss Fraser said to Rutledge as she served their plates, "It's odd to know the house is full — and to have no one here." But she seemed tired, as if she was glad she didn't have to make an effort at polite conversation. She had offered to lay a fire in the dining room and make it a proper meal, and he had refused to let her go to so much trouble.

"Do you do all the heavy work here?" Rutledge asked, carving the ham.

Elizabeth Fraser smiled. "Heavens, no! You've met Constable Ward, I think. His sister Shirley usually cooks and cleans for Mrs. Cummins. I'm merely filling in.

Ward's daughter-in-law is expecting her first child this week and Shirley is staying with her until she delivers." The smile deepened. "Harry Cummins suggested that Shirley bring her charge here while the men were searching for Josh. For safety. But Shirley told him roundly that any murderer who shows his face at Grey's Farm will regret the day he was born."

"She sounds formidable!"

"And yet she's the kindest person!" She gestured towards the hot pad in the center of the table, and he set the platter of ham slices there. "Thank you, that's everything, I think."

Hamish, a low murmur in the back of Rutledge's mind, was accusing him of letting down his guard. He tried to ignore the voice.

"Tell me about London," she said as she drew up her chair across from him. "Is it more cheerful now? Are the shops carrying more goods? I've been away so long —" It was the first time she had indicated where she was from.

Rutledge told her what he could, trying to make the city seem better than it was, for her sake. The war was finished but the peace was gloomy, defeated and exhausted.

"I used to go to plays," she said, "before

the war. And to concerts. It was always so exciting, waiting for the moment when the music began or the curtain lifted. Jewels glittering, satins and silks and feathers catching the dim light with a flash here or a gleam there. The men so handsome in black. But the war changed all that. Everyone in uniform, colors more sober and suitable to the long lists of heavy casualties. Styles gone with the wind of change, and even the players and the musicians seemed daunted by it all. One of my favorite actors died early in the war, and a violinist from the symphony lost an arm and never played again. So sad."

But there was more to the war than that, and she smiled, as if acknowledging his unspoken thought. "I know. But when change comes, you tend to feel the small sacrifices most, because they're more easily borne. The great sacrifices you try to shove out of your mind until there's a better time to grieve. As if there ever will be!"

"In the trenches, we wanted to believe that nothing had changed — that what we were fighting for was still there, just as we'd left it. But men would come back from leave and tell us the truth, and we'd try to absorb it without accepting it. I expect we didn't want to."

As they finished their meal, she said, "Tell me honestly, if you will. Who do you think could have done this terrible thing? Will it turn out to be someone we know? Someone we've met on the street or dined with or spoken to on the church steps? I *have* thought about it, you see, and I don't know anyone who could have killed *children* — most particularly not those babies, who couldn't tell anyone what they'd witnessed! It's so senseless — so cruel."

Rutledge wasn't ready to tell her about Janet Ashton's accusations against Paul Elcott. Instead he said, "I'm the stranger here, trying to find pieces of information to fit together, trying to look for evidence. You must tell me."

She stared at him in surprise. "But you're a policeman —"

Rutledge smiled. "That doesn't make me omniscient. Still. We ought to begin by considering people closest to the family. Could Paul Elcott have shot his brother?"

Shocked, she exclaimed, "Of course he couldn't do such a thing! And in heaven's name, *why would he even wish to?*"

He didn't answer that. "What about Robinson? He came home to find his wife and family gone, part of another man's life now."

"Hardly a good reason to kill them!" she retorted in distress. "To win them back — that's understandable. From what Grace said, there was very little left of the marriage anyway. Otherwise she couldn't have fallen in love with Gerald."

Which was, he thought, an innocent view of love and marriage. "How did they meet, Grace and Gerald?"

"He was convalescing in the village outside London where she was living. And he seemed to get on with the children long before he met her, making little things for them to play with. Invalids are encouraged to find ways of passing the time, and it helps, I expect, to keep one's hands busy." She frowned, as if remembering her own recovery after her accident. "At any rate, as I heard the story, he was one of a group of soldiers sitting under the trees on the clinic's lawn, and he'd carved a lovely little boat to float in a pail of water, which Josh adored. Grace came to see if it was proper for Josh to accept such a gift, and soon found herself reading to the men every afternoon. I gather it wasn't a hasty, thoughtless courtship. They appeared to be so happy together, as if their feelings ran rather deep and would last . . ." She lifted her hand as if to make light of her words.

"Did *she* tell you she was happy?"

"Grace? It was something you read in her face, whenever Gerald stepped into the room. The way she turned to greet him — the smile she always had for him. I must say, I was more than a little envious." She gave him a wry smile. "Every young girl dreams of that kind of love. Grace seemed to have found it."

"All right then. Let's consider Janet Ashton. Was she happy with her sister's decision to remarry and move north?"

"Grace never discussed her sister with me, Inspector. And you must remember — when Miss Ashton came to visit she went directly to the farm and stayed there. We don't have dinner parties and afternoon fêtes here in Urskdale. If she was in a shop with Grace, of course I'd make a point of speaking to both of them. But these were chance encounters, hardly an opportunity for anything more than idle conversation."

"I understand Miss Ashton wasn't here for her sister's second marriage."

She slid her serviette back into its ring. "It isn't pleasant, what you do, is it? Asking questions, prying into people's lives."

"Better than letting a murderer go free."

She looked at him. "I suppose that's true . . ."

But something in her face made him wonder if she believed it.

Late in the night, Rutledge awoke with a headache, and reaching for his dressing gown, went to the kitchen for cold water to bathe his face.

Silent on stockinged feet, he moved along the passages wondering if his fellow guests were awake or had finally found sleep, however fitful. The house was quiet around him, and he felt at ease in the darkness.

"You canna' see through the doors," Hamish reminded him. "Grief can make a long night!"

The front part of the house was drafty, cold air sweeping around his feet. Rutledge glanced at the front door as he passed, but it was firmly latched. As he stepped into the passage that led to the kitchen, the cold was like a sudden surge.

" 'Ware!" Hamish warned.

The door into the kitchen was standing ajar, and Rutledge stopped, uncertain whether someone else was there. The room was dark, but the cold was more intense. Who had come in, without disturbing the household? A man making a report would have pounded on the door.

Behind him the short passage seemed alive with an electric tension. Was there a murderer even now making his way through the house, searching for a victim? Or had he come — and gone?

Rutledge moved forward quietly, until he could peer through the narrow crack. There was no light at all — the curtains pulled, the stove banked — and yet the chair backs were curved silhouettes.

He shifted his position, trying for a better view of the room.

He could just see the strip of harsh light where the door to the yard stood open to the night.

Nothing moved. There was no sound at all.

But as he watched, someone rose to fill the doorway, a slim figure standing straight, no more than a shimmering silhouette against the snow, breath like a wraith blowing into the room with the cold blast of air.

It was Miss Fraser, standing in the doorway, staring up at the fell that rose beyond the yard, a great white mass that had no beginning and no end from where Rutledge watched, the sky blotted out by its shape.

She took one step and then another,

clutching at the door frame. And then after a long moment, she moved back, as if defeated, slowly subsiding into her chair again. With a last look into the snowy shadows of the fell, she wheeled herself back far enough to allow the door to be closed.

Rutledge heard the bolt slide home.

He didn't stay to be found there watching. Keeping close to the passage wall where he couldn't be seen if Miss Fraser turned, he reached the hall, and then without a sound was walking swiftly down the corridor to his room.

Hamish said, "She isna' as crippled as yon chair siggests."

Rutledge answered slowly, "I don't know. Was it wishful thinking? Or the torment of wanting what isn't there . . ."

"Aye," Hamish said, "It's no' much of a life for a lassie."

Breakfast was nearly ready when Rutledge came down to the kitchen again. But it was Mrs. Cummins standing by the stove, busy with a pan of eggs. She looked up at her London guest.

"Good morning, Inspector! I'm afraid I've burned the toast — but only a little."

The teakettle was whistling noisily, and

he offered to pour hot water into the pot for her.

Relieved, she said, "Would you? I seem to be all thumbs —"

He made the tea, found butter in the pantry off the kitchen, brought in the cream, and was setting the table when Inspector Greeley arrived.

Surprised to see Mrs. Cummins, he said, "Good morning, Vera. Inspector."

Rutledge said, "Any news?"

"Depends," Greeley said, watching Mrs. Cummins. "The searchers have been to every farmhouse, combed the ruins they knew of, looked anywhere a child could hide. They're ready to admit defeat. Three days, and nothing."

"What's your feeling about it?"

"The boy is dead, he has to be. Either frozen in the snow or tracked down by the killer. It was what we feared from the start. . . ."

Mrs. Cummins set the pan of eggs off the stove, humming a little to herself as if Greeley had been exchanging views on the weather.

"I hate to quit. I've never been one to quit," he said, pulling out the chair. "That tea fit to drink?"

"Just steeped." Rutledge poured him a

cup. Greeley drank it thirstily.

"Come and talk to the men. See if you can give them new hope," he said after a moment. "I've run out of words."

"They know the land far better than I do. But I'll try."

"Let's go, then. We'll take your motorcar. It's warming up, this morning, enough to melt the worst of the ice. We can make better time if you drive."

The two policemen found the roads either slushy enough to mire the tires or hard enough to make speed dicey. Greeley swore as they nearly got bogged down in the first drive they turned into. But they found a cluster of men in the yard behind the house, drinking mugs of tea and talking among themselves. The farmer, red-faced and weary, was gesturing towards the land that rose in the watery sun like a heavy blanket of snow and stone. The sky was a hazy blue.

The men turned at the sound of the motorcar, and came to greet Inspector Greeley, then to stare with curiosity at the stranger from London.

"Well, I've brought no news," Greeley began, raising his voice so that all could hear him. "But Inspector Rutledge here is asking us for one more effort, another day at least, a searching of the mind as well as the terrain, trying to think where a lad like that could find shelter — a place he might have discovered on his own, a small space we as grown men might not think about, but a lad could crawl into —"

Hamish said, "He's making the speech for you!"

One of the searchers interrupted Greeley. "We've done that and more. It's not our failure, it's the fact that he's not *there!*" His eyes were hard, red-rimmed from lack of sleep and exposure to the cold wind. "There's stock to be seen to, and our own families. We're so tired we're at risk of not seeing the next crevice that will break a leg. We've done all we bloody *can!*"

"I know you of all people wouldn't give up, Tom Hester, if there was any chance at all! But I can't help but think the lad's out there and terrified, so terrified he won't come out and be found for fear what's hunting him is the killer. He'll stay in that hole like a wounded animal, and it's up to us to do the finding."

Another searcher demanded, sourly, "Where's this hiding place, then?" He swept his arm across the landscape. "We've looked and looked, and there's nothing out there! The killer found him before we did, and it will be *spring* before the body comes to light! If it ever does."

Rutledge, listening, could sense the feeling of frustration and the exhaustion that depressed these men, and he said, without raising his voice, "I believe you've done all you could. I disagree with Inspector Greeley. I think the time has come to call off the search." Greeley turned in dismay.

The farmer, listening behind the men in his yard, spoke up. "How would you know? This isn't your country."

"I've walked here in summer —" Rutledge began.

Greeley was staring, angry now, as if feeling betrayed.

The farmer grunted. "Summer, is it? That's as different from winter as the moon is from the sun!"

"I'm as aware of that as you are. But if you, the people who know this landscape, have run out of answers, then I must respect your decision —"

There was a furious denial that they had run out of anything. The first speaker, Tom Hester, said with some heat, "I tell you, we've *looked — !*"

Greeley answered, "So you have —"

194

The farmer said, "The weather's broken. The light is better. We'll give it one more day —"

There was agreement among those nearest the motorcar. In the end, they set their mugs on the steps of the farmhouse and began to move off again, shoulders bent and heads down, but willing after a fashion.

Greeley watched them go. "Damn it, Rutledge, for a time I thought you were stabbing me in the back."

"They had to want to go," Rutledge answered. "They couldn't be driven to go."

It was the Cumberland and Westmorland temperament. Greeley had to acknowledge that.

They turned the motorcar in the muddy yard and went on to the next place where searchers had gathered, and the next. Only the last group refused to start again. As one man said, "You haven't been up there. Nothing could survive that storm, much less a lad Robinson's age. Not up there. And we've searched every house, every barn, every sheep pen, and every rock. I tell you, he's not there, nor never was, and I'm telling the truth as I see it!"

In the event, the man was wrong.

He had indeed searched — but he had

reckoned without the canny knowledge of a woman who trusted no one and nothing but her own wits.

# Chapter Fourteen

It was late in the morning when the frightened child came bursting out of the room where he'd slept and into the kitchen where the fire was already warm enough to take away the night's chill.

A woman sat at the table, her face red from windburn, her eyes tired and sunk into their sockets.

Skidding to a halt, the child stared at her as though half expecting her to turn into an ogre before his eyes.

She stared back. The dog, wandering in to flop down by the stove, heaved a sigh as if duty done.

"Hungry, are you? There's porridge on the stove. I'm lame, you'll have to fetch it for yourself. And there's ewe's milk in the pitcher. It's all I've got."

The boy stood there, mute.

"My name's Maggie. It's what my father

called me. I never liked it. What's your name?"

He shook his head.

Maggie shrugged. "As you like. But the food's there, if you're of a mind to eat."

His eyes were darting around the room, still wide with fright as he backed towards the outer door.

"There's nobody else lives here, if that's what you're wondering. Unless you count seven sheep in the shed, yonder. I don't have much to say to them, nor they to me. Keeping them alive is all I owe them. My father is buried on the hill. It's what he wanted."

She went on eating her porridge, not looking at him.

"The sheep in the shed got themselves hurt, one way and another. Silly buggers."

The child seemed to be breathing more regularly, as if his heartbeat had settled down. But his face was still pale, and he was trembling.

"That's Sybil. The dog. She found you in the snow and took a liking to you. God knows why. You didn't look like much to me, when she dragged me up to the hill to where you were."

He had reached the door and was fumbling for the latch.

"If you want to leave, that's your choice. But you'll eat first and put a coat on your back. I told you I was lame, and I'm damned if I'll drag your frozen carcass back a second time, just because Sybil here wants to keep you!"

Her gruffness seemed, oddly, to reassure him. After a long moment he sidled to the other side of the table, picked up a clean bowl, and then edged his way to the stove, to stand on tiptoe and dip hot porridge out of the steaming kettle.

The pitcher of milk was on the table, and he poured it without taking his eyes off the woman, as if expecting her to spring across the cloth to catch him.

She handed him a spoon without comment, and he backed across the room again to sit close to the dog before beginning to eat like a starving man.

"On the other hand, if you wanted to stay on a bit," she said conversationally, "I've got nothing against it. But you'll not make work for me, you hear? And you'll do what I can't get about to do. It's only fair if I'm feeding you!"

He listened, but said nothing. She was beginning to wonder if he was mute.

But when he had eaten his porridge and scraped the sides of the bowl, he got up and went to the sink, pouring water into the bowl and scrubbing at it.

Maggie took that as acceptance of her hospitality.

That done, he came warily to the table and took away her dishes, to scrub at them and upend them in the rack.

Satisfied, she got to her feet and limped towards a bin by the door. "Here's what I've been feeding the sheep in the shed. There's a coat belonged to my father in the room you came from. The sheep get a measure each. You'll have to carry a pail with you, with enough to feed all of them. I'd take it as a favor if you'd see to them. I'm still done in from last night."

She turned to find him staring at her injured leg. "I broke it once. It's stubborn and won't heal."

He had the grace to blush.

"Well, go on! They're as hungry as you were!"

He found the coat, shrugged into it, and buttoned it snugly although it swallowed him, the cuffs well over his hands. The boots he found under the coat were twice his size, but he laced them up. When he came back to the kitchen, Maggie stared at him.

"That'll never do!" She moved towards

him, expecting him to run, but he stood his ground. Still, his eyes widened anxiously as she reached out, lifted his arms, and roughly turned back the cuff on first one and then the other. Satisfied, she stepped back. "Go on, then!"

He filled the pail he found inside the bin, stuffed the measure in one pocket, and then with both hands gripping the handle lugged the heavy container out the door without asking for help. The boots slapped at the floor like a clown's.

He must have found the shed without difficulty, for he was back in a quarter of an hour, boots caked with snow, and his cheeks red from the cold. He came scuttling through the door as if afraid that out on the fells in the cloudy morning there was something ominous waiting for him. Maggie saw him surreptitiously bolt it.

She had tea waiting, hot and sweetened with honey. He drank it eagerly, and then washed up for both of them. After that he went to sit by Sybil, his hand smoothing her rough coat.

"Ever had a dog of your own?" Maggie asked, scrubbing at potatoes for the noon meal.

He shook his head.

"Well, Sybil's never had a boy of her own."

It was not ten minutes later when Sybil growled deep in her throat, rising to stare at the door. The boy dove like a terrified rabbit towards the room he had slept in, casting a pleading glance over his shoulder in Maggie's direction.

"It's a neighbor, wanting to know if I'm alive. He won't stay," she answered quietly, and then dragged herself painfully to the door.

But when she opened the door, there was no one outside. The yard was empty.

Maggie stared at the tracks, gave the matter some thought, and then made up her mind. She came inside, called through the bedroom door to the cowering boy that the neighbor's cat had caught herself a rat.

"She keeps the shed free of the wretched things, else I'd take a broom to her!"

Rutledge found his fellow guests in the kitchen when he arrived at the small hotel some hours later. He had dropped Greeley at the police station, aware that the inspector was not happy with the lack of results. The boy alive, witness to murder, was one thing. The boy dead, frozen to death, left the investigation to go nowhere.

It was a daunting prospect, and Greeley let it be known, as he stepped down from the motorcar, that he had done what he could.

"I'll help however I can. Everyone will. But it's up to you now. I've run out of opinions, and I've asked enough of the people here. You'd have to be a wizard to settle this business. All I can say is, I hope you are."

And with that he disappeared through the station door without inviting Rutledge to follow him.

An air of gloom hung over the kitchen, and the silence could be felt. Robinson was sitting with his head in his hands, as if in the depths of despair. Janet Ashton, her face pale with pain and grief, stared out the window at the fell behind the house. Miss Fraser was finishing the dishes, setting them to drain.

She looked up as Rutledge came through the passage door but didn't ask the question he could read in her eyes. He shook his head slightly, indicating no news, and she went back to the last of the pans, rubbing at it industriously as if to keep herself from feeling anything.

She said, "There are sandwiches under that tea towel. If you're hungry."

He was, and nodded with gratitude. Hamish, sensing the atmosphere, said, "She's glad to see you. It's no' been easy, this morning."

As if she had heard him, Miss Fraser went on. "Mrs. Cummins has one of her headaches. She won't be joining us for the midday meal."

Janet Ashton said, "I saw her on the stairs an hour ago. She'd been drinking. I could smell it."

"Yes, well," Elizabeth Fraser began, trying to smooth over the encounter, "I expect she's worried about her husband."

Robinson lifted his head out of his hands and said to Rutledge, "He's dead, isn't he? Josh? If you're trying to find a way to tell me, I'd rather know straight out."

"We haven't found him," Rutledge answered. "But yes, perhaps it's as well to prepare yourself for the worst."

Janet Ashton bit her lip and looked down at her hands. "I know what it's like to lie there in the cold, praying help will come. It's a wretched way to die!"

Hugh Robinson exclaimed, *"Don't —"*

Rutledge sat and reached for the plate of sandwiches. "The men are still out searching. At least there's that. I wish I could have brought better news."

Robinson said wearily, "That's kind of them. It can't be easy." He took a deep breath. "What about the person behind these murders? Have you found any evidence — anything that will help you find him?"

Janet Ashton asked, "Have you spoken with Paul Elcott? Dr. Jarvis says he's better today. If you're going to take him into custody —"

"Elcott?" Robinson demanded, staring from her to Rutledge.

"Early days for that," Rutledge answered her.

But before he could answer Robinson, Janet had turned to him and said, "Perhaps you can persuade the inspector, if I can't! Grace was terrified of Paul! Did she say anything to you about —"

Robinson cut across her words, his attention on Rutledge. "Nobody told me Elcott was under suspicion!"

"He isn't. Any more so than anyone else," Rutledge replied curtly.

Miss Fraser turned her chair to face them. "No, I can't believe — surely — !"

"Tell me who else would have harmed those poor children?" Janet Ashton demanded. "He's the only one who had a reason to kill the twins. Helpless babies, hardly old enough to know their mother's face — even a madman would have pitied them!" Spinning to accuse Rutledge, she said, "At least tell me why you're protecting him? Is there something you know that we haven't been told?"

Robinson said, "I went out this morning, before first light. Looking for anything, a sign — I thought if Josh saw me, heard my voice —"

Miss Fraser protested, "That wasn't very wise, was it? If you'd been lost, a search party would have had to hunt for you! And they're nearly at the end of their strength."

"I couldn't sleep," Hugh Robinson answered bluntly. "I lay in a warm bed, and all I could see was Josh, frightened, not knowing where to turn — no one to help him. It's worse than a nightmare! I'm not sure I want to live with that image for the rest of my life! Or can —"

"If you would only speak to Paul Elcott!" Janet Ashton interrupted. "Ask him if Josh was there — if he knows which direction Josh took! You're wasting precious time, time Josh can't afford! Don't you see that?"

Her voice was urgent, forceful. Rutledge could see in her face now a similarity to the sulky girl in Hazel Robinson's framed photograph.

He got to his feet, sandwiches untouched, and immediately Elizabeth Fraser put out a hand to stop him. "You've been out all morning —"

"Miss Ashton's right," he told her. "I've got to speak to the man. Better sooner than later. Can you tell me where to find him?"

"He has rooms over the licensed house — The Ram's Head — you'll see it just before the church, a two-story building with a sign over the door. The next one to that goes up to his rooms."

Rutledge thanked her and left. Janet Ashton half rose, as if she intended to follow him, but Elizabeth Fraser said quietly, "No, it's best if you don't." And she sank down again in her chair. The expression on her face was hard to read.

"Neither of you believe me," she said. "But I'm right, at the end of the day, I'll be proven right!"

Paul Elcott came to the door looking like a man who had spent the last three days drunk as a lord. But the reek of alcohol was missing, and Rutledge realized it must be the sedatives that Dr. Jarvis had given the man.

"Who are you?" Elcott asked, frowning. "What do you want?"

"Inspector Rutledge, from Scotland Yard. I'd like to speak to you if I may."

"They've got the Yard here? Good God! Greeley never mentioned that. Nor Jarvis." He held the door wide and Rutledge stepped in.

Paul Elcott was wearing trousers that appeared to have been slept in for days, and a rumpled shirt to match. His feet were bare, and he hadn't shaved. A dark growth of beard shadowed his features, and his hair hung over his eyes.

"I'm parched dry as a desert," he added. "We'll step into the kitchen, if you don't mind. I need something to drink."

But the fire was out in the stove, when they had climbed the stairs to the rooms over the licensed house. From the temperature there, Rutledge suspected the fire hadn't been stoked for days. Elcott stared at it, standing like a man lost, as if he had no idea what to do about it.

Rutledge said, "Sit down. I'll see to it." And he set about cleaning the ashes and laying a new fire. As he worked, he talked to the dazed man in the chair by the table. But Elcott didn't appear to hear him.

"I can't get that room out of my mind,"

he told Rutledge finally. "I tried, but as soon as I shut my eyes — Jarvis gave me something, and it fairly knocked me out." He shook his head as if to clear it. "Any news? Is that why you've come?"

"Not yet. How well did Josh know the countryside around the farm? Where could he have gone?"

"Josh?" Elcott said, as if the name was new to him. "I expect he knew it well enough. Boys explore —"

"Where would he choose to go? Which direction? Did he know anyone, play with other children in that part of the valley? Would he have come here, to you, if he escaped?"

"I doubt he'd come to me. I never liked him. I thought Gerald was a fool to take on a wife with two children by another man. And told him so to his face!"

"What did he say to that?" Rutledge turned as he finished washing his hands and drying them on a towel by the sink. The fragrance of wood starting to burn filled the room, but no heat reached them yet.

Elcott shrugged. He didn't seem to be able to focus his mind. "Have you seen the house?"

"I've been there. Yes."

"God! You should have been there before Miller and Jarvis took them away!" He shivered, and it had nothing to do with the cold room.

"How are you managing, getting this place back on its feet?"

"It's not going to happen," Elcott said harshly. "I've tried, but there's precious little money, and no hope of business picking up until late in the spring. I'm worn out with the effort." He had the air of a defeated man who had lost the ability to believe in himself. Or was it assumed?

"Will you inherit the farm, now your brother and his children are dead?"

Elcott looked at him in surprise. "I hadn't even thought about that —"

"It gives you a motive for murder," Rutledge pointed out mildly. He was watching Elcott's eyes. But they seemed more annoyed than unsettled by his words.

"Yes, well, I'm sure a hangman's noose would put an early end to that, if it were true," the other man answered sourly.

"Did Jarvis tell you? Miss Ashton, Grace's sister, is at the hotel. If you'd like to call on her. Do you know her well?"

Elcott's glance sharpened. "Oh, dear God, I never thought to send word to her! Or to Robinson. It never occurred to me. I expect I've Jarvis to thank for attending to it. Or was it Inspector Greeley?"

"She was already on her way here when she had an accident on the road. It was Dr. Jarvis who broke the news to her."

"I wonder what went through her mind when he did." Elcott rubbed his face with his hands. "She and Grace were as different as two sisters could be. It always struck me that if they hadn't been related by blood, they'd have nothing to say to each other."

"She told me that Grace was afraid of you. And she believed that you were jealous of her and her family."

"Well, there's a blood lie!" Paul replied. "I never liked Janet, and she never cared much for me. The ne'er-do-well brother who needed bucking up to make a man of him. She'd even told Gerald that in her opinion I was malingering, that the Army would set me straight. I never told her it was the Army's doctors who turned *me* down. Janet's the sort of managing woman I never cared for. Always wanting her own way, always seeing what she wished to see. But I never expected her to go this far!"

"Did Grace get along well with her?"

"Grace was blind to her faults. But then Grace was sweet-natured and saw no wrong in anybody. Myself, I don't know how Gerald put up with the woman. But he did, probably for his wife's sake. I'd wondered a time or two if Grace realized Janet had had her eye on Gerry long before Grace met him. If anyone was jealous of Grace Elcott, it was her loving sister!"

Surprised, Rutledge said, "I hadn't heard anything about that."

"No, she wouldn't have told you herself, would she? Well, she'd got to know Gerald when he was in hospital in London, recovering from surgery. She would come to write letters for the wounded, or read to them. And she fell in love with him. You didn't know my brother. Women liked Gerry; he had a way with him that attracted them whether he wanted it or not. Ask Elizabeth Fraser, she's had an eye for him, too! He did his best to discourage Janet, and was glad when they shifted him to the convalescent home in Hampshire. And there, quite by accident, he met the other sister."

"How did you learn this? Did your brother tell you — or more to the point, write to you?"

"I'm not a fool. I could see for myself. And Gerry did write part of the story to me when he was considering proposing to Grace. He was afraid it might present a

212

problem because of Janet. But as she was living in London and the doctors were expecting to release him to come home to Urskdale, he thought it could be worked out."

"Do you still have that letter?"

Elcott paused, staring at him. "I don't know whether I kept it or not —"

"It would be helpful, if you could find it." Rutledge kept his voice neutral.

"What I don't understand is why Gerry ever believed that Janet was moving to Carlisle for her sister's sake. Particularly after she wouldn't stand up for Grace at the second wedding ceremony. It was as clear as the nose on your face that she'd begin to meddle the first chance she got. And she's still doing it, damn her! I don't know why she's pointing a finger at me! She had a better reason for hating Gerry than I ever did."

"Why didn't she attend the second marriage?"

"What do you think? If Grace was forced to go back to Hugh Robinson, someone would have to console Gerry. But that wasn't how Janet put it, of course. She said she felt it wasn't right — that she believed it was her sister's duty to go back to her true husband."

"Did your brother tell you that?"

"He didn't have to. Grace was so disappointed you could see it in her expression when I carried the letter to her. Why else would Janet stay away, when her sister needed her to help put the best face on what had happened?"

"Did you stand up with your brother?"

"Of course I did! In my view, it was a God-given excuse to change his mind, dropped into his lap. But he loved Grace, the twins were his flesh and blood, and there was an end to it. I wasn't about to shame him in public." He turned aside, pulled back into his own misery. "I'd give anything to turn back the clock and find out it was nothing but a bad dream. That I could make it right again." His voice was so low Rutledge could barely make out the words. "I wish I'd left it to someone else to find them!"

Hamish said, "There's something on his conscience. It's no' giving him any peace."

Paul Elcott wouldn't be the first man to have killed in hot blood and regretted it when the passion of the moment had passed.

As an excuse to linger, Rutledge made a pot of tea. When it had steeped, he left.

Paul Elcott, whether hiding secrets or telling the truth, had said all he was going to say.

# Chapter Fifteen

Hamish remarked as Rutledge made his way back to the inn, "Jealousy sees what it wants to see. . . ."

It was true. Janet Ashton and Gerald . . . Hugh Robinson and Grace . . . Elcott and what? The family's land?

If Gerald's twins were killed, Paul Elcott would have clear title to the farm. It would be worth his while, if murder was his intent, to wipe out the entire family.

But what did Janet or Hugh have to gain? Why kill the object of one's love?

And the answer to that was all too simple. Love spurned turned easily to hate.

Had Inspector Greeley's supposition of events in the bloody shambles of the Elcott kitchen been wrong? Had he and Inspector Greeley seen it *backwards* from what actually happened? Had Gerald or Grace been the last to die, as a final punishment? But

Gerald had done nothing to defend his family . . . *Why?*

"There's no proof," Hamish pointed out, "how it happened."

And small chance of finding answers until or unless they managed to find Josh Robinson.

But Janet Ashton had had a revolver in her possession. . . .

Rutledge tried to picture her murdering the Elcotts. The slim, pretty woman he'd rescued from the snow didn't seem to be strong enough physically or emotionally to fire shot after shot into children — however managing she'd appeared to Paul Elcott.

"There's the sulky girl in the framed photograph," Hamish reminded him. "And you didna' ask Elcott if he owned a handgun."

It was true. The murder weapon was missing. Unless Rutledge himself had taken charge of it in the barn at the Follet farm. But there was no way — yet — to prove it.

Janet Ashton was waiting in the sitting room, where someone had got the fire going. Her ears must have been attuned to the sound of the front door opening and closing, for she was in the passage to meet Rutledge as he took off his coat.

"Well?" she demanded. "What did he have to say for himself?"

"He was hardly awake enough to defend himself," Rutledge answered. "The doctor had filled him full of sedatives."

"Yes, well, he would tell you that, wouldn't he?"

She turned to go back into the sitting room, and the pain seemed to come back again, as if held at bay by her hope that Rutledge would take Paul Elcott into custody. She sat in the chair by the hearth, and he could see how pale she'd become. "I wish I could do something besides sit here," she said to the room at large, rather than to him. "I wish I could go out and talk to him myself!"

"You'll stay away from him," Rutledge ordered. "Do you understand that? It's my duty to find out who's behind these murders, not yours."

She looked up then and there were tears in her eyes. "You've never lost anyone, have you? I mean, other than parents — natural deaths. You can't imagine the frustration and the grief, and the anger. I keep seeing them dead, my only family — and it's worse because I don't *know*." She was weeping, bereft and hurt.

Hamish said, "To listen to the lassie, she's told the truth from the start."

But Paul Elcott had just said she was clever and managing.

"I can't tell you they didn't suffer," Rutledge answered, sitting down across from her. After the cold of the wind, the fire seemed almost too hot to bear. "But it must have been very quick. They didn't respond — they didn't try to defend themselves. There was no time."

Was that the truth? Or did the woman before him know better than he ever could what had taken place in that snug kitchen with the snow piling against the house and the wind whipping it down the chimneys and into drifts against the barn?

"Did you love Gerald Elcott?" he asked after a moment.

Her face, wet with tears, stared across at him. "Did Paul tell you that?"

"He suggested it was possible."

"Gerald was my sister's *husband*. What good would it do me to shoot him? And if I murdered his family, how do you think he would have loved me, knowing what I'd done?"

"Revenge?"

She laughed shakily. "Revenge makes a

cold bed partner, Inspector Rutledge. If I'd loved him, I'd have found a better way to rid myself of Grace and then come rushing to help Gerald cope. Josh and Hazel were fond of me. I'd have made a place for myself in that house in no time at all! And it's a short step, don't you see, from housekeeper to wife, when a man needs someone to right his world. Paul was the only one who had a reason to kill the twins. For *me,* those babies would have been a stepping-stone. . . ."

But Hamish was pointing out that she hadn't directly answered Rutledge's question.

Yet in a way, hadn't she? It would be easier to lay her sister's death at Janet Ashton's door, than all five murders. And a good barrister could make that part of her defense. But twice Gerald had chosen Grace instead of her sister. Was that why Grace had been the last in that kitchen to die? To see what she had brought down on her family by not stepping aside and doing her duty to Robinson?

Young Hazel and Josh had kept their proper father's name. If Grace hadn't remarried Gerald and instead had returned to Robinson, the twins would not have borne Elcott's name. By law they would have been Robinson's. Or been branded illegitimate, if he'd refused to accept them. Had that been in her mind when she stayed with Gerald? To give him heirs to High Fell, and the children she was carrying a rightful place in their proper world?

What had motivated Grace Robinson Elcott? But there was no way of guessing what had passed through her mind. Or how much she'd known about her sister and Gerald Elcott. . . .

All the same, as Hamish was saying in the reaches of his mind, whatever happened at the farm, Grace Elcott was the pivotal factor.

She had taken the man her sister loved. By bearing the twins, she'd deprived Paul Elcott of his hopes of inheriting High Fell. And she had been given the chance of returning to the father of her older children, and refused it.

Which brought Rutledge back to motive. Greed. Jealousy. Revenge. The land — the lover — the wife . . .

Given the savagery of the attack, he would have added one other motive: Fear.

Yet who had been afraid of the Elcotts? What did they know that could have threatened anyone?

Rutledge roused Greeley from a sound sleep, much to the annoyance of his wife. "But he's hardly closed his eyes! Can't you let him have a little peace?"

She was a tall woman, her face angular and her features well defined. Dressed in black, with a white collar at the throat, she reminded Rutledge of a strict schoolmistress.

"Then you'd better come this way," she said with a sigh when he insisted. "I won't have him up and dressing again." She led her unwanted guest up a flight of stairs to the third door along a carpeted passage.

"I'm sorry to intrude on your sleep," he told the haggard man in the rumpled bed. "I need to find someone who can take me out on the fells. If I can't manage on my own, I'm capable of following a man who knows what he's doing. Give me a name, or send me someone."

"Good God, man, you must be mad. All right then, give me an hour —"

Sooner than that, a rough-looking, bearded man appeared at the kitchen door of the hotel and asked for Rutledge.

Elizabeth Fraser said, "Hallo, Drew. What brings you out at this hour?"

"I'm to take the policeman walking." His voice was gruff.

"Indeed?" she replied, surprised. "I think he's in his room. Come in!" She smiled and maneuvered her chair out of Drew's way. "Can I get you something?"

He stepped into the kitchen and looked around him, ill at ease. His fleece-lined leather coat was buckled around him by a stout belt, and his heavy-soled boots were crusted with snow. "I'll have some of that tea, if you don't mind!"

She was pouring his cup when Rutledge came through the door. "Ah," Elizabeth said, looking up at him. "I expect this man is the guide you've been waiting for. Drew, Inspector Rutledge, from Scotland Yard."

Drew nodded and drank his tea noisily. Rutledge said, "I'm used to the fells — but not in winter. I've got warm clothes with me, and boots. Gloves. A torch. A flask for tea. Is there anything else I need?"

"A better hat," Drew answered without looking up. "Your ears will be dam— be cold."

"You can borrow one of Harry's," Elizabeth put in quickly. "I'll just go and fetch it!"

She wheeled herself out of the door Rutledge held open for her. Behind her,

Drew was saying, "Mind, I'll know best when it's time to turn back."

"Yes, that's fair enough." Rutledge nodded. "I've got that map," he said, gesturing to where it lay folded and to hand on the sideboard. "And I've learned what it can tell me. But there's more to land than flat markings on paper. I need to see the valley from a vantage point where I can understand all the difficulties faced by the search parties. And the boy."

Drew grunted in acknowledgment. "There's one place best for that."

Hamish commented, "The hills here breed silence into a man. It was the same in the glen. Words counted."

Rutledge nearly answered him aloud, and caught himself in time. *If he can take me where I want to go, that's all that matters.*

They set out without another word. Drew walked with long, tireless strides, neither hurrying nor wasting time. The sun's rays angled over the mountains, sending stray fingers down to illuminate the far end of the lake, but it was not a strong light, this close to the solstice. It gave the dale an almost ethereal air, as if it might disappear before anyone could really grasp it. The snow, where it was undisturbed, looked as smooth as glass, and the deeper end of Urskwater was a blue-black. Here and there outcroppings had begun to poke their heads up through the crust of white.

"A sheep man, are you?" Rutledge asked, after a quarter of an hour.

"All my life."

"Why weren't you out with the searchers?"

"I've been and come."

They were well outside the village now, climbing the shoulder of the fell, angling a little west. Hamish, his mind on Scotland, began a long soliloquy comparing the fells with the Highlands, the difference in the colors of the soil, the shape of the rocks, the sense of isolation. It was a background accompaniment to the crunch of boots on snow and rock, and the breathing of the silent men.

After another hour or more, they had reached a point where they could see much of Urskdale. Above them, on the skyline, a rounded topknot perched almost nonchalantly, a stone afterthought. The Knob, which Mrs. Cummins had pointed out to Rutledge from the kitchen of the hotel. Below, Urskwater wound between the fells in a stretched *S*, and the valley seemed to widen at both ends, narrowing only a little at the middle. The village was nearer the top end of the lake, and The Claws projected in a great broken ledge far above where the road began to bend to reach the other side of the water. It was from there, that ledge, Rutledge found himself thinking, that the best view could be had. But the approach was rough, more of a climb than a walk.

At the far end, where the valley was closed, another peak rose, swelling gently and then showing a precipitous wall of scree where no snow clung.

It was easier to breathe here, on the slopes, where he could look down as well as above his head. As if he'd reached an unexpected equality with the land. His claustrophobia began, a little, to recede.

Drew was pointing. "There's the Elcott farm — the barn's just visible. No, to the left of that boulder shaped like a chimney . . ."

"Yes, I see it now."

"Look how it's situated. If you were the boy, which way would you go?"

Rutledge considered the setting. "It's impossible to say. There's nothing to stop him until he's well up the shoulder in any direction."

"Look at the sheep pens, high up on the slopes. You can see some of them. There — Over there — And there — To the left of the last one, some three hundred yards lower, is the ruin of the old Satterthwaite farm. And over to your right, near the top of that saddle, is a small stone hut built for walkers to take shelter in bad weather." Drew looked around him. "In the spring, there are wildflowers everywhere. Tiny things, that cling to the rock like the sheep."

He went on, identifying the landmarks, laconically naming the farms one by one. Specks of civilization in a wilderness of rock. Lanes, their snow cover already broken and dirty, wound with the land, sometimes disappearing into the distance without a sign of life.

It was a vast area, this valley and its mountains. Most of it impossible to cover well on foot. Rutledge, whose sight was very good, peered into the hazy sunlight, trying to identify what Drew could pick out so easily. Sometimes only a sharp-edged shadow betrayed a man-made structure. The dirty-white bodies of sheep, now finding grazing where they could break through the snow, were all but invisible, although Drew recognized them without trouble. Only when the animals moved could Rutledge see them. A needle in a haystack, indeed. . . .

"There're tracks and footpaths everywhere. If the Robinson lad found one, he could go some distance, depending on the depth of the snow. They twist and branch. Some of them have names, some don't. Some of them lead to the pens, some go nowhere in particular. He'd have to be lucky."

"We must assume," Rutledge replied, "that the killer came up the lane. Blocking the way back to Urskdale. And so the boy would have gone in another direction. The question is, did Josh try to circle around in the hope of reaching the village? If he chose the high peaks instead, why did he believe he was safer there? Because he couldn't be followed there? Or was he not thinking at all, just fleeing blindly?"

Surely Janet Ashton couldn't have followed him out into the snow, if she had murdered her sister and the children. She was more likely to find herself lost than the boy, and even his rudimentary knowledge of the slopes would put him at an advantage.

On the other hand, Paul Elcott had lived here all his life. It wouldn't matter which direction Josh Robinson took; the older man would be able to outwit him.

It always came back to one central problem. They'd have to find the boy before they could know the whole story.

Rutledge scanned the land again,

thinking about the boy. That night it was stormy, the air filled with snow, the ground possibly already invisible —

"That farm there — what did you call it?" he asked Drew.

"Apple Tree Farm. We'd asked there, and looked at all the pens."

"And on the shoulder of the hill — which one is that?"

"It's called South Farm. Nothing."

After a moment Drew went on. "Can you see the sheepfold well beyond the farm, on the rising land of what we call The Bones?"

"Where?"

"To the south, now, at an angle to the Elcott barn."

"Yes, now I see it."

"That's where Elcott kept his sheep in winter storms. Just under Scoat Ledge. We went over that bit with care, walking an arm's length from each other. If the lad went south, we never found any sign of him."

"Where were Elcott's sheep?"

"Either Elcott or the old bellwether took most of the flock to the safety of the pen. Some few are scattered about the ground, taking shelter where they could. But there might not have been time to find them all.

That's not unusual. It'll take days to collect them again, but they know, the sheep, how to find the flock for themselves. They aren't stupid, whatever people say."

How easy it would be, Rutledge realized, for the boy to burrow into the snow next to a ewe. One more white lump among so many scattered across the landscape.

But if that had saved Josh on that terrifying Sunday night, what had become of him when the danger had passed? Why hadn't he made his way the next morning to the police or to someone he trusted? What had made him so terrified of going for help?

"Tell me about the sheep," he said as he followed his guide higher, his breath coming hard as he climbed in the cold air. If the animals could survive, it might be a lesson well worth learning.

"What's there to tell?" Drew was barely winded. "They lamb in late April or early May, when the grass in the low pastures is greener and someone can keep an eye on them. Shearing is in July. The cur-dog — that's a cross between collie and sheepdog — helps bring them in and take them out."

"The sheep runs — are they close by each farm, fell land connected by sight and footpaths to the yard? Where a boy, even a city child, could come to know them well?"

The older man chuckled. "The fell that goes with a farm is where time and custom set it. I walk three miles to the start of mine. Elcott's runs behind the house and then skips to the saddle over there. A drift road runs between."

Had the boy found the drift road?

Rutledge watched his guide. The man seemed to find his footing with ease, as if he could peer through the heavy snow crust to the familiar track he knew was there. He himself was not always as lucky. Above all, the energy needed to force a way through the snow as they climbed depleted his stamina. But then, they were going straight up, rather than following the contour, and that counted for much.

Higher still, as Rutledge was catching his second wind, he could see a thin trail of smoke coming from what appeared to be no human habitation. But then as his eyes learned to pick out details, to recognize the line of shadow, the difference in how sunlight touched the snow on a roof, he asked, "Whose farm is that?"

"The Ingerson farm. Too far for a child to reach. Still, the party searching there roused Maggie. They got the rough side of her tongue for their trouble."

Ingerson. Rutledge could picture the map on the kitchen table, hear the voice of the messenger reporting, watch his hand tick off each farm. "Yes, all right, I know who she is. And over there — the Peterson farm. There's the Haldnes house . . ." He went on, giving life to the flat surface of the map, seeing for himself how the land lifted and changed, how the shape of the fells determined where men could farm or run their sheep. Where a boy could run.

If you could see the skyline, see the way the great ridges ran and knew how they dipped and changed their shape with distance, Rutledge thought, you could find your way. I've done it, walking in daylight on summer tracks I remembered. But at night, in a fierce storm . . .

Drew was watching Rutledge's face. "Aye, you begin to see."

Rutledge turned and looked back to Urskdale. The hotel was only a dot on the streaked line of the road, and the church seemed squat, unimpressive, and the shops like toy houses, lacking human definition.

His knees were stiff and he could feel the sweat on his body under the heavy layers of clothes. The thought of walking all that way back tired him.

"I can understand the problems of the

searchers," he acknowledged. "What I'd hoped to see was something — anywhere — that the boy might have known about, somewhere he could have hidden himself."

But the shadows on the landscape were deceptive. A boulder and its shadow could loom large as a house, a thin dark line could mark the top of a stone wall, gullies and breaks in the ground could lie smooth, filled to their rims. Gills ran black in the snow, threads of water with frosted fronds of grass or moss overhanging the icy edges. Nothing was what it seemed. The boy could lie in one of those deep crevices, and with the snow covering him, he would be invisible. Dead or alive, no one would see him.

Hamish, silent for some time, said, "It's as if the land has swallowed him up and willna' give him up again."

"All right, go on," Rutledge said, but Drew shook his head.

"As it is, it'll be well after dark before we reach the hotel again."

Reluctantly Rutledge heeded the warning. But there was the motorcar, and with that he could reach a handful of those outlying farms — he could try tomorrow himself.

With a last look at the broad expanse of

land all around him, the ranging hills and fells, he said, "What if the boy found shelter that first night, and survived? What then?"

"We'd have spotted his tracks. He wouldn't have moved until the snow stopped."

"You're telling me that you believe Josh Robinson is dead."

Drew took a deep breath, and then let it out softly. "Aye."

The single word was as cold as the icy patches under Rutledge's boots and the chill wind that swept down from the heights.

"Keep to my tracks going down," the older man cautioned. "As the light fades, you'll miss your step."

And Rutledge did as he was told, well aware of the treachery of the blown snow waiting for an unwary boot. He stopped once and thrust a hand into one of those seemingly flat stretches crusted with ice after the melting during the day, and his fingers disappeared up to the elbow into a fold in the rock.

A man, he thought, could dig deep and bury a handgun under a few rocks, and we'd never find it.

And then he hastily caught up with

Drew, watching the long shadows sweep down for an early dusk, and the lamps of Urskdale twinkling one after another as they were lit, like an untidy, bright necklace along the road.

# Chapter Sixteen

Dinner was late, but all the guests came to the meal, a somber gathering straining to make polite conversation and often falling silent before their own thoughts. Even Mrs. Cummins was there, toying with her food, listening to discussions no one else heard. From time to time she would interject a remark that had no bearing on anything being said.

Once or twice she asked if anyone had seen her husband, adding, "Harry is always the first to table."

And Elizabeth Fraser would answer, "He'll be home soon, you know. He has been out with the search parties."

But they were already making their way home, each man without hope to buoy him further. Even the final effort had failed. Word had arrived by way of Sergeant Ward in Rutledge's absence. The note had simply read, *We've come to the end.*

It also disturbed Mrs. Cummins that her guests were taking their meal in the kitchen, and more than once she offered to light the fire in the long dining room, where they could be comfortable. "It's such a lovely room —"

Rutledge had stepped in there earlier, to see for himself. On the western side of the building where no sun reached it until late afternoon, it had been uninvitingly cold despite the graceful stone fireplace and the ancient but beautifully polished oak chairs around the oval oak table with its lion claw feet. On the sideboard, a pair of Staffordshire spaniels had stared forlornly back at him, and the china pheasant on the lid of the huge soup tureen seemed poised for flight in the light from Rutledge's lamp.

The room hadn't been used, according to Elizabeth Fraser, in weeks: "Not since the middle of September — we haven't had any guests."

It would have taken hours of a roaring fire to defeat the winter chill in the walls.

"Tomorrow night, perhaps, when your husband is here," Rutledge replied, to distract Mrs. Cummins.

"I wish Harry had sent news," she answered fretfully. "Why do you suppose he hasn't? Do you think something could have happened to *him?* I always worry that something has happened. That there are more dead we don't know about —"

And then it was as if the pent-up emotions in the room couldn't be held back any longer.

Janet Ashton exclaimed impatiently, "Surely in all this time someone has seen *something.* A footprint, a depression in the snow where he could have taken shelter, even a lost glove. I mean, these men live here, they're supposed to know every inch of these fells in the dead of night in blinding rain! I've heard the sheepmen brag. How they found a lost ewe that everyone else had given up hope of finding. How they located an injured walker in heavy mist that filled Urskdale for days on end. How they can tell where they are by the feel of the stone under their feet or the smell of the wind."

Mrs. Cummins, alarmed, answered, "Are you saying that my husband and the others haven't done their duty? But surely that's not true. Mr. Robinson, do you feel that way?"

Before he could answer, Janet glanced across the table at Hugh Robinson's strained face. "I'm sorry, Hugh. I don't mean to dash your hopes, but it's the waiting — spirits rising every time someone comes to the door — plunging when there's no news — I can't fall asleep without jerking awake at the slightest sound. You must feel it, too. It's making all of us edgy."

Elizabeth Fraser, in an effort to distract her, put in, "Yes, and you must be in some pain, as well. Would you like me to send for Dr. Jarvis —"

But Janet had already turned to Rutledge. "I wish I knew what you'd said to Paul Elcott. I wish I'd been there. You don't know him, Inspector! How sly and devious he can be. Gerald never listened, either. He felt sorry for Paul, and he cosseted him, just as his mother had done. And just look how that ended!"

"Miss Ashton." Elizabeth Fraser's voice was firm. "This doesn't do any of us any good!"

Janet stared at her for a moment and then dropped her eyes to her plate. "I'm sorry. I've lost my sister. I know how afraid she was, and how Gerald thought she was just suffering from the melancholy sometimes associated with a difficult pregnancy. I just want Josh to be found! I want something of hers to hold and love. And I want justice for her, too. Inspector Rutledge hasn't lost someone to murder, has he? He doesn't understand what I — we — feel."

Rutledge, unwilling to be drawn into her arguments, said only, "We've all lost people we've loved, Miss Ashton. And it's natural to rail against what we can't prevent or change."

"I will tell you this." Hugh Robinson set down his fork as if he couldn't go on pretending to eat. "He's alive. Josh. I can feel it! Whatever the search parties may tell me."

"If he is, it would be a miracle," Rutledge warned. "You have to prepare yourself — in the event —"

"No, he's still alive!" His eyes met Rutledge's, despair in them.

"I don't see what Paul Elcott has to say to anything," Mrs. Cummins interjected. "Josh was Gerald's son, after all! Dear Gerald, he was such a *nice* man — I miss him so terribly!" Her face crumpled.

Elizabeth Fraser said hastily, "Josh is Hugh Robinson's son —"

Confused, Mrs. Cummins looked around the table. "I never heard of it if he was! The boy lived with Gerald, didn't he? Well, then —"

Rutledge caught Miss Fraser's eye and

shook his head. In an attempt to shift the subject, he said to Janet Ashton, "I've been meaning to ask you. Didn't you believe the policemen stopping traffic in Keswick, when they told you that the roads were impassable going towards Urskdale?"

He thought for an instant he'd read surprise in her eyes, but if it was there, she managed to cover it quickly. "I'm afraid I didn't believe them — I thought the storm would blow over. That I could make it to Urskdale, if I just rested the horse often and took my time."

Hamish said, "She didna' know they were blocking the road. She came through before word went out."

Elizabeth Fraser started to say something and then thought better of it.

Janet Ashton flicked a look in the other woman's direction and then went on, "There's something more. Have you considered the possibility, Inspector, that Paul Elcott will worry about what I can tell the police? Or that Grace might have written to me about her fears? I don't even have a key for my door here. Paul's free to come and go as he pleases. I could wake up one night and find him standing over my bed!"

Mrs. Cummins gave a little mew of terror.

"She willna' let go of it," Hamish said. "I'd wonder why she's pressing sae hard?"

Miss Fraser said, "If you'd like a key, I'll see that you have one. But I hardly think you have any reason to be afraid here."

Robinson spoke up suddenly. "I've met Elcott. I think you're wrong. I can't believe he's the man we're after. Unless there's some problem I'm not aware of?" He looked around the table.

"Of course not," Elizabeth Fraser answered. "Paul's very different from Gerald, but that's not unexpected. I'd say you and your sister were different as well, Miss Ashton?"

Mrs. Cummins put in, "I don't see why a problem with a weak bone in his leg should make any difference to the Army. He could still shoot, couldn't he? Harry went to fight, even if they sent him off to Egypt instead. He didn't like Egypt, you know. But it was better than being cannon fodder in France."

Ignoring her hostess's digression, Janet Ashton turned to Robinson. "I'm sorry," she apologized for a second time. "I can't help it. I lie awake at night struggling to find answers. And Paul is the only threat I knew about. But if you don't agree with me, if there's something I haven't thought of, I wish you'd tell me! Anything to stop the ache of wondering."

He turned his head away, unable to look at her. Rutledge, beside him, could sense the rising tension in the man. The hand holding his serviette clenched and he cleared his throat as if he found it hard to breathe.

"Hugh? Please help me. You've hardly spoken to me since I got here — did Grace tell you something —" Her voice broke on tears.

And then almost against his will, Robinson blurted, "God knows I'd rather have it be Elcott than Josh —"

There was a stunned silence as everyone stared at him.

Robinson's face was drained of feeling, as if he had reached the bottom of despair.

"What do you mean, rather Elcott than Josh?" Rutledge asked slowly.

"I'm afraid — Josh hated his stepfather. I can't believe he'd have touched his mother. Still, once the shooting began — I don't see how he could have *stopped*. And I keep asking myself why he *didn't* die with the rest of them — how it was he got away. And there's only one answer I can think of. He'd planned it quite carefully. He killed them all and escaped under cover of the storm. I can't sleep for wondering if he was trying to get to London and to me. That it's my fault, indirectly, that they're dead. Because, you see, I wouldn't take him to live with me, however much he begged. *God help me, I felt he was better off with his mother!*"

He began to weep inconsolably.

Janet Ashton gasped, hands over her mouth. And for once she was speechless.

# *Chapter Seventeen*

Elizabeth Fraser was the first to recover. "For *shame!*" she exclaimed, a flush of anger rising into her cheeks. "You can't believe such a thing — he's your *son!*"

"No, Hugh, that's nonsense. You can't believe that! Grace would have told me if he was that unhappy! And he wouldn't have touched his mother — or Hazel — he *loved* his sister —" Janet Ashton's words spilled over each other as she leaned forward across the table.

Mrs. Cummins, flushed with shock, got to her feet, overturning her chair. "No, please — I can't bear any more of this." She hurried out of the kitchen, almost the scurry of a timid and frightened animal.

Robinson pressed his hands to his face, as if the very bones ached. "If you want to know, that's why I came to Urskdale. Rather than send the gifts by express.

Don't you see? Josh had been telling me all the autumn that he hated it here in the North, that his mother no longer had time or patience for him, that she loved the twins best because she loved their father best. I thought it would help if I talked to him, face to face. That's why I have to find Josh now, to help him, protect him. Whatever he's done." He drew his hands down, his eyes haunted. "Do you think I like the idea? Do you think I don't want to believe in someone — anyone else — killing them? The doctor said it must have been someone they *trusted*. Please God, let it be anyone but Josh!"

Janet Ashton said, "Did you tell Grace what you're telling us? Did you talk to her about it?"

He shook his head. "I didn't need to. She assured me he'd outgrow it, that he was still struggling with the fact that I'd come home. And I told myself he was far too young to come and live with me —"

He broke off as Janet Ashton got up from the table.

"I won't hear any more of this — I was here when the twins were born, I would have seen for myself that he was troubled —"

But Hugh Robinson answered the

thought behind what Janet was saying. "Gerald had been good to Josh. I don't think it was something Grace wanted to discuss with anyone but me."

"Grief has turned your mind, Hugh," Janet declared. "You should never have gone into that house or asked to see their bodies — it was not something you should have done!"

Janet walked quickly out of the kitchen, as if afraid their voices would follow her.

Robinson turned to look after her. "Grace wrote me, just before I was taken prisoner, telling me how Janet had stepped in after I'd been shipped to France. How she'd helped with Hazel and Josh, even going to London to find work and make sure the children had everything they needed. It was Janet's spirit that kept my family together. I owe her more than I can ever repay. But there are things between a husband and wife that no one else shares." He folded his serviette with shaking fingers and got to his feet. "If you'll excuse me —"

As his footsteps faded down the passage, Elizabeth Fraser said into the silence that followed, "I wish I hadn't heard any of that. It's too horrible even to think about!"

"They're grieving. You can't always heed

what someone says in the first hours of grief." Rutledge had lost his appetite, the rest of his meal untouched on his plate.

Hamish stirred. "Then you didna' believe the man."

"Children don't always think about the aftermath of an action. Only about what they want," he answered, this time silently, for Hamish's ears only. "But I find it hard to believe that a child of ten could aim and fire a revolver accurately, six times."

"It's no' difficult in sae small a room. He couldna' miss at that distance. If he was fashed —"

It was true, anger could have given a child the steadiness of purpose and the strength he needed. It would be over with quickly, surprise carrying the day for him, and only then would he begin to realize the horror of death. But where had he found a weapon?

"If Josh killed his family, then he's better off dead on the mountainside."

"There was the lad in Preston. He was only eighteen."

"Arthur Marlton was driven by voices — no one has said that Josh was anything but sane —"

Rutledge became aware that Elizabeth Fraser was speaking.

"— It must be hard to listen to such things. Even a policeman can't be inured to that kind of suffering!" She began to collect the plates, but he could see that her hands were trembling.

He thought of all the suffering he'd witnessed, in the war — in the course of his duties. He was abruptly tired of judging, of looking at the cruelty of violent death. He was tired of probing into the souls of people and digging out the nasty secrets he found there. This kitchen, with its cozy warmth, its small pleasures, shouldn't be the forum for questioning the motives of murderers.

He found himself longing for the ordinary life that most men lived, with a wife — children — a house with a small garden. But what could he bring to such domestic scenes? A haunted mind, an overfamiliarity with death, a burdened conscience . . .

Hamish said, "You were never a man for self-pity."

"No. Not self-pity. Loneliness."

Rousing himself, he moved to help Miss Fraser. "I'm sorry dinner was ruined —"

She bit her lip. "Why couldn't it have been a stranger? It wouldn't hurt as much, somehow. You could hate a stranger and what he'd done."

"If it is a stranger," Rutledge told her, "then he's still out there. And if it wasn't a grudge against the Elcotts — if it was something else, madness even — he could very well kill again. Don't you ever lock your doors? People come in and out of this house at will!"

"And I'm helpless to defend myself? Or Mrs. Cummins?" she finished for him. "I can't think of anyone with a grudge against us."

"I expect the Elcotts didn't know of anyone with a grudge against them," he answered curtly. "Until the door opened and their murderer stepped into the room." He thought of something. "Did the Elcotts own a dog?"

"In the summer Gerald had had to put down his sheepdog. She was twelve, and failing. A beautiful animal. He named her Miata. Strange name for a dog, isn't it? He said he'd read it somewhere and liked it. I asked if it was Irish, and he said it wasn't —"

"I thought you didn't know the family very well?"

She had the grace to blush. "I knew Gerald to speak to. Everyone did. On market day most people come in to Urskdale for supplies and news. And he was that sort of man, open and friendly.

Not just with me, because I was confined to my chair. It was a gift he had. Small wonder that Grace fell in love with him. A woman can judge a man sometimes."

Paul Elcott had said that even Elizabeth Fraser had been attracted to his brother.

"Then how do you judge Paul?"

Miss Fraser shook her head. "He was the younger son. And not easy to know. Often in his brother's shadow. But that doesn't make him a murderer!" She turned to look up at Rutledge, her blue eyes full of unhappiness. "Do you think Hugh Robinson is right — that Josh *could* have done such a thing?"

"God knows," Rutledge answered her. "But Robinson believes it. For now. And it's tearing him apart."

The boy was never comfortable wherever he sat. His body, tense as a spring, seemed to be unable to rest. He moved from chair to chair, and then to the floor next to Sybil. Up again and around the room, only to huddle once more against the dog's warm body. His eyes darted in the direction of any unexpected sound, galvanizing him to run. Sometimes it drove her to distraction, this constant prowl.

Maggie watched him without appearing

to: scanning the face that seemed pared down to skin over bone, the eyes looking inward at something too dark to bring out into the light of day. It was, she thought, like sharing a house with a shadow. Silent, no substance, hardly companionable. A burden rather than a gift from the snowy night.

But she needed him. His body was young and strong, and it didn't matter where his mind was. He could feed the sheep; he could drag bales of hay to the horse and the cow; he could clamber up on the roof with a broom to push the worst of the snow off the eaves. He could carry in the scuttle filled with coal and bring in kindling to lay the fire. She sat in her chair, nursing her leg and cursing the pain, and patted Sybil on the head. Clever girl that she was. "He'll do," she thought. "I won't make it through the winter without him —"

When the last of the search parties had come in from the fells, Greeley walked to the hotel and summoned Rutledge to the cold sitting room. Standing by the hearth, he said, "Well. I've done all I can. A pity it wasn't more."

Rutledge, looking out into the street, replied, "Miss Ashton believes Paul Elcott killed his brother and his family."

Greeley's eyebrows rose. "Does she, by God!"

"He found the bodies."

"What's that got to say to anything!" the older policeman demanded, irritated. "Who else was likely to have gone out to the house, after a storm like that one, save Paul? To see if the family had managed, if they needed anything." He shook his head. "We look in on each other," he added grimly. "And if Elcott hadn't found them, your Miss Ashton might have. She ought to be grateful to him for sparing her that grief."

It was true enough. And Hamish was reminding him of the revolver in Miss Ashton's carriage. There was only the woman's word for the fact that she hadn't made it as far as the Elcotts' farm — she might well have been on her way *back* to Carlisle when Rutledge found her.

Rutledge said aloud, "I'm told Janet Ashton helped her sister care for the children, when Robinson went to France. She knew Elcott. She might know if Elcott had other enemies. I must ask her that."

"Oh, yes? Enemies who come in the middle of a storm to butcher his family in front of him?" Greeley responded scornfully. "Unless there was something that happened in the war. He served in France. Artillery."

"I don't see how the killer could have anticipated such a ferocious storm. Still, it covered his tracks as well as the boy's. The question then becomes how long had the murders been planned? Or had something happened to precipitate events?"

Greeley shook his head. "I don't know what to think. I wish to God this hadn't happened on my patch!"

The outside door opened, and they could hear a man scraping his boots on the threshold. Greeley opened the sitting room door, expecting to find one of his men reporting. The newcomer looked up at Greeley. "Any news?"

"None, unless you've brought it." Greeley indicated Rutledge. "Scotland Yard, come to help us. Rutledge, this is Harry Cummins. You've met his wife."

The owner of the hotel. The Egyptian sun had darkened his skin, and a little gray threaded his dark hair. Rutledge shook his hand and thanked him for putting him up for the duration.

Cummins, staring at Rutledge, seemed at first not to hear, and then said quickly, "We're not exactly overflowing this time of year. Er — what's the Yard's interest in our problems?"

"The Chief Constable felt the local people needed help."

"I see." He seemed to shake off the mood that had distracted him. With false heartiness, he added, "Yes, of course, I should have thought of that. I'm sorry, I'm still asleep on my feet!"

"There are two other guests," Greeley told Cummins. "Robinson, Grace Elcott's first husband. And her sister, Janet Ashton."

"A good thing Elizabeth is here to see to them. Vera would never have managed!"

There was an awkward silence. Then Cummins indicated his snow-wet coat. "I'd better be getting out of these clothes. We've done our best, Greeley. There's no sign of the boy anywhere out there. I never thought he would have turned east anyway. If so, why not come directly into town and to you?"

"Good question," Greeley agreed. "Well, go and change. I was just finishing my conversation with Rutledge here."

"How long will you be staying?" Cummins asked, looking at the man from London.

"Until I find some answers," Rutledge responded.

"He's no' happy to see you . . ." Hamish pointed out.

Cummins nodded, and went off up the stairs, trudging heavily. The slump of his shoulders spoke volumes.

Greeley, following him with his eyes, sighed. "Well, where do we go from here?"

"Ask your men to canvass the village. We want to know about any strangers they've seen. About any trouble the Elcott family may have had with their neighbors — or any quarrels. We also want to know what the relationship was between Josh Robinson and his stepfather."

Greeley's glance swung back to Rutledge and sharpened. "What's that in aid of?"

"Robinson admitted over dinner that he's afraid his son killed the Elcotts. That Josh was angry with his stepfather — or was jealous of the twins. It might be best if I speak to Josh's schoolmaster."

"My good God!" Greeley whistled under his breath. "That couldn't have been an easy admission! I didn't know Josh well enough to tell you if it could be true or not. But I'll send the schoolmaster to you. Tonight!"

"I give Robinson credit for being honest. There's still an urgent reason to find the boy, while we can still be sure how he died.

And where." Silently he added, *And if he had a revolver with him —*

"And how do you intend to go about that?" Greeley retorted. "Watch for ravens collecting around the body?"

"We can begin by finding out whether or not anyone in the valley might willingly hide Josh Robinson. Protect him. After all, as far as anyone knows, he's been orphaned, and they might take pity on him. A classmate, a friend of Gerald's. It might tell us which direction he tried to take."

"There's not a soul in Urskdale who wouldn't have told me as soon as they heard we were searching for him!" Greeley protested. "They were told he'd likely witnessed the murders and we wanted him safe. No, I have to say you're barking up the wrong tree with Josh."

It was an hour later when the school-master presented himself at the hotel.

A tall, thin man with graying hair and an air of the cleric about him, he introduced himself to Rutledge as Rupert Blackwell and said, "Inspector Greeley tells me you wish to speak to me."

Rutledge led him into the chilly sitting room and offered him a chair. "It's about the boy, Josh Robinson. Elcott's stepson."

"Ah, yes, I thought as much. I was with one of the search parties. It was discouraging. We tried hard, believe me!"

Interested, Rutledge answered, "Indeed? Where did you search?"

"I was with Cummins and two other men. We went to the east of the farm, and then swung a little south, to come full circle." Blackwell added dryly, "I was already in my bed when you sent for me!" The chapped skin of his face stretched in a wry smile.

"Then I'll make this as brief as I can. Tell me about Josh."

"He's a bright child — was —" He paused, as if unwilling to use the past tense yet. "Quite clever with his hands, eager to learn. It's my view he needed better schooling than we can offer here. He'd grown up in a very different world, you see, with wider horizons. Most of our youngsters have always been content to follow in their fathers' footsteps. They learn what they can, and as their schoolmaster, I'm not ungrateful. Of course, those same horizons made Josh something of an outsider. His stories about living near London sounded like boasting to the other boys. As a result he made few friends."

"Was he a troublemaker?"

"That implies a certain quality of leadership, doesn't it? The outcast is troublesome, unable to understand why he isn't popular, lashing out because he's hurt and lonely. Wanting to stop the pain he feels. I saw none of that. But I gave him books to read — explorers and the like, men who accomplished great things alone. The sort of thing a boy with a lively imagination should have relished. But there was something more — I could see that it wasn't only his unhappiness at school. These last few months he's been distracted, and his schoolwork had begun to suffer. He was more inward-looking. More — worried. When I asked him outright if all was well at home, he answered that he was content. But you could see that he wasn't."

". . . *men who accomplished great things alone* . . ." Had that well-intended reading matter made it possible for a boy to contemplate killing his family? It was a chilling thought.

"How did he get on with his stepfather?"

"Sad to say, I don't know the answer to that." There was a pause. "He missed school more than usual this term. His mother would bring him to me and make excuses. It was outright truancy, but I welcomed him back, hoping to smooth over whatever it was that was disturbing him. I did wonder — and I made a point to bring it up with Mrs. Elcott — if he would be happier with his father, and schools in the south. If he was torn, you see, between his duty to his mother and his love for his father."

"How did she answer you?"

"That he was her son, and she wouldn't let him go. I don't think it occurred to her that it might be better for Josh. And in my opinion — well, that's water over the dam, you might say. If Josh survives, he'll go to his father after all."

Hamish was saying something. Rutledge realized that he was pointing out that Blackwell might have put his finger on the reason behind Robinson's fears.

An unexpected motive . . . an unhappy, frustrated child's solution to his private demons.

"Is it possible that Josh Robinson was wretched enough here in Urskdale to take matters into his own hands? So that he could live with his father?"

Blackwell stared at Rutledge. "Good God! Are you suggesting — ? No, that's contemptible! We're talking about a *child* — !"

"A policeman doesn't have the luxury of making exceptions. I have to look at every possibility, no matter how distasteful it might be," Rutledge answered mildly.

"He won't be eleven until January!" Blackwell exclaimed, shocked. "You must be out of your mind! I'd as easily believe Harry Cummins or I could have done such a thing!"

Rutledge said, "With a revolver there's no thought — there's no strength required. You simply point the weapon and pull the trigger. And people fall dead."

Blackwell got to his feet. "I shan't waste breath on this question!"

"Is there anyone Josh might have turned to — anyone he trusted enough to make his way to them? You, his teacher, perhaps."

The schoolmaster stopped at the door. "I wish I could say he would come to me. But of course he wouldn't have." He shrugged deprecatingly. "I make it a habit never to show favoritism. I never gave that child any reason to believe he could trust me particularly. I never imagined there would come a time . . ."

Rutledge waited, and Blackwell added almost against his will, "That's my failure as a teacher, Inspector. Some men have the gift of inspiring the young. I merely teach them. For what that's worth." And he was gone, a gust of frigid air swirling into the hall in his wake.

★ ★ ★

Rutledge discovered Elizabeth Fraser sitting in the kitchen, reading. He was surprised to find her still awake, and wondered if she found it as difficult to sleep sometimes as he did. And then remembered her standing in the door in the moonlight, taking tentative steps as if testing her will. When the house was dark and silent . . .

She looked up as he came through the passage door and said, "Was that news?"

"It was Blackwell, the schoolmaster. Did you know that Cummins has come home?"

"I heard him in the passage, speaking to his wife. She's not — well — tonight, as you saw." She marked her place in the book. "You look tired. I've put your hot water bottle there on the table."

"Were you waiting for me?" he asked, feeling a surge of guilt at the thought.

"No. I was trying to stay warm for a few minutes longer." She smiled. "I was born along the south coast, where winters were milder. We seldom saw snow, and I used to dream of traveling to Lapland and riding in a sleigh. It sounded so exciting — to be wrapped in furs and follow the reindeer herds."

"Why Lapland?"

"Because my mother often read to me from a little book about a child of the North." Her smile faded. "I know the men can't search forever. They have farms and families and work to see to. But I can't help but feel we've somehow deserted Josh Robinson by giving up."

"I haven't given up," he reminded her. "We're just trying new directions. Tomorrow I'll call on several of the farms closest to the Elcott house. To see what they've heard or seen, to ask where we ought to look when this snow melts. To keep their minds on the possible, even if we've had no luck so far."

"Do you think — is Robinson right about his son? He knows him best, but I — somehow I can't comprehend a child killing his own family! I've seen Josh; he was a child with unruly hair and a quick smile, and sometimes an imp of mischief in his face." She paused. "There was loneliness, too. I must tell you that."

Rutledge walked to the window and raised the shade to look out at the night.

" 'Ware what you say," Hamish warned him. And Rutledge turned away from the window, angry with the cautionary voice in his head.

"I've only begun the investigation —"

"It's just as hard to imagine Paul Elcott shooting his own brother." Her face was troubled. "What if you don't find the killer? Ever? There'll be a cloud over Paul's head. And over Josh's, even if he's found dead. You must realize that accusations have long lives, sometimes . . ."

It was as if she knew what she was talking about. As if accusations against her had shadowed her life. It could explain why she was content to stay here, at Mrs. Cummins's beck and call.

Instead of answering her, he said, "Cummins doesn't sound like a dale man."

"No, he's from London. But he's lived here forever — for twenty years or more, I should think." She smiled wryly. "He's still considered a stranger. For that matter, so am I. He bought this hotel and has tried to make a success of it, but sometimes I think he wishes he'd never set eyes on it."

"His wife was saying that he'd served in Egypt."

"Yes, that's true. He didn't like the East very much. He never talks about it. I don't think he's ever been happy. Isn't that a wretched thing to say about anyone? But I can't help it. He's haunted by something." She stopped, suddenly embarrassed. "I shouldn't be saying such things to a policeman! Harry Cummins is a good man, I don't mean to make him sound otherwise." She glanced at the clock on the wall. "How late it is!"

She set her book aside and collected her own hot water bottle. "Good night, Inspector."

He held the door for her and watched her wheel her chair down the passage.

As he reached for his own hot water bottle, he glanced down at the book she'd left behind.

It was one of O. A. Manning's slim volumes of poetry. *Wings of Fire.*

After a time he went to his own room and lighted the lamp. The room seemed to be full of ghosts, crowding him, and a wave of claustrophobia swept through him, driving him to open the door again and step into the passage, where the cold air of the unheated wing of the house seemed to swirl around him. The lamp dipped in the draft, and he could feel the beat of his heart like a drum that was too loud, reverberating through his body.

Hamish said, "You canna' escape fra' what you are and ha' been. . . ."

Rutledge answered him in the silence of the passage, "I can't live with it, either."

# Chapter Eighteen

The next morning Rutledge, with the map on the seat beside him in the motorcar, turned out of the hotel yard towards the bottom of Urskwater.

He followed a rutted lane into the yard of Apple Tree Farm. Dogs met him with lowered heads and suspicious growls. A woman came to the yard door to stare at him, uncertain who he was and why he had come.

"Inspector Rutledge, from London," he called, without leaving the motorcar.

"My husband's in the barn —"

"Mrs. Haldnes? I'd like to ask you a few questions about the night that the Elcott family died —"

The uncertainty changed instantly to wariness. "I can't tell you anything —"

"No, I understand. Not about the murders. But I wondered — did your dogs bark that night? Did you find tracks in the snow where they shouldn't have been? Did your children appear to be worried about something?"

"A storm was coming. We had work to do. What were we likely to hear? Or to see? There's no reason to think the killer came this way, surely!"

"I was thinking about Josh —"

"I don't wish the lad any harm — my husband searched for him with the rest. But he wasn't friendly with my boys. They didn't get on well together."

"He was in dire need; he might have tried to find help anywhere he could."

"Yes, and we'd have done what we could, wouldn't we? But we never saw him."

Hamish said, "She wasna' the sort of woman he would turn to. She's cold, and no' very motherly."

Ignoring the voice, Rutledge said, "You're the closest farm."

"That's as may be. But the track over the shoulder of the fell isn't the best there is."

He thanked her and, when she'd called off the dogs, walked into the cold mustiness of the barn, meeting with an equal reticence in her husband. A sense of closing ranks.

But he could identify an undercurrent of

superstition as well — as if speaking of the Elcotts and what had happened to them might somehow bring the same fate down on this family. To be ignorant was to be safe.

Rutledge drove on to South Farm, and found the owner in the stable, mucking out.

He asked Mr. Peterson the same questions — and once more met a blank wall. Mrs. Peterson, driven by curiosity, came out to see what it was the stranger wanted.

"We didn't know the lad, not really. Of course we'd seen him on market day with Gerald or his mum," she told Rutledge. "But our children are grown, with lives of their own, and we had no reason to take special notice of Josh. I'd heard he was troublesome, but he seemed quiet enough when Gerald was about."

"Troublesome?"

"I'm only repeating what Mrs. Haldnes told me. I don't know firsthand."

Peterson's eyes slid towards the heights. "We did our best, searching. It was expected of us." But the dissatisfaction of failure lurked in his voice.

"And you're sure there were no strangers in Urskdale, the week before the murders?" Rutledge asked again.

"Well, if a stranger was bent on mischief, he wasn't likely to call attention to himself, was he?" Mrs. Peterson asked reasonably. "Not many of us look out our windows of a night, to see who may be passing."

"Besides," her husband put in, "no need to stir up the dogs, if you're willing to walk wide of a farm. There's a hundred tracks to choose from, besides the lanes."

But when asked why the Elcotts might have been killed, the Petersons, like the Haldneses, shook their heads.

"Gerald was a good man," Peterson said. "Hardly the sort to find himself mixed up in something nasty. And that young wife of his was very mindful of her place. People like that aren't likely to find themselves in trouble, are they?"

"His father, Henry, was a good man, too. And of course his uncle. Sound stock, the Elcotts," Mrs. Peterson agreed. Then she added anxiously, "I don't think I ever knew anyone murdered before. It's not something we're used to, is it?"

When Rutledge brought up Paul Elcott's name, a quick glance passed between husband and wife. "He's not Gerald, mind. But sound enough," Peterson replied. "A shame the licensed house didn't fly, but there you are. He's young, yet."

Mrs. Peterson nodded. "He reminds me of his uncle Theo. And look how he turned out!" It was, to Rutledge's ears, faint praise.

Hamish said, "A long shadow to live under for a lifetime."

It was an interesting observation.

"Does Theo Elcott live here?" Rutledge asked. No one had mentioned another relative until now.

"Oh, Theo's been dead since 1906," Mrs. Peterson assured him. Then, reverting to the murders, she said, "Henry would have been horrified. I just don't understand how something like this could have happened here in Urskdale!"

Driving away from South Farm, Rutledge marveled at the silence bred into these people. The willingness to shut their eyes, the refusal to be a brother's keeper. Searching was one thing. It was what they knew, the land they lived with. If someone needed help repairing a storm-damaged roof, or the loan of a team or plow, or a hand feeding livestock when he was ill, neighbors would come because they knew he would return the favor one day. It was a matter of survival, in a place where nature was against them all.

But whatever the Elcotts had done to

call the wrath of the gods down upon them, their neighbors wanted no part of it.

The lane leading to the last farm on his list was deep with snow. His tires struggled up the incline, spinning, the motorcar rocking from side to side like a ship in a storm. Only the slightest indentation defined the lane as it wound around a knoll and then traveled a good mile over hilly ground before finally straggling upward again and into a farmyard. The outbuildings were weathered, tired. The snow lay heavy on their slate roofs, and in the gray sunlight, there was a dreariness about them that struck him at once.

Glancing down at the map, Rutledge read the name by this particular square. It was the Ingerson farm. An old name, surely, going back to the Scandinavian heritage of many families in the North.

He pulled into the yard and saw that seven or so sheep were penned near the house. Smoke rose from the chimney but the yard was empty, and no dogs barked.

Getting down from the motorcar, he looked around him. There was nothing to be seen in the snow but the tracks of a man's Wellingtons and the prints of a dog.

Before he could walk up the flagged approach to the kitchen door, it opened, and a woman stepped out to stare at him.

She was middle-aged, her hair pulled back in a knot behind her head. It had been fair once but now was streaked with gray, though her eyes were a startling blue. She leaned on a cane as if walking was difficult, and there were deep lines of pain in her face. Behind her a black dog stood guard, growling, warning him to mind his manners.

"I'm Inspector Rutledge — from London," he began. "I'm looking into the deaths of the Elcotts."

"Maggie Ingerson," she answered with a brief nod.

"I've come to speak to Mr. Ingerson, if I may."

"He's been dead for ten years. My father. You'll have to make do with me, if there's anything you want to say."

"You live here alone?" Rutledge asked, glancing up and judging the size of her farm. In the hazy light he could just see one of the sheep pens that lay high on the shoulder of the fell rising some distance behind her house, a snake of stones already standing out above the banked snow. "It must be hard work to keep up this place on your own!"

"The man who helped me until 1914 got blown up at Mons. There hasn't been anyone else who could do what needs to be done. I've seen to it myself." It was said without rancor, but something in her eyes told him that she resented the war and mourned the man dead in France.

"I've come about the search for young Robinson, Gerald Elcott's stepson."

"I guessed as much. Have they found him yet?"

"Not yet. No."

She had a stillness about her that spoke of self-sufficiency without self-pity. A plainness, as if her life had not left much time for frills. She was wearing Wellingtons, a man's thick corduroy trousers, and a man's heavy coat. The red plaid shirt under it, visible at the collar, seemed her only concession to femininity, as if there was no time to waste on something there was no one about to appreciate.

"I'd like to ask if you heard or saw anything the night of the storm. If your dog barked for no reason — if you found any tracks the morning after the storm passed — anything that might help us locate the boy. You're not that far from the Elcott farm."

"On paper, that may be. You have to

273

take into account the elevation as well. Until the search party arrived, I didn't know I should be listening for anything out of the ordinary. And the wind was that fierce, you couldn't hear yourself think. The dog and I stayed by the fire and left the sheep to fend for themselves." She indicated her cane. "There wasn't much else I could do."

Rutledge could feel a rising thread of wind that seemed to come from the heights and gather strength as it rolled down towards them. The woman seemed not to notice it, as if inured to the cold. She was, as Hamish was saying in the back of his mind, of sturdier stock.

"I understand that not far from here there's a track that leads over the mountains and down to the coast road."

"Not so much a track as an old drover road. I daresay I could find it on a good day. I don't know many who could. It's not been used in a hundred years."

"Did anyone pass that way on the night of the storm?"

She laughed shortly. "It's not like London, Inspector. An army could have marched that way, and I wouldn't have seen them. Or heard them."

"Your dog might have."

"Sybil isn't the adventurous sort. I let her out, she does what she has to do, and she comes back in. She's a working dog. If whoever walked that track had two legs and didn't smell of sheep, she'd ignore him. Whatever he'd done."

Rutledge shaded his eyes to study the spectacular scenery that surrounded the farm. There was a beck tumbling down a rocky defile on the far side of the farm, disappearing in the direction of the lake. Far above, a ragged shelf leaned down crookedly towards the jumble of fallen debris that had once been a part of it. And higher still, the rounded shoulder of the fell turned and ran towards a fold of land that looked like a high pass.

As if she'd read his mind, Maggie Ingerson said, "He didn't grow up here. That boy. I don't see him running too far from home. In his shoes, that's what I'd have done. Stayed close and bided my time."

"It would depend," Rutledge answered, "on whether he was running from — or to — something."

She shrugged. "I never had a child of my own. I don't know the answer to that."

"There are five people dead —"

"And I didn't kill them. I liked Gerald

Elcott well enough, but I have all I can do to survive here. If the boy escaped, as Sergeant Miller says he did, then he's dead, too, and I haven't energy to spare in mourning him. In my view, he's better off dead. I know what it's like to live alone and have no one to turn to. I wouldn't wish that on him. Now if you'll forgive me, I need to rest my leg. Standing isn't good for it."

"Do you need help? Would you like to see Dr. Jarvis? Or to have someone bring you supplies?"

"It's Dr. Jarvis who's to blame for my leg. He told me he could set it again and it would be straight. But he was wrong. About that and the infection afterward. I manage with what I've got, and the rest I do without. Still, thank you for asking."

She turned and walked back through the door, shutting it in his face.

Rutledge stood there for a moment longer in the yard of the Ingerson farm, remembering what the woman had just said.

The assumption was that Josh Robinson had fled that house of slaughter and run for his life — and that theory had served to galvanize Urskdale, sending searchers in every direction.

But what if it wasn't what had happened that stormy night —

What if he was still somewhere close by his home, waiting for his father to come for him?

Rutledge started the motorcar and drove back the way he'd come.

When Maggie came back into the kitchen, she found him standing there, rooted to the floor, eyes wide with fear.

"I wouldn't mind *him*," she said, crossing to the stove to warm her hands. "He was lost."

The child stared at her.

"From London, he said."

The boy began to shake, as if from a fever. She thought at first he was having a seizure, and watched in concern, waiting for his eyes to roll back in his head. But he simply stood there, unable to move, in such a state of terror that she crossed to set her hands on his shoulders. He winced at her touch.

"What Sybil finds, she keeps," Maggie said firmly. "Do you hear me? If you want to leave, there's the door. Open it and go. If you want to stay, then you'll have to trust me." She moved on to her chair and sat down heavily. "The kettle's about to boil, and I've been on my feet long enough. If we're going to have tea, you'll have to make it. I'll cut the bread. And then we'll see about getting a little hay to the sheep on the hill. The snow's too deep, they'll be starving before it melts. I can't afford to lose them."

Massaging her leg, she said, "I hate being in debt to any man. It's not how I was brought up. But you're here, and I need you, and that's all there is to it."

He walked to the stove and lifted the heavy kettle as it began to whistle. It took all his concentration, and he set it carefully on the mat on the table before rooting in the cupboard for tea and sugar and cups.

Maggie watched him without seeming to.

"Do you have a name?" she asked. "I've got to call you something."

But he didn't answer, his face turned away.

She let it go.

Sybil, lying by the bedroom door, heaved a sigh, as if something had been settled.

Maggie, hearing her, said nothing.

When Rutledge arrived at the Elcott farm, there was another vehicle there already, a small cart drawn by an old horse.

He stopped the motorcar some distance away and went to the cart. Laying a hand on the animal's shoulder, he could feel the sweat, still warm.

The interloper hadn't been there very long.

A curious neighbor? Or someone else?

He strode across the muddy yard to the kitchen door and opened it.

In the light of a lamp on the table, Paul Elcott, on his knees by the wall, looked up with terror in his eyes, and then swore as he recognized Rutledge.

"God, but you gave me a start, man! Did you ever think to knock?"

"What are you doing here?"

Elcott gestured towards the bucket of water and scrub brush.

"Someone's got to clean this room. And if I'm going to live here now . . ."

One side of the room was nearly clean, the rusty stains only a faint streak in the paint now.

"I thought you lived above the licensed house."

"The bank won't give me any more money. Not with Gerald dead. I'll lose the place before the month is out. There's nowhere else to go."

Rutledge thought, *I don't envy him, living here with the ghosts.*

279

Hamish said, "Aye, but if he wanted the farm enough to kill for it, ye ken it's timely."

Rutledge looked again at the bloodstains, at the devastation that represented the abrupt end of five lives. Even when he first stepped through the door here, something had bothered him. A sense of evil and ugliness.

It was hard to believe that a child could have done this.

Elcott seemed to know what had been passing through Rutledge's mind. "I shan't have anywhere else to go!" he said in self-defense. "What am I to do?"

"Did your brother own a handgun?" Rutledge asked. If Josh had killed his own family, where had the revolver come from?

"He never had a hope of reaching it in time, if he did. With small children about, he'd have kept it locked up in his bedroom or out in the barn . . . If I'm to finish here before dark, I need to be about it." Something in his voice hinted at a fear of the dark in this place. . . .

"Yes, go on. I have other business here."

Elcott waited, but Rutledge didn't explain. Finally he got to his knees again and began to scrub, but the stiffness across his shoulders indicated that he was all too aware of the policeman by the door.

★ ★ ★

Rutledge walked outside, going through the barn with some care, looking for trapdoors, looking for some sign that someone had taken refuge here after the searchers had departed. But there was nothing. No makeshift beds, no sacks pulled into a dry corner, no cache of tins or biscuits or anything else a boy might live on. The same was true in the outbuildings. But then the police had already done this search earlier.

He walked out into the yard again and scanned the slopes of the fell, searching for — what?

Hamish said, "An observation post . . ."

To begin with, perhaps. But nearly a week had passed since the murders. Without food, with only cold snow for water, and with little protection during the cold nights, how could a child have survived?

But then this might have been a child with murder on his soul . . . and surviving was the reason for killing.

It would depend, Hamish was reminding him, on how far ahead the boy had planned.

Or, Rutledge found himself thinking, on how Josh Robinson had felt about the bloody shambles he'd fled. He could have carried out the murders and then, over-whelmed by the horror of what he'd done, he might have run too far and lost himself in the unfamiliar night, the unfamiliar snow. And never had the strength to find his way back.

Rutledge went back to the house, this time entering through the front door, climbing the stairs to the bedrooms.

Searching more carefully than he'd had a chance to do in Inspector Greeley's presence, he went through drawers and cupboards trying to find something that defined the dead. Letters — more photographs —

"It isna' a house wi' secrets," Hamish grumbled.

And that was true. Nothing was concealed. It was as if the family had never felt it had to hide anything. The handful of letters he came across were innocuous, hardly more than everyday accounts of events. Seven from Janet Ashton, three from Robinson. If there had been other letters, they were gone now.

He found a book of accounts in a desk in Gerald and Grace Elcott's bedroom, and turned through the pages, recognizing that the farm was relatively prosperous. Another factor pointing in Paul Elcott's direction.

An album of pressed flowers on a shelf by the bed must have belonged to Grace. She had collected these blooms, pressed them with care, and identified them on the page. As the guide Drew had said, in the short growing season there were wildflowers along the edges of the lake, and in sheltered pockets, if one knew where to look. Bog myrtle with its distinctive scent, the leaves and flowers of Mimulus, various ferns, the leaves of dwarf willow and dwarf sedge from the highest peaks. They were mixed with the more familiar marigold, rose petals, violets, and lavender.

Grace Elcott must have walked often through the countryside, adding to her store. He tried to picture her, holding her daughter by the hand, her son running ahead, going out to search for something new with each season.

But she had worked hard as well, cooking, making her own bread, hanging out the wash, ironing the clothes, cleaning the house, sweeping out the kitchen . . . and never complained. Transplanted from London to a harder life, perhaps, than she'd expected.

He put the album back in its place and

went on. The toy soldiers in Josh's room, the dolls in Hazel's, painted an ordinary picture of life here. He found a small coral necklace that had belonged to the little girl, wrapped in pretty paper and kept in a velvet box. A birth gift from her parents? But in Josh's room there was a pair of gold cuff links, broken and stuffed behind the head of the bed. . . .

Rutledge held them in the palm of his hand, wondering what they represented. A gift from his stepfather, secretly rejected? Or merely broken by an active boy who was afraid to tell his elders what had become of them?

In the parlor were books, *Peter and Wendy* and several volumes of explorations. A Bible. A book of household hints. A chess set and board. A pipe rack with a tin-lined tobacco box beside it. A small sewing basket with needles and embroidery threads in gay colors. A folded tea towel with an unfinished pattern along its border — a vase of violets with leaves trailing . . .

Domestic life. Ordinary, comfortable.

Rutledge remembered the hat with its cabbage roses. Grace Elcott had possessed a sense of style. A pretty woman, who had attracted two husbands.

Had she been afraid of Paul Elcott because he coveted not only his brother's farm but also his brother's wife?

He went back up to Hazel's bedroom to look again at the photograph of Janet Ashton. Where did she stand in this scene of death? The only revolver he'd found was hers. . . .

He was studying her petulant face when he heard Paul Elcott's voice from below.

"Inspector Rutledge? Are you still here?"

He went to the head of the stairs and called, "Yes. What is it?"

"It's Inspector Greeley. He's come looking for you. There's been trouble at the hotel."

# Chapter Nineteen

Inspector Greeley was pacing the yard when Rutledge came around the corner of the house.

"You're a hard man to find!" Greeley said.

"What's happened?"

"It's a ruddy nightmare. Robinson tried to kill himself. It was all Elizabeth could do to stop him! She's cut, too. A straight razor —"

Rutledge swore. "All right. I'll meet you there."

He cranked the car and got in behind the wheel. Greeley, behind him, turned his carriage and prepared to follow.

Rutledge drove fast, sending a spray of snow, meltwater, and mud behind him as his tires bit into the road.

Was it a bit of histrionics — or had Robinson let his grief get the best of him?

Hamish said, "If he cut the lass, it wasna' dramatics."

"Damn the man!" Rutledge snarled. "It serves no purpose, not here. Not now. He should have waited until his children were buried. He owes them that much."

But grief had many faces, and here was a man who had suffered through a prisoner-of-war camp after a bloody war. He had come home to a family that had, for whatever reasons, forsaken him. Now they were dead. And even in that, there was no peace.

Hamish grunted, as if agreeing with Rutledge's thoughts. "War changed us."

And the simple words carried a wealth of misery.

The back door stood wide. Rutledge could hear anxious voices from the kitchen and crossed the yard in long strides.

Hamish, his voice seeming to echo against the fell, said, "She's come to no harm —"

As he stepped inside he could smell the odor of fear and a heavier reek of burned toast. It was bitter in his nostrils.

The first thing he saw was the spattered blood on the floor. And shards of a broken teacup and saucer.

His mind flashed back to another kitchen he had seen not an hour before, and a man scrubbing the stubborn stains on the walls.

Dr. Jarvis was there, and Vera Cummins, her cheeks streaked with tears. And Elizabeth Fraser, pale and shaken, was submitting silently to the bandaging of her hand. Harry Cummins stood near the door to the passage, worry deepening the lines of fatigue, his eyes on Miss Fraser.

All looked up as Rutledge came in.

"What happened? Where's Robinson?" he asked.

"Robinson is in his bed. Under sedation," Jarvis said grimly.

"I was coming down the passage with clean towels," Elizabeth Fraser said, her voice trembling. "I heard a — a noise in Mr. Robinson's room. It sounded as if something heavy had fallen to the floor. I knocked, and then when there was no answer, I went in —"

She shivered, and looked up at Jarvis. The doctor was just tying off the bandage, a frown on his face.

She cleared her throat and went on. "He was on the floor. There were pieces of china all around him, and blood pouring from his wrist. He was just — staring at it.

And when he saw me, he tried to slash the other wrist. I fought to stop him. Mr. Cummins heard the noise, and then Miss Ashton came running to help as well. It took all of us to subdue him — it was as if he had the strength of a dozen men. And all the while he kept calling for his children. It was *horrible* — I didn't think I could prevent him from — If it hadn't been for Harry, I'd have failed. We got him out here and used belts to tie him to a chair until the doctor could be sent for —"

She stopped, then said faintly, "I was frightened he'd succeed."

Rutledge turned to the doctor. "How is he?"

"I think he's come to his senses," Jarvis answered. "He was apologizing profusely to everyone —"

Rutledge brushed past them and walked down the passage to the guest rooms. He opened Robinson's door without ceremony. As it banged against the wall, Miss Ashton, who had been sitting beside the bed watching her former brother-in-law, started at the sound, turning to Rutledge with wide, startled eyes.

Robinson looked up at Rutledge blearily, and with an effort lifted himself to one elbow. There were bandages on his wrists and one across his chin. Blood stained the floor and the white cloth on the table that had held the yellow pitcher and bowl. They lay on the floor in bits.

"What in hell did you think you were doing?" Rutledge turned back to Robinson as Hamish, in the back of his mind, urged caution.

Hugh Robinson said, "I — I don't know — I think — I think I lost my mind —"

"It was a stupid, dangerous thing to try! You've hurt Miss Fraser, you've frightened everyone in the house, and you've wreaked havoc here and in the kitchen — and you've gained nothing!"

"You don't know what it's like —" Robinson began, tears in his eyes. "You don't know — That child is my *son!*"

"All the more reason to keep your head and help him when he's found." He turned to Miss Ashton. "Is there a key to this door?"

"Yes — Miss Fraser passed them out last night, after dinner —"

"And the razor?"

"In the kitchen."

"All right. Robinson, you're locked in until I see you've got yourself back under control. Your meals will be brought to you."

He took the key, ushered Janet Ashton out into the passage, and shut the door.

She said, "He's grieving —"

"Nevertheless." He turned the key and dropped it into his pocket.

She followed him back to the kitchen, still protesting.

Hamish was saying, "Ye've lost your temper because ye've wasted the morning! It isna' right to take your failure out on others."

They reached the kitchen. The others watched him, disturbed by something they read in his face.

"Is he all right?" Mrs. Cummins asked. "He's a guest here; I can't imagine what went wrong! We've done all we can to make everyone comfortable, but it's hard, you see —"

He could smell the whiskey on her breath. "It was nothing you did — or failed to do," he told her. Then looking over her head to her husband, he added, "Perhaps you ought to take Mrs. Cummins upstairs to rest."

Cummins tore his eyes from Elizabeth Fraser's face. "I should stay to see if Miss Fraser is all right . . ."

Mrs. Cummins caught her breath on a sob and walked quickly out of the room, hurrying down the passage. They could hear her footsteps flying up the stairs.

"Your place is with your wife," Rutledge told Cummins curtly.

Reluctantly the innkeeper left the room, casting a last glance at the woman in the wheeled chair.

Miss Ashton declared, "I'm going for a walk. I can't sit here and do nothing!" She turned and followed Cummins down the passage.

Dr. Jarvis was replacing instruments in his satchel, wrapping them in cloth as he put them away. "I don't think Robinson did much damage," he told Rutledge as he worked. "To himself or to Elizabeth here. He was distraught, and overly emotional, but I don't think he had the heart to finish the job."

Miss Fraser was looking down at her hand. There was a rising bruise on her cheek where Robinson must have struck her as they struggled. Rutledge swore under his breath. He wanted to take Robinson by the throat and shake him. The force of the feeling surprised him.

Dr. Jarvis considered her for a moment. "Would you care for a sedative, my dear? Something to soothe —"

"No. I must see to the dinner —"

"I'll leave something then, in the event it's needed later. I have another patient to see to, a broken collarbone. Fell off his roof trying to push out the snow. If you need me, send for me."

He nodded to Rutledge, and was gone. From the yard they could hear him speaking to Greeley, who had just pulled in. The two men left together.

There was silence in the kitchen.

Then Elizabeth Fraser said again, "I was so *frightened* — *!*" Her voice was soft, as if she wasn't aware she was speaking aloud.

For want of something constructive to do, Rutledge began to make tea, and after a few minutes set a cup before her. She drank it down, her left hand shaking only slightly as she lifted it to her lips.

"Ask Mrs. Cummins or Miss Ashton to help you with the meal. You shouldn't disturb that bandage for twenty-four hours."

"You sound like Dr. Jarvis!" She smiled wryly. "But then in the war, you must have seen far more terrible injuries than mine. This will heal in no time."

He didn't answer her, standing at the window looking out, sorting through his emotions. He had saved Janet Ashton's life, but there was no sense of warmth between them. They had become antagonists over the murders, and her determination to force the issue kept her at arm's length from everyone. He wondered why Gerald had chosen one over the other. Because Grace was vulnerable, with two fatherless children, bringing out his protective nature? Was it in fact Janet Ashton's strength that had seemed unfeminine and hard to him? And was that why Gerald had been kind to Elizabeth Fraser? Because she was vulnerable in her own fashion?

Yet he himself had seen another side of Elizabeth Fraser. She possessed a gallant spirit, taking her disability in stride, earning her keep without complaint in this house of tensions between husband and wife. He wondered why she stayed. And again he came to the conclusion that need had forced her into what might become an intolerable situation.

Because Harry Cummins was keenly aware of her vulnerability, too.

"I understand, really I do," she was saying. "He's half mad with grief and frustration. But it's such a waste. There's been enough bloodshed already. What good — what possible good — could it do to shed more?"

"I expect he didn't think about good. Only about his own pain." Rutledge knelt and began quietly washing up the blood from the floor, collecting the bits of teacup.

"You needn't do that —" Elizabeth Fraser protested.

"Why not?" he asked, forcing a smile. "It's a way of dealing with my own frustrations."

She looked askance, but didn't take it any further.

Tipping the broken china into the dustbin, he closed the door to shut out the cold, clear air. The odor of burned bread was gone now, and the kitchen seemed chill, unfriendly, as if what had happened at the Elcott farm had finally spread to this comfortable and unlikely place.

Mrs. Cummins came down to help prepare the meal, and Rutledge left the women to their work. He had sat for an hour with Elizabeth Fraser, silence between them, her thoughts turned inward. He had offered what he could, his presence, without intruding.

Hamish, uneasy and withdrawn, was a third party in the room.

Just before Mrs. Cummins had come in again, Miss Fraser had said, as if closing the door on whatever was on her own mind, "Did you learn anything this morning? You seemed so hopeful as you were leaving. I could feel it."

"Not much, I'm afraid."

"Perhaps you aren't looking in the right place?"

"That's what Maggie Ingerson said to me."

"Miss Ashton is convinced that she's right about Paul Elcott."

"It would be convenient for her."

"Convenient? An odd choice of words, surely, Inspector! I don't see what she might gain from blaming him!"

But he said nothing. After a moment, Miss Fraser commented tentatively, "You *must* find out who did this horrible thing — as soon as you can! Urskdale won't be the same even so, but we have a better chance of putting events behind us if there's an end to it."

He couldn't tell her that he already had too many suspects — and far from enough proof against any one of them. He couldn't tell her that he was stumbling in the dark, looking for answers, no better than Inspector Greeley before him. And what if there *was* someone else out there, a stranger whom no one had seen in the storm — or worse, someone in the dale who had killed wantonly and could possibly kill again. . . .

He dared not concentrate on any one possibility to the exclusion of others. It would be too dangerous. This wasn't London, where constables across the city could keep an eye on each suspect and report daily. Here there were no eyes. And there was a good deal of empty landscape where people could move at will.

He admitted to himself that he didn't want the killer to be the child. It was too monstrous a thing to have done.

Hamish reminded him, "Aye, but ye ken, the duty of a policeman is no' to feel a partiality. It will blind you to what must be done."

Rutledge had done his best to be impartial in Preston. Odd to think that if the trial had been finished only a day early, he wouldn't have been sent north. He'd have been halfway back to London before the bodies had been discovered.

But if the trial had ended a day early, the fate of young Marlton might have been very different. The long and serious debate by the jurors as they considered the evidence was all that had spared him from the hangman.

As for duty, Rutledge understood that all

too well. He had sent young, green men into the heat of battle, because it was their turn to fight. He had had to close his eyes to the fact that they would surely die. In the end, chance had made the final choice. Or so he had tried to tell himself as he reported the long lists of the dead and missing.

The Scots under him had sometimes sat with a bowl of water on a black cloth, searching for a sign of what lay ahead. He never knew if it had worked.

What would he ask of the water, if he sat over a bowl right now? Where was the child? Or — who was the murderer?

Better by far for the snow to have swallowed up Josh Robinson than for him to be brought in for trial.

# Chapter Twenty

Greeley was at his office, his face haggard with fatigue. Even handing the investigation over to Rutledge had done nothing to alleviate his own involvement, and he seemed to carry around with him the haunting question of responsibility: Had he failed in his duty by not bringing in the killer himself?

As Rutledge walked in, he got up from behind his desk and said, "Dr. Jarvis tells me he's all right. Robinson."

"I have a feeling it won't happen again."

Greeley sighed. "I tried to persuade him not to look at the bodies — for this very reason. The loss alone was enough to drive any man mad."

He fished out a sheet of paper from a pile on the top of his desk. "This came for you. A man from Keswick brought it. I'd gone by the hotel to deliver it. That's how I walked into the middle of the chaos. I summoned the doctor and went looking for you."

It was a telegram from Inspector Bowles in London.

REPORT FINDINGS AS SOON AS POSSIBLE. CHIEF CONSTABLE ANXIOUS FOR RESULTS.

Rutledge read it and then shoved it into his pocket.

Easy enough to sit in London and demand solutions. Where was the evidence to bring anyone to trial?

Greeley said, "I'm told you were questioning people who have holdings closest to the Elcott farm. I'd been over that ground. It was a waste of time."

Taking the chair across from Greeley, Rutledge answered him indirectly. "It was an excuse to see for myself what the obstacles were. For instance, none of the three farms was a likely place for Josh Robinson to seek shelter. He didn't get on well with the Haldneses' sons, and I don't think that even in desperation he'd appeal to their mother. The Petersons are older, and he hardly knew them, which means he wasn't likely to trust them. Miss Ingerson is gruff and keeps to herself. She'd probably seem more frightening than sympathetic to a child."

"It's not likely he's in hiding," Greeley agreed. "Even if the killer lived in Urskdale, and the boy had named him, a responsible adult would report to me. Everyone knows what happened — I could depend on that." He paused. "This Miss Ashton. I've spoken to her a time or two, when she was in the village with Grace Elcott. I had the feeling she looked down her nose at us, that we didn't quite measure up to her London acquaintances. Have you spoken with her about her sister? It seems odd to me that Miss Ashton would choose to visit this time of year. Dr. Jarvis tells me she ran off the road near the Follet farm. If it wasn't urgent, why didn't she turn back long before Keswick, rather than risk life and limb? She might have been killed. There's an urgency there that smacks of knowledge."

The outsider . . .

"She tells me Grace Elcott was afraid of her brother-in-law, Paul."

"Well, there's nonsense right there! She must be covering up something!"

"If we can't find the child to tell us what he saw, we need to find the murder weapon and trace it back to its owner. Can you make me a list of all the people in Urskdale who own revolvers?"

Greeley said, considering, "With a little thought. I should have seen to that earlier, but there was the search on my mind. Let me see —" He pulled out a sheet of paper. "The Haldnes family. And theirs is all but useless, old as it is."

"Is it possible that their sons would let Josh borrow it for a few days?"

"This one would probably blow up in his face. They found it on a strand outside Liverpool while on holiday, rusted and full of sand. I doubt they could even load it."

Hamish grumbled, "Then it's no use on the list."

But Rutledge answered, "We'll keep it in mind."

"The Elcotts themselves had one."

Hamish said, "Then why was the lass bringing one to her sister?"

"Gerald's?" Rutledge asked on the heels of Hamish's words.

"Actually, the revolver belonged to Gerald's uncle, Theo Elcott. He worked in South Africa for a number of years. Something to do with the railways. He never trusted the Boers, and the story was he'd shot one of them when a commando attacked his station. I don't remember him — he left when I was still a boy, and he died of a fever in 1906 on the boat back to England. But he was quite a local hero, and we all knew about the famous revolver. It came back in his trunk, I know, because Gerald's father showed it to me. I can't tell you what's become of it since. I hadn't given it a thought for God knows how many years. I don't suppose anyone else has. And Harry Cummins —"

Mrs. Peterson had said something about Gerald's uncle. Rutledge interrupted Greeley. "Where is this trunk now? I don't remember seeing anything like that in the house."

"Nor do I. It could be Paul Elcott's got it."

"Is there anyone who knew the family well enough to answer a few questions before we go to Elcott?"

"Um, I daresay it would be the ironmonger. Belfors. He was a friend of Paul's father and uncle."

Rutledge stood. "Then it's time to ask him."

When Rutledge opened the door of the ironmonger's shop, Greeley at his heels, very blue eyes examined the Londoner as if weighing him up.

The man behind the counter was elderly, with shoulders that were still broad and heavy. His face was rugged, pocked with scars from working hot iron, and his broad hands were gnarled and twisted.

"What can I do for you, then?" Belfors asked, palms resting flat on the worn surface.

There was a clutter of goods everywhere: Barrels of nails and hinges and locks were stocked in front of ax heads, shovels, and spades. Gates for fences leaned against one wall, rakes and pitchforks on either side. And all manner of chains and hammers and spanners filled shelves. A sharp odor of metal mixed with the scent of pipe smoke filled the air.

"My name is Rutledge —"

"Aye, from London."

"That's right. I'm told you knew Gerald Elcott's father."

"His father?" He stared at Rutledge for a moment, as if this was a question he'd never expected. "He's been dead for going on ten years. But yes, we were in school together, Henry and I." Belfors straightened. "We courted the same girl for a time." A grin creased his face. "Until she married someone else."

"And did you know his brother, Theo?"

"The inspector here has no doubt already told you I did."

"Tell me about Theo Elcott."

"What's this about, then?" Belfors glanced at Greeley as if seeking an explanation.

But Greeley said only, "Answer the inspector, if you will."

"Theo was railway-mad. Since he was a lad. Read everything he could find about trains. That finally carried him off from here at the age of nineteen, and I saw him but once after that."

"Where did this passion for railways take him?" Rutledge asked patiently.

"Slough, for a time. Then he was offered a position in South Africa, and he took it. Did well enough for himself out there. But he died before he could return to England." Belfors glanced from Greeley to Rutledge. "What's this in aid of, then?" he asked a second time. "You don't think Theo's come home to murder people, do you?" There was a thread of sarcasm in the man's voice.

Greeley started to speak, but Rutledge was already answering. "Hardly. We're looking for his trunk. The one holding his belongings, the one that came back after he was buried at sea."

Belfors sighed. "I can tell you the answer to that. It was given to my sister when she went to Northumberland to live."

"And the contents? What became of those?"

"How should I know? Clothes and shoes and hats and the like? Donated to the Mission boxes, most likely."

"Did he bring any souvenirs out of Africa with him?"

"Ah. It's the revolver you want to know about, then! Why didn't you say so? The revolver he used to shoot the Boer. I saw it once. Henry brought it in to show me. He was that proud of his brother. To be honest, I'd have never thought of Theo as a brave man. He had his head in machinery when I knew him. But I suppose he must have been brave enough, when the time came."

Rutledge held on to his patience. "What became of Theo's revolver, do you know?"

"Henry is the only one who can answer that. And Henry, God rest him, is in the churchyard."

"Surely one of his sons would have wanted it. A token, as it were, of their uncle's courage?"

The bright blue eyes stared into Rutledge's dark ones.

"I never thought to ask, to tell you the truth. I never knew."

And Rutledge had to be satisfied with that. But he had the oddest sense that Belfors could have told him more, that he was holding back the whole truth and palming off this stranger from London with bland half-lies.

Who was the old man protecting?

Hamish answered the thought. *The only Elcott that's left. Paul.*

But Rutledge was groping for something else, something that seemed elusive and fragmentary. At length he said, "By any chance, did you offer to buy the revolver from Henry, when he brought it in to show you?"

There was a flicker of change in the steady blue eyes.

"Henry never wanted to sell it. Why should he? It was Theo's."

"Then who did offer to sell it to you —"

But the shop door opened and a customer came in. Belfors turned away, and the question hung in the air like a ghost, waiting to be exorcised.

Outside in the street again, Rutledge said to Greeley, "I want to go back to the farm and search before I speak to Paul Elcott. For now, I'd like to get a message to Sergeant Gibson in London. Can you see that it's taken care of?"

"I'll send Constable Ward to Keswick with it."

"He can drive the motorcar. That should take less time. And ask him to wait for a reply." Rutledge commandeered a desk and began to write.

He could almost feel Hamish standing just behind him, peering over his shoulder as he worked on a list of names for Sergeant Gibson.

The house was quiet when Rutledge returned to the hotel. He walked through to the kitchen to find himself a glass of water, and sat at the table, where he could see the fell rising beyond the gardens, and the play of light in the dips and hummocks of snow. There were more ribs of stone showing now, as the sun strengthened to warm the hard rock. The slopes seemed less oppressive, more tired, as if they had been waging a battle against the blanket of white.

It was odd, he thought, how in the years he'd come here to walk in season, he hadn't really come to know the people. Or, for that matter, to understand them. The days were spent on the fells, if the weather was good, and the evenings in their lodgings, where he and his father or his friends had talked about the day's experiences, comparing views, the difficulty of the tracks, the plans for the next day. Wastwater had been one of his favorite haunts, wild and beautiful, always a challenge — he could remember where he had walked even now. But he couldn't bring back the name of a single family he'd stayed with —

There was a light tap on the back door, and it opened.

The man coming in was from one of the first of the search parties to report to Rutledge. Henderson . . .

He nodded to Rutledge, and stood there in the doorway as if expecting to find someone else in the kitchen.

Rutledge said, standing up, "Did you want Cummins? Or Miss Fraser?"

"No. I've come to speak to you." Henderson seemed reluctant to go on with whatever had brought him there. "No word of the lad?" he said finally.

"Sorry, nothing."

"Umm. And the killer, are you any closer to finding out who it was?"

"We're continuing our inquiries," Rutledge answered. It was the standard reply when someone prodded the police. And then with honesty, he added, "I'm afraid we haven't found him yet."

"Umm."

"Is there something you've come across that might help us?"

Henderson looked down at the hat in his hand. "I don't know. But it was that strange."

Hamish was speaking in the back of Rutledge's mind, a voice that was a low rumble. "He's troubled . . ."

It was clear that Henderson was of two minds about what he had come to say. Rutledge held his tongue, waiting patiently.

Finally the man said, "I was bringing my youngest in to see Dr. Jarvis last night. He'd fallen — there was a lump on his collarbone."

"Broken, was it?"

"No. But he'd cried for an hour. It worried my wife."

"Yes, I can see that."

"Dr. Jarvis gave him something for the pain. And let him rest half an hour before going home. It was well after eleven o'clock before we were on the road again."

"Your wife was with you?" Corroborating evidence.

"No, just the boy and me. I had come out of Urskdale, and was just past The

Knob, and I looked up to see there was a light, high up."

The Knob was within view from where Rutledge had been sitting.

"Are you sure?"

"It bobbed, the way it would if a man was walking."

"And where was it going? Towards Urskdale or away?"

"Away. Towards the Saddle."

"That's above the Elcott property."

"Yes, that's right. I didn't see it for very long, the light. It was as if when he heard my team, he shielded the lantern. I looked again soon after that, but there was no more sign of him. Whether he went on or came down I don't know."

"It's not usual to see people on the fells at night?"

"Not one who hides his light." He shifted from one foot to the other. "I wouldn't want to make trouble for a neighbor."

"No, I understand that."

"All the same . . . it was like someone walking over my grave! I thought it was something you might want to hear."

"Yes, that's very helpful, Mr. Henderson. I appreciate your willingness to come forward."

"I don't make out why it should have bothered me. But it did."

"Can you guide me up there now, to see if there are any tracks?"

"I've already walked up. That's why I decided to come and speak to you. Mind, I wasn't able to go up until well into the afternoon. The sun had been at any footprints. All I could see was that someone had passed there before me."

"A man? Or a woman?"

He shook his head. "There was no way to tell. The sheep move about. The underlying rock encourages the snow to melt. Prints change shape. But someone had been there."

Henderson seemed to be uncomfortable with his decision to tell what he'd seen. After a moment, he nodded to Rutledge, clapped his hat back on his head, and was gone out the door.

As it closed after him, Hamish said, "Who moved about the fells at night?"

And Rutledge knew the name that Hamish was expecting.

But he didn't answer.

It was too late to go on to the farmhouse.

Either the revolver was still there — or it

had already been taken away.

Josh Robinson must have heard the story of his stepfather's uncle. But who had inherited the famous revolver? Had the boy looked for it when his mother was occupied with the twins, or his stepfather was out in the barn or up on the fell pastures? And had the timing of the killings been set when he found that revolver, for fear that his sister's prying or his mother's quick eye might prevent him from using it?

It was a chilling thought . . .

Hamish was saying, "You didna' fancy the valleys, coming back to them in the dark. What if the lad felt the same, away from all that was familiar in London? You're no' the only one who doesna' care to be shut in by the mountains."

What was there about this valley that had disturbed the boy? Even if he'd been unhappy at home, even if he'd had trouble making friends in a closed community he hadn't grown up in, even if he had wanted to go and live with his natural father, it didn't explain murder.

Was it Gerald's fault? What had he done to the boy? Punished him too harshly?

What might have turned the tide in a child's mind and made murder something he could contemplate?

Rutledge shook himself.

He couldn't put himself into Josh's shoes. Their experiences had been too different.

But thinking back to something the schoolmaster had said about Grace, that she refused to consider letting her son go to his father, he wondered just how long she herself would have been happy here. Had she seen her son's suffering and ignored it for fear it would feed her own?

Had the happy family façade been on the verge of collapse, and no one had realized it?

"There hasna' been another killing," Hamish was pointing out. "Nor is there likely to be. If it *was* the boy."

Then who had been walking across the heights late at night with a lantern?

Janet Ashton came in, intending to warm her hands at the banked fires in the stove. Startled to see Rutledge sitting there with the lamps unlit, she stopped and drew in her breath as if she would have avoided him if she had not come so far into the kitchen.

"I've walked until I'm cold to the bone. It didn't help," she said after a moment. "All I've done is make my ribs ache."

"If you'd like a cup of tea —"

"No. That is — thank you, but no." She went to the window and stood looking up at the fell, where the westering sun was painting faint colors across the snow. "I hate this place!" she said fiercely, almost to herself. "I hate what it did to my sister — and what it does to me."

"What did it do to your sister?"

"It was too hard a life for Grace. She was city bred, with shops and neighbors across the back fence. We'd always lived where there was some semblance of culture, some semblance of comfort. Here they heat the rooms they use, and the rest of the house is *cold!* And there were no servants to help her —"

"If you'd married Gerald, it would have been the same."

Caught off guard, she answered tartly, "If I'd married Gerald, he'd have stayed in the South!"

"He owns land here. He'd have wanted to come back and run his sheep; you couldn't have kept him away forever."

"But then I wasn't in love with him, was I?" she countered.

"I don't know."

She turned to stare at him, then took a deep breath. But whatever she was on the point of saying, she stopped herself.

"Why do you live in Carlisle, if you hate the North?" he went on.

"I told you. I was worried about Grace. I came up here to keep an eye on her. It's the only thing that could possibly have brought me here!"

"I expect," Rutledge said, "that if it came to a choice, the local people would prefer to see *you* charged with the murders of your sister and her family. You'd be taken away and hanged rather than Paul Elcott, and life could go on here as it had before. A very tidy ending."

"Is that why you haven't told Inspector Greeley whatever it is you suspect?"

"I don't know what I suspect," he told her honestly.

"That's probably true. You prefer to sit here in the comfort of this kitchen, with the soft, sweet voice of Elizabeth Fraser in your ear!"

Angry, he stood quickly and said, "You have no reason —"

"It's my sister who is dead. My niece and nephew as well. And what have you done since you came here? Nothing!" She was suddenly angry, too. "It wasn't poor Josh who killed them. You know that as well as I do! But you won't take the killer into custody. If you do, you'll have to leave Urskdale; your work will be done. And so — for now — Paul Elcott goes free. What are you afraid of? Your own judgment? What's wrong with you? The war? Were you wounded? Is that what makes you doubt yourself?"

When he didn't answer, she said, "My sister Grace was very much like Elizabeth Fraser. Don't you care about *her*? Or a little girl who had all her life ahead of her? Hazel was only *seven!*"

He had himself under control again. He said, "You're the only one with a revolver — so far. I can't prove that Josh Robinson had access to one. If he did, it makes a lie of your story that you came here in that storm to bring one to your sister. And the same is true of Paul Elcott. If he's the murderer, where's the weapon?"

"Somewhere out there in the snow. You'll never find it — he didn't expect you to find it. And if you wait for the weapon, you'll wait until spring. Summer." She shook her head. "Josh is dead. All of them are dead. I close my eyes at night and I hear them crying out to me. I want someone to pay for their pain and my grief. I want someone to remember that they were avenged."

"Justice isn't vengeance," Rutledge replied.

She looked him in the eye. "As far as I'm concerned, it's the same."

# Chapter Twenty-One

Miss Fraser sat at the table cradling her injured hand as she gave Mrs. Cummins instructions on preparing the meal. It would be a little late, she wryly told Rutledge as he brought in the last of the coal scuttles.

"No matter —"

Harry Cummins put his head in the kitchen doorway. "Mr. Rutledge. I'd like to speak to you."

Rutledge set the scuttle by the parlor hearth and turned to shut the door as Cummins stood by the cold hearth. The man was uneasy, his eyes moving around the room as if he'd never seen it before.

"I just heard you'd asked London for information about a list of people living in Urskdale . . ."

News passed quickly. Damn Ward!

"Yes, that's true." Rutledge dusted his hands and added, "It's not an unusual request. Routine, in fact. But the constable was out of line if he told you the names."

"But people may have secrets that aren't — in any way connected to murder."

"I have to be the judge of that," Rutledge replied.

"What do you do with the information collected for you? Do you make it common knowledge — do you, for instance, tell Inspector Greeley? Or anyone else?"

Rutledge's attention sharpened. "What's worrying you, Cummins?"

"I — I'm not worried. It isn't that. Curiosity . . . it's just curiosity."

Hamish said, "He wouldna' ask if it wasna' something that mattered."

"Well," Cummins went on, summoning a smile. "I daresay dinner will be a little late. I apologize."

"There's no need."

"I'm not much of a hand in the kitchen. It isn't something . . ." His voice trailed off. "I'll just see if there's anything I can do. Thank you for bringing in the coal — I'll see to it myself from now on."

And he was gone, leaving the parlor door wide. Currents of cold damp air made the flame in the lamp on the table flicker and dip.

Rutledge said aloud, to Hamish as well

as to the shadows, "I wonder how well he knew the Elcotts . . ."

The potatoes were not thoroughly cooked, and the meat was tough. But the people around the table said nothing about that as they ate their meal in silence. A gray-faced Hugh Robinson had been allowed to join them, and he kept his eyes on his plate as if ashamed of his earlier emotional outbreak.

It was Rutledge who turned to Elizabeth Fraser and cut the roast mutton for her and buttered her bread. She thanked him with her eyes but said nothing. Her bandaged hand was paining her — he could tell from the way she held it close to her body, cushioning it.

Mrs. Cummins was chattering about the food, begging everyone to let her know whether it was to their liking. Cummins toyed with his meal, and Hugh Robinson ate mechanically. Janet Ashton answered Mrs. Cummins at first and then fell silent. The ticking of the kitchen clock and the shifting of the coals in the stove filled the room, and the sound of the rising wind.

Hamish, stirred into life by the uncomfortable atmosphere, said, "It wouldna' be sae cheerful at a wake."

The wind was moaning around the eaves as they finished their flans. Mrs. Cummins began to clear away the dishes. Her husband rose to help her, his sudden cheerfulness forced and uncomfortable as he took them from her and stacked them by the sink. A fire had been lit in the small parlor, and he promised the tea tray there in a few minutes.

Janet Ashton was the first to leave the kitchen, and after a moment Rutledge followed her. As she went into the parlor, she said out of the blue, "When will we be allowed to bury our dead? It would be a kindness, if you'd tell Hugh."

"I'll speak to Inspector Greeley tonight," Rutledge replied. "There's no reason why you shouldn't make arrangements for a service."

Hugh Robinson was on her heels but appeared not to have heard the question. He sat in his chair like a lump, speaking only when spoken to.

Rutledge added, "You understand that you won't be allowed to leave. Even if the roads are passable."

"I didn't expect we could," Janet Ashton answered tartly.

Everyone had gone to bed and the house was quiet when Rutledge brought himself up out of deep sleep. He had learned that trick over the months and years in the trenches, where it was too dangerous to light a match to see the time. An internal clock worked nearly as well, allowing him to snatch sleep where he could and still wake up for a change in the watch or the next attack.

He got up, dressed, and then walked silently down the passage towards the kitchen. The fire had been banked, and the air was already chilly. He pulled on his boots, then buttoned his coat.

Letting himself out the kitchen door, he kept to the shadows as far as a small shed, and there leaned his back against the rough wall facing The Knob. He had borrowed field glasses from Elizabeth Fraser, glasses kept for summer guests, and he warmed them under his coat as he waited.

And for the next five hours he kept watch on the heights.

A little after four in the morning, he gave up. Hamish had been telling him for an hour that no one would walk this way, but he was reluctant to leave too soon.

By that time his feet were icy in his boots and his face where the scarf didn't cover it was stinging with the cold.

Why had someone been out there on the

heights last night and not tonight? A lost sheep — a shortcut home?

Then why had it disturbed a plain man like Henderson to see a shielded light just here?

"Because," Hamish said in the darkness, "it was too close to the Elcott farm."

Rutledge made his way back to the house and shook the snow off his boots before stepping inside.

Elizabeth Fraser was there in her chair, her hand raised in alarm as if expecting him to attack her.

Hamish had already hissed a warning, and Rutledge recovered first.

"What on earth are you doing here at this hour?" he demanded, taking off his hat so that she could see his face more clearly.

"Oh, my God, you frightened me!" she was saying, catching her breath on the words. "Where have you been? What's happened?"

"Nothing has happened. I — couldn't sleep —"

"No, that's not true," she challenged him, her voice still trembling. "There was someone out there —"

He wheeled to look over his shoulder, then turned back to her. "I didn't see anyone. I was walking back from the shed, passing the barn —"

She shook her head. "Not by the barn — it looked like a dog — and someone following it. Hunched over, staring at the ground."

"If that's true," he said, unable to keep doubt out of his voice, "you shouldn't have been here, you put yourself at risk. If someone had seen you —"

She heard his doubt. "I can't believe I dreamed it. It was *real!*"

"I don't understand how he could have slipped past me." But he wasn't sure that that was true. Standing there, cold and tired, his attention had wandered in the last half hour.

He looked back at the night, the silent fell rising above him, the looming shapes of outbuildings, the stark patterns of white snow and dark shadows.

A dozen men could be hidden there. . . .

And yet his sixth sense, which had made a difference between life and death for four years of war, told him there was no one in the yard.

When he turned again, she was looking up at him, her face a white oval in the pale light of the snow.

"It's happened again," she said in a whisper.

"Another murder?" he asked quickly.

"No." She spun her chair, maneuvering it around the table, where the light couldn't reach her. Out of the darkness she answered him. "I — see things sometimes."

"What are you telling me? Imagination? Dreams —"

"I don't know." He thought she was crying. "It's a curse. I can't be sure what it is. Sometimes my eyes play tricks. Or my brain. I don't know," she said again. "I wish I did. But it was so *real*. I couldn't move. I couldn't do anything but watch."

But Rutledge thought he understood. She had been walking in her sleep. It was, perhaps, what he had seen before, on his first night at the hotel. Her restless mind, driving her, sent her out of bed and on missions of its own, and this time, inadvertently, he had awakened her by coming in the door.

"I wouldn't worry about it, if I were you," he assured her. "You're safe now, and there was nothing out there but shadows moving with the clouds. Would you like a cup of tea? Something warm to send you back to sleep again?"

"You don't believe me," she said forlornly.

"My dear girl, I do believe you. I've

known men at the Front who saw whole armies coming towards them across No Man's Land. Straining their eyes to see how far away they were, and giving the alarm when there was nothing there. It's caused by anxiety when you know the enemy is forming up to attack, and the wait seems to tear at your nerve endings until you'd rather face it now than later."

"I have no enemy waiting to attack."

"We all do," Rutledge told her. "Sometimes it's just a fear of ourselves."

She was silent for a time. Then she said, "What is your enemy?"

He almost told her, there in the dark, where he couldn't see her face and she couldn't see his. But he was afraid to put his fears into words, and have to live with them tomorrow in the light of day.

"The war," he said finally. "And living when so many died."

"Yes. I understand that."

He could hear her turn her chair towards the passage door. "Will you latch the outer door for me, Mr. Rutledge?"

"Yes. Good night."

"Good night." Her voice came softly to him from the passage.

He stood there in the kitchen, feeling alone and terrifyingly empty.

★ ★ ★

The next morning, before anyone else had walked in the yard, Rutledge went out to look for prints. But the rain had begun at first light, and any that had been made in the dark were washed away. Even his own.

Necessity in the North was the main consideration in all matters.

And the rector who came every other Sunday to the little stone church to preach to the handful of villagers collected there in the cold sanctuary was called on to bury the dead while he was here. Mr. Slater was a middle-aged man who appeared to have a dour outlook on life, his eyes pouched and his eyebrows sprouting dark wiry hairs above the rims of his spectacles.

He went off to dine with Dr. Jarvis, and at two o'clock was prepared to conduct the funeral of the five victims of Urskdale's unknown killer.

There were a number of people present — not as many as Rutledge had anticipated, but Inspector Greeley, standing with him in the back of the unadorned plain stone nave, tried to explain. "Stock need tending to."

"But if the Elcott family was well liked,

I'd have expected half the village to be here. Stock or no stock."

The line of coffins before the altar was heartbreaking. The twins would be buried with their mother, who had died trying to protect them. Hazel had her own small casket, and someone had found a bouquet of white silk roses to place on the top. The empty space where her brother might have been seemed to stand out with a cold clarity, as if pointing out the failure of the men of Urskdale to find his body.

The rector spoke of Fate, and the need to be prepared to meet Death, since no one knew when and how it might reach out to pluck its next victim. Rutledge, listening, considered it a macabre funeral oration, raising the specter of a murderer roaming the dale in search of new prey. Even Inspector Greeley seemed to shiver at the images the thin voice carried to every cranny of the church.

And then, with surprising compassion, the rector addressed each of the family members in turn, painting a warm portrait of each of the five victims that may or may not have been true.

Rutledge, observing the mourners with a policeman's eye, read nothing in their features except sympathy as they sat patiently through the service. For the most part, they appeared to agree with Mr. Slater's words, and once or twice he saw women resorting to their handkerchiefs as the rector touched a chord of memory. Children, restless beside their elders, stared at the rafters and the single stained-glass window, and sometimes at the coffins. There were a number of boys close in age to Josh Robinson. Rutledge noted them, and saw nothing in their behavior to indicate they kept any secrets about their missing classmate. Mrs. Haldnes sat upright, as if in judgment, with her own sons around her. Mrs. Peterson had not come. The Hendersons were there, with a young child who fidgeted in pain. Henderson put his arm around the boy and drew him closer, as if afraid of losing him.

It was a somber party who gathered under dripping umbrellas in the churchyard. Beyond the yews, someone had scraped away the snow, and the sexton had managed to dig three graves in the soggy earth. With no flowers and the sun hidden behind heavy clouds, the rain an uncompromising drizzle now, and the rector reading the last words of hope and resurrection as if they were a curse, the depression of the mourners only deepened.

It was a bleak service, the wind howling around their shoulders, the ground gaping cold and hard. The rector was hoarse, his voice barely audible and half buried in his black muffler.

Paul Elcott stood as if alone, head bowed, face scourged with grief. Nothing in the slump of his shoulders and the tight grip of his hands on the bone handle of the umbrella indicated that he was comforted by the service.

Beside him was Hugh Robinson, face unreadable, his emotions locked too far away to be touched. His eyes weren't on the coffins but on the heights, as if saying good-bye to his son as well as his daughter.

Farther away, closer to the yews, Janet Ashton also stood alone, the veil borrowed from Mrs. Cummins shielding her. Rutledge couldn't read her thoughts behind the dark folds of silk, but her black-gloved hands held her body as if her ribs were aching and she felt the cold deeply.

Elizabeth Fraser was there, in her chair. She bit her lip once during the final words of interment, and ran a gloved finger over the raindrops that glistened on the black robe across her knees. Once she looked up and caught his eyes on her, and seemed disconcerted for a moment.

Harry Cummins had attended, but his wife hadn't come to the graveside, pleading dizziness. He frowned as he watched the coffins sink into the wet earth, and something made him glance towards Elizabeth Fraser as if he could sense what she was thinking.

Belfors, the ironmonger, was there with his wife. She was a fair woman with gray eyes, tall and slender and carrying her years well. They had brought Paul Elcott in their carriage. Friends and neighbors formed a ring around the raw earth, their faces a blend of sadness and uneasiness.

Hamish said, as the rain pattered down gently on Rutledge's umbrella, "It's no' verra comforting. I'd ha' had a piper for my funeral."

Rutledge winced, thinking that Hamish must be close enough to stand under the spread of black silk with him.

"No pipers here," he said under his breath. But the mountains ringing the valley and the wide expanse of black water in the lake would have echoed the chilling skirl and sent it back again a dozen times.

# Chapter Twenty-Two

The funeral's baked meats were sandwiches and cups of tea provided by Harry Cummins for those mourners who chose to accompany the survivors of Gerald Elcott's family to the hotel. Comforting words were quietly offered to Robinson, Miss Ashton, and Elcott, but no one mentioned the house at the farm, where bloodstains were still visible in spite of repeated scrubbings. And no one in Rutledge's hearing referred to the way five people had died.

But both would, as Hamish noted, be discussed in hushed voices on the way home.

Some had said their farewells at the church, unwilling to be caught on the road by December's early dusk. Jim and Mary Follet had come to the hotel, out of respect, but soon took their leave. Follet, shrugging into his coat in the front hall, commented to Rutledge that it was a sad day for Urskdale — and would be sadder still when everyone learned who was to blame. A few villagers lingered, most of them friends of Paul Elcott's, exchanging reminiscences with him. Mr. and Mrs. Belfors, who carried Elcott off with the last of the mourners, ignored Rutledge in their farewells.

Janet Ashton and Hugh Robinson sat together awkwardly talking for several minutes longer, and then Janet went to her room, saying she wouldn't be dining that night. Hugh soon followed. Since his attempt at suicide, he'd kept to himself.

Inspector Greeley saw them all off and then departed, with Dr. Jarvis following on his heels.

Harry Cummins excused himself and went to see to his wife. She had made a brief appearance in the dining room and then wandered away as if distracted by her thoughts.

Rutledge, standing by the dining room windows, wasn't aware that he was being watched. His eyes were on the dark line of Urskwater.

Finally Elizabeth Fraser's voice broke into the tangle of his thoughts. "You're tired. How do you expect to see clearly when you drive yourself like this?"

He turned, staring at her. "You know the right things to say, don't you?" he asked with surprise. Old Bowels, his superior in London, would have wasted no time in pointing out Rutledge's failure. Hamish knew his shortcomings. For years he'd grown used to judging himself harshly as well.

Elizabeth Fraser smiled faintly. "It's common sense, that's all. And to be truthful, because you're the stranger, you may well see us for what we are, no matter how hard we try to hide ourselves behind masks. That's what Inspector Greeley can't do, don't you see? He's lived here too long to step aside. You're to be his scapegoat, and after you've gone he'll blame you and Scotland Yard for any resentment."

It was an astute comment.

"I'm used to that," Rutledge answered, making an effort to smile.

And yet, as Hamish was reminding him, their murderer had to be one of a handful of possibilities. Josh Robinson. Janet Ashton. Paul Elcott. Even if the murder weapon never turned up, even if the motive for murder proved to be elusive, there would be something, somewhere, to point him towards the killer.

Was it because he'd saved Janet Ashton's life that he didn't want it to be her? What was it the Arabs of the desert believed? Save a person's life and that person was indebted forever. He belonged to his savior as surely as if he were enslaved. Not in the physical sense of enslaved, but in the emotional ties that lay between two people.

But he didn't want Janet Ashton to belong to him.

Perhaps, as Hamish was telling him, he just wanted to believe that her life had been worth saving. For better things than the hangman.

Restless, Rutledge retrieved his damp coat and hat and went to walk down the streets of Urskdale. The rain had stopped, but he tugged his coat collar up against the raw wind that continued to blow down from the fells, bringing the bite of snow with it.

The houses huddled along the road with a grim determination, the stone they were built of hardly distinguishable from the saddle looming behind them. Here and there a plum or apple tree grew in the gardens behind the homes, but for the most part no trees broke the stark line of the roofs. There was a bleak beauty here, but in winter, with snow piled high against stone walls and slate tiles, there weren't many people on the streets, and those who were out seemed to hurry, heads down, nodding briefly to others as they passed.

Many of the shops had been boarded up, closed while the storm raged and left as they were while the men were out searching the fells. It was, Rutledge found himself thinking, hard to keep shelves stocked when goods lorries and wagons couldn't get through. On the other hand, short of the drive to Keswick, these had little competition.

He couldn't help but remember what Janet Ashton had told him about her sister, that Grace had grown up in very different surroundings. How happy had she been here in Urskdale? Had the isolation and the loneliness made her regret her choice?

Hamish reminded him that she'd had the opportunity to leave when her first husband returned from the dead.

But she was pregnant again by that time. With twins . . .

Beyond the church, where the road curved to run along the top of the lake, he could see the bare earth where the bodies of the Elcotts had been buried.

You would think, Rutledge told himself,

that in such a tiny community, everyone would have known everyone else's business, and gossip might have pointed to some troublesome questions about the Elcott family — their enemies — their problems.

Hamish answered him. "There hasna' been time for gossip. No' wi' the storm and then the business of finding the laddie."

Which was true. But even when the gossip began, he would be the last to hear it.

Dr. Jarvis came out of a house door and seemed startled to find Rutledge in his path.

"Has there been news?" the doctor asked quickly. "Are you looking for me?"

"I wasn't," Rutledge answered pleasantly, "but I'd like to speak to you now that we've met."

"It's as cold as hell out here," Jarvis said, "but my surgery is just over there. I expect I've missed my tea, but I have some medicinal sherry that's warming."

He led Rutledge to a house that was larger than most, with a small surgery attached in what had once been the carriageway to the yard. Unlocking the door, he stepped inside and lit a lamp. Rutledge looked around with interest. A tiny waiting room and two doors on the inner wall, one to the examining room and the other to an office where comfort appeared to matter more than professional status. There were no windows, as the office abutted the house, but large paintings on the wall added brightness.

Catching Rutledge's eye on them, Jarvis said, "We had a local artist in my wife's father's day. More energetic than accurate, but they are appreciated by my patients."

The scenes were rustic renderings of the valley, views that added the garish colors of sunset or sunrise to a view from The Claws, with a walker poised on the ledge to look down at the lake. Another was of The Knob in a storm; a third showed a line of walkers traversing The Long Back. A smaller painting was of a deep and narrow defile where sheep were being herded by dusty men. The artist had caught the light and shadow to better effect than he had the sunset.

"What's this?" Rutledge gestured to the work as Jarvis handed him a sherry.

"One of the old drover roads out of the valley. Drift roads they're called. Closed by a rock slide two or three generations ago. I can tell you that's a fanciful view. Looks more like Cheddar Gorge than the reality. What did you wish to see me about? Not my paintings, I'll be bound!"

Rutledge said, taking the chair across the desk from him, "You delivered Mrs. Elcott's twins."

"Yes, that's true —"

"What was her mood through the pregnancy? Was she happy, looking forward to a larger family? And the children, Josh and his sister, how did they see this change in their lives?"

Jarvis thought for a moment. "Grace was happy enough, looking forward to giving her husband children of his own. Hazel was excited to have a sister. She was a sweet child, very motherly, helping prepare the cribs after we discovered Grace was carrying twins. Gerald was solicitous, worried about his wife, fussing over her."

"And Josh?"

"Josh was older — uncertain, I think, whether he would lose his mother's attention. She'd leaned on him, until Gerald came along. The boy was only just learning to share her. Now there were to be other children. I think it worried him. He asked me every time I came out to the farm if his mother was going to be all right."

"Jealous, was he?"

Jarvis stared at him. "Just where are you going with such questions?"

340

"The schoolmaster, Blackwell, believed Josh was unhappy and would gladly have gone to London to live with his natural father. But his mother wasn't willing to let him go, young as he was."

Reluctantly Jarvis replied, "I can't answer that directly. I can tell you two things. It was difficult for Josh, when his father returned out of the blue. He scarcely knew this stranger who'd been dropped back into his life. It was confusing for him emotionally. Hazel of course had only the faintest memories of Robinson, and seemed most comfortable with him. But Grace herself was troubled by her dilemma, which must have baffled her son. It's possible he didn't understand why, with his father home again, they shouldn't be a family now. I don't know. I'm speculating. I will tell you this. It was Gerald who was the rock from the beginning. Willing to let her choose."

"And the second thing?"

"Young Josh ran away from home the week before his mother delivered. I'd been summoned because she was experiencing false labor. With twins, it was important that I should be there. After I'd finished my examination, Hazel told me that Josh was missing, had been for more than a day.

Gerald had gone searching for him, but I was the one who found him. The same place, in fact, that Paul used to hide when he was a boy. It was a ruined sheep pen up by Fox Scar and the rocks had tumbled in such a way as to form a shallow cave. Josh was there sulking."

So the boy knew enough about his surroundings to hide from his stepfather. "Did he explain himself to you?"

"I didn't give him a chance. He was cold and miserable when I found him. I sat on the stone wall and told him that he'd worried his poor mother sick and she mustn't be upset like that, so close to her time, that it was dangerous. I told him I wanted to hear no more of such nonsense or I'd write to his father in London and tell him how unhelpful Josh was being. The boy promised to behave himself, and I took him down to his mother."

"And that was the end of it?"

Jarvis sighed. "The night Grace delivered, I came to the farm just after dinner to attend her. Josh was ill; he'd eaten something that disagreed with him. Retching and vomiting outside like a sick dog. He asked me something as I gave him medication for it. He said, 'Will I die?' and I told him roundly he would not."

"Was he relieved?" Rutledge asked. "To hear that he would survive?"

"I didn't have time to waste on Josh. The twins were large and I feared a breech birth. I was busy trying to save them."

Hamish said, "The boy was crying for help —"

"So he resented the arrival of the twins, you think?"

"Resented? I would've said he feared them, if that didn't seem so far-fetched. And yet after they were born, he was fiercely protective of them. As if to make up for any earlier hostility."

"How did Gerald Elcott treat Josh after the twins were born? Was the boy made to feel a part of this new family?"

"I never saw any difference in their relationship. Gerald told me once that he'd liked the boy from the start and was willing to be patient. It might have worked out quite well. But then the natural father turned up, after everyone had thought him dead. It must have been impossible for young Josh to decide exactly where his allegiance lay." Jarvis finished his sherry and offered Rutledge a second, but Rutledge shook his head.

"In my experience," the doctor said, "boys that age are nearly inarticulate. They can hurt inside and hide it very well. Even if they want to confide in someone, they often don't know where to find the words."

He took Rutledge's empty glass and set it on the tray by the bookcase. "I don't know what's behind these questions. They've disturbed me. I shan't rest until we get to the bottom of this wretched business!"

Janet Ashton was at the kitchen table, staring moodily out the window at the snow gleaming in the last of the light. Rutledge walked into the room before he saw her there, for the lamps hadn't been lit.

There was no unobtrusive way to back out. And so he came in and sat across from her. After a moment he asked if she were feeling better, and she nodded absently, as if her injuries weren't important compared to whatever was on her mind.

"Tell me about Josh," he said, then.

She turned to look at him, scorn in her face.

"No, don't tell me about Paul Elcott. And I asked you to tell me about the child — not defend him," Rutledge said equably.

She flushed. "So you did. An ordinary boy. Troublesome at times, and wild at others."

"How did he get along with his step-father?"

"Well enough. Josh wasn't bred to sheep farming. It's cold and wet and dirty work. The lanolin in the sheep's wool irritated his hands. Made them blister and crack. But he understood that sheep put the food on his table, and he tried to do what he could to help his stepfather. They seemed to respect each other, after a fashion."

"And after the twins were born?"

"He wasn't excited about the twins, before they arrived. Grace wrote to say that he was restless and unhappy, and she put it down to the pregnancy. She'd had a difficult one this time — I expect that bothered the boy. She was very sick in the morning for five months, and then after that, her feet and hands were bloated. But the delivery went smoothly enough, and she recovered quickly, amazingly so. She would laugh and say, 'I was eating for three, Janet, it was horrid! I felt like a *house!*'"

"Tell me about Elcott. What did you know about him?"

She got up to stand at the window, her back to him. "Actually I introduced Gerald to Grace. I knew him before she did." The words were reluctant, as if the admission was painful.

"Where did you know him?"

"I lived just down the street from Grace, in Ellingham. Hampshire. I went to London — it was the first year of the war — for six months, trying to help my firm overcome the shortage of men. I was a typist, and I became a clerk and then actually drove the delivery lorry for a time. When Grace wrote that Hugh had been killed, I went back to Ellingham. It was Gerald who gave me a lift. He was on his way to see a friend in hospital there. I rather liked him, and he came to see me a number of times before he was sent back to the Front. It was chance that brought him together with Grace. After he was wounded, and had gone through surgery in London, they sent him to Ellingham, of all places, to convalesce. As it happened, I was too busy to go down to visit him. I was trying to earn a living for my sister and myself. When I did get there, all Gerald could talk about was Grace. I realized he'd fallen in love with her. I told him it wouldn't do, she was only recently widowed, six or seven months before. But he wasn't listening —"

She turned and smiled at Rutledge. "I'd fallen in love with Gerald, worst luck. And it wasn't me he loved. I was the wrong sister . . ."

When he said nothing, she added, "I had a reason to kill Grace, if you like. Jealousy. But I would never have harmed Gerald. He was no good to me dead!"

At ten o'clock that night Rutledge's motorcar returned from Keswick.

Constable Ward, getting down stiffly, said, "I've only half what you wanted. Sergeant Gibson will be sending on the rest in a day or two."

He held out a sealed envelope. Rutledge opened it as he walked back into the parlor. In the lamplight he read the contents, refolded the sheet of paper, and stood there deep in thought.

Constable Ward broke the silence. "If you don't need me —"

"Yes," Rutledge said, turning, "it's fine. Go home. I'll have a reply in the morning."

When the constable had gone, Rutledge read the sheet of paper again.

One paragraph stood out.

*I spoke with Gerald Elcott's commanding officer. He tells me Elcott was the chief witness against a private soldier who was found guilty of shooting and severely wounding his sergeant under cover of a German attack. Elcott's view was that the shooting was deliberate, because the sergeant had had words with Private Bertram Taylor some hours before over a woman. After sentencing, Private Taylor called Elcott a liar and threatened him. That was three years ago. A fortnight ago, Taylor was being transferred to hospital for what appeared to be a heart seizure. He managed to overpower his guard and escape. He hasn't been seen since. No one thought it necessary to warn Lieutenant Elcott . . .*

A brief description of the escaped prisoner followed.

"It may be," Hamish said in the back of Rutledge's mind, "that Inspector Greeley has finally got his stranger . . ."

# Chapter Twenty-Three

In the night Maggie heard the boy crying.

She got out of bed, her feet chilled by the cold floor, and walked quietly to the door of his room.

The crying stopped.

She walked on, got herself a glass of water, and let Sybil out into the dark yard. The dog growled deep in her throat. But it was a fox trotting by, his long brush visible in the moonlight. She could hear the sheep in the pen stirring, but they were more than a match for a fox. It was a wolf that worried Maggie, not four-legged but two. Hunting her lamb.

The ax stood by the door, ready to hand.

But Sybil came back soon after that, and Maggie closed and barred the door.

When she crawled back into her cold bed, she listened for a moment. The room next to hers was quiet. Either he'd cried himself to sleep or he had heard her stirring and buried his head in the bedclothes.

After about five minutes, she heard Sybil scratch lightly on the door of the boy's room. The door opened quietly, and she heard the click of Sybil's nails as she crossed the room, and then nothing as the dog jumped up on the bed that had been Maggie's father's.

Satisfied, she pulled her blankets higher and settled herself for sleep.

When Rutledge brought him London's information the following morning, Inspector Greeley ordered copies made of the description given of Private Taylor, and asked Sergeant Miller to make certain these were distributed to everyone in Urskdale.

"I'll see to it," he added, "that word also reaches the farms. But they were questioned about strangers earlier. None was reported. A needle in a haystack, finding any trace of Taylor. If he had any sense, he's made for the London stews where he can lose himself."

Rutledge recalled what Mrs. Peterson had said, at South Farm: *If he was bent on mischief, he wasn't likely to call attention to himself, was he?*

"It's an off chance," Rutledge agreed.

"Still, I like Taylor a damned sight better than the suspects we have in hand. It makes no sense to me that that child killed his family. It makes no sense that Paul should have done it. He's not a man with backbone, if you follow me. I don't know what to think about Miss Ashton; she's a dark horse. But it's hard to imagine a woman shooting children. What else did your sergeant come up with?"

"Janet Ashton gave up a very good position in the City to move to Carlisle. Her reason for leaving was her sister's ill health."

"I'd never heard that Grace Elcott was ill! Other than the pregnancy, that is. Go on."

"There's very little information about Hugh Robinson. He was a prisoner of war, came home to be treated for a stubborn infection in his back, and when he was dismissed, he took up his old position as a bookkeeper at a firm in Hampshire."

"That tallies." Greeley leaned back in his chair.

"Nothing on Paul Elcott."

"Not surprising. He's lived all his life here in Westmorland."

There was one other name on Rutledge's

list, but he said nothing about it to Greeley.

Word of Taylor had already preceded Rutledge to the hotel. When he arrived, Janet Ashton demanded to know if there was any truth in the story that they had found their murderer.

"Because I don't believe a word of it! Gerald never said anything to me about this man you're looking for. And Grace would have told me if he had said anything to her!"

"Apparently during the leave when you met him, Elcott was testifying in the court-martial. There was insufficient evidence for Taylor to hang, but he was convicted on lesser charges. The man was in prison," Rutledge told her. "And in spite of his threats, he was in no position to carry them out. I daresay it was an experience Elcott preferred not to talk about."

She shook her head. "You didn't know Gerald! He wasn't the sort to ignore danger!"

"The authorities didn't send word to him that Taylor had escaped. Elcott had no warning."

"So you're satisfied that the case is solved. We're free to go. And if the police

352

ever find this man Taylor, they'll charge him with my sister's murder, and you'll be in Derbyshire or wherever the Yard decides to send you next, and it won't *matter!* Another feather in your cap for closing the case —"

"You aren't free to go anywhere until I tell you that you can leave," Rutledge answered harshly, on the point of losing his temper. "As for Taylor, it's possible he's guilty. But until I'm satisfied on that score, this investigation is not closed!"

He turned on his heel and stalked down the passage to the kitchen.

Elizabeth Fraser was there, and she looked up at his angry face.

After a moment she said, "Is there anything I can do?"

"I'm going to be out for a time," he told her. "If anyone asks for me, I'll be back as soon as possible."

He was cranking the motorcar when Cummins came around the side of the house. As the motor caught and he was opening the driver's door, Cummins called, "Inspector? I need to speak with you —"

Rutledge shifted the motorcar into reverse. "If it can wait until I come back —"

"I don't know," Cummins said, flustered.

"I want to ask about the information you got from London."

"Then it can wait." He put the motorcar into gear and turned towards the road. The snow was melting enough now to splash as he drove through the ruts. And it took him no time at all to reach the farm of Maggie Ingerson. But the lane was still high with unplowed snow, and he swore as the wheels bit and slipped up the long incline to the yard.

She came out before he could stop the motor and get down to knock. She said nothing, waiting for him to speak to her.

"I need your help," he told her. "You told me the last time I came that you were one of the few people who could find the track that led over the fells to the coast road."

"I told you I could find it on a good day," she answered him warily.

"It may already be too late. But I want to see for myself if anyone has taken that track out of the valley."

"And how am I to do that? With this leg? I'd hardly make it to yon sheep pen, and I'd be exhausted and in pain. You'd be no better off than you are now, and I'd be worse."

"It's possible someone came into

Urskdale by that track —"

"It hasn't been used in years! How was he to know it was there, in the first place? And how did he manage to find it, in a storm like that one?"

Hamish said, "The woman is right. It isna' possible."

Rutledge answered him. "Anything is possible." But he wasn't aware until the words were out of his mouth that he'd spoken them aloud.

"You're no' thinking clearly —"

But Maggie had taken the comment in stride. "That's right. Men can fly now, can't they? But it's not likely I ever will. And it's not likely this late in the day that you'd manage to see any footprints even if you found the old drift road. The snow's melted all week. The rain took a good bit of it off the heights. It's a wild-goose chase."

"Is there anyone else who could take me where I want to go?"

"Gerald Elcott might have known where to look. Drew Taylor might —"

"Taylor?" Rutledge asked quickly. "Is that his last name?"

"That's right. You know him then?"

"He took me up the fell that rises behind the hotel. For a better look at Urskdale."

"You might ask him, then. But I'm no use to you. And my soup's on the boil and will be all over the floor if I don't go in and see to it." She turned and went back into her house, closing the door firmly behind her.

Rutledge swore.

"Taylor's no' uncommon a name."

It was true. He turned the motorcar gingerly, then paused to look at the prints of Wellingtons in the snow around the sheep pen beyond the shed.

Surely on virgin snow, tracks might still be visible —

He drove down the farm lane faster than was safe, in a hurry to get back to Urskdale.

Drew Taylor lived in one of the houses that straggled out of the village just beyond the church. It was stone, low to the ground, and seemed to belong to a generation long gone.

Rutledge had got Taylor's direction from Elizabeth Fraser, asking her if Taylor had had any sons in the war.

She shook her head. "He never married. He's not the sort — if you wanted the perfect lighthouse keeper, it would be Drew. He prefers his own company."

Knocking at the door now, Rutledge looked at the garden that lay to one side of the house. It was well kept, the autumn's debris cut and taken away, the roses set in the one sunny corner heavily mulched far up their stems. Behind the house he could see barns, sheds, and, higher up the long shoulder of the hill, grazing sheep.

After a time Drew came to the door, opening it to stare at Rutledge.

"I've come for information," the policeman said.

Taylor waited.

"I've just spoken with Maggie Ingerson. She tells me you might know how to find the old drift road that led over the mountains to the coast."

"It was closed by a rock fall in my father's father's time," he said.

"To sheep, perhaps. What about one man? Could he find the way in and make it over the slide?"

"What's this in aid of?"

"It's important to be certain no one came into — or went out of the valley — that way. Where no one could see him."

Drew grunted. "Late in the day to be looking for signs of that. Snow'd covered any prints long before we got up there to the rock fall. Just as it had the boy's. Besides, a stranger would have to know where the beginning or the end of the track was, wouldn't he? To find his way? He wouldn't be likely to stumble across the old road and just like that, know what it was or where it led. Not this time of year."

"But it could be done. If you were set on reaching the valley by the back door? And someone had told you how."

"It's possible," Drew grudgingly answered him, unwittingly using Maggie Ingerson's words. "But not likely."

"Then show me, if you will, what we're talking about."

The man shrugged. "Well, then. I'll just get my coat." He shut the door in Rutledge's face and was gone for some five minutes. When he came back, he was wearing heavier shoes, a scarf, and his thick coat.

Rutledge had expected to be directed back to Maggie Ingerson's farm, but Drew Taylor sent him instead to the Elcotts.

They arrived to find Paul Elcott's carriage there, but Drew told Rutledge to drive on for some two hundred yards beyond the house. A broad track led to a pen where the sheep were brought in for shearing, and stopped just beyond.

They got out there.

Drew led the way past the pen, and began his steady climb up a track that was apparently clear to him but invisible to Rutledge. Other boots had packed the snow to an icy crust, indicating that a party of searchers had started from here. But after an hour or more, Taylor struck out in a different direction.

At one point when they had stopped on the high shoulder, Rutledge asked, "Did you have relatives who served in the war?"

Drew Taylor looked at him. "I'm the last of my name here. Why?"

"Gerald Elcott knew a private soldier by the name of Taylor. They served together, for a time. Or so I've just been told."

"Gerald asked me the same question when he came back to the dale." He turned and began to climb again. "Common enough name."

In another hour they had reached the long ridge and made their way along it. Another rank of mountains, lower but just as rough, forked off to the south and east, towards the coast.

"On a clear day you can see the sea from here," Drew Taylor told Rutledge. "The drift road you want cuts in over there. See how the ridge dips and flattens? You can run sheep up and over it. And horsemen could follow, if they started up from the Ingerson farm and cut over. Still, that was chancey. Mostly it was the sheep, the cur-dogs, and drovers on foot."

"I have in mind a man, determined and alone."

"And I've told you before, it's hit or miss. In a storm and at night —" He shook his head. "I'd not attempt it, myself."

"They bring charabancs up to Wastwater, don't they? Filled with sightseers?"

"But that's an easier route. You'd never get one into Urskdale, save by way of Buttermere. And there's nothing at Urskdale to make it worthwhile."

"What's that hut there, the one where the roof has fallen in?"

"A shieling, a shepherd's hut. My father's father told me that William Wordsworth walked there once, and called it a tolerable view. But whether it's true or not, I can't say."

"And the rock fall?"

"We can reach it from here." He described the route to take.

Rutledge followed his pointing finger. Another hour or more, at the least. And more to the point, without landmarks, how would anyone find his way from there to one of the nearby farms? The Elcotts at High Fell . . . Apple Tree . . . South Farm. The Ingerson holding. By guess and by God, if at all.

He could feel the stiffness in his knees from the climb. In snow it would have been far more difficult, and the risk of getting lost would be high.

But what if the interloper had come during the daylight hours, and stopped at the hut where Wordsworth had admired the view? Got his bearings there and then waited for dark? Who was to see him but a passing raven? The storm, catching him up, would have persuaded him that he was safe from detection. And afterward, after the murders, he had only to wait on the other side of the rock fall until the worst of the snow had abated . . .

Hamish said, "A man would have to be intent on revenge, to attempt it."

The sun was moving faster than they were walking. But Rutledge told Taylor, "I want to see the fall. Did any of the search parties look on the far side of that?"

"To what end? It's not likely the lad could get across it!" He moved on, breaking through the crust of snow with the surefootedness of one of his sheep. After a time he pointed to where the ravens had been at the torn body of a seagull blown inland in one of the storms.

"The fate of the lad," Hamish said. "If he got this far . . ."

Trying to stave off discouragement, Rutledge kept on. Taylor seemed tireless, his legs moving with precision over the stones and folds and loose scree that Rutledge couldn't see.

After a time they came to the rock fall that had turned this road into a footnote in the history of Urskdale. As far as Rutledge could tell, the spread was a good fifty feet wide. Jagged edges protruded through the snow, and when he reached out to test their stability, Rutledge could feel the unsteadiness of the larger stones on top. Already many of them had tumbled down to form small hillocks and traps for the unwary foot.

With good light and steady nerves, it would be possible to clamber over the fall. Just.

And sheep were not stupid, as someone had pointed out to him earlier. No bellwether or dog would risk seeing the flock trapped here. And it would take blasting and long weeks of digging to make even a single track through the debris.

Rutledge looked at it, and then began to

fight his way up the shambles of rock and loose scree.

"Here — !" Drew Taylor began, and then fell silent.

Rutledge struggled upward, slipped and banged a knee, found his footing again, and moved on. He was young and agile. But the snow was heavy, making hand-holds hard to pick out. And then without warning, he began to fall as a single rock moved under his boot and dislodged its neighbors as well. With nothing but his fingers to break his descent, he bumped down the hidden obstacles and landed hard on his back.

For an instant he lay there, winded. Drew came hurrying across to him, but Rutledge waved him away. There was a scrape on his cheek, his shins had been bruised in five or six places, and an elbow ached. But nothing was broken, and gathering his feet under him again, he stood.

"That was foolish," his guide scolded him. "Break a leg, and who's to drag you out of here, with darkness coming on?"

Rutledge clapped his hands to dust the snow off his gloves and then brushed down his coat and his trousers. His hat had gone rolling, and he picked it up. The palm of his right hand was stinging and he took off his glove to look at it. There were bloody punctures in a half-moon crescent.

"What the hell — ?" he began, reaching for his handkerchief to wipe away the blood.

It was an odd wound for a rock to make. And it looked like nothing he could identify.

Turning back to where he had fallen, he considered the ascent he'd tried to make. By instinct, he'd taken the line of least resistance. Closest to the wall — and the lowest point. The most logical place.

After a moment he began to dig in the snow where he'd landed.

Drew squatted on his haunches to watch.

It took several minutes to find what his hand had come down on hard enough to break the skin in five places.

He held it up for Drew to see.

A heel from a boot. With the nails still embedded in the leather. He turned it over and matched it to the wounds on his palm.

"Someone has climbed over this slide. Or tried. The question is, when?"

"Last summer, I'd say. We had a number of Cambridge lads here. Not much money and not overmuch sense. We brought one of them down with a broken ankle. From

The Knob. In my book, he was lucky he didn't break his neck!"

By the time Rutledge had reached the hotel again, the moon had risen, casting a cold silver light over the fells, etching them against the sky. It was very late.

Every bone in his body ached. All he wanted was his bed, and a night's sleep. His hand stung where the nails had gone in, two of them deeper than the others, as his weight had come down there first. It had been difficult to crank the car when they reached the Elcott farm. But Drew Taylor had been eager for them to be on their way, as if he expected the ghosts of the dead to come out of the kitchen door in their bloody shrouds.

Paul Elcott's carriage was gone, and the house was dark. Moonlight touching the upper windows gave them an eerie brightness, almost as if someone had lit the lamps in the bedchambers.

Up on the fell, something was moving. A line of sheep slowly made their way to a place flat enough for them to settle for the night.

And then Drew Taylor said into the silent darkness, "He must have stood about here, where we are, that night. The killer.

365

He could have seen that the lamps were still lit in the kitchen, and known where to find the family. Or he might have waited in the barn until he could be sure they were all there. What went through his mind, do you think?"

It was an unexpected question from a man who ordinarily had little to say. And he waited, as if wanting an answer.

Rutledge looked at the yard, the shapes of the outbuildings, the peak of the house roof, the shadow of the fell behind.

"Anticipation. He couldn't know how it would turn out."

"No. I think it must have been hunger. A wanting so deep he could taste it."

And Drew Taylor climbed into the motor-car, without looking at Rutledge.

# Chapter Twenty-Four

Rutledge woke to Hamish's voice.

"The heel of a shoe isna' evidence of anything."

The voice seemed to be there with him in the room, and he kept his eyes tightly closed against it.

"It proves someone was there at the rock fall."

"Aye, I grant you that. But a heel canna tell you *when* it was lost. Or fra' whose shoe. Or if the wearer walked sae far out of curiosity or murderous intent. Yon rock fall is in plain view. It's the old drover's road that climbed to it and passed on beyond it that's been lost."

Rutledge had left the motorcar idling long enough to put a message under the knocker on Greeley's door last night, asking him to contact the police along the coast.

*Tell them to question hotels and shop-keepers about any holiday-maker who had shown an unusual interest in an old drift road coming down from Urskdale — or who was curious about other ways to reach the dale.*

"It's a wild-goose chase."

"It's a beginning," Rutledge retorted. "If we don't get to the bottom of this, a clever barrister for the defense will."

Hamish made no answer.

After a time Rutledge opened his eyes to an empty room.

It had slipped his mind that Harry Cummins was eager to speak to him. It was brought home again when Cummins waylaid him in the passage as Rutledge was on his way to the kitchen for tea and a late breakfast.

Cummins was pressing, and took him into the empty dining room where Rutledge could see that he'd been waiting for some time. A dish of half-smoked cigarettes sat by the one chair pulled out from the table.

Without preamble, the innkeeper said, "It's about the names of people to investigate that you sent to the Yard."

"Yes?" Rutledge answered warily, thinking of a name he had not given to Greeley or anyone else.

To his surprise Cummins asked directly, "Am I on that list?"

"Why should you be?" Rutledge countered.

"Because you've had your suspicions. I've read them in your face."

"Not all the answers have come back," Rutledge replied evenly. "Is there anything you want to tell me before they do?"

"I — I just need to know if my name is there! I haven't done anything — not to the Elcotts. But I'm used to — it's — something personal — I'd rather not have it talked about. Not here, where everyone knows one's business before the day is out."

"It might be best, then, to tell me what you're hiding."

"I'm not hiding — at least nothing to do with murder. It's a very private matter. You don't understand what it's like, sometimes. Surely you've done something you're not especially proud of!"

The expression on Rutledge's face tightened, and Harry stepped back, his hand on the chair behind him.

"I didn't mean — Look, forget I said

anything. It's just that everyone's nerves are on edge. You can feel it. Even Elizabeth isn't herself. She snapped at me this morning, and she's never done that. Never. If she can be unsettled by all this, it isn't — surprising — that others should be." He turned away, towards the window. "If only you could take into custody whoever it was killed the Elcotts! We could be at peace again."

"How long have you known Miss Fraser?" Rutledge asked.

He turned so quickly he nearly knocked over the chair. "Elizabeth? For about four years, at a guess. Why?"

"How did she come to Urskdale?"

"I — I offered her a position here. To be company for my wife while I was away fighting. Elizabeth had just recovered from her accident. She wanted to get away from pity; she wanted a quiet place where no one cared how or why she was bound to that chair." He gestured around him, as if the cold dining room was sanctuary. "It suited us both."

"Tell me about her accident."

"Truthfully? I don't know what happened. I was in Green Park in London early one morning, walking off too much whiskey the night before. And she was sitting there in her chair, crying. I went over to her and asked if there was anything I could do. She said, 'Talk to me until I've got myself together again.' And I did. Fifteen minutes later, she thanked me and there was an end to it."

"Go on."

"I met her on the street a day or so afterward, and she said, 'I remember how lonely the Urskdale mountains are, and how the afternoon light glints on the lake. I'm afraid I don't remember your name.' I took her to a shop for tea, and we talked for a bit. I think I told her how unhappy my wife was. It had been worrying me and there was nothing I could do. You can't very well tell the Army to go hang! I don't know if I suggested she come here to be with Vera, or she did. It didn't matter. I was grateful. A fortnight after that, I put her on the train and said good-bye. I sailed three days later. But she wrote to me while I was away. Vera couldn't. She'd begun drinking, you see. She was certain I'd be killed. So many were . . ."

"And you knew nothing about Elizabeth Fraser, before sending her north? That was damned trusting!"

"I was desperate. She seemed gentle and kind. My wife's family hadn't spoken to her since we were married. Vera needed *someone*. My God, what else was I to *do!*"

Greeley arrived as Rutledge was preparing to leave the hotel.

"What's this about the old drift road?"

"It's another way into the valley," Rutledge told him.

"Yes, but not a *likely* way."

"It wasn't likely that Josh Robinson survived. But you searched for him. I intend to be thorough in this matter as well."

"I'll send someone to inquire, although it's time wasted. Even the summer walkers don't venture that far. It's rough going in good weather, and the views are no better than others easier reached. Not when you've got Wastwater or Buttermere to choose from."

Rutledge reached into his pocket for the heel. "What do you make of this? I found it on the Urskdale side of the fall."

"Hardly evidence of murder. God knows how long it has been there."

"What do you know about Drew Taylor?"

"Drew? He's lived here all his life. His mother was eighty-seven when she died and was rumored to be something of a terror. Little wonder he never married! I doubt there's a woman in six counties Mrs. Taylor would have thought fit for her son. You aren't suspecting him next!"

"Curiosity. Elcott served with a man called Taylor. There was ill feeling between them. I wondered if there could be a connection."

"Elcott never had much to say about his war. And Taylor's got no family."

"Indeed." Rutledge got up to set his plate and cup on the sink. "I want to talk to Belfors again. Are you coming with me?"

Belfors was just opening his shop. He nodded to the two policemen, and led them inside. "I expect it isn't a new spade you're after," the ironmonger said.

"The revolver that Theo Elcott brought home from Africa —"

"He didn't bring it home. He died on the ship of a fever."

"Where is it now?"

"I don't know. Henry — Gerald's father — showed it me. He didn't tell me what he'd done with it."

"Was that the only time you'd seen it?"

Belfors's eyes flicked away, and he ran a cloth over the counter as if a speck of dust had caught his attention.

"I can't remember, to tell you the truth."

Rutledge nodded to Greeley. "I'll have this man taken into custody, if you please, Inspector."

"On what charge?" Greeley demanded, caught off guard.

"He's concealing evidence."

Rutledge turned on his heel and walked out the door.

Behind him he heard Belfors call, "Here — !"

But he kept going.

At the tiny police station, he went into Greeley's office without a word to Sergeant Miller, and shut the door behind him.

It wasn't long before he could hear Greeley coming through the outer door, Belfors loudly complaining of injustice and threatening to take up this vile behavior with Rutledge's superiors.

Sergeant Miller added his voice to the fray, demanding to know what Belfors had done.

Rutledge could hear him. "Surely he's not our murderer, sir? Mr. *Belfors?*"

Hamish scolded, "It wasna' necessary!"

Rutledge didn't answer him.

After a time Greeley opened the door to his office and said as he came in, "Are you satisfied? This is irregular behavior!"

"Irregular, perhaps, but I don't like being lied to. In half an hour, we'll see if Mr. Belfors has decided to cooperate."

In the event, Belfors was still seething when Rutledge went back to the single holding cell to speak with him.

"I'll have a word with the Chief Constable about this, see if I don't."

"When you're charged with being an accessory to murder, he may take a different view."

The words sobered him instantly. "I've killed no one!"

"Perhaps not. I'd prefer to let the courts decide." Rutledge started for the door.

Belfors said, "Look, you've got it *wrong!* I haven't seen that weapon in years. And I'm not about to cause trouble for other people on the basis of some boyhood *prank!*"

Rutledge paused at the door. "Mr. Belfors, I only wanted to know under what circumstances you'd last seen that revolver. If you feel your conscience won't let you answer my questions, I have no choice but to let a judge ask them."

"Damn you! Henry Elcott was my friend. His sons were my friends —"

"Curiosity killed the cat, Mr. Belfors.

You asked Henry Elcott to show you his brother's revolver. Did you stand there at the counter in your shop and hold it in your hands? Did you sight down the barrel and rest your finger on the trigger? It's what most men would do. Vicariously reliving someone else's exploit. No one else from Urskdale had killed a Boer. It was exciting. You could picture the man striding into Theo Elcott's railway station, to shoot him before he could use the telegraph to warn of the commando's whereabouts. Or perhaps he was plotting to take over the station and use it to ambush a train. It was a favorite Boer tactic, to disrupt British lines of communication. And Theo Elcott, who was train mad and not the sort to shoot anyone, had done what neither you nor Henry nor any other man from Urskdale had had the chance to do." He paused. "And that's why you knew the weapon when you saw it again."

Belfors stared at him.

*"Who was it?"*

"I tell you, I won't betray him —"

"Was it Josh Robinson who had brought that gun in to sell to you? Knowing you might like to have it, because you'd known Theo better than most?"

"It wasn't the boy!"

Rutledge remembered Belfors and his wife standing beside Paul Elcott as the bodies of his brother and his brother's children were lowered into the earth.

"It was Paul, wasn't it? He reminds you of Theo. Quiet, not the sort to dazzle the world as Gerald had done. You're fond of Paul. And you've kept an eye on him since his father, Henry, died."

Belfors stood there, saying nothing.

"You're a bastard, did you know that?" he finally snarled.

"It's not going to help either of us if I run out of patience, Mr. Belfors. I think it might be wise for you to tell me the rest of the story now."

Silence. At last Belfors answered grudgingly. "He was only fifteen. He knew I'd liked Theo. He brought me the revolver and told me his father wanted to sell it but not to a stranger. Did I want to buy it? I suppose he thought I'd believe him, but I went to Henry and asked if it was true, if they were selling the revolver. And Henry told me it wasn't true."

"Why did Paul want to sell the handgun?"

"He'd had an argument with his father. Paul was angry and hurt, and I expect he was selling the one thing of value his family had, in order to run away."

"Was the argument over who was to inherit the farm?"

"He never said. I don't know. Henry was furious about the weapon and took Paul out behind the barn. I felt responsible for getting the boy in trouble, and I kept the revolver for a time. But Paul didn't hold what had happened against me; he realized I'd have had to ask Henry before I bought the handgun. Gerald came in one day and asked for the box it was kept in. He had a proper message from Henry, and I gave Theo's revolver to him."

"And what was Paul's reaction to that?"

Reluctantly Belfors answered him. "He said — he said he would take it back one day, with everything else that was due him. It was no more than a boy's rash threat! Paul wasn't vengeful. And he was facing his father's death, sooner rather than later. A boy of fifteen isn't able to handle his emotions well. You can't take that as proof he shot his brother!"

But as Hamish was pointing out, it meant that Paul Elcott had known where to find a revolver. If he had wanted to use one.

Rutledge said, "I'll go and speak to Elcott — before I order you released."

And he left the fuming Belfors there in the cell.

Elcott was at the farmhouse. The kitchen was nearly clean, and a pail of fresh paint was being applied to the walls, a cheerful and sunny pale yellow. The table-cloth with the roses, the chintz covers to the chairs, the hangings at the window had been taken away. A bolt of fabric stood in a corner, a cream background with blue cornflowers in bunches scattered across the cloth.

He glanced up as Rutledge knocked and then entered the house.

Rutledge said, "It looks better."

"I can still smell the blood. I don't know if I can ever live here. There's a shed out back that I could turn into a reasonable place. I don't know." He stared at the walls as if he could see through them to the stains he'd been at such pains to hide.

"Who is looking after your brother's sheep?"

"I've been doing that. With help from neighbors. They've been kind. Most of the stock seem to have survived the storm. Thank God for small mercies." He set down his brush. "You didn't drive all the way out here to ask after the sheep."

"No. I've come to look for your uncle Theo's revolver."

A range of emotions swept across Elcott's face. "I was wondering how long it would be before someone remembered that."

"You should have told me from the start." Rutledge came into the room and set his coat and hat on the back of a chair. "If you had nothing to hide."

"I didn't think about it. Not at first. You don't. My God, what I saw in this room wiped everything else out of my head!"

"What became of it?"

"Theo's revolver? It went to Gerry. And Gerry was set on passing it on to his sons."

"There's only your word for that, of course. Where's the revolver now?"

"I would guess it was upstairs where Gerry kept it. I haven't looked. I feel — uncomfortable — going through his belongings. It's as if he's still here, watching me!"

"Then show me where it should be. I'll do the searching."

Paul Elcott washed his hands and dried them on a rag he used while painting. "Come with me."

Hamish commented, "He sounds like a man on his way to his hanging."

They went through the door to the kitchen passage and to the chilly main rooms of the house. Paul Elcott led the way up the stairs to the bedroom where his brother and his wife, Grace, had slept.

Rutledge made no comment as he watched Paul open a chest that stood against the far wall.

It was made of oak, carved and polished, and the feet that held it up from the floor were round knobs of the same wood. It held blankets, linens, and an assortment of bedclothes.

Elcott stood aside and let Rutledge lift them out and set them on the bed.

At the bottom of the chest was a rectangular box of dark wood, the initials *T.A.E.* burned into the lid and under them a relief of mountains, one of them long and flat on the top. Table Mountain in Cape Town.

Hamish warned, "It will be there. Cleaned and oiled. He's had time to see to it under cover of the painting."

Rutledge took the box out and passed it to Paul Elcott. When the lid was opened, Rutledge saw that the box was a small traveling desk. A square of wood was covered in green velvet held by strips of tooled leather, and one end could be raised on brass struts to form a gentle slope, making writing easier when sitting on the ground or in a chair.

Elcott pulled out a hidden knob and took out the board. Underneath was a tray for pens along one side and compartments for a square jar with a cork stopper for ink and for stamps along the other. The larger space in the center held stationery and envelopes. It was large enough and deep enough to conceal a revolver as well.

But there was no revolver inside.

Elcott slowly raised his eyes to Rutledge's face. "I swear — I never touched it!" he said in a strained voice.

"Then where is it now?"

"God knows — your guess is as good as mine. With children in the house, Gerry may have taken it out and hidden it in the barn or somewhere, thinking they wouldn't find it. He never told me — he wouldn't have. I — I was foolish once. I did something — *I don't know why it isn't here!*"

Motive. Opportunity. Means.

Paul Elcott could have taken the revolver at any time. While the twins were being christened. While his brother was out on the slopes with the sheep. While Grace was in the village doing her marketing. On Sunday morning when the family went to worship in the church . . .

Hamish was saying in the back of his mind, "Gerald Elcott couldna' reach it in time. If it was there."

But Josh Robinson might have known where it was. Children were often more aware of what was happening around them than adults recognized. Gerald might even have shown him the revolver, hoping to give his stepson a sense of pride in his new family. Little dreaming that one day the child would take it out and use it to murder his family.

"Are you going to take me into custody?" Paul Elcott demanded, his hands automatically shutting the little desk. "I didn't do it. *I swear before God!*"

There was a long moment of silence in the room. Elcott's face, locked in fear and uncertainty, waited. Then he bent to set the box again in the bottom of the chest, set the rest of the contents on top, and closed the lid.

Rutledge said, "I'm not taking you into custody now. There isn't enough evidence. Yet. But I warn you against leaving Urskdale."

Paul Elcott straightened up and said with desolation in his voice, "I don't have anywhere else to go."

# Chapter Twenty-Five

Rutledge gave Greeley the order to release Belfors and then went back to the hotel.

Where was the missing revolver? Had Elcott taken it? Had the boy? Was it lying somewhere in the snow even now? Or had Gerald hidden it so well that no one had found it yet?

"You canna' take Elcott into custody until you know," Hamish warned him.

There was no way of judging who had pulled the trigger . . .

He walked into the hotel kitchen, his face grim.

Elizabeth Fraser looked up from the potatoes she was peeling, and set the knife aside as she saw his expression.

"What's happened?"

"God knows — Nothing. As soon as I find one bit of evidence, it's ambiguous — I don't know how to weigh it. You shouldn't be doing that. Not with your hand!"

"Yours doesn't look much better," she told him, pointing to the holes in his palm. "How on earth did you hurt yourself?"

He looked down at his hand. "I — was clambering over rocks, and I must have cut it."

"You didn't do that sort of damage on a stone. Here, let me see."

"No, it's all right." He took off his coat. "Why did you come here for Harry Cummins? What's between the two of you?"

She laughed. "Nothing but gratitude. I needed sanctuary and his wife needed a — companion. We served each other's purposes. He loves her, you know. But she won't let him. She holds him at arm's length, and it drives him mad sometimes. He was fond of Grace. She was young and pretty and lively. What he had once loved in his wife. The contrast was painful. He longed for his wife to be herself again."

"Are you telling me Cummins fell in love with Grace Elcott?"

"Of course not. She was a reminder of what he'd lost. That's all. It was like holding up a mirror to the past. He said to me once that he had asked too much of his wife. And he bore the guilt for that. But he wanted more than anything for her to — come back, as it were."

"He told me that her family had turned away from her because she'd married him."

"Yes. One of the tragedies that have driven a wedge where there shouldn't be any."

"Why did they turn against her? What had he done?"

"I can't tell you — this is a personal secret. It has nothing to do with murder!"

"Then I'll go directly to Cummins."

"No — you mustn't! He isn't aware that I know. And he mustn't learn how I discovered the truth. It will hurt him." She made a deprecating gesture. "It was in a bout of drunken self-pity that Vera told me. She asked me afterward if she'd said anything out of line. 'Betrayed any family secrets,' was the way she put it. And of course I had to tell her she hadn't. It would have sent her directly to the bottle again if she'd realized —" She looked up at him, her eyes pleading. "I respect Harry. I respect how much he's suffered. *Don't ask him!*"

"Then you must tell me and let me decide for myself whether it's important information or not."

Her face judged him, and he could feel himself flush under her scrutiny. "I understand that we have five unsolved murders," she said quietly. "Six, for all we know! But it doesn't give you the right to hurt people. That makes you no better than the killer."

He found himself wanting to plead with her for understanding, as if her good opinion mattered to him. What was it about this woman, bound to a wheeled chair, that made a man feel the need to stand tall in her eyes?

Before he could say anything, she went on in the same quiet voice. "It wasn't what he'd done. It's what he was. They were furious with her for marrying a Jew. Even though he'd changed his name and didn't practice. No one else knows — except me."

"Edward the Eighth had a number of Jewish friends." But even as he said it, Rutledge knew that that had done little to change the stigma for ordinary people.

"They were rich. It — made a difference."

"And so the Cumminses moved here, where he could pass as a Gentile, and build a respectable life."

"Until the war, when no one had the money for holidays. Nor the spirit. The hotel — like Urskdale as a whole —

counted on walkers. When they didn't come, life was hard for everyone here."

"What brought you north?" he asked again. "If it wasn't Harry Cummins?"

"A broken heart," she answered. "But that's none of your business, Inspector."

Mrs. Cummins was sitting in the small parlor, forlornly leafing through an album of photographs. A fire was blazing on the hearth, and the room for once felt reasonably warm. She looked up as Rutledge came in. "I'm so sorry, I shouldn't be in here — this room is always reserved for our guests. But it's so much easier to heat than anywhere else."

"Why not enjoy it?" Rutledge asked. He sat down in the chair on the far side of the hearth from her. "You're our hostess." He paused and then said, "Have you always lived in Urskdale?"

Hamish broke in repressively, "It's no' right to take advantage of her!" But there were things Rutledge needed to know. And he could see that Vera Cummins was especially vulnerable just now. As if sitting in her own parlor had reminded her of what had been — or ought to be.

"Oh, no, I came from London. Kensington," she told him. "Do you know it?"

"Yes, indeed. Does your family still live there?"

A frown shadowed her face. "I don't know. They haven't told me. We aren't — close."

"Did Miss Fraser know them?"

"No, I asked her that when she first came here. But she didn't. Elizabeth's family lived in Chelsea. Near the hospital, in one of those lovely old houses. I should have liked to live there after we were married. But of course Harry wasn't — happy in London."

"And so you came here."

"Actually we went to Warwick first. But it didn't work out. We had no friends to speak of. It was very lonely." She smiled wryly. "I didn't know the meaning of that word lonely until we came here."

"Why?"

"We weren't born here. My grandfather was from Buttermere, but he's been dead for years. Oh, people were nice enough, but they kept us at arm's length. Harry needs people more than I do, and I could feel that weighing on him."

But he thought she, too, had missed being a part of what social life there was here. "Is any of his family still living?"

"Oh, no. That's why he — could do what

he did. Walk away, so to speak. There was no one to hurt. But it hurt him inside, I know it did. I thought perhaps he blamed me . . ."

He could see, watching her face, the toll life had taken on her. "Were you grateful for Miss Fraser's help while Harry was away in the war?"

"At first I was suspicious. I thought he'd sent her here to kill me."

"Kill you?" Rutledge asked in astonishment. "Why on earth —"

"Because she'd already killed someone. Didn't you know? I thought a policeman would."

"Elizabeth was quite frank about it, when she came," Mrs. Cummins went on. "She said it wasn't fair if I didn't know. She'd told Harry, too. Harry's always collected lost sheep. I saw him a time or two talking with Josh Robinson. For all I know, he thought I was one of his lost souls. No, that's not true, not at first. We loved each other very much." She raised a hand to her forehead as if to clear her mind. "I sometimes forget that."

"Did you mind that he was a Jew?" Rutledge asked gently.

"How did you know?" she asked in astonishment. "Is it so obvious?"

He smiled, while Hamish called him traitor to his promise. "I'm a policeman, after all."

"Yes, of course. But you seem too nice to be a policeman. Elizabeth tells me you're such a gentleman. She's quite fond of you."

"Harry —" he reminded her, embarrassed.

"No, I didn't care if he was a Hottentot! My father cared, though. He told me he would never speak to me again if I married beneath me — that's how he saw it! — and of course I didn't believe him." Tears came to her eyes. "I didn't even have a trousseau. I wasn't allowed to take anything from the house except the clothes I stood up in."

"That was cruel of him!"

"Was it? I've wondered if I was the one who was cruel — to disobey him."

Shifting the conversation, Rutledge asked, "Did you get along well with Miss Fraser, after she came here?"

"Everyone loves Elizabeth. I envy her that. Even Harry loves her, after a fashion." She sighed. "I think more than anything Egypt changed Harry. I think being so close to Palestine made him realize what he'd lost. He wrote long letters to me about how much he wanted to go to

Jerusalem. And I couldn't answer them. I was so terrified that Palestine would take him from me!"

She set the book aside and stood up. "I could fight another woman for him. But I couldn't fight his heritage. I kept hoping that that man Lawrence, the one in all the newspapers, would see to it that the Arabs got all of Palestine and the Jews were thrown out. It was the only way I'd ever win the battle for Harry's soul."

# Chapter Twenty-Six

Rutledge got to his feet as Mrs. Cummins walked from the room. He couldn't be sure how much of what she'd told him he could believe. Or whether years of drinking heavily had warped her memories.

Hamish said, "She's to be pitied."

"People who make great sacrifices for love often live to regret it." Rutledge was thinking of Jean, but it was Hamish who brought up the name of Fiona Mac-Donald.

"*She* didna' regret loving me."

Rutledge stared into the fire.

He was tired of the grief and pain of others. He hadn't healed sufficiently himself to take on more suffering.

"*How do I find this killer?*" he asked into the silence. "I can't seem to put a finger on the truth. I can't seem to sort out the people and see them clearly. I can't seem to find the thread that will lead me to the answer."

The Scot's voice seemed to fill the room. "First you must look at the key . . ."

When Maggie had latched the door on Rutledge, she stood for a moment, resting her leg, her back to the cold wooden panels.

"It's a bloody Picadilly Circus!" she said under her breath. Her eyes fell on the Wellingtons by the door. Then she looked up at the frightened boy waiting tensely across the room.

"Well, we're rid of him. But with so much coming and going, I'd recommend feeding the sheep after dark from now on. There's no use calling attention to ourselves, unless we need to."

Taking off her coat, she hung it from the hook beside her. Sinking into her chair with relief, she put her head back and considered the ceiling. "If I knew what it was you were afraid of, I'd do better by you."

But he said nothing.

She pointed to the table. "There's pen and paper there. I can go on talking to myself, if that's what pleases you. But my father, God rest him, always told me that facing the monsters under the bed gave you power over them."

He didn't seem to understand what she was saying. Heaving herself out of her chair, she crossed to the table, found a clean sheet in the assortment of papers she kept there. Taking up a pencil, she concentrated on drawing for several minutes.

The boy stole closer, for a better look, and she shifted in her chair so that he couldn't see what it was she was doing.

Then, satisfied, she leaned back, set the pencil down, and got to her feet.

"That's what terrified me at your age. Now I'm going to rest for a little. This leg aches like the very devil! There must be a change coming in the weather."

She walked to her room, closed the door, and sat down on the bed.

The boy crept to the table to see what she had drawn, and stood there fascinated.

A blackness against greater blackness, shaped like a hulking human figure, its broad shoulders crowding out everything else. It loomed above a child's narrow bed, menacing in the extreme. The image was crudely drawn, but the power of it was immense, the pencil strokes bold and vigorous, as if the memory was real and fresh.

Underneath, Maggie had scrawled *The Man of the Mountain*.

He had listened to Mr. Blackwell's classroom account of the man who had lived in one of the shielings on the mountains and crept down at night into the village, hungry for human flesh. It was an old Norse legend carried to England by early settlers in the region, and with the passage of time had come into local folklore as a threat for naughty children.

*"If you don't mind your mother, the Man of the Mountain will come for you. Wait and see . . ."*

*"If you're not back by dark . . ."*

*"If you fail to say your prayers . . ."*

Mr. Blackwell had called it superstitious nonsense, but there were those in the classroom who had surreptitiously crossed their fingers against invoking the Man. He had more reality than the Devil and was closer to home. The schoolmaster had also told his students that the Man owed much to *Beowulf*, but the boy hadn't recognized the name. Someone living in another valley, he thought.

To the boy, an outsider over whom the power of the legend held no sway, it was no more than a delicious tale meant to send a shiver down the spine.

He smiled a little as he looked at Maggie's work. And then, turning the sheet over, he studied the blank paper for a time.

Then he picked up the pencil and with shaking fingers made his own drawing before hiding it deep in the pile on the table.

After the boy had gone to bed, Maggie looked for and finally found the sheet. She was chilled to see a stark outline of a gallows, with a dangling, empty noose.

A swift foray into the kitchen was unsuccessful, but Rutledge found what he was looking for in the barn.

The cow, which the neighbor had been caring for while Harry Cummins was away, lifted her head from the manger where hay had been strewn for her, and stared at him with dark, soft eyes.

He spoke to her as he went out, and she went on placidly chewing.

Rutledge left the hotel to drive back to the Elcott farm. Paul's carriage was there, but he didn't go to the kitchen to find the man.

Instead, he got out of the motorcar and walked around to the front door.

Moving quietly, he went up the stairs to Josh Robinson's bedchamber. He went carefully through the boy's belongings again, frowning as he worked. Clothes, shoes, stockings, belts — a cricket bat and ball —

And then he remembered the set of broken cuff links. Taking them, he put everything else back where he'd found it.

Outside again, he climbed the slope behind the house. The going was still difficult, but he took his time and watched where he set his boots.

Far up on the shoulder, where the scree began, was the Elcott sheep pen.

A pregnant ewe had taken shelter there, scraping at the snow cover in search of grass. She sneezed as Rutledge came towards her, and then edged nervously away.

He kept walking, heading for the ruin of a hut higher up.

The roof had fallen in, snow had banked high against the walls, and there were heavy tracks all around the hut. It was here that Paul Elcott had once retreated. And here that Josh had retreated the day his mother had gone into false labor.

The search party had been thorough, poking their staffs into the drifts and trying to probe the narrow opening under a part of the collapsed roof that formed a tiny shelter. If there was anything to be found, they would have seen it. But even they, in the first aftermath of the storm, might have missed something that the rain and sun had brought to the surface like old bones.

Rutledge knelt and looked inside.

This was the likeliest place for a child to take shelter. Jarvis had been right. And although the search party hadn't found him here, small traces might have been buried deep in the snow, impossible to see in the light of a lamp or torch.

What he was about to do would be accepted as truth.

Reaching into his pocket, he took out one of the cuff links and dropped it into a crevice between stones in the corner nearest what had been the door.

Satisfied, he squatted there and looked at what he'd done. The cuff link was completely out of sight. He got to his feet and dusted off his gloves.

Paul Elcott had stepped out into the yard, shielding his eyes as he looked up the fell towards Rutledge.

Rutledge lifted a hand as if he'd just realized Elcott was there, and began to descend the slope, Hamish arguing with him every step of the way.

By the time he reached the yard, Elcott had closed the kitchen door and stored his painting gear in the barn. He stood there by his carriage as Rutledge slipped and skidded down the last hundred yards.

"What possessed you to go up there? It's been searched, that hut."

Rutledge, breathless, shook his head. "I'm sure it was. The report said nothing was found. But the snow has melted considerably. I was luckier. I came across these."

In the palm of his hand he held out a stub of candle and a burnt match.

"Someone was there. Either the night it happened, or afterward. I expect it was Josh. But it might have been the killer."

Elcott stared at the candle. "You can't be sure —"

"No. Of course I can't. I didn't have any tools with me. I'll come back tomorrow and look again."

"It doesn't make sense. I mean, if he was there — if he had a candle — why didn't he come out when the searchers were calling his name?"

"You may be right," Rutledge said, with reluctance. "But this candle hasn't been out in the weather long. Who else has been up there, if not the boy?"

"Gerry might have been —"

"I can't see Gerald taking a candle and hunkering down in the hut. But I'll come back tomorrow and take my time."

He cranked the motor and stepped into the driver's seat.

"Did you ever go up there as a child, and hide? Is it a likely place?"

"I — yes. I could see the yard, and come down when my father was in a better temper," he admitted reluctantly. "But I doubt Josh ever did that."

"I wouldn't say anything about this in Urskdale. Until I can be sure what the candle means."

"No. Of course not. I — I'll be working out here again tomorrow. You'll let me know —"

"Yes, I'll be sure to do that."

At the hotel, Rutledge found Mrs. Cummins in the kitchen boiling carrots for dinner.

He took out the candle stub and held it out.

"I found this above the Elcott farm — in a hut that's beyond the sheep pen. Does it look as if this candle is one that could be bought here in Urskdale?"

She studied it. "Harry has a box just like it that he bought in one of the shops. He keeps them in the barn. What's it doing up in a hut? That's an unlikely place to store candles!"

"I can't be sure what it means. I'm going back tomorrow to search again. There was no time to do more — I didn't have a spade or a torch with me."

Mrs. Cummins said, "You ought to ask Sergeant Miller to go with you. He's a good man with a spade. You should see the garden behind his house!"

"Thank you. I'll do that."

It was Janet Ashton who made a comment at the dinner table about the candle.

"I can't see that it's important. That candle you found. I mean, Josh had probably played up there a hundred times. He liked walking about on his own."

"I don't know that it matters," Rutledge agreed. "But I'll have a look tomorrow. I could have missed something today."

"It's silly," she said doubtfully. "But you know your own business best."

"What troubles me," Rutledge said, "is that the boy may be alive somewhere. I'm considering sending out search parties again. Who else could have been using a candle in that hut? What was he waiting for? Was he looking for you, Robinson? Or afraid to come to the authorities? And if it wasn't the boy, someone was waiting, possibly watching the farm. You can see the yard quite clearly from there. It's an ideal observation post."

"For what?" Harry Cummins asked.

"Opportunity," Rutledge answered him. "He might not have been certain whose farm he'd come across. Or how many people lived there. What the best time for attack might be. In short, reconnaissance."

"What you're telling us is that it was a cold-blooded attack. Well planned and scouted," Robinson retorted. "No one living in Urskdale would need to do that. Josh wouldn't have to conceal himself and spy. And I refuse to believe he acted with such chilling premeditation."

"That's why I'm going back. The candle and match prove nothing. But if the searchers missed this, what else did they overlook?"

Elizabeth Fraser said, "It's a frightful thought. That someone could sit and watch, like a monstrous animal in search of prey. But even animals have a reason for what they do. Why should someone stalk and kill the Elcotts?"

Mrs. Cummins said, "Oh, don't! I don't want to know! That someone could be out there right now, watching *us*."

"My dear, it's supposition. You needn't be afraid! Not with this many people about. You're safe!" Harry Cummins assured his wife, and then deliberately turned the subject. "And that reminds me, Mr. Rutledge, if you're intending to send your motorcar back to Keswick, I'd like to ride with the constable — we're in need of supplies."

There was an apple pudding for dessert. As he finished his, Rutledge said, "I'm sorry — I haven't had a chance to speak to Inspector Greeley. If you'll excuse me, I'll do that now and turn in early."

He rose from his seat at the table and went to his room to get his coat and hat.

Passing the dining room five minutes later, he could hear the discussion going on.

And Elizabeth Fraser was saying, "I really think it was unwise to tell us what he'd found. Or for us to speculate this way."

But Janet Ashton was furious. "I don't care how many candles he found, or where he might have found them. It's not proof that will stand up in a court of law, and for all we know it has nothing to do with our killer. It's a waste of time, and I for one think we ought to tell the Chief Constable as much. Inspector Rutledge saved my life, and I'm grateful. But I am tired of sitting here waiting for him to get to the bottom of this wretched business."

Hugh Robinson's deeper voice cut across something that Harry Cummins was about to say. "What if Josh came back, waiting for me? He might have taken shelter in that hut, thinking I'd be sent for and would come looking for him. It's possible, for God's sake! We're dealing with a ten-year-old!"

"Elizabeth is right," Cummins intervened. "It's not proper to be talking about this. My dear, shall I bring in the tea tray, or will you?"

Rutledge found Sergeant Miller at the police station, thumbing through a catalog of gardening supplies.

He looked up at Rutledge and said, "Something I can do for you, then, sir?"

"I need your help. Will you drive me now to the Elcott farm, and then bring the motorcar back here, and leave it in the yard of the hotel?"

Miller frowned. "I don't understand, sir. Take you out there and leave you? What's that in aid of?"

"Let's call it an experiment, shall we? As far as anyone knows, I'm at the hotel, asleep. And you'll say nothing to the contrary. Tomorrow morning, at first light, you can come and fetch me again."

"You think you're on to something, then?" Miller's face was alert, intrigued.

"Possibly. Yes. Will you do it?"

As if indulging a superior's whim, Miller answered, "I'll just get my coat, sir, and we'll be off."

When Miller had left him at the farm, Rutledge looked up at the still, silent house, and felt a chill.

He was not superstitious, and yet the horror of what had happened here had left its mark.

The odor of fresh paint met him as he let himself into the dark kitchen, and he flicked on the torch he was carrying to make his way across the floor.

Hamish had been arguing incessantly with him for hours, and Rutledge found himself on the brink of a headache.

He climbed the stairs up to the small room where Hazel Robinson had slept.

It looked out across the yard and up the fell. He walked to the window, pulled up the only chair in the room, and settled down to watch. As his eyes adjusted to the darkness, Rutledge began to pick out details. The path he'd taken earlier. The sheep pen. The hut. And looming over them was the fell, massive and dark and somehow sinister.

Around him the house creaked and

stirred in the cold night air. He could imagine people walking about downstairs, the way the floorboards groaned in the dark. Or someone on the roof above his head, moving stealthily.

War had inured him to the stirring of the dead. He sat there and waited.

The hours seemed to drag by. Watching the stars, he could see that time was passing. He had scanned them in the night at the Front, when all was quiet. The silence before an attack, when it wasn't safe to light a match for a last cigarette, and faceless men coughed or stamped their feet, their nerves taut as they pretended to sleep. The unrelieved tension had been telling.

Hamish was reminding him of the sniper who had crept forward, invisible, deadly, eyes sweeping the English lines for any indication of where a careless man might be standing, where the tension might drive a soldier to peer across No Man's Land and think anxiously about tomorrow.

"There will be no sniper here," Rutledge answered him aloud, startling himself as his voice filled the small room.

It was well after two when he thought he heard the trot of a horse coming down the lane.

His eyes told him nothing was there, that the night was still empty.

Hamish was intent behind him in the darkness; Rutledge could feel it. How many nights had they stood shoulder to shoulder in the trenches, patient, alert, and yet drowsing as only a soldier can . . .

Yes, it was a horse. He could see it now, moving up the lane, a stark outline against the whiteness of the snow. The figure on its back was an uneven bundle of dark clothing, head and shoulders hunched together against the cold.

Man or woman? There was no way of knowing.

He waited, and the horse slowed as it approached the house, reined in and guided to the shadows cast by the barn.

It stood there for a time, not moving except for the swish of its tail and the occasional nod of its head as it chewed at the bit.

There was no saddle.

Rutledge could see that now.

After a time the figure stirred and dismounted. Holding the reins, it stared up at the house, and Rutledge almost had the feeling that whoever it was could see him, back from the window though he was. He kept very still.

Finally, as if convinced there was no one about, the intruder began to climb the track that led up from the yard. Easily seen, silhouetted against the snow, even without the torch that was flicked on to guide feet through the ruts that Rutledge and Drew and the searchers had made, it was not difficult to follow.

In time it reached the sheep pen and then moved on to the hut.

Rutledge, with only Hamish for company, waited.

The light seemed to lose itself in the hut's thick walls. He could see that whoever had come in the night to search was being thorough.

And it was a long time before the figure turned and made its way down the long treacherous slope.

Rutledge had already slipped out of the house and was standing in the deep shadow cast by the shed where sheep were brought down to be bred or birthed.

He could hear the crunch of snow even before he saw the beam of the torch. Tired footsteps, making no effort to hide their approach, came nearer with every breath.

And then, as the torch's light grew brighter in the churned snow, Rutledge stepped out of the shadows. Dark and half seen against the house.

A cry of alarm was cut off as the intruder realized that a man, not a ghost, stood in its way.

Then it turned and tried to run back the way it had come.

Rutledge, faster, was at its heels, and as it missed its step on the stony track, he caught up to it and brought it down.

The bundled figure writhed in his grasp, crying out in pain.

"No — my *ribs* —"

He rolled off Janet Ashton and swore.

"What the hell are you doing out here at this hour of the night?"

She answered, "I could ask you the same thing! God, but you frightened me!"

She was shaking.

"Come on, up with you."

He gave her his hand and helped her to her feet.

"Back to the house," he ordered, "where I can light a lamp and see you."

But she pulled away from him in a fierce effort to free herself. "No! I won't go in there! You'll have to carry me, fighting all the way!" Her voice rose as she struggled.

"The barn, then," he said roughly, catching her arm and dragging her with him.

The barn was marginally warmer. With the stock taken away to be cared for elsewhere, there was none of the comforting security of animals in their stalls. He took her into the depths of the cavernous darkness and shone his torch into her face. Tears streaked her cheeks, but she stared defiantly back at him.

"What brought you here?" he asked.

"I was afraid whatever it was you thought you'd discovered here would distract you. Josh lived on this farm! He might have used a candle up there in the hut any time. You don't understand him, the way he worried about his mother, the way the twins changed his life. I can imagine him slipping out of bed and running away for an hour or two, to get his head together again. But that's no proof he's a murderer. I don't care what Hugh says, I knew Josh just as well — better, probably — and he isn't a *murderer!*"

"It was a foolish thing to do. To come here — alone — at night."

"Yes, but I found something up there — look!"

He expected her to show him the cuff link he'd concealed hours earlier.

But in the palm of her gloved hand was something entirely different.

He turned the torch to see it clearly.

It was the black button from a man's coat.

Hamish mocked, "She's as clever as you."

# *Chapter Twenty-Seven*

Janet Ashton closed her fingers over her find. "All you have to do is look for a coat with a missing button —"

"I don't believe you found it there!"

"Why not? Because you overlooked the button earlier? It's sheer folly for me to play that game. Oh, I know you think I was as likely to have killed them as Paul — or Josh. But you can't have three murderers in a family, can you? If you have to choose, who will it be — ?"

She broke off as the horse gently blew, as if it had picked up a scent it didn't like.

"Shhh —" Rutledge said, turning off his torch and stepping swiftly to the barn door.

There was someone above the shed, on the hill.

Rutledge slipped to the shed and laid his hand across the horse's nose, to keep it quiet, all the time talking to it in a low voice as he urged it out of sight.

Janet Ashton was beside him. "Who is it?" she demanded in a fierce whisper. He could feel her shaking as her hand came to rest on his arm. "I could have run into him!"

"Shhh —" he said again. "Here, hold on to the horse. Don't let him make a sound!"

And he was gone, out of the shed and into the starlit yard.

Above him he could see movement, but the line of sight here wasn't as good as it had been in the upper floor of the house.

But the figure didn't seem to be moving towards the hut. Instead he seemed to be looking at the house from the fell. Searching for a better angle.

What was it he wanted? A man, surely — not a boy.

Hamish said softly in his ear, "Taylor, the escaped prisoner . . ."

Was it? Rutledge waited, silently urging whoever was there to come down the hill and into his line of sight.

But he stayed high, watchful as an animal. His attention was focused on the house still, and Rutledge realized that he would be hard to see from Hazel Robinson's bedchamber. The line on which he seemed to be moving was bare rock, brought to the surface by the rain and the sun's warmth. A shadow on a shadow, he thought, like a fish in a pool.

And then, finally, he was coming down.

Rutledge ducked out of sight, and said to Janet Ashton, "Stay here with the horse. Whatever happens. If he's armed, he might fire at anything that moves."

"Don't leave me here," she begged. "I don't want him to find *me!*"

"He won't. You're safest here."

He was back at the shed door, listening.

The crunch of boots could be heard indistinctly. All at once, the sound stopped. And then turned away, moving fast.

Rutledge swore under his breath.

A good soldier could sense danger. Could sense the shift in the silence that told him someone else was there, concealed and menacing. Whatever alerted the man on the slope, he was taking no chances. By the time Rutledge started up the track, the man was lost in the darkness.

He could crouch down and stay unseen, like a rabbit outwaiting the fox. It would be impossible to spot him until one was nearly on top of him . . .

*Nevertheless,* Rutledge thought, *I've got to find him.*

But it was useless. After an hour of trying, Rutledge was forced to give up.

When he came back to the shed, he discovered that Janet Ashton was gone.

But who was the other shadow up there on the hill? Where had he been heading, the house or the hut, before something had alerted him to his own danger? What would he have done, left to his own devices?

It was just before dawn when the sound of the motorcar roused Rutledge from an uneasy sleep.

Sergeant Miller, square and sensible behind the wheel, said, "I hope it was worth missing sleep over, this wild scheme of yours."

"It was a quiet night," Rutledge answered him.

Miller grunted. "That's as may be, sir. You were lucky. Anything could have happened out here, and you had no way of summoning help."

When he got to the hotel, Rutledge stepped into the barn and looked at Harry Cummins's mare. She was standing in her stall, asleep.

When he touched her neck, he could tell

she'd been ridden, the sweat still stiff there in the hairs.

That explained how Janet Ashton had come to and returned from the farm — bareback, because with her sore ribs she couldn't have tossed a saddle over a mount's back.

Then how did the other night stalker get there? And what had brought him, if not the lure of the candle purportedly found in the hut?

When Rutledge came down to the kitchen for hot water to use to shave, Janet Ashton was sitting in the predawn darkness, holding a cup of tea.

"I suppose you intend to arrest me now. Returning to the scene of my crime."

"You could just as easily have run into the murderer as you did me. And he could well have circled back while I was out there on the fell."

She inadvertently shivered. "That never occurred to me, or I'd have stayed here. Are you going back today to look for tracks?"

"That won't do much good. The search party made it impossible to tell who was coming or going."

"And so now you can't decide whether

to take me into custody or trust your judgment that the other idiot out there in the night was the man you want."

"I'm prepared to arrest both you and Elcott and then let the courts make sense of it!"

She caught the edge in his voice. "You haven't thought, have you, that Paul and I might be in this together . . ."

He took the candle stub from his pocket. And the cuff link he had kept.

"The boy broke this, either by accident or in a fit of temper. Do you know who gave them to him?"

She didn't need to look at it. "Hugh gave them to Josh on his birthday. Grace let him keep them in his own room. It was a mistake, I can see that now."

"Why would he want to destroy them?"

"I expect he felt Hugh had deserted him. By not coming here and taking him back to London. Perhaps Hugh is right, Josh was unhappy and vengeful. But that doesn't make the child a killer."

Rutledge's loud knock at the door woke up Paul Elcott well before eight o'clock.

He came to the door of the licensed house with his hair tossled and his pajamas shoved into his trousers. Rutledge looked down. His feet were bare.

"What is it? What's wrong?"

"I want to have a look at your boots."

"*Boots?* Good God, man, are you mad? It's barely morning!"

"Nevertheless."

Elcott led the way up to his quarters and opened the door to the wardrobe. "There they are. The other pair is by the bed."

In the close quarters of the room, Rutledge could smell the gin. It permeated the bedclothes and Elcott himself.

He lifted each shoe and examined it.

Dry, clean except for paint smears on one pair, and not newly polished.

"Are these all that you have?"

"I'm not a rich man!" Elcott said defensively. "That's the lot."

"I'd like to look at the coat you were wearing at the funeral."

"Search the wardrobe and be damned!"

Rutledge found the dark cloth coat and ran his hands down the side where the buttons belonged.

One was missing.

How had the coat fit at the church? He tried to bring back the image of Elcott standing there beside Belfors and his wife. Could the button have been missing then? In the rain, streaking coats and hats with long dark shafts of wet, such things would have been difficult to note.

But he made no issue of it, putting the coat back where he'd found it.

"When did you start drinking?" he asked instead.

"If it's any of your business, it was after I had my dinner. Such as it was. I don't have the heart to cook these days. And precious little appetite after working in that cursed kitchen. I'd sell High Fell, if I thought my father wouldn't come back from his grave and devour me. Instead I'll have to learn to live there. Call it Dutch courage, the gin. It's left over from last summer's stock."

Rutledge stood in the middle of the room, noticing that it was warmer than usual. "Have you had your breakfast?"

Elcott swore. "I got up about six and made myself a cup of tea. There's no law against that, the last time I looked."

But a stove would dry boots very efficiently. Was that when Elcott had begun drinking, to cover his night's activities?

Elcott went on, "I thought you'd be at the farm, by this time, spade and torch in hand. Looking for whatever it is you expect to find there."

"How did you get on with Josh?"

"Well enough. I told you, I thought

Gerry was a fool to take on a ready-made family. And I didn't like the boy. But that's not to say I'd harm him."

"But the Robinson children were no threat to you, were they? They couldn't inherit from their stepfather."

"I asked Gerry about that. How things stood. I mean, it's one thing if the children are Elcotts by blood, quite another if they have no ties to the land or to Urskdale. He told me the farm wouldn't be left away from our line."

"Did you believe him?"

"There wasn't much choice, was there? But yes, I think he was telling the truth. He was bred to that land, more than I ever was. Josh was ten. He had no ties here, except his mother and sister. It might have been different if the boy was a babe in arms —"

He stopped, realizing what he'd all but said. "Have you finished what you came for, Inspector?"

"I'd like to see the kitchen, if you don't mind."

"I do mind, but that's beside the point. You know the way."

Rutledge examined the small kitchen. Any rags that might have been used to clean shoes would have gone into the fire.

Hamish was complaining, "For all your fine lies, you've got nowhere!"

There was a bit of mud under the table, where Elcott might have sat in the chair drawn up to it.

But there was no way of telling whether it had come from walking in from the stable or from climbing the fell.

Rutledge thanked Elcott and left.

His next call was on Hugh Robinson. The man was already dressed and having breakfast in the kitchen. Rutledge quietly went to his room and looked at his boots.

Nothing.

He went back to Robinson and said, "Did you go to the farm last night?"

"The farm? God, no. If I never see it again, it will be soon enough."

"I thought perhaps you might have wondered if your son was there, hiding. And went to look for him."

"I'll admit I thought about it —" He broke off as Elizabeth Fraser wheeled herself into the room.

"Harry isn't feeling well this morning. I knocked and he told me he thought he felt a migraine was coming on."

"You'll no' see his boots this morning!"

Her bandages had been changed and

were thinner. But she couldn't lift the heavy teapot, and Rutledge poured a cup for her. She thanked him.

Robinson went on, "I don't know whether to mourn my son — or hold on to a slim thread of hope. What do they do to children that age, if there's been murder done? I can't sleep for thinking about that. Surely they don't hang them — and prisons are no place for a boy. What do they *do*?"

Rutledge found himself thinking of the young man who had just been committed to an asylum. As an alternative, it offered little hope to a grieving father. Yet it had seemed to be a kinder choice to that man's parents. "It will be left to the judge to decide what's best," he answered, watching Elizabeth Fraser's face. "That's his duty. Mine is to sift out the truth from the evidence. Where is Miss Ashton?"

"Still asleep, I expect. I saw her as she let herself in after a long walk. She says she finds it hard to lie down with her ribs still aching. And she's grieving for her sister. I saw her in the churchyard when I was doing my marketing yesterday."

Mrs. Cummins opened the door and then stopped on the threshold as if uncertain of her welcome. She was more than a little tipsy, her eyes wide and not very focused, her hand trembling on the knob.

"I had the most awful dream last night," she said to the room at large. "I was here in the kitchen and something came in that door from the yard. I could see it, but I didn't know what it was. The room was dark, and I was so afraid. I — I could see blood everywhere. And I didn't want to *die*."

Her voice broke on the last word, and Elizabeth went swiftly to her, to comfort her.

"It was only a dream," she told the other woman gently. "There was no one here. No one had come to hurt you."

"Still — it was so *vivid* —"

Elizabeth took her trembling hands. "You don't have anything to fear, Vera. Inspector Rutledge is here — he'll protect us from any harm."

"But he wasn't here. I went to his room and he wasn't here! I wish I knew where Harry had put his revolver. I'd sleep with it under my pillow —"

Rutledge went back to the ruined hut as soon as he could. Climbing with Hamish's voice in his ears nearly masking the crunch of snow, he could feel the mantle of fatigue settling over him.

"You canna' hope to gain anything with such tricks! It was foolish."

"If I'd caught whoever walked here last night —"

"But you caught the lass instead. And ye believe her!"

"I don't believe her."

"Aye, but ye looked for a missing button on yon coat."

"Elcott has been out here painting day after day. She could have gone into The Ram's Head at any time and twisted one of the buttons off. He wore heavy sweaters painting, not his one good coat."

"Do you ken, you're always making excuses for the lass!"

"I'm not making excuses for anyone —"

"Aye, and ye've no' arrested anyone!"

They had reached the hut, and Rutledge dug deep between the stones where he had hidden the broken cuff link.

His fingers searched diligently, working at their task with care.

But where the cuff link had been hidden, there was nothing.

The question was, what had been done with it? And who had taken it?

Janet Ashton, Paul Elcott, or a player who was not even on the board yet?

Hamish said, considering the implications, "It wasna' taken to condemn the boy. And a stranger wouldna' ken where to look."

"It might well have been Hugh Robinson. He may be regretting his rash confession about his son and decided to conceal evidence. Sparing the boy's memory."

"It would be a kindness . . ."

Maggie had found it hard to wake the boy in the middle of the night, but she got him out of bed and into the Wellingtons as he grumbled, half asleep still.

"We must see to the sheep. And it's better, with people lurking about all the day long, to do that after dark. I told you."

But he held back.

"What's wrong? Are you afraid of the dark, then? There's nothing out there to hurt you. And Sybil will be with you. She's worth an army! Look at that tail wagging! Do you think she'd let you go into danger?"

The boy's hand went to the thick soft fur at the dog's throat, behind the collar. His fingers smoothed and kneaded the fur. And then he took the pail from Maggie and went out into the cold night.

Maggie stood outside the door to keep

watch. Half afraid he might run away if given the chance, half afraid something would pounce out of the darkness at him.

"Which is the most ridiculous thing —" she scolded herself.

But she couldn't bring herself to go inside until she saw him coming back, lugging the pail, with Sybil at his heels.

Once the dog stopped to sniff at a patch of snow, and the boy turned to it. With his back to her, Maggie couldn't tell whether he'd spoken to the dog or simply touched her head. She trotted along beside him then, seemingly undisturbed by the fact that he was mute.

Sybil's love was uncritical and unconditional.

Maggie sighed with relief when they were safely in the yard once more.

"What will Sybil do when he's gone?" she asked herself as she held the door wide. "And what will I do?" was the thought that followed on the heels of the first. She brushed it away, angry with herself.

The boy was going nowhere. She and her ax would see to that.

# Chapter Twenty-Eight

Greeley had sent a message to the hotel, enclosing a telegram for Rutledge.

"The baker's boy," the message read, "brought this with the morning post. And I've also had reports from the police along the coast. The latest known query about the old road to Urskdale was last summer."

"It closes the door on the man, Taylor," Hamish pointed out.

"Not necessarily," Rutledge answered as he opened the telegram. He stood stock-still, staring at the printed words.

CHIEF CONSTABLE UNHAPPY WITH PROGRESS. YOU ARE RELIEVED. MICKELSON WILL BE IN NORTH NEXT TRAIN.

It was signed "Bowles."

"Aye, and I'd warned you," Hamish told him bluntly.

Relieved . . .

It had never happened before, though Bowles had sometimes blustered and threatened as panic overcame reason. Mickelson was one of his cronies. What would the man do?

With Bowles breathing down his neck, Mickelson would wrap the inquiry up quickly, smoothly, ruffling as few feathers as possible in the course of his duty. Josh Robinson would be pronounced the killer. There would be a brief sensation in the press, and Bowles would make sad pronouncements on the state of young people since the war, so many men killed, women left to enforce standards . . .

It would read well, and there would be further comments at speaking engagements, pointing to the role of the Yard in bringing swift justice to those who broke the Sixth Commandment. One of Bowles's favorite texts.

Nothing would be said about breaking the Ninth Commandment, with regard to bearing false witness.

Elizabeth Fraser, who had handed him the message, asked softly, "It's bad news, isn't it? I'm so sorry. You'll be making an arrest, then."

He was still lost in thought, but he heard her last words.

"The Yard will, yes," he answered. Folding the telegram, he shoved it in his pocket, then said briskly, "I have work to do."

In his room, he sat down at the small writing table under the windows and began to make a list of what he knew — and what he didn't.

On balance, the facts were evenly spread out before him. The spur towards murder was weighted evenly under each name.

Janet Ashton: Jealousy. When her sister had refused to go back to her first husband and leave Gerald free to marry again, had the plot to kill been set in motion?

Paul Elcott: Greed. He'd had no problem with his brother's marriage to a widow with children of her own. But when the twins were conceived, there was the impediment to his inheritance of High Fell. When they were delivered safely and thrived, he must have been desperate, as The Ram's Head fell apart around him.

Josh Robinson: Revenge. The twins had tied his mother more closely to Gerald Elcott, and Josh had run away once, missed school often, and from what the schoolmaster had said, was unhappy in the North, with few friends to make life bearable. And when he'd been told he was too young to live with his father, had he decided that the only way to be free was to murder his family?

There was Bertram Taylor as well, who had carried a grudge against Gerald Elcott. And Hugh Robinson, who had been forced to give up his own family through no fault of his own. And even Harry Cummins, who had been attracted to Grace. But if that were true, why kill her? Or had her happiness embittered him, sending him there in the snow to wipe out a family he envied?

Hamish said, "Hav' ye no' thought of the wife? Jealous of the woman who had caught her own man's eye?"

Far-fetched though it might be, Rutledge added Vera Cummins to the list. For frail as she seemed, there was a tenacity and a force under her drunkenness. She loved Harry, doubted him, was troubled by him — and failed to live up to what he had wanted from her.

He looked in his papers for the reply received from Sergeant Gibson on his earlier query. An unexpected answer, but Vera Cummins had confirmed it.

Elizabeth Fraser had been tried and found not guilty of murder.

The charge was killing the man she was engaged to marry.

A bare-bones report from Sergeant Gibson, with none of the flesh that lent humanity to a case.

The victim, Ronald Herring, had been a conscientious objector. The K.C. had pointed out that perhaps Herring was a moral coward, and the accused had been ashamed of his convictions. When he refused to release her from her engagement, she had taken matters into her own hands. Or in Sergeant Gibson's words, "rid herself of a man who didn't have the backbone to step aside."

Tried and found not guilty . . .

But perhaps the jury had been sympathetic.

Conscientious objectors and cowards, even men who had suffered from shell shock, were despised by people who had watched sons and fathers and brothers mown down in France. Women had been particularly hard on those they felt were malingering. Many had handed out white feathers to any man not in uniform, and a special uniform had been designed for those given medical discharges, to protect them from harassment.

He had hoped that it wouldn't be necessary to ask for the details of the case. Elizabeth Fraser was bound to her chair. She couldn't possibly have reached the Elcott farm in the snow.

Yet he had seen her standing. And she herself had told him that the doctors had found no physical reason for her disability.

Mickelson would probe into the case. He had to forestall that.

Rutledge put aside his papers and went to the kitchen, hoping to find her alone. He could hear the voices of Cummins and Robinson from the small parlor, and walked quietly past.

Mrs. Cummins was in the kitchen, trying to find something in one of the drawers of the dresser. She looked up as Rutledge came into the room and said fretfully, "I can't seem to find my scissors — I was sure they were here just this morning!"

"Let me search in the drawer for them."

He went through the detritus of twenty years, a magpie's nest of things that had no other home. A broken spoon, stubs of pencils, a bit of torn lace, part of a steel hat pin, and lengths of colored thread. In the bottom, tangled in string, was a small pair of embroidery scissors.

She took them as if he'd handed her the

Grail, holding them to her breast.

He happened to look up at her face just then, and saw something in her eyes that chilled him. He nearly reached out to take the scissors back again.

It struck Rutledge that she had played a role for years. The drunken, needy wife, who clung to her husband and bound him to her with pity. Terrified he wouldn't come home to her, terrified he might have sent his mistress to live with her for the duration of the war, terrified that his sacrifice for her might have been greater than his love for her, Vera Cummins had become someone Harry couldn't leave because he believed he'd been responsible for who and what she had become.

The tyranny, Rutledge thought, of the weak.

She glanced away, as if fearful that she'd somehow betrayed herself.

"I don't know what we'd do here without you," she said bleakly. "You don't know how frightened I am sometimes. It's so lonely here, so much empty space beyond my windows . . ."

Her voice trailed off as she started for the door.

"Mrs. Cummins —"

"Yes, Inspector?" She was poised to hurry on.

"I'd like to speak to Miss Fraser, if you'd ask her to come to the kitchen."

She tensed. "Is there anything wrong? It was I who burned the toast again this morning —"

He smiled. "No. It's — my hand. I hurt it, and I'd like her opinion about seeing Dr. Jarvis. Unless you'd care to look at it?"

"Oh, no! I'll just call Elizabeth —"

She went hastily out of the room, and he crossed to stand by the window, trying to force his mind to blankness, to seal off what he was feeling and thinking.

By the time Elizabeth Fraser wheeled her chair into the room, he was in control of his emotions.

"Vera tells me your hand is hurting you —"

"That was only an excuse. I know it's cold in the dining room but we can be more private there. Would you mind?"

She searched his face. "What's wrong?"

"Will you come with me?"

Wheeling her chair towards the dining room door, she replied, "I think I know what it is you want to ask."

He held the door for her and watched her roll the chair to one side of the hearth.

"I told you once that it must be difficult to pry into the secrets of people you suspect. I told you too I thought it was rather horrid."

"Yes." It was all he could say.

"Tell me first why you think I could be capable of killing Gerald and his family."

"I don't suspect you —"

"You suspect all of us. I can see it in your eyes, watchful and giving away very little." She studied his face. "It troubles you, doesn't it, to hunt people down."

"I did enough of it in the war."

"All right. What do you want to know?"

"About your trial."

"I was acquitted. You can't try me twice for the same offense."

"I never suggested . . ."

"No."

"Look. The Yard is sending someone else to take over this inquiry. He won't be as — kind. I'd rather end the investigation before he arrives. I need to know why you were tried."

"Someone else? Was that the bad news —" After a moment she went on with such sadness in her face that he wanted to stop her and tell her he was wrong, he didn't need to know.

"Ronald was a man of the utmost integrity. I respected and admired him. We'd known each other for two years when he fi-

436

nally asked me to marry him. But then the war came along. And he refused to serve. He said that killing — for any reason — was wrong. That it was a last resort that governments chose to avoid working out a settlement in which they might lose something. It was horrible — the way he was treated. He got the white feather over and over again, until he was afraid to go out without a uniform on. But he stood by what he believed. And I honored him for that."

She took a shaky breath. "His parents supported his decision at first. But then something rather odd happened. Have you heard of the Angel of Mons?"

He stared at her. "Yes. Some of the men fighting in Mons in the first days of the war swore they'd seen an angel one night. They were being forced back. The angel seemed to cover their retreat. It meant different things to different men. Many of them refused to talk about it."

"Yes. Well. Ronald's brother died at Mons. And his parents turned against Ronald, then, telling him that God was surely on our side. That Ronald was going against the will of God. It was nonsense; they were grieving. I'm not sure they realized what their constant barrage of criticism did to him. He took it to heart, and I watched him suffer as he tried to come to terms with what they wanted. And then . . ."

She faltered, her voice refusing to go on.

Rutledge waited, his back to her, until she could speak again. Finally she said, "I stopped at his flat after a friend's birthday party. Sometime in the evening he'd turned the gas on and killed himself. I'd seen him at tea, and he'd tried to be cheerful for my sake. He hadn't expected me to be the one to find him, but I'd been given a book I thought he might enjoy. I'd hoped it would pick up his spirits, as it had mine."

Her voice changed. "I was so *angry* — angry with myself for not seeing his desperation, angry with his father for being so heartless and refusing to understand, angry at his mother for her stupid comparisons with his brother. All I could think of was protecting Ronald from this last indignity. 'A coward to the end,' his father would have said. 'Couldn't face the Hun, the way our Willie did. A disgrace to Willie's memory!' And so I took the blame."

"What do you mean?" He had turned from the window, a dark silhouette against the light. Her knuckles were white on the arms of the chair, her face drained of expression.

"I wrote a note. In it I said that I'd watched Ronald suffer the indignities of others, and I couldn't go on. And so I'd ended it for both of us. But I was afraid if we died together, it would appear to be a double suicide. I went out, shut the door, and let myself be struck by a lorry coming down the road."

"My God," he said quietly.

"Melodramatic, wasn't it? Foolishness in the extreme. But I couldn't think of anything but the fact that he was dead and I wanted to die too. Instead, I woke up in hospital with the police by my bed." She sighed. "My friends at the birthday party — it didn't occur to me that they might be asked — could prove that Ronald was alive earlier when they met me at the flat. The woman who owns the building had seen him on the stairs half an hour after I'd gone. He'd put the cat in the back garden. She swore she hadn't smelled gas then. But of course, she wasn't happy with a murder in her house. The suicide of a coward gave her some standing on the street. And so — his parents learned the truth after all. They were in the gallery at the trial. I could almost see them gloat. And I couldn't walk.

They felt God had punished me sufficiently, too."

"Did you kill him?" he asked her bluntly.

She lifted her face to look at the candlesticks about the hearth, ornate Victorian silver with twining ivy running up the shaft to form the cup for the candle. "I loved him so dearly. I could have done it, I think. But I didn't." She took a deep breath. "And when Harry asked me to come here, away from London and the gossip, where no one knew — I thought I could forget. But you don't, do you? The past stays with you, like a shadow."

"And Gerald?"

"Ah, yes, Gerald. He wasn't at all like Ronald, and yet if I watched, sometimes I'd catch a glimpse of Ronald in him. His fairness, the way he walked, that sparkle in his eyes when he was excited about something. I took such pleasure in that! Even, sometimes, Gerald's laughter would catch me unprepared. I would hear it in a shop, and turn quickly — Have you never lost someone, and then looked for them in other people?"

He'd lost Jean, even though he'd come back alive from France. She had been terrified of him, sitting irrational and suicidal in hospital. And he'd seen her only once afterward, in London just before her marriage to someone else. Had he looked for Jean in other women? Or found in other women the traits that he had missed in her? In Aurore — or Olivia Marlowe? Even Fiona . . .

"I don't know," he answered simply. "I expect I haven't loved as deeply as you did."

Elizabeth Fraser smiled, but it was more with sadness than humor. "I never want to love anyone again. It hurts too much. Am I free to go now?"

"Yes —"

But when the door closed behind her, Hamish said, "Did you believe her, then?"

Rutledge found he couldn't answer the voice in his head.

The screams brought Maggie up out of a deep sleep. For a moment she lay stock-still, disoriented and uncertain. Then she found her shawl and threw it around her shoulders, hurrying to her father's room without stopping to light the lamp.

He was sitting up in bed, on his knees, his eyes wide but unseeing.

She stood there for an instant, then awkwardly put her arm around the boy's heaving shoulders.

But her touch was shocking to him and

he whimpered as he curled himself into a ball in among the bedclothes, his screams rising in pitch as if afraid of what she would do to him. Yet she thought he didn't recognize her in the middle of whatever nightmare held him in its grip.

"Sybil!" she called to the dog, but it was already on the floor by the bed, hunched and whining.

She could hear words now, incoherent but terrified.

"What is it?" she asked him, her own voice shaking. *Tell me what's wrong!*

He lifted his face out of the coverlet and stared at her, and she thought this time he was wide awake, no longer in the throes of his dream.

"I killed them," he whispered. "I watched them die. There was so much noise. And then I ran. I didn't want to hang."

He pointed his finger as if he held a gun. "Bang! Bang-bang, bang! Bang! Bang —"

She had to reach out and shake him to stop the sound, recognizing it for hysteria.

Afterward he just sat there and cried.

Sybil jumped on the bed then and tried to comfort him.

Sitting at the kitchen table in the dark, staring at nothing, Maggie could feel the

442

cold settling in. The stove had been banked for the night, and she didn't have the energy to make herself a cup of tea.

"What am I going to do?" she asked the shadows. "Papa, what am I going to do?"

But her father was dead and buried on the hill.

After a while, when her feet felt half frozen and her head had begun to ache along with her leg, she heard a voice saying aloud, "Nothing has changed. I don't see that anything has changed."

She was startled to realize that it was her own voice.

Soon after that she got up and went to her bed. But it was hours before she finally fell asleep again.

The next morning he didn't seem to remember anything about his outburst in the night.

And when he was washing up the dishes, she surreptitiously took out the gallows drawing he'd made and burned it in the stove.

# Chapter Twenty-Nine

That night, Rutledge drove down the Urskdale road towards South Farm, where the Petersons lived. Leaving his motorcar on the road, he walked partway up the lane, and found a bare patch of rock where he could stand and watch the long outline of the ridge that rose to The Knob and then leveled off as it fell to The Long Back and dwindled towards the south. It was cold, wind whipping down the lake and scudding clouds sailing overhead, obscuring the stars.

From here he was invisible to anyone on high ground, and he could still reach the village faster in the motorcar than anyone on foot. The question was, would this be another nightwatch that failed to bring him any answers?

Turning to look across the mere, he could just see the ragged outline of the fells blotting out the sky. Somewhere in the distance to his right, the clank of a bell told him where sheep were on the move. He could hear his own breathing. And then a rock, dislodged by a careless hoof, rolled and bounced for what seemed to be twenty feet or so.

"If I cough," he thought, "it will be heard for miles . . ."

The feeling of claustrophobia settled around him again. Pinned where he was by the fells, isolated and lonely, he was one man in a wilderness of stone that seemed to press in on every side. He couldn't push it aside and escape, he couldn't choose his way out. Not without wings.

Shaking off his bleak mood, he pulled his collar up against the wind, and shivered in his heavy coat.

After a time, he had to stamp his feet to keep them warm, and the stars swung across the sky with silent precision that measured the minutes. He kept time by them instead of his watch as the hours crept by.

And then, faintly, across the Saddle, he could see the pinprick of light as a lantern bobbed slowly across the ground.

There was no way to intersect the path the walker had taken. But Rutledge was, this time, perfectly positioned to track the small glow as it moved.

For a long time it seemed to follow an erratic course, and with the map in his mind, Rutledge could tell when it veered off to stop at the sheep pens, the deeper crevices, and the old ruins.

Searching for what? A revolver? A child? Or perhaps some other bit of evidence that the police were not aware of?

But Rutledge wanted to find out.

Hamish, standing watch with him in his mind, kept up a running commentary, reminding him that time was short and that Mickelson could arrive the next morning, or in the afternoon. "Better to finish what needs to be done, before the wrong person is hanged."

"I'm doing my best —"

"You havena' used your eyes, they're too blinded by the woman."

"I tell you, there's no key!"

"Aye, but there is. Think, man, you're no' this puir a policeman!"

"All right, then. Tell me what I've missed!"

"Go back to the woman!"

"She's not a suspect. She was acquitted."

"Aye, and you're too blind to see what I'm saying —"

The disembodied lantern had come

some distance from town now. Rutledge swiftly retraced his own steps to the motorcar and cranked it. Getting in, he heard Hamish say, "The headlamps."

But Rutledge hadn't turned them on. Driving blind in the darkness, praying not to plow into a ewe on the roadside, he pushed his speed as much as he dared. For a moment Urskwater shimmered in a white sheet, before the moon raced under another bank of clouds. He could understand, he thought, why the Norse and the Danes had woven Nature into their stories, giving it a sinister life of its own. He'd been told on one of his visits to the region with his father about the Old Man who haunted the fells of Urskdale, and he wondered how many people like Mrs. Haldnes kept their shades lowered at night and never looked out. If Henderson hadn't been driving his son to the doctor's surgery —

The village loomed ahead, dark and quiet. Long before he reached the hotel, he stopped the motorcar and left it standing, striding quickly the rest of the way. Once he stumbled in a rut left by a cart, and cursed under his breath.

He made his way around to the back of the hotel, letting himself in the kitchen door, as he'd come out.

Elizabeth Fraser was there in the darkness.

"Dear God," he said, startled.

"I heard you go out," she said softly. "I thought you'd like something warm to drink when you came in."

"There's — business I must attend to first. But thank you."

He went past her chair into the passage. When he reached Hugh Robinson's room he stopped to listen to the low roll of snores inside. Opening the door silently, he looked into the room. Robinson was sleeping on his side, his face turned away towards the only window. But there was no mistaking him.

Rutledge went on to Janet Ashton's door. He couldn't hear anything beyond the panels and gently opened it half an inch. She lay with her face turned to a long streak of moonlight coming through the window. As he watched, the light faded and there was only the slim shape under the blanket and a pale oval framed in dark hair.

He shut the door again, and made his way silently out of the house to where he'd left the motorcar. He drove it into the hotel yard and left it there. Then he walked down through the town. There was a lamp lit in the doctor's surgery as a night-light, but the rest of the house was dark. Shops were shuttered, and the streets were empty. The ghostly shape of the church tower was lost against the bulk of the mountain behind it. Across Urskwater, a dog barked, and the sound traveled to him clearly. Another answered closer to the village.

He might have been the only man left alive in this alien world, he thought. But try as he would to walk softly, his boots crunched on the ridges of dirty snow and icy mud under his feet, and anyone lying awake could hear the sound of his footsteps echoing in the night. The last thing he wanted were lights coming on as curious heads lifted shades to see who was about.

The Ram's Head was dark, but he tried the door. Locked. In Urskdale, until the murders, almost no one locked his door. Either Paul Elcott was cautious, or he'd made certain no one would be able to find him gone, his bed empty.

Rutledge crossed the street to where a baker's shop offered some shelter against the wind. He pressed into the frame of the door, making himself all but invisible.

It was a long wait. From time to time the

creaking of the sign over The Ram's Head could be heard, and he thought, "Rusty and uncared for." It was in a way, a description of Paul Elcott's view of himself and life.

Stiff from the cold and from standing so still, he shifted his position finally and nearly betrayed himself when his heel struck the lower part of the door with a resounding *thud*.

A light came on in the floor above his head, shining out into the street. The window sash went up. A voice, angry and hard, called, "Who's there? What do you want?"

Rutledge stood stock-still. It was impossible for the man in the window to see him where he was. After a time he heard the voice saying to someone inside, "It's the blasted wind. Nothing more. I can hear it rattling the door."

The window shut with a bang, and the street was once more quiet.

A cat walked by, carrying a mouse in its mouth. The moonlight, fitful at best, played tricks with shadows, and Rutledge thought of the nights in the trenches when tired eyes could read movement in the wire when there was none.

Hamish said, "Whist!"

Rutledge listened. A crunch of steps. He thought it must be nearly five o'clock. Time enough for whoever had been out on the heights to reach Urskdale again — before an early rising farmer saw the silhouette of an intruder in his pasture or sheep run and came out with his shotgun.

The lonely figure walking down the street kept to the center, as if fearful of ambush. It moved wearily, as if burdened by its thoughts as well as lack of sleep.

Rutledge stood where he was, waiting.

The figure was perhaps five shops away, and still coming towards him.

Even though he knew for a certainty that he couldn't be seen, Rutledge kept his breathing light and shallow.

If it was Paul Elcott, he would soon turn towards The Ram's Head.

Two shops away now . . .

And then the unknown night walker was even with the licensed house that stood as a monument to Elcott's failure in life.

But to Rutledge's surprise, he didn't go in. He kept on walking.

After a time he was lost in the shadows of the churchyard yews. Rutledge could hear the church door open, the heavy wood dragging on its iron hinges.

*Who the hell* — Rutledge cut short the

451

thought and strained to listen.

"Ye'll lose him if you wait here!"

"I'll lose him if I walk to the church. I can't open the door without making noise."

"He may no' come back this way."

And after ten minutes, it appeared that Hamish was right.

Rutledge stepped out of the baker's shop doorway and, keeping to the shadows, moved on to the church. He walked softly, watching his way.

And still no one came out of the building.

When he reached the door, he hesitated, but this was a small church with only the one entrance. There was no other way in — or out.

For another ten minutes he waited on the church porch, and in the end did his best to open the door silently, only wide enough to allow him to pass through.

Inside he let his eyes adjust to the deeper gloom, for the stained glass window let in very little light.

No one stirred. He began to wonder if his hearing had betrayed him and the church was empty. Or had it been a trick all along, and the walker had only opened and closed that door before vanishing in the direction of Drew Taylor's house?

Taking out his torch, he swung it from side to side, slowly and quietly making his way down the aisle. He had to be certain.

It wasn't until he had reached the front of the church and the altar rail that he found his quarry.

Paul Elcott lay on the floor, where he had fallen asleep from sheer exhaustion as he prayed — or waited in vain for peace.

Rutledge took Elcott by the shoulder, and the man all but leaped to his feet, shocked and terrified, lashing out as if to drive away a ghost.

"It's Rutledge. Wake up. This place is cold as the tomb. Come back to The Ram's Head. I want to know what you were doing out there on the fell tonight."

"I swear, you nearly gave me an apoplexy!" He was still breathing hard. "Good God." And then, "What the bloody *hell* are you doing here at this hour!"

"I might ask the same of you."

"I must have fallen asleep. I didn't hear you come in. I didn't think anyone would be in the church — where were you hiding? And why are you spying on me!"

"Hardly spying. I saw you come back into the village. Where have you been?"

"Out, walking." He retrieved his shuttered lantern and fumbled to light it. Shadows raced around the stone walls as his hands shook.

"Beyond South Farm. Hardly an evening's constitutional!" Rutledge switched on his torch.

"If you must know, I've been looking for the boy. If he's dead, there's no one to speak up and tell what happened that night at the farm. He's my salvation, that boy. Whether I like him or not, whether he killed them or not, my life's in his hands." He set the lantern on the seat of a chair and looked up at the altar. "I can't sleep. I work all day, and then I walk at night. It's taking its toll. I began hallucinating tonight. I could see the boy, but I couldn't tell where he was. I went stumbling after him, and then I realized it wasn't a child after all, only a ewe." He faced Rutledge again. "If I can find out what happened at the farm, I could sleep again. Instead, I shut my eyes and see them lying there. I didn't even realize the boy wasn't among them. It was so — grisly. I'd never seen anything like it."

There was a ring of truth in his voice, but Rutledge wasn't convinced.

Elcott must have read his reaction on his

face. "I don't understand why you won't take Janet into custody. Is it because she's a woman, pretty and persuasive? Or do you know something I don't? Why have I been left to my own devices to defend myself? No one cares what becomes of me! Except perhaps the Belforses." A note of self-pity had crawled into his voice. "There's no money for a fine barrister from London or even Preston. I'll hang, if you put these murders off on me."

"And you claim you've been out looking for the boy?"

"Yes. Hell, you just missed me the other night. I'd heard from Robinson that you'd found some candles or something up in the old ruin. I went to see if there was anything else. I know this land better than you. If he'd been living rough, I thought I could find out where it is he's hiding. Track him. I told myself he'd come to me. Out of desperation if nothing else. His father hadn't searched for him, after all. I thought he might be glad of me."

"You think Robinson could have found him, if he'd gone to the farm, called his name — made some effort to lure him out?"

"Who could say what a terrified child might do? And it's hard to blame Robinson for not trying overmuch. He's afraid he'd only be delivering his son to the police and the hangman. Better for him to be dead, quickly, painlessly, of exposure. You can tell it's eating the man alive, this waiting for answers!"

"You might just as easily have put paid to the boy yourself, if you'd come across him."

"I tell you, he's my salvation! Why in hell would I want to kill him!" He stirred uneasily. "All right, you've found out it was me walking about in the night. God knows how. But you did. Now go home to bed and leave me alone. If you can't take me into custody, then have the decency to leave me alone!"

As Rutledge walked back to the hotel, Hamish said, "He makes his case verra well."

"If he's not guilty, then he has. If he is guilty, then he's built himself a very fine defense. Tomorrow morning — this morning — I'll have Greeley take him into custody."

"Because ye're satisfied?"

"No. Because among other things, I want an excuse to search his rooms."

Elizabeth Fraser had gone to her room when Rutledge returned to the hotel. But there was a warm bottle for his bed ready on the table.

As he closed his door, he realized how tired he was. He took off his coat and hat and set them in the armoire. For the last time?

Twenty-four hours, he told himself. It was not long enough to finish what had to be done.

As he fell into a deep sleep, Rutledge heard Hamish's voice.

*You havena' found the key!*

It seemed to echo around the room.

Greeley was thunderstruck. "You can't believe Paul Elcott killed his brother! I know you've considered him from the start, on the spiteful word of Miss Ashton, but I never dreamt it would come to this!"

"No? Then perhaps you've got a better solution to these murders?"

"Miss Ashton. I've never been completely satisfied why she was on the road to Urskdale in such a storm. For my money, she was on her way *back* to Carlisle when you found her in a ditch! But you refuse to consider that."

"I haven't refused. I've slowly come to the conclusion that she's been lying from the start." For according to the farmer Jim

Follet, Janet Ashton had been crying inconsolably even before she'd been told that her sister was dead. But had she reached the Elcott house? If she hadn't, what was it that frightened her away? Aloud he said only, "But we can't prove that at the moment."

"Speaking of proof, where's Theo's revolver? If that's what Paul was supposed to have used."

"Truthfully? I don't know. Out in the snow somewhere. Flung there by the killer or dropped there by the child. Or still hidden in the barn to keep it out of the hands of an inquisitive boy. Elcott may well have taken it off to war with him, for all we know."

"Well, then, you have precious little reason to take Paul Elcott into custody." Greeley got up from his desk and began to pace the small office, studying the thin, tired face of the man seated in his extra chair. "I tell you, I don't understand you. It's all very well to come here from London and give assistance. I grant you, I needed your help to see beyond this crime. But to judge a man on so little evidence — it smacks of desperation! Is there something you've been keeping from me?"

"Just do as I ask, if you will."

Greeley's mouth tightened. "Then you're grasping at straws."

"It's true. But if I don't have better answers for you in twenty-four hours, you have my permission to release Elcott."

And with that Greeley had to be satisfied.

News swept through Urskdale with the speed of wildfire. Belfors was one of the first to storm into the police station and engage in a shouting match with Greeley.

Janet Ashton, on the other hand, was irritatingly quiet when Rutledge told her the news. He had expected her to be smug.

"I'm glad it's over with," was all she said. "Grace and the children can rest in peace."

"And Gerald?"

"Gerald." She said the name with sadness. "I did love him, you know. I never understood why he couldn't have loved me as well. It broke my heart. And I was very foolish to think I could change his mind."

He said, "It could be that you were too strong for him. Grace was vulnerable. He may have found that attractive. Many men do."

"Yes. I've watched you fall under the spell of Elizabeth Fraser. She's stronger than you think. The difference is, she knows how to conceal it." It was a bitter admission.

He tried to disregard her accusation. "What was your first thought, when you saw they were all dead? That Paul had killed them?"

Stunned, she stared at him. "When I saw — *What are you saying!*"

"I think you knew what had happened. Before Jarvis told you."

"Be damned to you!" She got up swiftly and swept from the room, slamming the door behind her.

Paul Elcott's rooms were an indication of his condition. A man on the brink of failure, with nothing to show for years of hard work while his brother was in the war, nothing to show for his attempt to strike out on his own.

Rutledge went through his possessions with distaste. How envious had Elcott been of his brother? he wondered as he searched.

Hamish said, "It's in the nature of a child to be envious."

Had Henry Elcott, the father of the two boys, always found Paul lacking, and had his mother always made excuses for him, protecting him? The incident with Theo Elcott's revolver, when a young and rebellious Paul had tried to sell it, was a reflection of the knotted relationships. And the fact that Paul hid on the fellside when he was unhappy at home told its own story.

He should have been sympathetic to Josh, another lonely boy . . .

Thorough as he was, Rutledge could find no boots without heels. They might already have gone to the rubbish heap. There was no hidden revolver, although Rutledge searched the bar and the saloon and the kitchen as well as the rooms upstairs. Only a coat with a missing button — but there was only Janet's word that she'd found the button in the hut above High Fell Farm.

Above the hearth on a corner of the mantel was a pretty vase, out of place in such dreary lodgings. The sort of thing a woman might buy, for the sake of the roses that clambered up to the neck. Pink roses like those in the kitchen and on Grace Elcott's frivolous hat.

Rutledge had seen it there before, but hadn't given it more than a passing thought. It was something Grace might have given Elcott. Or that he might have planned to give her.

He looked at it, and then lifted it down from its place of honor. Something inside rattled.

With Hamish already alive in his mind, Rutledge turned the vase upside down and spilled the contents out into his hand.

A black button rolled into the palm of his hand. A black button, like the one that Janet Ashton had claimed she'd found in the ruined hut. But there was no sign of the broken cuff link that had once belonged to Josh Robinson.

Rutledge went to the cell where Elcott sat morosely staring at the floor. Unshaven, wearing the same clothes he'd had on climbing the fell in the night, he looked both pitiable and exasperating. A man without spirit who seemed to prefer to wallow in his defeat than strive to overcome it.

The gray walls, the cot to one side, and the slop jar in one corner seemed to reflect the stale, colorless atmosphere of prison.

Holding out the vase with the clambering roses, Rutledge asked, "Can you tell me where this came from?"

Paul glanced at it and resumed his study of the floor. "Grace gave it me. She thought it would brighten my rooms. She liked roses. Flowers of any kind."

Tilting it, Rutledge let the black button slide into his palm. "Is this from your coat? It's missing a button."

"I wondered where that had got to." He frowned, sticking out a finger to touch the button almost as if to see whether or not it had reality. "That button was loose at the funeral. I was going to sew it back on and never got around to doing so. What was it doing in the vase?"

"And this?" Reaching into his pocket, Rutledge held out the cuff link. It was the second of the pair, retained for interrogation purposes.

"That belongs to Josh. A birthday gift from his father."

"Gerald?"

"No, Hugh, of course. It's broken." Elcott turned it in his fingers. "A pity. It's gold. Grace would have been angry if she knew Josh had been so careless."

"Did you find it up there in the hut?"

"I never found it anywhere. It was too dark, and then you came at me before I could light my lantern. Are you now reduced to manufacturing evidence against me?"

It was hard to tell if he was lying or telling the truth. Rutledge let it go. "I've a feeling Janet Ashton reached High Fell the night it snowed. And something made her turn around and go back the way she'd come. Do you know what it was?"

"Ask *her!* I've told you until I'm tired of telling. I never killed them!" But there was undeniable wariness in his voice.

"If you know anything about her movements, then you'd be better off answering my question."

Elcott sat there, stony-faced and silent.

"Did she reach Urskdale at the beginning of the storm? Did you see her or her carriage?"

"Ask her!"

Hamish said, "It may be he doesna' want to gie away too much!"

Rutledge left, taking the vase with him and setting it on Greeley's desk, with its contents. But he kept the cuff link in his pocket.

# Chapter Thirty

He cornered Janet Ashton in the kitchen. She looked up in alarm when he strode in, closed the door at his back, and leaned against it.

"Enjoyed your walks, have you?" Rutledge asked. The tone of his voice was pleasant enough, but his eyes were hard.

She opened her mouth to say something, and then shut it firmly.

"They've been very useful," he went on. "Everyone was sympathetic. You were injured, grieving, the waiting was too much for you, and so you did what you could to keep your spirits up. Elizabeth even saw you at the churchyard. Paying your respects to the dead."

"They *are* my dead!" she told him flatly.

"And the churchyard is close enough to The Ram's Head that you could see when Paul Elcott left for the farm. It was easy enough to put the broken cuff link in the vase on the mantel. He seldom locks his doors."

"I don't know what you're talking about," she retorted. "You're saying, I think, that I've tried to make Paul Elcott look guilty. It's true. But I took back the button I'd twisted off his coat after the funeral. It was hanging on the coatrack in the hall while everyone was in the dining room. I thought I could use the button. Afterward I felt ashamed of myself. Grief does strange things sometimes. And I was so *angry* that you'd done nothing."

"And the cuff link?" He took it out and showed it to her, as if he'd found that in the rose-twined vase as well.

"No, you can't blame that on me as well!" she snapped indignantly.

"Where did you run into Paul Elcott, the night you arrived at High Fell in the early hours of the storm?"

The switch in subjects caught her off balance. "I never saw him!"

"But you did, that's why you're so certain he's guilty. You saw him leave the farm — you'd heard him arguing with Gerald. There in the barn? Or in the yard? Where you could see them and not be seen by them. But you heard something, didn't you? Loud voices, words both of them must have wished later that they could take back?"

It was a shot in the dark, but she was staring at him as if he'd just produced a crystal ball. A small change in the line of her jaw, a sudden tension around the eyes, told him he was on the right track.

"Paul saw you. Or the tracks of your carriage. You might as well tell me the truth. It might go a long way towards proving he was there, and angry enough to kill. A witness, since we don't have Josh to tell us what happened afterward."

The temptation was there, he could feel it. But she was wary, thinking through what could condemn her and what would surely put the noose around Paul Elcott's neck.

"He will use it to convince his lawyers that you should be in the dock in his place. And in turn, they'll use what he knows to cast doubt on his guilt. A reasonable doubt . . . that's all the jury is required to feel. He'll go free, and there's no possibility of trying him a second time."

He had to admire her for having the courage to stand there and resist him. He remembered how little she'd cried out as he'd pulled her from the overturned carriage. In spite of the pain . . .

"On the other hand," he carried on, "there're a good many pieces of evidence against you." He began to tick them off the fingers of his left hand. "James Follet will testify that you possessed a revolver. The police at the barrier in Keswick can testify that you never passed them — going in either direction. When I asked if you wanted us to contact any family you might have in the vicinity, to let them know you were safe, you told me you had none. If you hadn't killed your sister, how could you know she was dead? Fourth — the button you took —" But she stopped him before he could finish.

"*I didn't know!* I came here to *talk* to Grace. Not to kill her! I wanted her to go back to Hugh, now that the twins were born and she'd finished her duty to Gerald. My leave was nearly up. I had to make a decision. Either stay in Carlisle or return to London. I couldn't put it off any longer!"

"If you were only expecting to talk to her, why bring a revolver?"

She turned away. "I have told you."

"Gerald had a weapon. Grace could have used that if she'd needed it. Your story doesn't *hold*."

She said nothing.

"Then tell me. What happened at the farm?"

The tension in the room was so great that Hamish seemed to be there, just behind him, and yet his back was touching the door. Then, before he could stop himself, he stepped away from the door, so that he was no longer crowding the voice that was always there.

She must have thought he had given up, and was leaving.

"It had just begun to snow when I got there." Her voice was muffled. "They were still alive. And you're right, Gerald was just outside the barn, and he was talking to Paul. I left the carriage in the lane and walked towards them. I could hear Gerald very clearly. I could see his face. He was absolutely furious. He was saying, 'Get out of here. Get off my farm and never come back. I don't want to see you here again, do you understand me?' And then Paul said something I couldn't hear. But Gerald answered, 'Blood ties be damned! That can never excuse what you've done. Be clear on this. I love my wife, I love my children. And I'll guard them if I have to. You stand in far greater danger from me than we do from you. So there's an end to it, before you do something you'll always regret!' At that stage I went hurrying back to my carriage, for fear Paul would turn to go and on his way find me there eavesdropping. And Gerald was not in any state for me to come riding up unexpectedly! I turned the carriage and drove to the church, pulling the horse around to the back where no one could see me. And I sat inside for a good hour, before venturing back to the farm."

She put her hand to her face. He couldn't tell if she was crying or not. But she managed to continue. "The church was dark. Quiet. Peaceful. I went back to the farm then, hoping Gerald might still be in the barn. The snow was worsening, and he'd stock to bring in. I looked, but he wasn't anywhere to be seen, and I assumed he'd gone to look for his sheep. So I went inside. Grace was nursing the twins. I don't know where Josh and Hazel were — I was just glad not to find them with her. She looked so happy, holding the babies." Her voice broke on the last words.

"Was she surprised to see you?"

"Oh, yes. She hadn't expected me before Boxing Day. I asked her if there was any way that both of us could be happy. I asked if she felt anything at all for Hugh. After all, he was the father of two of her children. She must have cared once! I reminded her that in the eyes of the Church she was still married to him. And all she said was, 'You're living in a dream, Janet. It has nothing to do with Hugh, don't you see? I told you when you wouldn't come for the wedding: I don't think I'd go back to him even for the children's sake — even if anything happened to Gerald. We fell out of love before the war, I know that now. We're strangers.' And then Gerald came in, and I asked him to his face if he could ever love me."

Her shoulders began to shake. "I went back to the church. The snow was heavier, and I left the carriage in the lee, where the horse was protected from the wind. I wanted to freeze to death there in the church, and have them find my body. I wanted my death to be on Gerald's soul. I wanted everyone to know he'd killed me."

"It was a cruel thing to do."

She whirled. "Not as cruel as his rejection of me! It was unbearable, and yes, at that time, I wanted him dead!"

"And so, with your revolver, you went back . . ."

"No! I was a coward. I raged and cried until I was exhausted, and then I set out for Carlisle. I got to Keswick and the horse couldn't go any farther. So I stopped in Keswick, at a small hotel I knew there. I must have come to my senses at some point. Finally, two days later, against all advice I started back to Urskdale. When the poor horse went off the road, and I couldn't move for the pain, I thought, I can't die without making amends! I *must* make it up with Grace somehow. And then, when I'd given up hope, you came."

"She's concocted a verra pretty story," Hamish objected. "But she's lied before."

"We can find out if you really stayed in Keswick," Rutledge warned her.

"Then you'll learn I'm telling the truth," she flung at him. "Why in God's name would I have come back to see them all dead? Even I can't hate that much!"

If she'd stayed at Keswick, he told himself, it would explain why she hadn't seen the police barricades in the road. . . . More to the point, why the police hadn't seen her.

"And when you heard what had happened, you believed it was Paul who had killed your sister and her family."

"Oh, yes. If you hadn't found my revolver and taken it, I think I would have shot him myself. Don't you see? She — Grace — died not knowing I'd had a change of heart! And all that's left now is to be sure whoever killed her — them — *hangs!*"

# Chapter Thirty-One

Rutledge said into the sound of her weeping, "You are certain it was Paul Elcott you saw standing in front of the barn, talking to Gerald?"

"I'd take my oath on it!" She found a handkerchief and dried her tears angrily, fighting for control. "In a court of law!"

"Then why didn't you tell me this in the beginning? Why play games with coat buttons?"

"Because I was *there*. And because you're right: Paul would just as happily see me hang, instead. Otherwise he wouldn't inherit that bloody farm, which is why he killed them in the first place! I've seen Inspector Greeley looking at me, I've read what was in his mind. I'm the outsider, I have no place here, and it won't disturb his precious valley if I'm taken off to trial. I'm *expendable!*"

Rutledge let her go then. It was Hamish's voice he could hear as he walked out into the yard and looked up at the fell.

"You canna' believe both!"

"She's willing to swear he was there. As he'll no doubt swear she was. In the end, they may well cancel out the testimony on either side."

"She had a revolver," Hamish reminded him.

It was a sticking point in the evidence against Janet Ashton — and a stumbling block in the evidence against Paul Elcott.

And if Elcott was searching the heights, it could mean he hadn't found the boy the night of the murders. Indeed, had reason to suspect Josh hadn't died straightaway.

Hamish urged, "Time's short. You canna' leave the choice between them to Mickelson!"

Rutledge said aloud, "There's something about her account that doesn't feel — right."

His intuition and his knowledge of people had always been his strengths as a policeman. What, when all else failed, he could rely on to take him through the tangle of half-truths and lies and misdirections to find the guilty party.

And now, when he needed them most,

they seemed to elude him. "I shouldn't be questioning anyone. I've been relieved."

Hamish repeated, "You canna' leave it to yon flunky from London."

He had lived with these people for over a week and gotten nowhere. Was it possible Mickelson would see more clearly how the scant evidence stood? Or muddle it further in his driving need to please Chief Super-intendent Bowles?

Mickelson was ambitious, he was quick, and if he made mistakes, he could live with them, where Rutledge couldn't.

If Rutledge didn't get there before him, it was possible that the wrong person would hang.

And time seemed to be melting away like the snow . . .

Walking back into the house, he made his way to Hugh Robinson's room and knocked lightly on the door.

"Come!"

Robinson was sitting by the window, an unopened book in his lap, staring out at Urskwater.

"I'd rather think Josh died of cold than that someone drowned him," he said to Rutledge as he stepped into the room. "He wouldn't have suffered."

"I don't think drowning is likely," Rutledge told him. "If the killer found him, then the revolver was quickest. If he got away, the weather took him."

With a sigh, Robinson turned. "I've heard you arrested Elcott."

"Yes, and that's why I need to speak to you now. You knew Janet Ashton for a number of years. You said she did everything possible to help your family through the war."

"Yes, it's true. I have a good deal of respect for her. It couldn't have been easy, two women struggling to keep a home going for two small children who had no idea what was happening around them." He smoothed the crease in his trousers. "Grace told me she'd tried to explain to Josh that I'd gone missing and was very likely dead. But I'd been away for two years by that time. He didn't really understand the difference. Janet told me Josh believed I'd stopped loving him. That hurt."

But might explain the broken cuff links?

"Do you think it could have been your sister-in-law who killed Grace and her children?"

Robinson considered him. "Why did you send Elcott to jail, if you aren't sure in your own mind?"

"It's more a matter of leaving no stone unturned."

"Then I'll tell you what I think. Janet was probably in love with Elcott, although I've never asked her outright about that. It would explain why she moved north even though she had an excellent position in London. That's her business, and not mine. Do I believe that after all she'd done for Grace, she was hurt and angry that Grace had taken away the man she thought she loved? Yes, that's probably the case. I just can't picture her walking into that house and shooting living people."

"And Elcott?"

"I don't know him well. Janet claims he wanted to inherit High Fell. It could be true. Would he kill to get the farm? I can't answer that."

"What you're telling me is that you still believe your son is the — murderer."

Robinson winced at the word. "I don't know anymore. I'm beyond thinking. If you want to know the truth, I'm beyond caring. They're dead, I can't bring them back, and I just want to walk away and never think about any of it again." His eyes begged for understanding. "I thought the war was hellish enough. I expected to dream about it for the rest of my life. But

477

when I close my eyes, it's not the trenches I see. Not now. Hazel's little face — Josh falling asleep, alone and unprotected in the snow. The blood in that kitchen. And I don't know how long that will go on."

Rutledge had no answer to give him. He had not learned how to face his own nightmares.

"Will you testify at the inquest? It will be held in Keswick, once the roads are better. In another three days . . ." Mickelson would press forward on that.

"I don't know what I can tell them. I — At this stage, I'm reluctant to blacken my son's name. But if you think —" He stopped, shaking his head, uncertain.

"Let your conscience guide you. Don't let an innocent man go to the gallows if you think you can stop an injustice."

Rutledge left the room, and his last view of Robinson's face was daunting. He was looking down at his hands, an expression of despair twisting his features into a mask of pain.

Harry Cummins found Rutledge sitting alone in the dining room, going through his policeman's notebook.

"I'm told that Paul Elcott has been taken into custody."

"Yes." Rutledge's answer was curt.

"I'm glad there is resolution. I just didn't expect it to be someone I knew."

"It often is someone you know. In a murder case. There aren't that many wandering madmen to choose from." The bitterness in Rutledge's voice was apparent.

"I'd heard that Gerald had enemies — the war."

"London came up with a name. Bertram Taylor. The man hasn't been seen in days. Not since his escape from prison. I doubt we can consider him a real possibility."

"Yes. Well. I've known Paul for some years. He never gave me the impression of a man ridden by greed. Envy, perhaps . . . But Miss Ashton must be right, it's what drove him to do this. I've just not come to terms with it yet." He paused, studying the palm of his hand. "Will you and Miss Ashton and Mr. Robinson be leaving soon? Now that there's someone in custody . . ."

You could see, Hamish was saying, that he was concerned about losing his paying guests with the long winter months stretching out ahead.

"I'll be leaving tomorrow. Their situation will depend on other factors. A Mr. Mickelson will be arriving shortly. He's the man to ask."

Cummins, no fool, looked at him sharply. "You've been replaced."

"I will be. Yes."

The play of emotions across the innkeeper's face was revealing. "Look, about what I said earlier. It isn't important — I hope there won't be any need to pass on my — my personal concern."

Rutledge said, "I see no reason to cause trouble for anyone."

Cummins smiled, relieved. But at the door, he said, "It's been difficult, sinking roots into the hard, stony soil here. For my wife's sake, I'm glad there's been nothing to shame her."

It was a sad remark to make.

When Rutledge didn't answer, he said, "Well . . . I must look to the fires. Please let us know if there's anything we can do. For Paul."

Maggie watched the boy feeding the dog, coaxing Sybil to eat. But the dog was too busy licking the boy's pale face.

"I don't think she cares much for toast. Put some of the drippings on it. She'll like it better."

He got up and went to the bowl Maggie kept by the sink. Sybil, knowing what he was about to do, went with him, drooling with anticipation. Her tail wagged furiously.

How could Sybil be wrong about him? Or had he killed in a moment of madness, long since carried away by the cold and the snow?

She refused to believe what she'd heard with her own ears. But that chilling "Bang! Bang-bang! Bang —" echoed in her brain. He had been there when the killing was done. That much was certain. The searchers had all but said he could be a witness. What they hadn't said was that he'd done this terrible deed. But perhaps they hadn't known, in the first rush to find the only survivor . . . Perhaps that came later.

She cursed her bad leg. She daren't go into Urskdale village to listen to the gossip. The journey there and back would put her in bed for a week. Longer. The London policeman had come three times. Suspicious, wanting to know about the old drift road that went over the Saddle and through the narrow cut that led south. A child could never have made that journey, not in summer even. What was it about the old road that intrigued the policeman? That one man could pass there, without being seen in the village?

Closed to sheep it might be, but her father had made his way over the rocks when he was sixteen, and found the way to the coast. His father had given him a lashing with the leather belt for frightening his mother by disappearing for several days. But he'd had pocket change with him and bought a small pillow slip with *Morecambe Bay* embroidered on it to beg forgiveness, saying that he'd not realized it was so far to walk.

It was the only time her father had ever left the dale. He'd told her once that the sea wasn't much to look at and he'd decided that roaming didn't suit him after all. . . .

She went to the cupboard where her father had kept his belongings. The boy, idle now, watched her as she rummaged through the shelves. Frustrated, she leaned against the wall for a time until she could muster the energy to begin again.

And then she had a better idea and went out to the barn, dragging her foot after her as she searched for the clothes that had belonged to the sheep man who had died at Mons. A flat cap . . . leather, like some of the Londoners wore. Or so he'd said, jauntily clapping it on his head and laughing at her. She'd told him he looked a fool, but he had laughed again and said, "The girls in shops don't think so." She called him cheeky, and had turned away, hiding her smile. But she had understood why the girls in the London shops found him dazzling . . .

Sentimental she was not, though he had been a wonder with the sheep, a blessing after her father's death. She took the hat out of the suitcase it had lived in for the duration of the war and carried it back to the kitchen. The boy was curious, but she didn't tell him what she was planning.

An hour with an old cloth and saddle soap made the hat look better, and she turned it this way and that, studying it.

It would do.

She took it back outside and tossed it into the snow that had drifted higher against the shed.

When the Londoner came back, she was ready for him.

# Chapter Thirty-Two

Elizabeth Fraser found Rutledge still in the dining room. She had brought with her a pot of tea and some sandwiches, a cup and saucer, and the sugar bowl and creamer.

"Everything looks better on a full stomach," she said, edging her way through the door, the tray balanced on her lap. He hurried to help her, taking the tray from her and setting it on the tea cart by the hearth.

"Tea. The English panacea for everything short of the end of the world . . ."

She looked up from spooning sugar into his cup. "You're trying to be clever. Arresting Paul. Is it working?"

"Yes. No."

"Who really killed Gerald and his family?" She handed him his cup. "Or do you even know?"

"There's something I've seen —"

"Then it's all right."

"You don't understand." He bit into the sandwich of roasted pork and realized that he *was* hungry. "What's the most common thing to be found in Urskdale?"

"Sheep," she answered readily, and he smiled in spite of himself.

"Yes, all right, the next most common thing?"

"Rock. Of all kinds. Slate. Basalt. Volcanic."

"And it doesn't show tracks. And even if it did, the snow would have obliterated them."

"That's true, but —"

He took the broken heel out of his pocket. The ring of nails gleamed dully.

"So that's what cut your hand!" she exclaimed, staring at it.

"Indeed. Someone lost this, and you can't walk on rock with a damaged shoe. After a time, it takes its toll on the foot and the ankle. If you'd come all the way from the coast and had to walk out again, what would you need straightaway?"

"A shoemaker. Barring that, a new boot. But you'd have to send to Keswick for it."

"Yet I've looked, and no one had a damaged boot."

"And there wasn't time to replace it . . ."

"Exactly."

She tucked the tea cozy over the pot and thought about it. "If you're saying that this damaged shoe belonged to the killer, I know where he could find a new boot. If they were of a size. Gerald's."

Rutledge smiled. "Hamish was right. He'd said something about asking the woman."

She was perplexed. "Hamish?"

"Never mind. I'm going to be out for a while. Say nothing about the heel, will you?"

He drove to the Elcott farm. Without Paul there to paint, the house had taken on a forlorn air. As if it had been abandoned.

Rutledge walked into the kitchen by way of the yard door. The smell of paint was still heavy in the air. And without heat the room had a chill that was permeating. As he pulled off his gloves, he tried to picture it as he'd first seen it. With bloodstains marking where five people had died.

No one had stepped in the blood. No one had stopped to make certain that each of the victims in this room had died. It was the last thing a child would attempt to do. An adult would be aware of the blood on the floor and avoid it. Especially with a torn heel.

There was a rectangular wooden box by the yard door which held an assortment of shoes. Wellingtons in various sizes, heavier boots for walking across the fells. And a pair of pattens for gardening.

He went through them one by one, matching them up into pairs.

And all the pairs were there. Each had heels, worn in some cases, fairly new in others, and a few caked with mud.

Rutledge stood looking at them for a moment, as Hamish said, "He wouldna' be sich a fool as to tak' only one . . ."

"Then where is his cast-off pair? The one with the missing heel and its mate? Am I on the wrong track?"

Hamish didn't answer.

"The barn, then."

"Aye, but what if the heel was lost as he left the dale?"

"We'll cross that bridge when we come to it."

Rutledge carefully piled the shoes back into the wooden box and went out, shutting the door behind him.

The barn took a long time to search. He worked methodically, his mind busy with all the possible hiding places. Dust rose from the corners as he dug out old spades and tools, a yoke for a team, chains of various lengths, the broken wheel of a barrow, and an assortment of oddments that had sat idle and unused for generations. He raked out the stalls, searched the mangers, went through the tack room, and then found the ladder to the loft. It was in a far corner, buried under damp and rotted straw, that he finally found what he was looking for: a heavy walking shoe without a heel. And its mate.

Hamish said on the drive back to Urskdale, "Ye ken, this still doesna' prove much."

When he had tried to fit the heel onto the shoe, the match had been good. And he looked at the size of the shoe. It would fit most men, he thought. Well enough to make walking comfortable over a long distance. He himself could wear them.

But Hamish was right, that the wearer was still in doubt — the time of losing the heel still in doubt. What if it had been Gerald himself, out searching for one of his sheep, who had worn these? Or his father, for that matter.

Rutledge had gone back to the house and measured the sole of the boot against the larger Wellingtons and leather shoes in the box.

Close enough . . . They could indeed be Gerald's.

Once in town, he went straight to the police station and asked to see Paul Elcott.

"Would you try on these shoes for me?" Rutledge asked as he opened the door.

He stared at them. "What on earth for? They aren't mine."

"Just try them, if you please."

Elcott unlaced his own boots and put his feet into the pair Rutledge had brought, then stood up.

"They fit well enough."

"They're yours, then?"

Elcott laughed. "They couldn't be mine. They're London made, at a guess. I've never been able to afford boots like these. Gerald's, then. He bought clothes for himself in London before he came home again. Afraid what he owned wouldn't fit anymore."

"Then he'd have no reason to hide them," Rutledge said, and was gone.

He asked Harry Cummins and Hugh Robinson to try the fit next. Robinson's feet were nearer to the size of the boot than Elcott's, but on Cummins they were nearly a perfect match.

Cummins looked down at them. "A shame they've lost a heel. I could do with a new pair . . ."

★ ★ ★

Maggie Ingerson came to the door at the sound of Rutledge's motorcar pulling into the yard at dusk.

"You again," she said.

"I want to ask you about that old drift road over the fells —"

"I've told you what I know. You'll have to be satisfied with that, unless you can speak to the dead. My father claimed he took it once. But that was before I was born, so I can't be sure whether or not it was the truth or bragging."

"Why did he take it?" Rutledge watched clouds slide down over The Long Back.

"For a lark, I expect. That was the way he was."

"How long do you think it would take to reach the coast?"

"I can't answer that. In daylight and good weather? The better part of two days. It's not so far as the crow flies, but there's the elevation to consider. In heavy snow, longer than that. You're not thinking that boy could have got out by the road?"

"No. I doubt he had the strength to walk that far."

"Then someone coming in."

"Yes."

She pointed towards the sheds up the

rise from the barn. "Then you might want to go look at what Sybil brought me last night. I left it there by the shed when I fed the sheep."

He switched off the motor and got down to walk up the hillside towards the shed. The prints of a dozen Wellingtons went up and down ahead of him, mucking up the snow. It was hard to separate them now, overlapping in the slush and mud.

When he had reached the shed, he turned and looked back at her.

"That's right, just there. Maybe a little to your left . . ."

He looked around at the snow by the shed, and saw that something had been dropped in one place.

Pulling it out, he could see that it was a leather cap.

Hamish said, "Ye've got the boots, and now the cap. That's how he came and went."

Rutledge slapped the snow off the hat and examined it. He would have sworn it was made before the war, when leather was better quality.

Taylor? He'd been in prison, he wouldn't have had access to newer clothes . . .

He walked back to the woman standing there leaning on her cane, watching him.

"The dog brought it? From where?"

"How am I to know? I sent her to bring in some sheep that were straying towards the Petersons'. That was two nights ago. She came back with this in her mouth. If it belongs to Peterson, you'll oblige me by taking it back to him. I'm not well enough to get there and back."

"You're certain that the dog went in that direction?"

"Sybil's been running sheep for seven years. She does what she's told, and there's an end to it."

"Thank you, Miss Ingerson. I'll speak to the Petersons."

She watched him drive back down the lane, well satisfied.

When she went back inside, the boy was standing there with the ax in his hands.

Rutledge stopped to speak to Mr. Peterson, finding him sweeping tracked snow out of his barn. He greeted Rutledge warily and waited for him to explain his business.

When Rutledge showed him the cap, he answered forthrightly: It didn't belong to him.

"But that's not to say the Haldnes boys weren't making free with my property.

They're a rowdy lot, and up to any manner of mischief."

And so he called next at the Apple Tree Farm, and showed the cap to Mrs. Haldnes. She was trimming a pie to set in the oven for dinner and wiped her floured hands on her apron before taking the cap. She examined it as closely as if she were a prospective buyer. And when she'd finished, she handed it back to Rutledge.

"Never saw that before, that I know of. Not the sort of things my lads wear. Where did you say you'd found it?"

But he hadn't said, and didn't answer her a second time, much to her chagrin.

A pair of boots. A cap. But not the man who had worn them. A pity, Rutledge thought as he turned into the hotel yard and switched off the motor, that neither of them would clear Paul Elcott . . .

"Aye, paltry matters, until you find their owners."

"Owner." Rutledge corrected Hamish out of habit. His mind was on other things.

He fully expected to walk into the hotel and find Mickelson there before him.

But as it happened, he'd been given one more day of grace.

# Chapter Thirty-Three

Rutledge took the cap and the torn heel to his room. They would have to be handed over to Mickelson when he got there, along with any other information that he felt was pertinent.

He stared at the cap, his mind elsewhere, and then slowly began to actually look at it.

What was it Hamish had said not ten minutes ago? *Owners* . . .

He'd grown up with dogs. They had been in his house and in his life for as long as he could remember.

Why would a dog sent out to manage the sheep bring back the cap of a man whose scent she didn't know?

The cur-dogs, as Drew Taylor had called them, were working animals, bred to it and trained to be an extension of their owners. In Scotland with his godfather, he'd seen a young Border collie round up geese, so strong was the instinct. The fast run . . . the sudden drop . . . the eyes that registered everything and anticipated just the right move necessary to bring a herd together, hold it, or cut out part of it. Some animals worked on whistled signals, some on hand signs, and some were so well trained to certain tasks that they could be sent out on their own.

But he was not the expert. And he knew someone who was. . . .

He dropped the cap into his suitcase and went back out to the motorcar.

It was dark by the time he reached Jim Follet's house.

A good sheep man . . .

Follet and his wife were just finishing their dinner and invited him to have pudding and tea with them. Bieder, no longer on guard duty in the barn, lay stretched out on a woven rag rug, head on his paws. His eyes looked up, acknowledging a stranger in the house, and then went back to whatever drowsy contemplation he'd been enjoying.

Rutledge could see the curiosity behind the smiles of his host and hostess, but he had told them the truth when he had walked into their kitchen.

"I'm here to learn something about your dog."

"My dog — or any dog trained to sheep?"

"Any dog."

And then Mary Follet was asking for news of Miss Ashton, and Follet himself wanted to know what had possessed Rutledge to take Paul Elcott into custody.

"I can't for the life of me see him committing such a horrendous crime!"

"Early days," Rutledge told him. "There's still much work to be done before we're certain of anything."

Follet didn't appear to be mollified.

By the time they had finished at the table and Follet had carried him off to the parlor, Rutledge had given them all the news he had of Urskdale, even to reporting on the Henderson child with the bruised collarbone, and thanked Mrs. Follet for the pudding.

Mrs. Follet had commented at length on the funeral service and how sad it was to see a family buried together. "But it was good of them to put the babies with their mother, rather than in separate little coffins . . ."

"A kindness," he agreed.

Follet said, as they shut the parlor door

and sat, "I daresay it's not my wife's cooking that's brought you here again. If you've put Paul Elcott in jail, then you've been satisfied that Miss Ashton is in the clear. I never knew what to think about her. Out in the storm —"

"I'm not satisfied with anything," Rutledge answered frankly. "And I shall have to speak to someone in Keswick before I can be sure she's in the clear. What I need at the moment is your skill with sheepdogs. How they're trained, how you work them, what they do — and won't do, while minding the sheep."

Follet complied, describing how he could tell when the litter was no more than ten days old which had the instinct to be a good working dog and which didn't. "But that's my years of experience speaking, you understand. Something about how alert they are, how they play amongst themselves. And I'm seldom wrong." He smiled and turned to the subject of training, "which is little more than building on what the dog already has in him or her," and how a younger dog could be taken into the field with a more mature animal, to learn. "The best pair I ever had were mother and daughter," he finished. "I'll never see their like again. Cassandra and Zoe, they were called, my daughter's choice of names that year. I taught them, and they taught me. It was a rare sight, to watch them work sheep. I'd take them down to the dog trials, sometimes, for the pleasure of seeing them show up every other animal there."

Rutledge said, "When a dog is sent to carry out a certain task — to work — can he or she be easily distracted?"

"Not unless the flock is in danger. We've had rogue dogs a time or two, killing where they could. But it's not something you see all that often."

"If your dog was working and came across — say, a glove you'd dropped — would he bring it back to you?"

"No. Still, I had a bitch who carried about any gloves she could find. You'd have a care about where you set yours down, she'd be on to them that fast. But not while she was with the sheep. She was single-minded then."

Rutledge got to his feet. "You've been very helpful. I appreciate that."

"I'd like to know what it's in aid of. With the matter closed."

"Someone told me she'd sent her dog to move the sheep, and it brought back an article of clothing that could have belonged to the killer."

"That's possible, of course. But I'd be doubtful. He may have stopped and sniffed at it, if he'd known the owner and recognized the scent. Out of curiosity. But not while working."

"Can you be reasonably certain about that?"

"I'd take an oath on it."

Rutledge took his leave shortly thereafter.

And in the motorcar on the way back to Urskdale, he said aloud to Hamish, "Maggie Ingerson lied to me. The question is why. And what did she expect to gain from it?"

At dinner Rutledge announced that he was being relieved of duty as soon as the new man arrived. This was met with no more than curiosity until he told them that the new man would require their presence until he was satisfied that the case was closed.

"And he'll be satisfied that Paul killed my sister?" Janet Ashton demanded. "I don't see the need for another inspector to come here if there's been an arrest!" There was alarm in her face, and it quickly spread around the table as Rutledge went on.

"I've ordered Elcott released tonight. There's insufficient evidence on which to continue holding him."

Consternation reigned, everyone talking at once.

"It was a *trick!*" Miss Ashton exclaimed. "Nothing more than a trick!"

Hugh Robinson said, "Are you telling me that you believe Josh —"

Harry Cummins looked quickly at his wife, and then his voice rose over the others. "We've just been able to sleep of nights —"

But it was Mrs. Cummins who put the cap on the discussion. "I never thought it was Paul," she said. "I never thought he'd harm a fly! But I expect I do know who killed them. I never liked George Standish over at Hill Farm. He's always putting on airs. I wouldn't put it past him to kill anybody!"

There was a smugness in her face as her eyes ran around the table.

"You can't mean that!" her husband exclaimed. "You hardly know him."

"I've said I never liked him . . ."

Cummins's eyes met Rutledge's over her head. Pleading in them.

"Yes, thank you, Mrs. Cummins," Rutledge said hastily. "I'll look into that myself."

She subsided, her attention returning to her plate. Cummins's fingers were shaking as he set down his knife and fork. He said quietly, "Standish is probably — He began taking in paying guests at the farm last summer. It rather cut into our own business. My wife was — understandably unsettled by it."

Elizabeth Fraser, sitting beside Rutledge at the table, added under her breath, "He's *seventy* . . ."

Rutledge said, "How well did the Ingersons know the Elcotts?"

Cummins threw a grateful glance in Rutledge's direction. "I expect they knew them as well as any of us did. I don't think there was a particular friendship. Miss Ingerson's father died some years ago — he was Henry Elcott's generation. Maggie has always been rather — reclusive. Perhaps that's the best word. There was no son; she took over the farm herself, and proved soon enough that she ran it as well as her father had before her. But it drained all the life out of her. When the man who helped her with the sheep died in the war, she did what everyone else had done: made do as best she could."

"That was the opinion I'd formed," Rutledge answered. "She's forthright and apparently unflappable. If she hadn't had a problem with her leg, she might have been out with the searchers."

Mrs. Cummins said, "It's Dr. Jarvis's fault, that. He didn't have the sense to leave well enough alone. There is no hope of her finding a husband, crippled as she is."

Elizabeth Fraser flinched, but Mrs. Cummins had turned to look at her husband. "I expect she knows all about the old road over the fells to the coast. She showed Harry where it was, and how it ran. But that was years ago, wasn't it, my dear? When she was much, much prettier . . ."

Restless in the night, Rutledge got up and dressed, then made his way out of the house. The walls seemed to close in on him, and Hamish was busily reminding him that Inspector Mickelson would arrive the next day.

"It wouldna' be politic to stay on after he's reported to you."

But Rutledge ignored him.

He had never dealt with a case where so many people were intent on misdirecting the course of the inquiry — each for his or her own ends. Lies, obstruction, muddled evidence, finger-pointing. As if mourning were not enough. Elcott and Miss Ashton had argued with the victims. Even Robinson was so intent on his own troubled role in the family's past that he wouldn't or couldn't look elsewhere. The ironmonger, Belfors, was protecting Paul Elcott out of habit, and because the information he could give the police was proof that Elcott knew where a revolver was to be had. Greeley wanted to live in peace with his neighbors long after Rutledge had moved on. Harry Cummins was intent on protecting his own secret. And his wife was not trustworthy as she pursued her own nightmares.

Of them all, Elizabeth Fraser had the least to win or lose. But she, too, had a past that made her vulnerable. Would Mickelson look at that and hear the whispers that she had cared for Gerald Elcott more than she should, and decide to point his finger in her direction?

He clenched his teeth and swore. There was nothing he could do about that now. He had had his chance to come to a suitable conclusion.

He could see all the twists and turns of the interviews he'd conducted. He could see where each of the people involved had something to hide. Except for Maggie

Ingerson. Why should she offer up a cap that had nothing to do with the south road?

Unless she, like Belfors, saw in Paul Elcott the local man being sent to the gallows by outsiders who were glad to let him take the blame . . .

All of them — Cummins and his wife, Miss Fraser, Miss Ashton, and Hugh Robinson — were not native to Urskdale. They would have had no defenders, if the tables had been turned. Even Follet had put in a word for Elcott and expressed his doubts about Janet Ashton.

An independent-minded woman like Maggie Ingerson might just do her bit to set him free.

But — who could have told her that he'd been taken into custody?

Rutledge looked out at the snow that still lay deep in corners, against northern walls, and wherever traffic hadn't trampled it into mud.

The storm had once covered every footprint. But even in this light he could squat on his heels and see fresh tracks. The hobnails of Drew Taylor's boots. The worn pattern of Cummins's Wellingtons. His own shoes. Miss Ashton's smaller soles. Beyond them the prints made by the search parties climbing the fell.

If the snowfall had been lighter, Greeley might have caught his man simply by tracking him. Case closed.

Rutledge turned to the house and his hand was already on the latch to the yard door.

Hamish was saying something, and he stopped to listen, but under the voice was something else. A memory.

He tried to bring it back. And lost it in Hamish's last words.

*"Ye've got til teatime tomorrow. Ye canna' afford to sleep."*

Rutledge lay awake another hour, reviewing all he'd seen and done here in Urskdale, raking through his actions and his unconscious observations.

By four in the morning he had drifted into an uneasy sleep, drained by his failure.

And when dreams came, they were mixed and morbid, as if in punishment.

He could see the boy running, dragging his feet, and the Elcotts lying dead in the snow, scattered like soldiers after an attack, limbs bent and bodies trampled by sheep. Overhead an artillery barrage lighted the sky, and he could hear Hamish calling the boy's name, pointing to the mud where Rutledge could see his footprints clearly in bloody snow.

The artillery barrage was louder, the shells exploding in his face, and he came out of deep sleep with a start, his heart pounding in time with the pounding on his door.

# Chapter Thirty-Four

When Rutledge opened his door, the thin, balding man standing there rocked back on his heels and said in a high, clear tenor, "It was the very devil of a journey, and I'm going to my bed. You've been relieved."

It was Mickelson. Behind his back his men called him Cassius, for his lean and hungry look. The name fit, for he was notorious for his ingratiating manner towards his superiors while behind their backs he ruthlessly promoted himself. A greengrocer's son, he had climbed high and expected to go higher.

Rutledge was left standing there while Mickelson strode to the door of the room Harry Cummins had assigned him.

Cummins cast an apologetic glance in Rutledge's direction as he asked his latest guest if all was to his liking.

Rutledge shut his door again and stood

there. He felt empty. He had fought for six months — seven — to rebuild his career. And it had come down to this.

Hamish said, "You canna' be certain he'll do any better."

But that didn't take away the stigma of being relieved. Of being seen as failing in his duty. Bowles would take pleasure in seeing that word got around, and he would never let Rutledge live it down.

"He's no' so clever. Only ambitious . . ." Hamish pointed out softly.

Rutledge took a deep breath. For his own sake, he must somehow find the answer that had eluded him from the start — that had eluded all of them. For his own self-respect.

Standing there, he remembered his dream. There had been something. He tried to recapture the swiftly fading memory of it. Artillery, and bloody snow. But the artillery had just been Mickelson pounding on his door, regardless of his sleeping neighbors.

And then he had it. Not the blood, not the dead lying about. What he had seen were the boy's footprints in the snow.

For he had seen them, those same dragging prints. In life. Not a child fleeing in terror, but a child shuffling in shoes too large. His heels leaving not a crisp mark like a man's but a blurred smudge.

Rutledge went back to his bed and slept for two more hours. After packing his belongings, he made his way quietly to the kitchen, where Elizabeth Fraser had already put the kettle on to boil.

"Will you help me?" he asked her. "Nothing quite as dangerous as putting your head into the lion's mouth, but all the same —"

"Yes, of course. I heard that Inspector Mickelson is here. Is it a message for him?"

"No. For Inspector Greeley. I asked him last night to let Paul Elcott go home. Would you tell him for me that I've left for London, and as you were cleaning my room, you found a shirt that I'd forgotten. That you'd like to send it on to me."

She stared at him. "But where will you be?"

"Don't ask me to tell you. But, as a favor, let Inspector Mickelson sleep as long as he can."

A smile spread across her face. "Have you found the boy? I always believed that somehow you would!"

His face betrayed nothing. "As far as

anyone is concerned, I've left Urskdale."

Nodding at him, she turned to the kettle. "I understand now." Her mind was busy, jumping ahead of his. "There's meat left from dinner last night. I can put up some sandwiches. Do you have a Thermos?"

"That's thoughtful of you. I'll take my case out to the motorcar and fetch it."

When he had cranked the motorcar and come back into the kitchen, she handed him a packet of sandwiches and then filled his Thermos.

"I'm sorry to see you go," she said simply. "But Godspeed." She held out her hand and he took it, held it for a moment, and then turned away.

Rutledge drove to the Elcott farm and beyond it, to the shearing pens where he had stopped once before with Drew Taylor. The shed was open on one side, and he drove the motorcar into it.

He knew Mickelson. The site of the murders had been cleaned and painted over. The victims had been buried. If he came here at all, he would listen to Greeley explain where and how the bodies had been discovered. And then he would go back to Urskdale and begin to question the people closest to the crime.

Paul Elcott was not likely to go far afield even if he found the courage to go on working at the house. And unless the weather came down again, the Elcott sheep would be left to their own resources.

The motorcar wouldn't be found for a day or two at best.

He took the packet of food with him, and the Thermos, and set out on foot.

There would be a vantage point somewhere where he could watch the Ingerson farm. In his pocket were the field glasses he'd used before at the hotel. And in his mind was the map, with the comments that Drew Taylor had made when they surveyed the terrain together.

It would be uncomfortable and cold where he was going, but in France he had suffered much worse conditions. What had driven him then was a desire to die. What was driving him now was the feeling that he must vindicate himself or lose all he'd achieved in the long, fearsome struggle to heal.

He thought fleetingly of Elizabeth Fraser. But that was far, far down the road.

Hamish demanded, "And if you find the lad, then what?"

Rutledge couldn't answer him.

Maggie walked into the kitchen and said to the boy, "I'm grateful for your willingness to defend me if you could. But that ax is sharp, and if you get hurt, who's to help me then?"

He lowered the ax and sheepishly put it back where he'd found it, by the door.

She went about her work in the kitchen and ignored him for a time. Then she sat down and began to talk to him about the animals he was caring for.

"Sheep fall into different lots. Can you tell a ewe from a gimmer shearling? Or a tup from a hogg? A wedder from a wedder shearling?" She could read the scorn in his face. "Of course you can," she answered her own question. "Still, it never hurts to learn the skills of the man you're taking on to work for you." She asked him a question or two about the wool clip, and saw that he understood her.

Finally, as if it were of no importance, Maggie said, "I don't think he'll be back. I've seen to it. The man from London who keeps coming here. But we'll give it a night or two before we take any chances with bad luck."

The relief in the drawn little face touched her heart.

But later in the evening after the fire had burned low and she was sitting at ease in her chair, her leg for once comfortable, she remembered another expression on his face, as he held the heavy ax in both hands.

And she found herself wondering what he would have done with it.

"You're a fool, Maggie Ingerson!" she scolded herself. But a twinge of pain in her leg reminded her that beggars couldn't be choosers.

When night fell, Rutledge moved again, taking up a position in a sheep pen. The grazing animals moved silently along the slopes, hooves scraping away the snow for whatever nourishment they could find. A ewe stared at him briefly and sneezed before moving on. Finally they settled for the night, lumps of dirty white were hardly different from the snow around them. One was near enough that he could hear it breathing, and he found the sound comforting.

There were stars overhead, great sweeps of them, and he picked out the winter constellations one by one. His feet were nearly numb now, the icy crust under them offering no warmth. And the wind picked up an hour later, the soft whistle of it coming over the western fells promising a deeper cold by morning.

It was nearly three, he thought, when the square of lamplight brightened the yard door of the Ingerson farm. He brought up his field glasses and thought he could just define Maggie's bulk in her old coat, standing against the light.

She seemed to be sniffing the air, almost like a cornered animal searching for danger. And then she moved away from the door.

The dog leaped out into the yard, and scrambled towards the pen by the shed where Rutledge had seen some dozen or so animals kept safely while they healed or re-gained their strength. Behind the dog, stepping out the door came an oddly shaped figure that seemed to be half gnome, half monster.

A superstitious man, Rutledge thought, would have a wild tale to tell about what was living in Maggie Ingerson's house.

The Norwegians had their share of small monsters, and the Irish, too.

But Rutledge didn't need Hamish to tell him what was walking up to the pen, bun-dled in a man's coat that was as long as he was tall, Wellingtons that were too large scuffing through the snow, a pail of some sort in both hands.

It was a boy, and unless Maggie had more secrets than he'd guessed already, the boy was Josh Robinson.

Rutledge spent a very uncomfortable night in the shearing shed, once he'd reached it again. He thought about the feather bed he'd left behind at the hotel, with a warm bottle at his feet and a dying fire in the kitchen that wrapped its heat around cold shoulders and frozen ears.

But the elation he felt kept him from sleeping.

Tomorrow he would brave the ogre in the farmhouse and ask Maggie Ingerson what she thought she was about.

It was Hamish who kept bringing up the question of what would become of Josh Robinson once the fact that somehow he'd survived was known.

What do you do, if a child has killed?

And what could he tell the world about what had happened that Sunday evening when the snow was thick and the door had opened on Death?

By morning the house was hushed. Smoke coiled from the chimney, but there was nothing else to indicate whether the people inside were asleep or awake.

Rutledge made his way down the slippery, icy rocks towards the farm. He was stiff with cold, and in no mood to brook obstruction. By the time he had reached the house, he was sweating under his heavy coat.

But he knocked with firmness on the door, rather than pounding.

After a time it opened and Maggie stepped out to confront him, almost close enough to him there in the little space between her and the shutting door to touch him.

"I know the boy is here. I'm cold, tired, and I need to come in and warm up. It would be better if you didn't make a fuss."

She stared at him, her face hard, revealing nothing. "I don't know what you're talking about. And I know my rights. You can't come in without a warrant to search."

"I'm here as a private citizen. Not a policeman. Open the door, Miss Ingerson. You can conceal the boy, but not his tracks." He pointed to the scuffed prints that crisscrossed the yard. Then he handed her the flat black cap. "You shouldn't have shown me this —"

Before he could stop her, she'd caught his arm in a grip as strong as that of any man he knew. She pulled him after her away from the door, determined and menacing.

"Step through that door, and you'll step into an ax," she told him.

He felt colder than he had on the hillside in the night. "Then it's true," he replied, feeling depression sweep through him. It was the answer he'd least wanted to hear. Josh Robinson was a killer.

"I don't know what's true and what's not," she said angrily. "But that lad is in no condition for a rough policeman to badger him. He'll do you an injury, and I'll be held to blame!"

"If he's dangerous, why have you harbored him all this time? Miss Ingerson — his father is waiting for him in Urskdale village. His aunt is there. They will do all that's possible for him."

"You don't understand! He's not speaking, he lives in terror of being found, and he's come to trust me. Leave him alone!"

"You know I can't do that. You have no *right* to him!"

"He was half dead when the dog found him! He'd have been dead in another hour. By rights he's mine. And I won't let you touch him."

He remembered what he had once thought concerning Janet Ashton. That in many cultures when a man saved the life of another man, he was owed that life.

"Miss Ingerson —"

"No. Go away and leave us in peace. *I won't let you have him!*"

She dropped her hand from his arm and turned towards the door, her mind on the ax, praying the boy hadn't moved it. She wasn't afraid of this man, and she could put an end to it. Even the hard, cold soil could be scratched away enough to leave his body where it would never be seen again. She was not going to be deterred, and if the boy had been her own flesh and blood she wouldn't have fought any more fiercely for him.

But Rutledge had turned as swiftly as she had, his hand on her shoulder. "Let me talk to him. Otherwise, Paul Elcott will be blamed for what happened. Let me at least ask him —"

She stopped so short that he bumped into her. "What's Paul Elcott to me? Where's he when the sheep need to be brought in or feed dragged up to the high pens? Where's he when the pasture grass isn't green in April for the lambing, and I have to take the cart and hunt for fodder to keep them alive? He'll outlive me, this boy, and see to what I can't. He's got no one else to care about him and neither do I!"

"He has to go to school — he has to live with his father — he can't be enslaved to fetch and carry for you or anyone else! You can't keep him like a lost dog you found in the snow!"

"I haven't enslaved him! I've given him a bed and food and Sybil to hold on to when the nights are dark and he cries out. I've given him work to take his mind off what he's seen. All you want him for is to hang him or lock him away in an asylum where he's got nothing. *Tell me that's better!*"

Rutledge dropped his hand. "It isn't. I grant you. But there are five dead, and we can't walk away from them!"

"The dead feel no pain. They don't hurt when they drag their leg into bed at night, and they can't give him human comfort. We need each other, he and I, and there's an end to it."

"Let me talk to him. Let me see if I can find out what happened that night. Let me do the right thing."

"Bugger the right thing," she retorted. But she was close to tears, and she used the rough sleeve of her coat to wipe brusquely across her eyes. "I wish you were dead! I wish you'd never come here. That's why I gave you that cap, so you'd go look south of here along the coast, and leave us to go on as we are!"

"It was never in the cards," he said wearily. "You know it and so do I."

They stood there, staring at each other, faces tense, eyes blazing.

After a time she said, "If I don't let you see him, you'll bring more policemen here and scare the boy into fits."

And then she turned towards the house. "He's not going to take you away," she called out. "I swear it. But I've got to bring him in."

There was no response. And then the door opened and Josh Robinson stood there with the double-bladed ax in his hand, defiant and ominously silent.

Beside him Sybil stood guard, her ruff raised and stiff, and growls sounding deep in her throat.

# Chapter Thirty-Five

What does a man say to a child who may be a killer? What could mitigate the nightmare that must be locked in his mind?

"Ye willna' have a second chance," Hamish warned quietly.

"Josh? My name is Rutledge. You may call me Ian, if you like. I've come from London to find you —"

Rutledge stayed where he was, and kept his voice level, as if there was no danger in the confrontation between them. Feeling his way.

The defiant face drained of color and the boy began to shake. But the ax was still clenched in his hands.

" 'Ware!" Hamish cautioned.

Rutledge quickly revised what he was about to say. "I was a soldier, like your father. I've been through some rough patches in the war," he went on. "But nothing like you've been through. If you will let me come in and talk —"

"He's mute," Maggie said, just behind him.

"Fair enough. I'll ask you a few questions, Josh, and you can nod your head or shake it, to let me know if I'm right or wrong. I'm not here to harm Maggie Ingerson. She's a very brave woman, and I have a high regard for her."

"Ask him if he'll go away again and leave us as we are," she told Josh. "Then you'll know where he stands!"

The boy's eyes switched anxiously from Rutledge's face to hers and back again.

"She knows I can't go away," the policeman answered honestly. "For days now we've been afraid that you were dead. We were worried, we searched everywhere, well into the night sometimes. Your aunt Janet is in Urskdale, at the hotel. More than anything she wants to know you're safe. She's grieved for you, fearful that you'd lost your way in the snow or were hurt, unable to call for help. And your father has come from Hampshire —"

A shriek of anguish was ripped from the child, and he slammed the door so hard it seemed to bounce on its hinges.

And Rutledge, moving swiftly towards it,

heard the fever pitch of his anger from inside.

"You're lying — you're lying!" he shrilled over and over again, and they could hear the ax striking the floor in rhythm with the words.

They stood in the cold, side by side but without speaking until the thuds stopped and the screams became broken sobs. It seemed, Rutledge thought, like hours before silence fell, and he looked at Maggie.

"Go in and comfort him."

"He doesn't like to be touched."

"All the same — and leave the door wide."

She finally did as he asked, opening the door with some trepidation, and a wave of warm air thick with the smell of cooked porridge washed over them. The boy lay on the floor, his arms around the dog, the ax forgotten. But in the floor were raw gouges where he had pounded the edge into the wood.

"Sybil has done more than I ever could," Maggie said, a forlorn note in her voice. She stooped to brush the tear-wet hair out of the child's face and he flinched.

Rutledge stepped in behind her and managed to shut the door. The heat of the room was stifling after his long night in the cold. He pulled off his coat and set it with his hat on a pail by the door.

Maggie had gingerly retrieved the ax and held it now as if she was debating using it.

Rutledge knelt on the floor. "I could do with a bowl of that porridge," he said, "and a cup of tea. You won't need that." He nodded to the ax.

She looked down at the blade of the ax and then set it aside. But she didn't move.

"I won't hurt him. Go on. Make his breakfast, and I'll share it. I need to reach him, and that may be the best way."

Reluctantly she went to the dresser and found three bowls. Rutledge looked at the curled-up figure of the boy, and then gently picked him up in his arms. It was as if Josh had burrowed so deep into himself that he wasn't aware of what was happening, for he put up no resistance. Rutledge carried the child to the chair where Maggie usually sat — where her father before her had sat, although Rutledge wasn't aware of that — and settled down, still holding the boy.

By the time Maggie had the porridge on the table, Josh was asleep.

It was two o'clock in the afternoon before the boy woke up. Maggie had spent most of that time trying to persuade

Rutledge to leave him where he was.

He opened red-rimmed eyes, puffy from crying and sleep, and stared at Rutledge without emotion.

For hours Rutledge talked to him. About Sybil, about the sheep, about Maggie, about Westmorland and London, whatever he could think of that had nothing to do with murder or policemen.

It was long after midnight before Rutledge, nearly hoarse by that time, got a response.

Josh looked up at him and said: "Will you hang me now?"

Rutledge said, "You can't be hanged. You're too young. And I don't know what you've done to deserve such punishment. I wasn't there —"

Maggie stirred, unwilling to force the child to relive what had happened that night in the snow.

"I was," Josh said, simply. "I killed them. All of them. Murderers always hang. It's what he told me. My father."

For several seconds Rutledge sat without moving. And then he said, "Gerald was the last to die, then?"

Maggie got to her feet and went to the

sink, where she leaned on her hands and stared out the window.

The boy shook his head. "No. He was the first. And then — then Hazel. After that, Mama. And the babies. He let me go then, told me they'd come and find all the bodies, and I'd be hunted down like a mad dog and hanged. I ran. He had the revolver against his head, by that time. And I heard the shot before I'd gone very far. But his voice came after me, over and over, no matter how hard I ran, telling me it was my fault, all my fault for not wanting to come and live with him. But Mama understood, and wouldn't make me do it. I was so scared she'd die when the babies came, and they would send me to London after all. Mr. Blackwell had told her that's where I belonged. And Paul, he said none of us belonged here, that we weren't Elcotts at all, even though Mama had married Gerald and Gerald called me his boy. And Greggie Haldnes told me I ought to go back to London and stop putting on airs at his school —"

He went on, spilling out a litany of small indignities and mistreatment and insults that had made him tragically vulnerable.

"Did you tell these things to your mother?"

He shook his head. "Dr. Jarvis said I mustn't worry her, that having twins was dangerous, and I wouldn't want to be responsible for what happened then."

Rutledge nearly swore, biting off the words.

"Are you sure it was your father, in the kitchen that night? Are you sure you didn't just imagine him, because you wanted him so much?"

Josh shook his head again vigorously, and rolled up the sleeve of his heavy shirt.

Maggie caught her breath in shock.

Deep bruises, only just turning green and yellow, ringed his thin arm in the shape of a man's fingers gripping hard.

"He made me watch. He held on to me and made me *watch* —"

By the time Rutledge had stemmed the tide of confession and helped Maggie feed Josh Robinson and put him to bed in her father's room, he was hardly able to keep his own eyes open. He could see in his head the horror that the boy had carried for more than a week, the images raw and frightful. But the last hours had taken their toll. When he came back to the warmth of the kitchen and sat down in Maggie's chair, he said to her, "I'll rest for half an hour. And then I'll go and do what has to be done."

"Yes. It's for the best. You look like I feel. I'll just lie down a bit myself." She lowered the flame on the lamp, banked the stove, and then went into her room, shutting the door.

The silence in the room, the ticking of a clock somewhere else in the house, and the warmth finally overwhelmed Rutledge, and he slept.

It was nearly three quarters of an hour later when he woke and couldn't remember where he was.

The room was dark, the lamp blown out. As his eyes adjusted to his surroundings, he got up and held a match to the wick, cupping his hand around the flame until it had caught. Settling the chimney in place again, he stood where he was and looked around the room.

All was as it should be. Maggie Ingerson's door was shut, as was the boy's. Sybil lay by the yard door, head on her paws, but her eyes gleaming in the glow of the lamp. He glanced at his watch. Too late to wake Mickelson or Greeley. He'd have to fetch his car soon and bring it around —

His eyes swung back to the yard door.

The ax was gone.

He crossed the room in four strides and flung open Maggie's door. Blankets were piled on her bed in the shape of her body, the coverlet drawn over them. In the dark it seemed she was sleeping, but a shaft of lamplight spilled across her pillow from the kitchen. And she wasn't there.

# Chapter Thirty-Six

Rutledge threw on his coat and headed for the door. Sybil refused to let him pass, growling and baring her teeth at him. Swearing, he turned and saw a door to another part of the house, shut off, cold and dark. But he went down the passage until he came to the front hall and the main door. He let himself out and trudged through the snow there to the lane that led to the main road.

He was a man, longer strides, younger, healthier by far.

But she had already made it to the Urskdale road, dragging the ax behind her.

When he caught up to her, Maggie swung it around in a circle, keeping him off.

"Let me go. He deserves to die, that bloody bastard! It's certain they won't hang him on the boy's word. They'll put the boy into an institution instead, and treat him as if he's mad. *None of this would have happened if you'd left us alone!*"

"Miss Ingerson — Maggie — listen to me. You'll never reach Urskdale. You can't make it that far. And if you did, they'd hang you for what you're intending to do."

She still held him at bay. "What good am I with this leg? Sometimes I think dying is all that's left, and I'm not afraid of it. At least I'll do one deed worthy of the name before I'm done."

"Maggie. I can see that Robinson hangs. I'll give you my word, I'll swear on anything you ask. Come back to the farm, before the boy wakes up and finds you gone. He needs you now, and he will need you in the days to come. *Don't do this!*"

She stood there in the starlight, staring at him.

He never knew what decided her.

She swung the ax in a wide circle, the sharp blade shimmering in the ambient light.

He thought for an instant that she was going to attack and kill him, and then she let the blade go, whirling and singing and gleaming, until it finally buried itself in the snow thirty feet away. And as it flew, she howled like a trapped animal, or a Viking warrior, a sound that sent the hairs on the back of his neck standing stiff and wild as if he'd stumbled onto something pagan, lost in the mists of time.

He got her to the house, and then went back to retrieve the ax and store it in the barn. It had been a long and painful journey for her, the cold and the strain of going so far telling on her. But she walked with her back upright and her head high, although he could see the streaks of tears down her face. He said nothing about them, and when, exhausted, she finally let him take her arm, he gave her the support he would have offered a comrade on the battlefield.

It was after four when he made the long journey back up the hill towards the sheep pen, and then over the saddle to the shed where he had left his motorcar.

It was cold and at first refused to crank. But after the third try he got it started and climbed in.

There was something he needed to do before he reached the hotel or spoke to Inspector Greeley.

The door to the rooms Paul Elcott used on the second floor of the licensed house was unlocked, and Rutledge went in, confident he would find Elcott asleep. He took the dark stairs two at a time, and opened the door to Elcott's bedroom, saying, "It's Rutledge. There's something you need to know —"

There was no light, only a shadow across the window, moving in an erratic pattern. Tired as he was, he stood there for an instant, trying to make sense of that curious motion as it came towards him and then retreated.

Hamish exclaimed, "Too late!"

Rutledge dug his torch out of his pocket and turned it on. The brilliant burst of light blinded him. But behind the flash, he could see Paul Elcott hanging from the ceiling where a lamp had once been.

It took him no more than a matter of seconds to kick the upended chair out of the way and shove a table under the dangling feet. And then he was on top of the table, his pocketknife sawing at the rope above Elcott's head. As the last strands parted, Elcott's body jackknifed, and hit Rutledge hard, knocking both of them to the floor. Winded, Rutledge lay there fighting for breath, and then he rolled to his knees. The torch, arcing in a half-circle, threw the room into bright relief and then shadow.

Elcott was gagging badly. Rutledge loosened the rope around his throat and turned him over, pushing air into his lungs as if he were a drowned swimmer.

Elcott was still struggling to breathe, and in the glow of the torch, kicked under the bed now, his face seemed suffused with blood.

Rutledge left him there, ran down the stairs, and up the street. He began pounding on Dr. Jarvis's door, calling to the house to wake up.

Jarvis testily put his head out of an upper window. "What now?"

"It's Elcott — get over there *now!*"

"Rutledge? I thought you'd gone back to London, man!"

"Hurry. Or he'll be dead before you reach him."

He turned and raced back the way he'd come. Hamish was loud in his mind, reminding him that he hadn't searched The Ram's Head —

Elcott was breathing, the sound of each rasping inhalation carrying down the stairs as Rutledge came up them.

He lay as he'd been left, on the floor, and his eyes were open. As Rutledge found a lamp and lit it, he blinked and then began to struggle as if fearful of whoever was behind the light.

"It's Rutledge. What the hell were you trying to do, man!"

Some of the tension seeped out of Elcott, and he lay still, concentrating on trying to breathe.

Jarvis was pounding up the stairs, shouting Rutledge's name. He'd put a coat over his pajamas and shoved his bare feet into his shoes. He stopped short in the doorway, staring first at Elcott, and then his eyes traveled up to the dangling rope overhead.

"My good God!" was all he said, hurrying to his patient.

After a time he rocked back on his heels. "It was a near-run thing! But the bone here" — gesturing to the front of the throat — "hasn't been broken. And he was lucky his neck didn't snap."

He turned back to Elcott. "Whatever possessed you to do such a thing, man? The inspector here had ordered you released without prejudice. It was over —" He stopped and got slowly to his feet.

His eyes sought Rutledge's. "Or was this a confession of sorts?"

"It was meant to be."

As the doctor had worked, Rutledge had retrieved a single sheet of crumpled paper stuck through by a pin to Elcott's pillow. He held it out now.

There were four words on the sheet, printed by a man under great stress — or duress. *I did do it.*

Jarvis said again, "My good God!" And then, "You shouldn't have stopped him. It will all have to be done again —"

"He didn't hang himself," Rutledge said. "Did you, Elcott?"

The dazed man on the floor shook his head vehemently and struggled to sit. His limbs seemed to have a mind of their own, arms folding as if no longer able to hold his weight.

He tried to speak but his throat closed over the words.

Rutledge said them for him.

"It was Hugh Robinson, tidying up before Mickelson could dig into the past as I had done. It might not have worked twice, his act of grieving. He couldn't pretend to a second suicide attempt. Elcott?"

Elcott's eyes were on Rutledge's face. He nodded vigorously, a sound like a growl coming from his damaged throat.

Jarvis picked up the overturned chair and sat in it, his mouth open.

"Let's get Elcott to the bed," Rutledge told the stunned doctor. But it was a moment or two before Jarvis could comply.

Elcott sank into the pillows, and tried again to find his voice. When it came it was no more than a harsh, raw whisper, hardly audible as words.

"Smoth— smothered me — pillow. Then left — dangling — toes on chair back. Could— couldn't — rise up — loosen noose. Lost my bal—ance trying. Fell off."

It was a hard way to die, choking slowly to death.

Jarvis wiped the palm of his hand over his mouth. "*Robinson,* you say?"

"Robinson. Carefully planned and executed, from the start," Rutledge told him.

"He killed them all? But *why?* Why in God's name — they were his own *children!*"

"Revenge." He stood by the bed. "And you were to be the scapegoat," he said to Elcott. "I'd failed, but he was afraid the new man would be luckier."

Jarvis got to his feet and went to the kitchen, rummaging in the dresser and the pantry. He came back with three glasses and a bottle of whiskey. Without a word he poured a finger for each of them, but had to hold Elcott as he sipped. The raw spirits sent him into a gasping fit.

Rutledge was saying, "Jarvis, I want you to stay here with him. I'll find Constable Ward and send him to keep you company. Don't leave until I've come back again. Do you understand me?"

"Yes, yes. You'll find Ward sleeping in the back of the police station. Greeley has had someone there since the — er — murders."

The doctor was right. Ward had prepared himself a cot in the cell, the door open, his shoes on the floor within easy reach. The constable's snores could be heard from the outer office.

He listened groggily as Rutledge briefly explained what he wanted done.

"With respect, sir, I've been told you're relieved." He rubbed his eyes with his fists, then stretched to ease his shoulders.

"If you want to leave Jarvis and his patient to the mercy of the killer coming back to see the results of his handiwork," Rutledge told him curtly, "by all means follow the rules. Meanwhile, I'm going to speak to Greeley."

Ward was already shoving his feet into his shoes, and reaching for his tunic. "Then I'll be on my way, sir. Mr. Greeley did leave orders to be called if there was any new developments."

Rutledge sat in the prim Greeley parlor for half an hour, speaking rapidly and carefully to his counterpart.

Greeley, half asleep when he began, was wide awake by the end.

"I've never heard the like!" he said grimly. "But what put you on to him? Along the coast they swore no one had asked directions about the old road."

"He didn't have to ask. He must have heard about it and spent some time during his summer holiday, searching it out for himself. It was useful, and even though he was caught in the storm, he'd have made some sort of provision even for that. He's not a man to leave much to chance."

"And the bastard made me take him to see his dead. To count them, more than likely!"

"It was a good excuse for his staying in his room much of the time. Waiting for his son's body to be found."

"Should we summon Inspector Mickelson and tell him what's happened?" Greeley asked. "As he's in charge . . ."

"If we go to wake Mickelson now, Robinson will hear us. His room is just across from the inspector's. He'll think we've found Elcott, and he may come out into the passage to ask if there's news. Better to wait until everyone has come to the kitchen for breakfast."

"And you say Ward's with Dr. Jarvis and Elcott?" Rutledge confirmed it and Greeley went on, "We'll just step around to Sergeant Miller's house and put him in the picture. We'll not take a man like Robinson without trouble." Greeley started for the door. Then he stopped. "Where's the murder weapon, then?"

But Rutledge was ready for the question. "It was Theo's revolver. I daresay Robinson disposed of it somewhere between Urskdale and the coast. There had to be a weapon that Josh could have used. Otherwise, no one would believe the boy had killed them all."

"I'd like to be there when the bastard hangs!" Greeley said vehemently, and hurried away to fetch his coat.

# Chapter Thirty-Seven

A gray, overcast day greeted them as Rutledge, with Greeley and Sergeant Miller at his heels, walked down the street towards the hotel.

"We'll have to tell Inspector Mickelson," Greeley was fretting. "Else it won't be done properly."

"One look at your face, if he sees you in the passage, and Robinson will know what's afoot. We'll send Sergeant Miller around to the back. I'll try to find Cummins and have him make sure his wife and Miss Fraser are safely locked in their rooms. You must go as quietly as you can to Miss Ashton's room and tell her there's been a message for her from Carlisle, and she's to see Constable Ward at the station straightaway. She's in the same passage with Mickelson and Robinson. It's essential to get her out of there."

"And Miss Fraser? Who's to see to her," Miller asked, "if she's already in the kitchen?"

"That's your duty, Sergeant. Step into the kitchen and tell her there's been an accident at the neighboring house. Ask her if you can wheel her next door while you go for Dr. Jarvis."

"But what about Mickelson?" Greeley asked again, anxious for the official stamp to his actions.

"First we must see to it that everyone is safely out of harm's way," Rutledge repeated impatiently. "We can't trust Robinson! He's killed five people in cold blood and left a child to die of exposure. He's tried to hang Elcott. We don't know if he's armed — don't know if he'll try to take hostages. Mickelson would give you the same order: Avoid any more bloodshed."

"Makes sense, sir," Sergeant Miller put in. "We ought to do as he says."

They had reached the hotel. Miller strode purposefully to the back. Rutledge and Greeley entered quietly, and Rutledge made his way up the stairs to find Cummins and his wife.

He tapped lightly, and then turned the latch. Mrs. Cummins was just putting the cap back on a bottle of gin, and she stared at him angrily as he came through the door. "What are you doing in my bedroom?" she demanded. "Leave at once or I'll scream the house down!"

"I'm sorry to disturb you but there's been an emergency. I'm looking for your husband —"

"He's downstairs, helping Elizabeth with the cooker. There's something wrong with it, she says."

He swore silently. "Then may I ask you to stay here, in safety, until we've finished —"

"You've come to arrest Harry! Is that it?" She stared at him. "Is it because he's a Jew? You can't seriously believe —"

"Mrs. Cummins, I am merely asking for your husband's help in a search for someone stalking the streets," he improvised swiftly. "If you stay here and lock your door, you'll be safe enough."

He backed out of the room and she hastened to take the key from him, on the point of locking herself in.

But from below there were loud voices, and the sound of footsteps running down the passage.

Rutledge passed her the key and was gone, down the stairs.

Greeley was just coming out of the passage, disheveled, a bruise rising on his jaw.

"Miss Ashton was already in the kitchen, so I woke Inspector Mickelson — Robinson heard me and knocked me down. Mickelson is after him!"

Rutledge didn't wait; he was racing down the passage with Hamish at his heels, the presence so real it sounded as if the Scot was just behind him.

There was a loud and angry exchange from the kitchen, Mickelson's voice and then Robinson's. Mrs. Cummins was halfway down the stairs, crying her husband's name. Rutledge ordered Greeley to stop her but she ducked under his arm and ran on.

As Rutledge opened the kitchen door, Vera Cummins darted in ahead of him, running to cling to her husband. Cummins was standing beside Elizabeth Fraser, staring in bewilderment as Mickelson tried take Robinson into custody. Janet Ashton was just reaching across the table to take up the sharp knife lying there. She was quick-witted, already caught up in what was happening. Her eyes were on Robinson's face and Rutledge heard her say, "Hugh? Is this man telling the truth? Was it you or Paul I saw that night in the snow? *Hugh?*"

Rutledge halted on the threshold, unwilling to press Robinson harder while the women were within his reach. But Greeley plowed into him, pushing him into the room. Robinson turned at bay. His face was furious. And all the while, Mickelson's piercing tenor challenged him to stop where he was and give himself up.

Rutledge, seeing the knife flash in Miss Ashton's hand said, *"Janet —"*

Mickelson wheeled on Greeley and demanded, "What's Rutledge doing here!" Robinson, as the inspector's back turned to him, flung out his hand and lifted the flatiron from the shelf along the wall. He swung it hard.

Mickelson went down, blood bubbling out of the cut on his cheekbone where the edge of the iron had caught him.

Greeley shouted, "Here — !" and barely had time to duck as Robinson hurled the iron at him. It struck the dresser, sending chips of wood flying in every direction. Vera Cummins had begun to scream in terror, but Janet Ashton was already advancing on Robinson with the knife, her face twisted in murderous fury.

Sergeant Miller came through the door and stopped short.

Rutledge called to Janet Ashton to stop where she was, and Miller, seeing the knife, lunged forward to pin her arms to her side.

Robinson, seeing the sergeant between himself and escape, reached under his coat and drew a revolver. He swung the barrel from Rutledge to Miller, and all movement stopped abruptly.

"If you want to die, I'll oblige!" he told the room at large, and then the barrel steadied, pointing directly at Elizabeth Fraser. Then, his eyes on her, he demanded, "Where's your motorcar, Rutledge? Speak up! I don't have much to lose by shooting her!"

Rutledge said, with far more self-possession than he felt, "It's by the church. Take it and go. I won't stop you, and I'll see to it that no one else does. You'll have reached the road to London before we can get word out. There's petrol in the tank, and money in my luggage in the boot. You can go anywhere you please and disappear." He watched the barrel of the revolver.

Greeley said, "You can't let him go! It's your duty —"

"I've given my word. Step out of his way, Greeley. If Sergeant Miller will open the door and let the ladies leave? Robinson, I'll even offer myself as hostage for the good behavior of the rest of them. I won't give you any trouble."

Robinson said, "Where's the boy? I'm not leaving without the boy."

"He's dead," Rutledge lied. "There's nothing more you can do to him."

"You couldn't have known I was there, unless you'd talked to him!"

"We don't need his evidence. Elcott survived, you see. He told us what you'd done. There's only one reason you'd try to hang him —"

"That's impossible — he couldn't have lived!"

"Oh, but he did. You left him teetering on a chair back. A note on the bed. After half smothering him with a pillow. I walked in just in time."

Robinson swore. "All right, then. The motorcar. Greeley, get out of my way. Faster, man, I'm impatient!"

Greeley backed against the wall, keeping his hands in plain sight.

Robinson glanced around the room one more time. Then he made to step over Mickelson, who was groaning as he began to regain his senses. For a split second Robinson took his eyes off Rutledge to glance at the man on the floor, making certain he wouldn't be tripped up. But the revolver was still pointing steadily at Elizabeth Fraser.

And then she spoke for the first time.

"Hugh?" She called to him, standing up from her chair and taking a step in his direction. "I hope you never close your eyes in peace again!"

Robinson had never seen her on her feet before. His attention was riveted on her. She had given Rutledge his only chance to act, but before he could move, Mickelson rolled on the floor in a desperate attempt to catch at Robinson's leg. Robinson was too swift for him. He sidestepped the clutching hands and fired.

The shot was deafening in the room, and Elizabeth Fraser gasped and spun as the bullet caught her.

With a roar of rage, Rutledge launched himself at Robinson, pulling him down with the strength of two men, and Miller was leaping over the table, crashing into both of them.

Greeley stooped to retrieve the flatiron, his eyes on the struggling men. But before he could use the iron, the revolver went off a second time, and then Rutledge had wrenched it out of Robinson's grip and flung it across the room where it skidded to a stop almost at Vera Cummins's feet.

Rutledge had his adversary pinned to the floor, and he was battering Robinson's face with his fists. Mickelson was pinning his legs.

"Miller, in the name of God, fetch Jarvis!" Rutledge shouted.

Janet Ashton had run to Elizabeth, and was cradling her head as Cummins began stuffing serviettes into the bleeding wound, frantically calling her name. Vera Cummins stood like a ghost against the wall, frozen there, her eyes on the blood.

And then Robinson wasn't moving. Dazed, Rutledge got to his feet, and lunged to Elizabeth Fraser's side, clasping her hands, telling her that she'd been damned foolish, begging her to hold on.

She opened her eyes and smiled up at him. "Couldn't — lose him," she said. "Boy's dead? Truly?"

"No. Quite safe. My dear girl, shut up and stay still."

She coughed, and a delicate pink froth spread over her lip.

Janet was smoothing her hair as she shut her eyes and sighed a little.

Mickelson and Greeley hauled a bloody and defiant Hugh Robinson to the police station, with Sergeant Miller behind them with Theo Elcott's revolver in one large, steady hand.

Jarvis, bending over Elizabeth Fraser and working steadily as he gave orders to Janet Ashton, said over his shoulder to Rutledge, "Get the rest of them out of here."

But a shaken Cummins was already leading his wife to the door.

Rutledge could hear Janet asking, "Is it true or a lie to comfort her? Is Josh alive?"

"He's safe for the moment —" His attention was concentrated on the woman on the floor.

Hamish was saying, "You canna' stay! Leave the doctor to his work."

But Rutledge was unable to move. "Don't let her die," he prayed. *"Don't let her die!"*

Janet demanded, "I have to know — tell me! What happened that night!"

Jarvis said, "Here — pay attention."

Hamish said, "It was for you she got in his way. To give you time."

"Damn Mickelson and Greeley both to Hell," Rutledge said between his teeth. But he knew the blame was his. He should never have trusted either of them to act outside the bounds of express duty. And he cursed himself for not acting alone, as he so often did.

"You couldna' ha' been sure you would tak' him on your own."

It was true, but it no longer mattered.

"If she dies, I'll resign," he silently promised God. "I've seen enough death and killed enough people."

Jarvis turned. "Rutledge? Lift her and carry her to her bed. I can't work here. I need more linens, a list of things from my surgery. Miss Ashton can see to that —" He began to give her instructions.

Rutledge came to kneel on the floor, gently putting his hands under Elizabeth Fraser's body. She seemed so fragile, and he cradled her close to his chest as he carried her out of the kitchen and down the passage to her room. He could feel her blood, warm on his hands.

Jarvis opened the door and pointed to the bed. "Put her down and find me pillows, as many as you can. And then hot water. The teakettle — a basin."

Rutledge went to do his bidding, moving in a nightmare. He came back with pillows scavenged from the other rooms and helped the doctor lift Elizabeth so that she could breathe more comfortably. Then he brought the kettle and a basin.

The doctor grunted as he took them, and said testily, "Where the devil is Miss Ashton? I need those powders!"

But she was coming down the passage,

Mrs. Jarvis at her heels with a basket of tins and jars and bandages.

"Now get out," Jarvis said to Rutledge.

"Is she going to live?" he asked, not moving from the bedside.

"No thanks to you. It's going to be nip and tuck. Greeley told me in the street — if you'd moved sooner, this would never have happened."

Greeley, Hamish snorted, was busily covering his rear.

Rutledge backed out of the room and stared for a time at his bloody hands.

*If she dies,* he told himself, *I'll have both of them on my soul!*

He looked in on Mickelson, whom Sergeant Miller had brought back to his room after safely delivering Robinson to gaol. His cheek was still bleeding, and his face was bruising quickly. Rutledge thought, "It must hurt like the devil!" And was glad.

"If you hadn't moved, I'd have tripped him up!" he said testily as Rutledge walked into the room. "I hope to hell your evidence is better than your timing!"

Rutledge left without answering.

He retrieved the motorcar and went back to the Ingerson farm.

Maggie was sitting where he had left her,

her face haggard, her leg stretched out in front of her on its accustomed stool.

The boy was there, sitting hunched over the dog, as if it was the only comfort he knew.

Maggie looked up and saw the blood. "What's happened, then?" she asked Rutledge.

"He'll stand trial. The boy may not need to testify. Robinson tried to kill Elcott, and nearly succeeded."

"And the aunt will want the boy."

"I don't know. I'll bring her later. She's needed now."

"How do I tell him? He's sure his father's dead, there with the others. That he turned the gun on himself. I can't make him listen."

"Don't try. It's better if he starts to forget." He went to the boy and sat down on the drafty floor beside him. "Josh. I knew another young man who heard voices in his head. They were wrong. And so are yours. After a while, they'll begin to fade. You'll go with your aunt Janet to London and back to the school you remember. It's finished."

"I don't want to go to London! I want to stay here, with Sybil and the sheep. My stepfather told me once I had the makings of a good sheep man. I don't like Aunt Janet. She made Mama cry."

"We'll see what can be done, then," the man from London promised. And then he rose. "I must get back to the hotel."

"You're asleep on your feet."

"It doesn't matter."

"It will if you drive into Urskwater."

"Miss Fraser is badly wounded. I have to be there. If — she doesn't live."

And he was gone, back down the road again, the rain beginning to pelt down on the bonnet and dance over the windscreen.

They wouldn't let him into her room.

But Cummins told him she was sleeping comfortably. "Nicked the lung, and two ribs, but that's all. It was a brave thing she did!" he ended admiringly.

"It was indeed." Rutledge felt as if his knees were ready to buckle under him, and his eyes seemed to be blurring with exhaustion. "Where's Mickelson?"

"I turned him out." Cummins said it with infinite pleasure. "As soon as he could walk. He's gone to stay with Greeley. Mrs. Greeley won't like that, but then I've never cared for Mrs. Greeley. Meanwhile, her husband has sent Constable Ward to send a telegram to London and to speak to the Chief Constable. They'll blacken your name between them, Greeley and Mickelson, I've no doubt of that. But it's to be expected."

"Yes," Rutledge agreed. "I've grown used to it."

"It won't stick. I spoke to Constable Ward before he left. He's always been rather fond of Miss Fraser. I explained to him how it came about that she was wounded and who's to blame. He's a man of few words, is Ward. But he's no fool. The Chief Constable will be on the phone to London before the telegram arrives. And that strutting little gamecock Mickelson will have to mend a few fences. Now go to your bed, or we'll have another patient on our hands!"

But Rutledge refused to consider it until Cummins opened the door to Elizabeth Fraser's room and let him see for himself that she was resting and not in pain.

Janet Ashton was sitting by the bed, and she tiptoed out of the room to say to Rutledge, "You must tell me about Josh!"

He said only, "Will you want him in London with you?"

That took her by surprise. "London? I — I haven't thought that far ahead. But Hugh's not here, is he? I don't have much choice. Oh, dear . . ."

"If you don't want him, he's found a dog he loves and a woman who loves him. I'd not meddle there if I were you. Not for a while. Not until he's healed."

And he left her there, closing the door to his room and finding the bed with some difficulty.

At length he slept. But not before he had answered the question that Hamish had been drumming in his head for the last few hours.

"I shan't stay to see how she feels. It wouldn't be fair. Not yet. There's the invitation from my godfather to spend Christmas in Scotland. I must make my peace with him. Then there's Dr. Fleming . . ."

But Hamish said into the darkness and silence, "I'll still be here . . . Dr. Fleming or no'."

# About the Author

**Charles Todd** is the author of *The Murder Stone*, *A Fearsome Doubt*, *Watchers of Time*, *Legacy of the Dead*, *A Test of Wills*, *Wings of Fire*, and *Search the Dark*. He lives on the East Coast, where he is at work on his next novel, *A Long Shadow*.

The employees of Thorndike Press hope you have enjoyed this Large Print book. All our Thorndike and Wheeler Large Print titles are designed for easy reading, and all our books are made to last. Other Thorndike Press Large Print books are available at your library, through selected bookstores, or directly from us.

For information about titles, please call:

(800) 223-1244

or visit our Web site at:

www.gale.com/thorndike
www.gale.com/wheeler

To share your comments, please write:

Publisher
Thorndike Press
295 Kennedy Memorial Drive
Waterville, ME    04901

2-19-14